THE HIT

Patrick Quinlan

THE HIT

headline

First published in Great Britain in 2009
by HEADLINE PUBLISHING GROUP

1

Cataloguing in Publication Data is
available from the British Library

ISBN 978 0 7553 3552 7 (Hardback)
ISBN 978 0 7553 3553 4 (Trade paperback)

Typeset in Fournier MT by Palimpsest Book Production Limited,
Grangemouth, Stirlingshire

Printed and bound in Great Britain by Clays Ltd, St Ives plc

Headline's policy is to use papers that are natural, renewable and
recyclable products and made from wood grown in sustainable
forests. The logging and manufacturing processes are expected
to conform to the environmental regulations of the country of origin.

HEADLINE PUBLISHING GROUP
An Hachette UK Company
338 Euston Road
London NW1 3BH

www.headline.co.uk
www.hachette.co.uk

For you and I, may we learn to face
hardship with grace and good humour.

'... it is unavoidable that we should look on the aims and hopes of the present day with ill-concealed amusement, and perhaps should no longer look at them. Another ideal runs on before us, a strange, tempting ideal full of danger...'

— FRIEDRICH NIETZSCHE

3 November: On the Water

Earlier that night a man's brains had been blown out.

The bullet had passed through his forehead and blasted apart the back of his skull in a spray of blood and bone.

Now, clumps of hair and scalp were drying on the wall. His corpse sloshed in ten inches of water at the base of that wall. The corpse, the wall and the water were inside the main cabin of the *Sea Dog*, a derelict houseboat fighting a hurricane more than a mile out from land.

Above the boat, torrential rain and wind tore open the sky. Below, angry swells threatened to capsize her. She was forty feet long, fourteen feet wide and shaped like a floating shoebox. Smashed windows ran along her length like haunted eyes. A six-foot deck protruded like a fat lip at her stern. She was driven before the squalls of the hurricane like a refugee before the gun butts of the storm troopers.

Inside, the low ceiling gave her main cabin the feel of a cave. The cabin was smashed, blown apart, with chunks of furniture, shards of glass and the remnants of a marine radio floating in the water. Worse, the dead man was not alone.

Other corpses floated in the room. Here was a naked man, face down with his head smashed in. Here was a large woman in a nightgown, on her back with a pair of scissors plunged into her chest. Both people were dead, yes, but both were moving and sliding like seaweed with the surges of the ocean. Worse even than the bodies, were the pieces of other bodies torn apart in the explosions.

Only one person remained alive on the boat.

He stood knee-deep in seawater. He clung to the metal support near the centre of the cabin. Sometime in the past, the pole had been welded there to make up for the *Sea Dog*'s compromised integrity. But the man who gripped it knew nothing of this. He stood, his left arm thrust through a bright yellow life vest. His shirt was red with blood, so wet that it stuck to his torso.

I'm the survivor, he thought.

He stared down at himself, soaking in the blood's pattern. It reminded him of the Rorschach blots shown to mental patients. Like those blots, this blood took shape and told a story, a story the survivor knew. The memory elicited a sound from him now, a grunt of horror, of which he was not even aware.

He snapped alert. He could save the luxury of remorse for another time and place. He was on a boat, it was going down, and if he didn't do something soon, he was going down with it.

As if to amplify this, another boomer hit the side of the boat. The survivor felt the wave coming and braced himself for it. It sucked the craft back into its maw. Right before it came there was silence, no movement, no wind, no rain, just a shadow looming on the wall before him and a feeling of emptiness and terrible anticipation in his soul.

When it hit, he lost his grip on the pole and pitched forward. He went down, dunking himself, head banging against the floor. Everything slowed and went dark, and he thought the boat had rolled over. Then he came up gasping.

The *Sea Dog* remained aright. She was three feet deep in water now. The bodies floated about the cabin like big rubber dolls.

He clutched the life vest to his chest.

He picked himself up and lurched through the galley. He stumbled out through the gaping hole in the wall to the deck. The Yorkshire terrier was out here, eyes bright and alive. It had belonged to someone who lived on the boat. Now it belonged to no one. The dog yapped at him from its perch on the bench bolted to the deck. Its tan coat was soaked and matted and its festive red bow was pulled askew. Its body shivered with the fear that comes easily to small dogs, and its teeth were bared as if to attack. But its tail wagged in greeting.

'Hey, Versace,' the man said. 'Hey, buddy.'

Maybe they were a team, he and that dog.

He stopped to consider this idea. Meanwhile the boat surged forward and the rain beat down. Far away, he caught a glimpse of the lights from land. It seemed as if he could almost touch them.

That's where he was headed. Land. He imagined the streets of the town there, shops boarded up, the few remaining people hiding in their guesthouses. Maybe one bar was still open, the local crazies in there drinking and laughing and playing darts while the stoplight outside swung in the wind and the storm bore in.

He turned to Versace again, just as another roller smashed the side of the boat. The man went down, almost over the side and into the sea. He clung to the deck like a rat as the water washed back over the side. Versace was above him now. The Yorkie barked madly, yap yap yap. The man could barely hear it. He was cheek to cheek with the deck, his hands pressed flat as though the pressure itself would hold him there.

There was nothing to consider. The dog was on its own.

The man pulled himself up on to the bench. Versace tried to climb in his lap, but he pushed the dog away. He peeled off his shirt and pitched it into the water. He yanked on the life vest and cinched it tight. It took him precious seconds figuring out how to tighten the vest.

Another wave hit the boat. The old beast took it hard and again nearly rolled, tossing the man like a rag. He couldn't stay a moment longer. He feared the water, but the boat was going to break up, sooner rather than later. Maybe a wave would cut it in half. Maybe it would dash itself on a reef, or on some rocky headland. Either way, it was going to the bottom of the sea and taking its unholy cargo with it. He wanted to be gone before that happened.

The time had come.

He stood and tottered to the edge of the platform. The sea roiled and raged just below him, water slopping over the deck. He checked the life vest one last time. He pulled all the straps as tight as he could, taking a deep breath at the same time.

Behind him Versace yapped once more, as if to say goodbye.

The man closed his eyes and let the ocean take him.

1

Jonah Maxwell felt like shit.

'What's this bastard's name again?' he said.

It was an overcast day in the Bronx, and he sat in the passenger seat of a parked car, once again about to tangle with a dangerous fugitive. He was sweating even with the window down, and just the slightest nip of cool air reminded him it was already late October.

It was supposed to be an election year and this would normally be the climax of it, but they'd cancelled the election a month ago after the Vice-President got blown up in his car. The President himself had gone underground, mouthing TV platitudes to the rudderless nation from a bunker under a mountain somewhere out west. The talking heads chattered about the government rescheduling the election for a date in the spring, or maybe next fall. Or maybe never, Jonah figured.

Didn't matter, anyway – we might not make it to next spring. The doomsday chorus, growing louder every day, was calling for the end of the world just before Christmas, which was the abrupt stopping point of the ancient Mayan calendar. About six weeks from now. The Mayans had watched the stars move for thousands of years, and had projected those movements well into the future. For some reason, they decided that the stars would stop moving on the twenty-first day of this coming December.

Jonah sighed. The end of the entire world. He could almost believe it was true, and it did nothing to calm his nerves. Bad nerves made him sick to his stomach. He closed his eyes, trying to control his breathing, trying to control the tingling in his head, hands and feet – trying to find his centre. Street sounds came to him. He could hear the rumble of the elevated subway line over on Jerome Avenue. Closer, children shouted about a block away. Salsa played on a boombox.

The car he sat in was a tiny Honda Civic hatchback parked on a quiet side street. The car had rolled off the line cherry red twenty years before, stock, with an AM radio, windows that rolled up and down by hand and not even so much as air-conditioning for the New York summers. Now it was mostly red with one blue quarter panel, rust beginning to eat through everything. The dashboard was caked in grime. The odometer claimed a quarter of a million miles.

Gordon Lamb, the Honda's master, sat behind the wheel and pored through the papers on his lap. Even with the seat pushed way back, there wasn't much room because of his belly and legs. He had a two-day beard and his hair stood up as if he had forgotten to shower that day. Jonah called him Gordo, short for El Gordo, a nickname coined by a funny Dominican whore Gordo had spent the night with years before. She'd had trouble with the whole name Gordon, so she'd dropped the n. It was perfect. In Spanish, El Gordo meant 'the fat one'.

He and Gordo made an odd couple, maybe. Jonah: a slim, muscular, well-dressed black man – café au lait because of his white father – who made the ladies swoon, and Gordo: a big, heavyset bear of a white man whom you might mistake for a lumberjack.

'The name's Foerster,' Gordo said. 'Davis Foerster.' He spelled it aloud and shuffled some paper around. 'Also known as Mark Foster. Also known as Foster Davidson.'

Jonah glanced out the window. From the looks of it, from the smell of it,

Jonah guessed that garbage pick-up in this neighbourhood had happened two or three weeks before. Along the edge of the sidewalk, in the shadows of the apartment buildings, overflowing garbage bags were piled high. Assorted kitchen scraps and other trash were strewn all over the street and sidewalk. Bomzhies, junkies, and scavengers of all types came and ripped open the plastic bags, looking for food or anything of value to put in their old supermarket shopping carts and trundle home. As Jonah watched, a large rat crossed the street, well-fed, in no hurry, moving from one mountain of trash to the next.

Meanwhile, Gordo launched into the story as if he hadn't told it half a dozen times before. 'Foerster's the perfect scumbag. Been up to petty shit since he was a teenager, but somewhere along the line it started getting serious. Cops wanted him for questioning on a year-old forcible entry and rape. A man fitting his description knocked on a 75-year-old woman's apartment door late one night, forced his way in, pushed her down and raped her. Took about five hundred in cash she had lying around the place. Case remains unsolved, but looks a lot like two earlier ones where the old ladies got killed.'

Jonah took another deep breath, letting Gordo's words wash over him.

'In any case,' Gordo continued, 'two weeks ago, Foerster lands in their laps. He gets picked up on a breaking and entering and attempted rape. Cops want to roll him up on the old lady case. They figure if they can break him on the one where they still have the victim alive, maybe they can break him on the other two. But all of this coincides with the latest general amnesty for nonviolent prisoners. The city swings wide the cell doors, and lets five thousand inmates – mostly drug offenders – walk. At that moment, there are two men with very similar names on Riker's Island. One is called Davis Foster. One is called Davis Foerster. True to form, they let the wrong one go. Foerster gets off a prison bus in Queens and disappears. Too late, the city realises its mistake, and quietly issues a fifty-thousand-dollar reward for his capture, hoping to get him back inside before the newspapers realise they did the bad thing again and released another maniac by mistake. Tough for a cash-strapped city, but good for people like us.'

Gordo raised an eyebrow.

'Most interesting thing? A little bird told me the FBI contacted the city cops about this guy two days after he walked. The feds also want to talk to him, and they're not saying why. He's not officially wanted, mind you. They just want to ask him a few questions.'

Gordo dropped the paper he was holding into his lap.

'All that said, who are you to him?'

Jonah gestured at the jumpsuit he wore. The name Jake was stencilled in white across his right breast. The jumper felt too small for his chest and round shoulders, and wearing it made him feel silly. He was too pretty to pass as an exterminator.

'I'm the guy who's here to kill his roaches,' he said.

They went through the drill every time. The skip's name, his description, the layout of the place, how they were going to nail him. They had gone over it the night before on the phone, but one more time never hurt. Gordo liked to be thorough, and if it meant they made the collar, then Jonah didn't mind.

Gordo moved two photocopied maps to the top of the heap. One was a building floor plan, the other a zoning map of the neighbourhood. Jonah leaned over to get a better look.

'OK,' Gordo said. 'This is the apartment, five C, rented by the so-called Mark Foster. It's a studio, right? And you can see the fire escape is outside this window, which is in the kitchen and dining-room area. If you flush him out that window,' he switched to the neighbourhood map, 'then you can see over here that he has to come down to this alley.' He looked up and peered down the street. He pointed to an opening between Foerster's building and the boarded-up building next door. 'Which is that alley right there. And that's where I'll be standing.'

'What if he goes to the roof?' Jonah said.

'If he goes anywhere other than the alley, you call me on the walkie-talkie,' Gordo said. 'But he won't. His first reaction will be to get down to the alley and disappear. Also, his building is free-standing and he probably knows it. It's gotta be fifteen feet across to the next roof, maybe more. So he'll figure if he goes to his roof, he's trapped up there.'

Gordo closed the file and placed it on the back seat.

'But once he commits to going for the alley, then he's really screwed.'

'What if he has a gun?'

Gordo shook his head. 'Not his modus operandi. In his entire life, he's never once been picked up with a gun.'

'Easy pickin's, then,' Jonah said.

'Cake,' Gordo said. 'Twenty-five thousand dollars each for a ten-minute gig.'

Inside his apartment, Davis Foerster slumped and smoked a Camel while he pulled the stuffing out of a gash in the upholstery of his easy chair. A bottle of beer was propped against his crotch. His feet rested on the worn parquet floor. The walls around him were bare except near the light switch, where over the years hands had smudged the area almost black.

The bruises around Foerster's eyes had faded. His hair was growing back over the scar that had run across his scalp like a railroad. The middle and ring fingers of his left hand were still wrapped in a dirty plaster cast that extended down to his wrist. Only his thumb, pointer and pinky were free.

He blew a smoke ring towards the ceiling and stared at the thirteen-inch colour TV on the stand in front of him.

No cable, and the reception in this building was so bad, he only got one channel clearly. There'd been continuous power cuts all day, and when the power finally came back on, he was treated to the spectacle of an afternoon talk show with a bunch of fatties lined up on stage, all of them sitting and blathering about how it felt to lose a hundred pounds and change their lives. The host was a cheerful woman whom America had watched rollercoaster from fat to skinny to fat and then skinny again. She'd tried all the fad diets, and had worked out with all the trendiest workout gurus. So this weight thing was a topic close to her heart.

The camera panned the studio audience. Housewives with tears in their eyes. A couple of the saps even had handkerchiefs out. A person weighs five hundred pounds, Foerster thought, loses a hundred, and still weighs four hundred. How does that change their life?

'That really touches me,' the host said to one of the porkers.

'Fuck you,' Foerster said.

Foerster didn't need to lose weight. If anything, he needed to gain some. Get some size to him for the next time he got in a tangle. With a little more size, maybe he wouldn't have ended up in the joint again.

Another smoke ring, a little one chasing through a big one.

His mind wandered, back to the most recent fall he'd taken. He had climbed through a window this time. Windows were the easiest, especially a couple of floors up. On hot nights, people left them open. All the way, a crack, it didn't matter. He'd just picked an open one along a fire escape and climbed up there. He'd slipped inside and stood in the living room.

Pretty nice furniture in there. Somebody in the place was still working. He remembered hearing a car go by outside – a cop car? No other sounds. The good stuff was usually in the bedroom, top dresser drawer in most places. Cash, maybe some gold. The place had wall-to-wall carpet, which was good – his feet would make no sound. He followed a short hallway. He passed a narrow door. It looked like a closet. Another closed door, maybe the bathroom. A sharp left turn and here was the bedroom. There was a sleeping form alone on the double bed. Foerster allowed himself another silent inhale and exhale, watching and listening. He could tell by the size and shape of the body, and by the hair sticking up from under the sheet. It was a woman.

That was better than money.

He went for her, of course. It was a stupid play and he knew it as he stood over her. But she aroused him and it clouded his thinking. Women didn't always arouse him, and he had to take the opportunities when they presented themselves. He slid into bed with her, working on his zipper. She made a sort of welcoming sound, like a sigh. It should have tipped him off. In her sleep, she thought he was somebody else, somebody who was supposed to be there.

It didn't tip him off, though. It got him excited instead.

Later, the cops were happy to fill in the gaps in his knowledge. The husband got up in the middle of the night, went into the bathroom and fell asleep on the can with the door shut. When Foerster grabbed the wife, she gasped, then screamed, and hubby woke up. The big boy came storming in and found Foerster on top of his lady. The next thing Foerster knew, the storm broke loose. Hubby let Foerster have it with a wind-up clock, a lamp, a glass candle holder, a metal magazine rack. They went around and around the room, the wife still screaming, the whole building waking up, Foerster trying to escape, trying to get his zipper closed while the husband clubbed him with everything within reach.

He made it back out the window, bleeding a river down his face. He didn't get far. Two pigs in a patrol car picked him up a block away. He banged into parking meters and shit as he ran, half blind from all the blood in his eyes, half mad from the pain, his zipper still stuck halfway down.

A funny scene, even Foerster could see the humour in it. But it turned ugly once he got back to the joint. He spent a night in the precinct house, took a trip to the doctor, then spent three nights in the monstrous jail on Riker's Island.

The wounds he got in jail were worse than the beating from hubby. The black guys in jail didn't need to beat him up. They just got him three or four at a time, stuffed a sweaty doo-rag in his mouth, held him face down and did it to him. Jesus. And the fucking COs didn't give a shit. It was all in fun, right? A guard even told him he should act like a man, stick up for himself more. The piece of shit said it while standing at the cell door, looking down at Foerster spreadeagled on the floor, cons sitting on each arm, a big two-hundred pound shrieking porch monkey grinding away on top of him.

Foerster didn't give it easily, though. They did him, but he fought them first, and he got his shots in. He could say that much for himself. No matter what happened, they hadn't broken his spirit. But he couldn't imagine what serious time would be like and for a second it had looked as if serious time was on the cards.

As it turned out, the cops knew about the old woman. Maybe they didn't know for sure, but they suspected. He thought about the woman for just a second, got an image of her. A white-haired biddy, with a clean, honest face. The skin round her throat sagged and creased like an elephant's knees. He had seen her on the street a couple of times. She plucked something in him, like a finger twanging a guitar string. So he had taken her. He hadn't planned it that way, but Foerster hardly ever planned these things. His desires came to him from some other place – he could go for weeks at a time without feeling anything. But when the thing started flowing, he always flowed with it. It felt natural. It felt right.

His mistake had been to let the old woman live. He had seen something in her eyes that night. They'd remained wide open and staring the whole time. She looked so gentle, like a doe paralysed by the headlights of an onrushing truck. He couldn't finish her. Not with those big eyes looking right at him.

He had wondered how long she could put him away for. Ten years? Twenty years? Life?

Foerster shook his head. No way. He was never going back to jail.

He stood up and got another half-cold beer out of the box. He tapped the empty on the edge of the sink till it cracked, then he placed it on a rickety white table piled high with similar empties. He once hit a guy in a bar three times with a beer bottle and it didn't break. Then he learned. Crack 'em just a little and they break on the first shot. Nobody likes to get a head full of glass.

He stood in the kitchen with his next beer and looked around. Shabby ass apartment. Roaches in the cabinets. He didn't even have sheets on the bed, just an old mildewed mattress and a quilt. He needed to start treating himself better. First and foremost, he needed to stay out of the joint.

On that end, he was in good shape. He had stopped showering in case the cops came while he was naked with the water running. Instead, he was dressed and ready to go at all times. Every dollar he had was in his pocket. He had his bottles, and leaning in the corner he had his table leg. If all else failed, he had practised his escape route till it didn't even scare him any more. There was a trick to it, one so dangerous no coffee and doughnut cop would ever attempt it – why get killed over nothing?

Foerster glanced at the kitchen window, where a threadbare curtain billowed in the breeze. He was waiting here, and he didn't like it. He wanted to get moving. Tyler Gant – his man down south – needed him for another science project. It was easy work, the kind of thing a smart tenth-grader could probably pull off, but Gant didn't seem to realise that. Pretty soon, one of Gant's goons was supposed to come to Foerster's door with an envelope. When Foerster opened that envelope, he was supposed to find $5,000 in cash. Then he was supposed to get in a car with the goon and drive down to Dixie.

Shit. Five grand in cash, and Foerster hadn't even done anything yet? This job must be something pretty big. Wouldn't it be nice if the goon showed up here today?

Just then, the doorbell rang.

Jonah stood in the bleak hallway and faced the solid green door to apartment 5C.

Weak light filtered through a translucent window at the other end of the hall. Solid glass bricks half a foot thick. Some kid had probably gone out the original window by accident, ended up with a broken neck in the street. Those glass bricks gave the only light – the overheads were all out. At night, this would be one dark hallway. On the wall, some new Picasso had drawn a mural in black magic marker, a big penis rubbing between a pair of breasts.

'Every nigga has 2 scheme 4 da creme,' read the caption underneath.

Nice building.

Sounds echoed through the halls. Laughter. Somebody shouting. Running feet. TV sets – the power was on. Water dripped somewhere. Plunk, plunk, plunk.

Jonah's body shook, a little nothing tremor maybe nobody could see but him. He always got nervous before one of these gigs. It wouldn't have taken much to throw up – if he thought too hard about his finger approaching the back of his throat, that might do it. Taking a shit would have been even easier. All he had to do was sit down.

In one hand, he held a clipboard with some bogus papers attached. In the other, he held a small black canister of pepper spray. It contained five bursts that could travel up to ten feet. The blasts would last one second each, fifteen per cent OC every time. OC stood for Oleoresin Capsicum, fifty-dollar words, but Jonah knew what they meant in plain English: STRONG SHIT. If he sprayed that stuff in Foerster's face, the blood vessels in the man's eyes would swell up, forcing them shut. His face would burn and the pepper would get down into his throat and lungs. He would start coughing up his insides. He would be under Jonah's complete control.

Jonah slid the canister into his right back pocket.

The left back pocket was where he kept the handcuffs. They were chain-links, nickel-plated all steel construction, and rated for police work. Gordo had scammed them from somewhere.

Jonah reached up to ring the bell one more time. Someone shuffled on the other side of the door. Jonah took a half-step backwards.

'Who is it?' said a scratchy voice.

'Mr Foster?' Jonah said. 'Mr Mark Foster?'

'Who wants to know?'

'Exterminator.'

'What?'

'Exterminator. I'm here to spray your apartment, sir.'

The peephole in the centre of the door slid open. Jonah stepped in front so Foerster could get a good, long look.

'What's your name there,' the voice said, 'Jake?'

'Jake, that's right.'

'Who do you work for, Jake?'

'The landlord sent me. Manor Property Management. I'm checking through all these apartments because of a roach infestation. Do you have any roaches in there, Mr Foster?'

'How do you know my name?'

'Your landlord gave me all the names.'

'My landlord can fuck off.'

Jonah sighed, just a working man getting nowhere with a customer. 'Sir, I'm going to have to come in there sooner or later. There's a roach problem in this building. If I have to call the office, they'll just get the maintenance guy to let me in.'

He waved the clipboard as if that would tell the story.

The door opened a crack. Foerster kept the security chain on. An eyeball peered out at Jonah. 'They have to give me twenty-four hours' notice. You know that, right? You can't just walk in here without notice.'

Jonah slid his right foot into the crack. Foerster tried to slam it shut but the foot was already there. Jonah shouldered the door hard. Once. Twice. Three times and he could feel the chain going. Four times and it was loose. Five and he blasted the chain housing out of the wall. Then he was off balance and inside the apartment.

They faced each other in a kind of stand-off, Jonah startled by the looks of the man. Unshaven, Foerster held an empty beer bottle in one hand – the hand with two fingers wrapped together in a cast. He was pale, almost a shade of yellow, as if light was bad for him. His skin hung on bone, like a vampire's would.

'Davis Foerster. I'd like you to come with me, sir.'

Foerster smiled, a wan and sickly sight.

'You a cop?'

'No, I'm not. I work for the courts. Why don't you come along peacefully? That way nobody gets hurt.' Jonah started to reach back to take the cuffs out.

'Sure,' Foerster said. He smiled that terrible smile again. He seemed relaxed, relieved even. 'I'll be right with you. Just hold this for me, will you?'

He threw the beer bottle. They stood five feet apart, maybe less. Jonah ducked too late. The bottle bonked his head and shattered, spraying glass and beer all over him.

He backed away into the hall again, but things went funny. The hallway was black, and bright white spots – call them stars – shot across the dark field of his vision. They sparkled and left trails of glowing dust in their wakes. They looped and spiralled. Spiders spun cobwebs in the corners.

Then his vision came rushing back, brushing away the darkness. He was down on one knee like a man proposing marriage. Things had gone wrong right from the start. He fumbled the walkie-talkie out of his jumper. He'd better call Gordo quick.

He looked up and it all moved in long sloow mo. Foerster came out of the apartment. Now he had a thick wooden table leg. He carried it like a slugger in the on-deck circle. A long screw stuck out from the business end. The screw would attach the leg to a table. It looked nasty, like it could poke a nice hole through somebody.

'C'mere,' he said. 'You wanna fuck with me, right?'

He swung the table leg full bore. Jonah jerked away, but the swing connected with his hand and knocked the walkie-talkie flying. The handset bounced off the wall, then hit the floor and broke into pieces. Jonah crawled backwards, pulling out his pepper spray. Foerster kept coming. Jonah shoulder-rolled and came up firing like a shortstop. He pressed the button on the top of the canister, but he aimed too low. The spray hit Foerster in the shirt.

Foerster gaped down at the wet stain and Jonah charged.

He hit Foerster hard and it was like tackling a scarecrow – there was no real substance to the man. He bulled him back into the apartment. They flew through the doorway and crashed to the floor. Jonah lost the pepper spray. Foerster lost the club.

Jonah landed on top. They wrestled. This close, Foerster smelled like cigarettes and body odour. Jonah was bigger and stronger, but Foerster raged with desperation. He screamed in Jonah's ear, and squirmed away like an eel. Jonah reached for Foerster's waistband, snagged it with his finger, lost it.

'Shit!'

Jonah rose to his feet and picked up Foerster's club himself. He adjusted his grip on it. The weight felt good. That screw stuck out thick and mean.

A glass bottle shattered near his head. He looked up. Foerster stood behind a paint-peeling white table. It was piled up with empty bottles – beer bottles, wine bottles, hard stuff. Foerster grabbed another bottle and threw it. Jonah ducked and it smashed against the wall. He felt the wet tingle of the glass.

'Get the fuck out of my house,' Foerster said.

Jonah ran down his options. He thought fast. The club might break this guy in half. Look for the pepper spray instead? That meant turning his back. Lost seconds. Time for Foerster to move. Fuck his M.O. – did he have a gun in the fridge? Maybe. Under the pillows? Jonah didn't want to find out.

Let him have it with the club? Of course.

He moved in.

Foerster threw another bottle.

Jonah swung.

He connected, spraying beer and shards of glass all over himself. He took another step forward.

'This is a citizen's arrest,' he said.

Foerster threw again. He threw to the right and high. The bottle smashed harmlessly. He picked up two more, one with each hand, and let fly. His aim was gone. Beginner's luck that first time. Jonah charged him, the club raised high. He brought it down like a woodsman splitting logs – knees bent, legs planted, his thighs and back doing the work, the force of it like electricity through his body, grip so firm his knuckles stood out in white.

The club smashed the empty bottles, then sliced through the table. The table broke in half, then separated and fell in. Glass went flying, a fountain of glass. The sound was like a car crash. Foerster dropped way back, then dove out the window.

'He's coming out! He's coming out!'

Jonah went to the window and stuck his head through it. Foerster aimed a kick. His foot whistled just past the edge of Jonah's nose. Jonah ducked back.

He counted to three then poked his head out again.

He caught a glimpse of Foerster's head going down the stairs. Jonah dropped the bat and clambered out on to the ironwork. It had been white once but now was flaking with rust. Across the alley was the old fire escape to the abandoned building next door. He went to the railing and glanced around five stories below. Gordo's round moon face stared up at him.

'He's coming down!'

Gordo raised his arms upwards like he was praising his maker. 'Bring him to me.' His voice echoed off the brick walls.

Jonah hit the stairs, taking them two at a time. He reached the first landing, turned the corner and two seconds later stood at the top of the next flight. One floor down, Foerster was perched up on the handrail like a bird on a telephone wire, grasping the stairs behind him with one hand.

It was three stories to the street and Jonah thought he had a jumper.

'Foerster! Don't do that!'

Foerster didn't even give him a glance. He let go of the stairs, bent deep at the knees and launched himself out into nothing like a squirrel from a tree.

Jonah's stomach lurched.

Foerster flew across the alley and crashed into the neighbouring fire escape half a floor below. He hit it railing high, catching the railing in his stomach. The whole fire escape shook with the impact. Foerster hung on, legs dangling, and yanked himself up and over the railing. He fell on to the landing and rolled over, holding his gut. Then he began crawling up the stairs.

Jonah watched as Foerster, gaining his feet now, reached the landing across from and a little above his own. Foerster stopped and leaned on the railing, breathing hard. Right there, but just out of reach. He looked over at Jonah and flashed his nasty smile.

'Nothing to it if you have the balls,' he gasped. Then he continued on his way.

Jonah leaned over the side again. Gordo's big face still loomed there. It hadn't seemed like such a terribly long way down just a minute ago. Now it looked like the Grand Canyon.

'I can't reach the ladder on that side,' Gordo called. 'It's folded all the way up.'

Of course. Foerster planned it that way.

Jonah surveyed the situation. Crunch time had come. Lose the skip and you might never see him again. It was one of the first rules Gordo taught him. The skip makes you and gets away, tomorrow he's gone. Wherever he can get to. It could be New Jersey, but it might as well be Bangkok, as far as you're concerned.

Well, if a skinny bastard like Foerster could do it . . .

That decided him. A moment later, Jonah was up on the railing. Precious seconds ticked by. Between his shoes he saw all that open space. Gordo's face watched from the bottom of a deep well. Ten miles across the alley, and a little bit below, the landing of the opposite fire escape beckoned. Everything seemed to swim and spin.

Now or never, said the demon.

Climb down and forget the whole thing, said the angel.

He bent like he had seen Foerster bend, a full squat. He imagined himself leaping and landing on the other side. Like shooting a free throw, that's all. See it happen and then do it. In his mind, he saw it happen. To his fevered imagination, it looked like an elf dancing from mountaintop to mountaintop.

See it happen. See it happen.

Do it.

He launched, everything in his legs.

The ground rushed up. The fire escape came at him on an angle. He fell too long and he was sure he had missed it. Then he hit like a meteor. The railing caught him in the stomach and his air whooshed out. He slid, grabbing madly for anything. The rail jammed into his armpits, his hands found grips, and he held on for dear life. The iron shook all the way up, and for a second he thought his extra weight would bring the whole thing down. It didn't. They made those things to last.

Far away, he heard a long whoop that told him Gordo was cheering.

Jonah pulled himself over the railing and collapsed to the deck. He gave himself a moment to let his wind come back. The cool metal slats pressed against his face. He was shaking a little, but not badly. He was alive and the chase was still on.

He groped his way to his feet. Foerster must have felt him land. Jonah needed to move fast. He climbed, dragging up the stairs at first, then catching a rhythm and starting to hit it. One landing, around the corner and more stairs. Another landing, no idea where Foerster was now. Did he go in a window?

Jonah kept pushing, guessing the roof. He passed another landing, then another. Did he hear breathing above him? He kicked the engine into another gear. He reached the top landing, eight floors he thought, he wasn't sure. Some view up there. The city, impossibly vast, stretched away in every direction. Near the horizon, something big was on fire, belching thick, dark smoke. He didn't have time to dig it because there went Foerster, twenty yards ahead, tearing ass across the black tar.

Jonah had sprinted in high school. He had big legs. He took off and for an instant he remembered those days. He could almost see the crowd up in the dim rafters surrounding the old armoury track. Back when Jonah ran, they used to pile up metal cots in the infield for the hundreds of homeless men who came there at night to sleep. Back then, the track was still made of wood, and any kid who fell down while jockeying during a race was guaranteed to get ripped up by splinters. Jonah never fell, though. He was too much of a beast. He thought back to the thundering hoof beats as the ancient track shook under his powerful foot strikes.

Foerster didn't have a chance.

Jonah closed the gap by half before Foerster reached the building's edge. A low brick wall marked the end. Foerster never slowed. He hopped on to the wall, launched and disappeared. Jonah was uncertain. He slowed, then came to the wall and stopped. The next building was lower and five feet across an air passage. Foerster was over there, still moving.

Jonah leapt up on to the wall, hesitated for a second, then took the gap easily. He touched down on a gravel roof.

They were on a row of packed-together narrow buildings.

Foerster reached the next gap and vaulted over it. Jonah gave chase, gaining again. He felt, rather than saw, the chasm open and close below him. His eyes were on Foerster's back. They jumped from roof to roof, dodging antennas, Jonah growing closer all the time. They reached the end of the block and Foerster turned right. He crossed to a long and wide gravel roof that was lower still. It was a pretty good jump but Foerster did it no problem and Jonah was too turned on to stop now.

He landed in a starter's crouch, Foerster just ahead of him, and this roof opened up like a football field. Here his legs would do their damage. He sprinted, and became aware of the handcuffs pressed hard to his ass in the back pocket of his jumpsuit. He would need them in a minute.

Closer. Foerster two steps ahead.

Their long shadows mingled on the gravel below them. Legs and arms pumping. Closer still. Be patient, Jonah told himself. Time it right.

Foerster made a sound, more like a caveman grunt than a scream.

Jonah dove and hit him waist high. He wrapped Foerster's legs and they slid together across the roof, the tiny stones tearing the blue jumper, digging into Jonah's flesh. Foerster scrabbled like a crab. He kicked, he scratched. Jonah looked for handholds, but found none. Foerster slipped away.

Again.

Jonah nearly laughed. This fucking guy, was he worth all this?

The answer: oh, yeah. Jonah needed the money.

He jumped up and continued the game. Foerster was running for the next low wall, bent over and limping now like a monkey. That tackle had hurt him – his small body took the brunt of it. Jonah pursued. Foerster reached the wall, jumped up, and then stuck his arms out like a tightrope walker crossing the gorge. Sure enough, the next roof was a big jump, fifteen feet, and Foerster walked the length of a piece of thick flat lumber about two feet wide. He reached the other side and leapt down. Jonah stopped. There was more lumber piled here, three or four big pieces.

Another gap. Another long fall.

Across the way, Foerster grabbed the beam and yanked it out from Jonah's wall. He let it fall into the abyss, and it clanked and clattered all the way down to the alley below.

'Heads up!' Jonah shouted. He leaned over and watched it go, but there was nobody down there. At the bottom, in the alley, all manner of garbage was piled high. He gazed across the abyss. Foerster was there, just beyond Jonah's reach.

Patrick Quinlan

Maybe Foerster had known nobody was in the alley, maybe he hadn't. What if people had been picking through there today? Foerster could have killed somebody.

'Let me guess,' Jonah said. 'You don't like jail too much, am I right?'

Foerster leaned on the opposite wall, catching his breath. 'Ever been?'

'Can't say that I've had the pleasure.'

'Never been, but you put people in for money,' Foerster said. 'That makes as much sense as anything.' He turned his back and began to walk away. Then he stopped. 'You're a fucking hypocrite, you know that? You and everybody like you.'

He kept walking.

It wasn't over, though. Not like that.

Jonah picked up the longest piece of lumber in the pile. The damn thing was heavy. He pictured ninety-pound Foerster here days before, muscling one of these things around to build that bridge, then coming back every couple of days to make sure it was still there. Jesus. The motherfucker was a boy scout. Jonah slid the lumber out over the alley, pushing down hard on his side to keep the other end up. He slid it. He slid it some more. It was too short. It fell away, banging and crashing on its trip down.

'Fuck!'

He heard laughter. He looked up and there was Foerster, leaning against the elevator shaft and smiling at him.

Foerster pantomimed a guy checking the time. 'I could watch this all day,' he said. 'But I got places to be, all right?'

2

The hot sun made her feel sexy.

Thirty-three-year-old, bikini-clad Katie Gant reclined in a lounge chair on a massive stone terrace, floppy sun hat shielding her eyes. The terrace looked over the backyard of her giant Tudor-style home in the suburbs of Charleston, South Carolina. It was a bright afternoon, and from her lounge chair she could drink in the sloping and closely manicured back lawn, the sparkling blue water of the in-ground swimming pool, even the riot of plantings tucked against the back of the house that made up her own kitchen garden, which had seen quite a bountiful harvest this year, thank you. Although her eyes were open, she saw none of these things.

She had a lot on her mind.

For a little while, as the perspiration beaded and slowly rolled down her skin, she imagined a shirtless young man in jeans shorts and flip-flops down there cleaning the pool. Her husband was away on business, again, and frustrated housewife Katie was trying to get that sculpted Adonis of a pool boy to climb the steps to her. She couldn't hold the image, though, and gradually it faded and was replaced.

She remembered a morning fishing trip with her dad when she was a little girl down in Beaufort, when at first light they flushed a heron out of the reeds by the shore. The great gangling bird flapped its huge wings and took off across the bay. It was so graceful, that bird, once it got going, gliding just a couple of feet above the water. A few minutes later, the sun came up over the saltwater flats, Dad was tying her bait, and all the world boiled down to just the two of them in a nine-foot aluminium jonboat. At that moment, she never wanted to leave. She wished that time would stop for ever.

Yet she had run away from Beaufort soon after graduation. By eighteen, the town was too small to hold her. She was confident, she was blonde, she was beautiful – everybody told her so – and she loved to talk and meet people. The world seemed to hold such promise. There was so much to do and see, and she couldn't wait to get started. Some kids were going to college, but she knew college would always be there when she was good and ready for it. First she wanted to taste adventure.

She moved to Washington, DC, with some vague sense that powerful people, movers and shakers, lived there. This was closer to the excitement, but somehow she always seemed to just miss out on it. Part of the problem was the jobs she could get. Secretarial jobs – she was always somebody's secretary. One day, while working as an assistant at the law firm of Benton and Hoffman, she spent seven hours pushing the green start button on a Xerox copy machine. That morning, the machine developed a glitch. It would copy only one page at a time. She needed to make a dozen copies of a government contract that was nearly two hundred pages long. For some unexplained reason the job had to be done that day. And for some reason, also unexplained, they couldn't send it out to Kinko's or Copy Plus. So Katie did it.

'Good job today, Katie,' her boss said, and meant it.

When the day was over, she went home to the apartment she shared with two other girls and cried. At the age of twenty, her employer valued her because she could stand in one place all day long and push the same button more than two thousand times in a row.

Where was the promise? Where was the adventure?

The copy machine debacle helped her realise she wasn't cut out for the business world. It wasn't just that she felt humiliated. It wasn't that she had been treated like a machine, or part of a machine. It ran deeper than that. She saw that if she were in her boss's position, there was no way she could demand that someone push a button two thousand times. It was a soulless, spirit-crushing thing. She wanted no part of it. She was too sensitive, she felt things too deeply.

As it turned out, she was actually an artist. When she was a child, she had loved to draw and to paint, and a life-drawing class she took on eight Saturdays reminded her of this. She moved again, this time to Dewey Beach, Delaware, where there was open space, open air and open water.

It was a party town on the Atlantic Ocean, and she partied right along with it. On summer weekends, it seemed like half of the mid-Atlantic region descended on the beaches. She worked as a waitress, first at a bar and grill, then at a seafood place, then at a steak house. Sweating through the menial jobs didn't bother her any more. She was having fun.

All-night keg parties at rented waterfront townhouses always seemed to end at dawn with eight or ten people nude in the surf. Katie was always one of them. Riding through town in late summer on the back of some guy's motorcycle, high on pot, the sun sinking in hues of red and orange and gold. Steamy lovemaking sessions on the beach, in the outdoor shower, on the back porch, on sandy sheets, with all sorts of guys. A sun-bleached surfer one summer. An artist, like herself, who came to paint the fall foliage one November, and who stayed through till the following April. A married fireman from Philadelphia who shared a ramshackle house with five other firemen, and who came to town every two weeks. Her first and only black man, a retired football player named Ray.

Ray had spent three years on the Kansas City Chiefs without ever getting into a regular season game. The way he saw it, he made all that money and didn't get hurt, and that made sense to Katie. She broke it off with him when he tried to get her into a *ménage à trois* with a hard-bodied black woman he brought over from Baltimore.

'Come on, baby,' Ray said. 'Look at that sexy thing over there. You know she looks good.' The woman leaned against the living-room wall in Katie's small apartment. She had long braids and high cheekbones and tight buns. She looked damn good in a bikini. She had a body to envy, and her big brown eyes said she knew it. Her presence, and the question at hand, made it loud and clear that Ray was already sleeping with her.

'Fuck you, Ray. No means no. It's just not my thing.'

Ray held Katie's face in both hands. He had soft hands for such a strong man. 'Let her taste you, then. I guarantee she'll drive you wild. She wants to do it. Ain't that right, Bevie?'

'Mmmm-hmmm. She looks good to me.' Bevie had a gap between her two front teeth. She said it meant she was sweet down below.

'Tell you what, Ray. Both of you. Out of my house.'

But she felt sad and empty when he was gone. Even now, years later, he was still her image of the ideal physical man. She wasn't tall, but she had a lot of body – she reminded herself of Marilyn Monroe. Ray was so big and strong he made her feel like a small and delicate flower. It was a beautiful feeling, while it lasted.

After Ray, she spent fall and winter collecting unemployment cheques and walking the empty beach. When she looked in the mirror, she caught the first glimpses of something she had thought she would never see. Age. She was twenty-seven. Her skin had seen too much sun. Her body had seen too much alcohol and maybe too many lovers. She counted them and the number only came to twenty-one, less than the number of years she had been alive. She had come close with quite a few others, so close that she almost counted them, but didn't. Twenty-one had received the gift, she decided. Still, it was more than she'd like. For the first time, she considered that she would like to be a virgin again.

The next one, she thought. I'll take it slow and I'll love him, and he'll be the one I marry. It'll all be innocent and like new.

Almost a year later, the next one was Tyler Gant. Handsome, fit and tough – in those days Tyler was every inch the newly retired cop. For a while it had been good with him, good enough to get married. He had taken care of her like no man before him – he was the first man who really had the means to do it. But things between them had turned dark and cold, and now their marriage, their love, was like a dead thing lying at the bottom of that pool on the rolling lawn below her.

The heat hit him like a blast from a furnace.

When the airplane door opened, Tyler Gant stepped from the sleek corporate jet into bright sunshine. He wore a suit of summer linen, and the air-conditioning on the plane had let him forget how hot it would be here on the island. He climbed down the narrow steps to the airstrip's tarmac, which shimmered in the heat. The black tar almost looked like it was bubbling. Gant was the only passenger disembarking from what had probably been designed as an eight- or ten-seater, but was laid out more like somebody's living room. He'd sat in a recliner reading the *New York Times* for the whole two-and-a-half-hour flight. Bad news from everywhere – modern civilisation was falling apart and there didn't seem to be a damned thing anybody could do about it.

Four men in khakis and loose fitting, short-sleeved shirts waited for Gant at the bottom of the steps. They all wore wraparound sunglasses. They all had big shoulders and forearms. Their faces were nearly identical – stone-faced and expressionless. He guessed they all had guns in their waistbands. Hired help.

They didn't ask him how his flight was. They didn't offer him a glass of iced tea. They directed him to a corrugated tin shack near the side of the runway. They entered with him and one of them directed him to remove his clothes. The shack was nothing more than one room with a couple of chairs and a desk. It had a dirt floor.

Gant took everything off, right down to his BVDs. As he did so, he handed the articles of clothing to the men, each one pawing through his pockets, feeling the linings of his jacket and slacks, looking for hidden compartments in his shoes. They found nothing – no weapons, no wires, no *nada*. Gant stood barefoot in the middle of the room, his toes gripping loose dirt, the men hovering around him. They eyed his slim and muscular body, only a flicker here and there betraying the thought – this man is sixty years old? Barely concealed menace came off them in waves.

'You guys want to do a cavity search?' he said.

One of the men smiled. 'We trust you, Gant. You're one of the good guys.' He gestured at Gant's clothes hanging on the back of the chair and draped on the table. 'Get dressed,' he said, and the four gorillas stepped outside.

Gant put his suit back on, but there was no mirror to check his look. He made a Windsor knot without benefit of his reflection, the knowledge where it always had been – in his hands. He came out of the shack and a white Lincoln Town Car was now waiting for him. A black SUV was parked in front of it, and another black SUV brought up the rear. Energy crisis, what energy crisis? The commercial airline industry had disintegrated, and Fielding sent a plane to pick up one person. In the United States, fuel riots were a weekly event, but here Fielding sent a motorcade of gas-guzzlers out to the airport. Maybe it was all designed for show – here on fantasy island money and resources were not an issue. Maybe none of it was really true, a Potemkin stage play put on for Gant's benefit. One of Gant's guiding principles was not to trust first impressions – often enough, things were not what they seemed.

He climbed into the back seat of the Lincoln. A man sat there, thin with round wire-frame glasses, nattily attired in a grey three-piece suit, sandy hair brushed back from his face. He extended a bony hand from a thin, fragile-looking arm. The arm could have been a loose thread at the end of his sleeve. Gant shook the hand, and the grip was firm enough. As Gant settled in, the little convoy rolled out. In fact it drove right down the middle of the runway towards a high chain-link fence at the far end – the exit. The limo driver was a dark shadow on the far side of a smoked-glass partition.

'Mr Gant?' the man said. 'I'm Elliott Howe, Mr Fielding's personal assistant. How was your flight?'

'Smooth,' Gant said. 'No complaints.'

'Would you care for a drink?'

'Not at the moment. Thanks.'

'Mr Fielding is eager to meet with you.'

'That's good news. I see he trusts I don't have a bomb planted up my ass.'

Gant wasn't one to suck up oxygen making small-talk, and he didn't like having happy gas blown his way – especially not three minutes after a strip-search.

The car motored along a narrow, winding concrete highway lined with palm trees and dense undergrowth. Their little motorcade seemed to be the only cars on the road. Gant didn't bother to look closely at the trees and other plants for what he knew he'd find. The island flora were sick – the rainy season was already lurching towards its end, and for the second year in a row it had barely rained at all. The climate patterns had changed here, abruptly and without calling the weatherman for permission.

Even in good times, many local people had been poor. A steady trickle of tourism had kept the island alive. Now the tourists were mostly gone. They had evaporated along with the gasoline and the good corporate jobs and the Wall Street funny money. With no rain, the meagre crops the folks here had planted to save themselves were dried out and dead. There was trouble in paradise. Poverty was bad enough, and sustained drought made it worse, but events were quickly moving to the next level. The island government – dominated and manipulated for many years by the man Gant was about to see – had collapsed. People were going hungry. Roaming gangs of men, armed with machetes, had seized some of the land and homes of the wealthy.

Every few minutes, the Town Car rattled over some rough road, or slowed to a crawl to pick its way across a monster chuckhole. Road maintenance was no longer a priority, it seemed. On the right, a maxi van, that Third World taxi service deathtrap, zoomed by going the other direction. The driver leant on his horn as he passed. The maxi went by so fast that Gant didn't notice much about it. He was left with the impression that maybe a dozen people were packed inside. All he knew for sure was that the van was still operational, the driver still had access to gasoline, and there was a slogan painted in bright colours on the front of the van: *Angel Eyes*.

On the left, across more undergrowth, Gant caught a glimpse of the turquoise ocean. On the right, through the bushes and on the other side of a dilapidated green fence, Gant spied cinderblock homes and tin-roof clapboard shanties in a riot of fading colours. Gant knew that many of the roofs were outfitted with cisterns to catch rainwater. The whole set-up had been described to him months ago. But the cisterns were hardly much use these days.

High above the roofs and etched against the sky, he noticed the grand prize – a large water tower. It caught his eye for a few seconds before he looked away. He'd seen aerial and ground-level photos of it, of course, but had never seen it in person. The communities on this island were served by two old towers, this one the Town Car was passing and one other. The water was pump-driven up into the towers from the tiny local reservoir, the pumps powered by diesel gas. The water pressure in people's homes was created by gravity as the water came down from the towers.

The towers themselves were very low security – you could simply cut open a chain-link fence and, in each case, climb a staircase a few storeys up to the tank. Each of the tanks had vents that could easily be forced open. It was mind-boggling, such open access to a vital community resource like water. For a moment, Gant found himself lost in thought about it.

Suddenly, up ahead, two children darted out from the grasses on the right. They were black kids, boys, dressed only in shorts. Each boy hurled something at the car, throwing their projectiles ahead of the car's path, timing it perfectly, nailing the spot where the car would be in another second.

It was some kind of red fruit. Gant heard the first one hit somewhere at the front of the car – maybe the windshield. The second one crashed into the window next to Gant's head. It made a loud THUMP, then hung there for a moment, stuck to the glass, weird, pulpy, almost obscene. The centre of it looked like the mouth of some kind of suckerfish, with ruby-coloured tendrils extending away like the arms of an octopus. Then the whole mess slithered to the bottom of the window and fell away. In its wake it left a path of slime, like a snail might leave behind.

'The car is bulletproof, of course,' Howe said. 'Including the windows.'

'They're throwing away food,' Gant said.

'Yes, very foolish. Maybe it was rotten.'

Gant smiled. 'Those little kids are probably pretty good at throwing a base-ball. In another couple of years, maybe they'll be just as good with a firebomb. Or a grenade.' The thought pleased him somehow.

Howe smiled in return, but it looked more like a wince. 'That's one of Mr Fielding's concerns. But hopefully, things will never get that far.'

The car slowed to a stop on a curve. Up ahead and to his right, Gant saw two of the men from the airstrip climb-out of the lead SUV. They both had compact machine guns cradled in their arms. Suddenly there was the blat of automatic weaponry. Gant's heart skipped a beat at the sound. He looked back to where the kids had been – they were both OK, running through the high grass towards the shanties. The gunmen had fired into the air.

'Not very sporting,' Gant said. 'Firing on children, even over their heads, could be counter-productive.'

Howe was unapologetic. 'We live in a profoundly active balance of terror with the neighbours, I'm afraid. We don't shoot children, but we do try to demonstrate who is in charge on this island. Increasingly, it's a lesson that seems lost on their parents.'

Gant just looked at Howe. He took a good, long look. Howe was a man who had probably never fired a weapon in anger during his entire life. But Howe held Gant's stare, his eyes never wavering. It was easy to be a tough guy in the back of a limousine.

'I guess that's why we hire a person like Mr Tyler Gant,' Howe said. 'To remind everyone just who's in charge around here.'

Gant glanced at the red smudge on the window. 'Actually, you hire me when no one is in charge, and you want me to fix that.'

The car and its SUV escorts started again. They exited the main road and followed a narrow, well-paved lane uphill through thick green foliage. The ascent was steep for a moment, and then very steep. Gant sat back in his seat, almost like an astronaut waiting for take-off. He felt the heavy Town Car working to manage the hill.

The entrance to Fielding's estate was at the top of the hill. Gant took in the security – the place seemed well guarded. The procession waited while the main gate slid open, then each car passed through in line. Unlike out at the airstrip, here the security team made no pretence. Two men stood near the booth with Uzis carried lightly in their hands. The perimeter fence was wrought iron and very tall – the gaps were too narrow for even the skinniest kid to slip through.

Gant glanced upwards and spotted bands of circular razor wire at the top. Beat that fence – a determined mob could probably take it down – and you faced about thirty yards to an identical wrought-iron fence, with identical razor wire on top. The thirty-yard gap between fences was a dog run. Gant spotted half a dozen Rottweilers roaming free in there. Beat the dogs, beat the second fence, and you probably confronted ten or more slack-faced, dead-eyed professional killers with automatic weapons. It would take something just short of a revolution to breach these grounds – hundreds of people, too hungry to fear death. Either that, or a sudden outbreak of empathy and reluctance to fire among the security team.

The house itself was a palace. When the Lincoln pulled to the top of the circular driveway, Gant made a quick calculation. Old quarried stone plantation house, around two hundred years old, fully restored, probably thirty rooms. Gant's own large home – a mansion by many people's standards – would fit tucked neatly into a far wing of this house.

He exited the car and immediately felt the breeze – the air wasn't nearly as heavy up here. Ahead of him, Howe jogged briskly up the stone front steps. Gant carried his own bag and followed him. They turned around. The front of the house faced inland – a sweeping panorama downhill across the brown and green island, the township far below, and in the distance, a white sand beach. Here and there, wisps of cloud clung to the treetops – maybe a few drops of rain in those clouds, but not much. On a few of the hillsides, Gant spotted homes similar, but perhaps not as grand, to this one.

'Quite a view,' Gant said.

Howe shrugged. 'That's nothing. Wait till you see the view from the veranda, and from your bedroom.'

In the foyer a simple white cross, seven feet high, dominated the space in front of the wide spiral stairway. Gant thought of the garish depictions of Christ on the cross from his Catholic upbringing – super-realistic, emaciated, bleeding from the nails piercing his hands and his feet and from the thorns pricking his head, wild eyes rolling heavenward in anguish. It was the stuff of nightmares, and had made an impression on Gant. But none of that for Fielding. Fielding's own brand of fanatical Christianity was crisp and clean – it had abstracted ol' Christ right out of the picture.

Howe led Gant to the second floor and down a wide, cool hallway. Their feet echoed on polished stone. They passed through a doorway and here was what must have been Fielding's office – fifty yards away, on the far end of what might have once been a ballroom. Gant could almost hear the strains of music and laughter from those long ago times – the good old days. As they walked across the open space, Gant could see the desk, positioned to the right of the open balcony. To the left of the balcony was a sofa and two chairs. Two men sat there, each sipping from a teacup. Gant recognised one of them, a man with white hair, from photographs. He was Roscoe Fielding, the owner of this house, and the master of all he surveyed. Gant didn't know the other man. They rose as Gant and his minder approached.

'Mr Gant,' Fielding said. 'Good of you to join us. Do you know Representative Harting?'

'I'm afraid I don't.' Gant extended his hand to the congressman, who took it in his soft paw. Harting was a beefy man of indeterminate age with a swoop of sandy brown hair. He wore a light brown sports jacket over a dress shirt, open at the collar, and khaki shorts – the prep school look. It was enough to make Gant dislike him instantly. Even worse, Harting's chubby cheeks and the spot of red on each one made him look like a spoiled twelve-year-old who spent much of his time indoors playing video games.

'Jim Harting, Tyler Gant,' Fielding said. He put a proprietary arm around Harting's big shoulders. 'Jim is one of the good ones. He's one of ours.'

'Fighting the good fight,' Gant said. 'Don't let me interrupt you.'

'Roscoe and I were just finishing,' Harting said, with a hint of a Southern twang. 'He told me y'all had some important business to talk about, and I'm here for a couple more days, so . . .'

'He has plenty of time to grab my ear, should he need to,' Fielding said.

Howe smoothly escorted the Honourable James Harting out. Gant took a seat across from Fielding. Fielding was thin to the point of pain. His bony wrists extended a few inches past the end of his white cotton sleeves. His eyes seemed sunken back into his face. The face itself looked like it was written on wrinkled parchment.

'The tea is still hot,' Fielding said, gesturing to the pot on the table. 'Hot tea on a hot day, it makes you perspire. Cools you off some.'

'No thanks.'

Fielding poured himself another cup, his hands shaking just a bit. 'We see you already moved the money from the account we set up for you.'

Gant smiled. 'One bank account is as good as another.'

'Do you trust us?'

Gant shrugged, didn't say anything.

Fielding waved the issue away. 'It's your money. Do whatever you want with it. Anyway, that's not why I asked you here. I thought it was time for us to meet. You'll find that I'm a man who isn't much one for chit-chat. I like to get down to business right away. And I like to speak plainly.'

Gant thought of the politician who had just left. He looked like a chit-chatter and double-talker, if ever there was one. 'I'm all for speaking plainly,' Gant said.

Fielding nodded. 'Good. Then here it is. We've paid you a lot of money, and as I say, that's OK with me. But I'm concerned. I find you much less forthcoming with information than I'd like. We've had no status reports from you. You're hesitant to talk on the telephone or to submit anything in writing, and I understand that reluctance. But you also refuse to send any of your people here to make a report, and that I don't understand. Our mutual friends told us to expect these things from you, so I've been patient, but my patience is wearing thin. I'm beginning to suspect I've been taken for a ride. I can't tell you how much that upsets and disappoints me.'

Gant felt nothing as a result of Fielding's little speech. He'd been through this type of thing before. Clients, at some point in any operation, especially one as uncertain as this, always needed to be reassured. They needed a hug, and they needed a grown-up to tell them everything was going to be all right. In fact, Fielding had lasted longer than some others before reaching that place.

'I'm here, aren't I?' Gant said. 'I'd hardly come waltzing through all of your gunmen if I were, as you say, taking you for a ride.'

'Agreed. I feel a little better already, just having you as my guest.'

'So then, what would you like to know?'

'Well, by now I was expecting to see . . . something. Some action. Since you're here, would you like to update me on the project's status?'

'Why? Don't you trust me?' Gant said.

Fielding smiled the tiniest bit. He moved a few papers aside on the table, and came up with a manila folder. He opened it and looked at the one sheet of white unlined paper inside. 'Tyler Gant. US Army Twenty-fifth Infantry Division, Vietnam. Two tours of duty, 1969–1971. Philadelphia Police Department, 1972–2003. You've spent most of your life in service to your country and your community. That's to be commended. You should be proud.'

'I don't make a fetish out of it,' Gant said.

Fielding laughed. 'They said you were a wiseass. I like that in a man, but only so much.' His face became serious. 'You know, I'm only five years older than you.'

'I know.'

'Well, how do you do it? How do you stay so young?'

'Believe me, I'm nothing like I used to be,' Gant said. 'I feel the time passing.'

'But still,' Fielding said. 'It's remarkable.'

Gant shrugged. 'I only drink the best whiskey. That helps. And I've been blessed with good genes.' He didn't mention the two days a week with a personal trainer, the five-mile runs, and the yoga nearly every morning. He didn't mention the fruit and vegetable juicing, and the four days of fasting each month. They probably had all that in a file, in any case. 'My father turned eighty-nine this year. He just came back from his fall hunting trip. Took down a ten-point buck. Clean shot to the head.'

'Amazing,' Fielding said. 'How's he getting along in these dark times? Does he find it hard?'

'He's a tough old bird. Says he's seen it worse. He was alive during the Great Depression. That was, of course, worse than now.'

'I'll grant that's probably true,' Fielding said. He paused, seemingly lost in thought for a moment. 'Mr Gant, I'm concerned. That's all I'm saying. You come highly recommended. I'm told you're among the best at what you do, but I feel like you've left me in the dark here.'

'Do you really want to be in the light? In matters such as these, highly sensitive matters, I operate under the assumption that the less the client knows, the better for the client. I think you should take a moment before you answer. Do you really want to know what's happening?'

Fielding didn't hesitate. 'Yes. I want to know.'

Gant took a deep breath, then nodded. 'We are very close. There's a boat anchored off the East Coast of the United States, exactly where doesn't matter at this moment. A small laboratory has been built aboard the boat. Not state of the art, but quite good under the circumstances. It has everything necessary. A person I trust, and who has experience in these matters, built the lab based on very specific guidelines. Some people I do business with have acquired a quantity of a certain substance, an organism, and they will deliver it to the boat when I give them the go ahead. A scientist is en route to the boat. He was unavoidably detained very recently, so the work is a little behind schedule, but I can tell you that soon he will be in place. Once he is, the work will proceed very quickly. After that, your men can meet us at the boat, and we'll make the transfer.'

Fielding nodded. 'You'll accompany my men back here on the plane, of course. To make sure the operation ends smoothly?'

'Of course. I'll probably bring at least one of my men with me as well.'

'The scientist,' Fielding said. 'He's a good man?'

Gant chose not to answer the question. 'I've worked with him before, and our previous work has been a success. What we accomplished in the past is likely what brought my name to your attention.'

He paused, then looked deeply into Fielding's eyes. 'The question now becomes, are you sure you want to go through with this?'

Gant saw *the look* come into Fielding's eyes. He had seen it many times before, in many other sets of eyes. It was a hunger, like a vampire thirsty for blood.

'Mr Gant, this house has been my primary residence for the past thirty years. I'm an American, but this island is my home. I buried my wife here. I raised two children here. I've run my businesses from here. Many good friends of mine have been driven away, forced off the island, by the tyranny of the mob. Innocent people have had their homes taken, have been murdered, and far worse.' Fielding's thin, weak hand clenched into a fist. '*Worse than murdered*, do I need to explain the meaning of that to you? And some of the men doing these things were policemen less than a year ago. But this isn't Rhodesia, or Zimbabwe, or whatever you want to call it. A few of us are still here, and we're not going anywhere. We will not be terrorised and we will not be driven out. I am totally committed to the course of action I've asked you to take.'

'And the media reaction?' Gant said. 'What will you do when CNN and the BBC are broadcasting footage of corpses being buried by bulldozers? What will you do when the Marines come ashore, with investigators from the Centres for Disease Control? What will you do afterwards? How will you stay here? This is going to be a land of the dead.'

Fielding waved his hand, as he would wave away a mosquito. 'Please don't underestimate my ability to influence media coverage, or to influence the US government response. Let's just say that members of Congress are among the least powerful of my friends. Anyway, this is a tiny island, barely worth mentioning. I'm sure you read the newspapers – people are dying everywhere. If a few thousand people here suddenly succumb to an infectious disease . . .'

He shrugged and paused for several seconds. Then he nodded. 'And what am I going to do in this land of the dead, as you describe it? For one thing, I'm going to stay and see my enemies defeated. Then, after an appropriate length of time has passed, I'll repopulate the island with immigrant workers who can better appreciate the blessings available here. To put it another way, I am completely prepared for the consequences of the operation.'

When he finished, a silence drew out between them.

'Have I answered your concerns, Mr Gant?'

'I guess you have. And I assume that means your operatives are ready?'

'They've practised night-time attacks on the water towers half a dozen times now, without being detected.'

'And you've taken the precautions I suggested? You have bottled water and food stockpiled? Your people are ready to defend this perimeter?'

'I do, and they are.'

'I want to tell you something. It's a hell of a thing, what's going to happen. I hope you'll feel as gung-ho about it afterwards as you do now. Personally, I think you probably won't.'

'I'm surprised to hear you say that, Mr Gant. You sound like a man suffering from regrets. Will you lose sleep over this project? Have you lost sleep over similar projects in the past? If so, then I'm afraid I have the wrong intelligence sheet here.'

Gant stared into Fielding's deep black eyes. 'I've been around death a long time, Mr Fielding. It doesn't bother me. In fact, it's been my constant companion. If I'm away from it for any length of time, I start to feel lonely.'

Fielding smiled. 'That's good. That's very, very good to hear.'

Gordo hummed a happy tune.

An hour had passed since they missed Foerster, and he and Jonah were in Kelly's Bar, a dark and moody watering hole with two shamrocks in bright green neon adorning the front windows. The place sat along a grim and desolate strip of road, across from a cemetery. The nearest open shop was halfway up the street, a place that installed alarm systems. Also, there was a scrap metal dealer next door, a sign announcing 'We Buy and Sell' hovering above a barbed-wire fence, but Gordo had never seen anybody go in or out of there. Kelly's itself was long and narrow inside, like a tunnel, and always smelled

of beer and piss. On the plus side, they had their own diesel-powered generator under an awning behind the building, and they weren't reluctant to use
it. As a result, the jukebox in the far corner and the colour TV bolted to the
wall over the bar always worked.

Gordo had the beers in hand, pints in frosted glasses. Despite the day's
fiasco, he felt pretty good. It was a temporary setback. Before leaving the
scene today, Gordo had gone upstairs and snatched some unopened mail
he found lying around the apartment. There was good stuff in that pile of
envelopes, he knew there was.

When Gordo arrived at the table, Jonah was slouched on his stool, ignoring
Foerster's mail. Instead, he held a wet cloth napkin packed with ice against
his forehead. He said he had gotten hit with a bottle, and he had an evil lump
to prove it. The lump had cracked open and was oozing a sort of liquidy pus.
Maybe there was some glass in there, Gordo didn't know and didn't care. He
had bigger things to think about. For one, Jonah had shown him something
today. That leap across the fire escapes, that took the prize for guts. That was
probably why Gordo felt so good, just knowing he had a partner with the
stones to do that.

For a moment he saw the Jonah others saw. Light-skinned black man, son
of a black mother and a white father. He had softer features than a lot of
black guys – a leaner nose, thinner lips. Jonah was a solid, handsome dude,
like an actor or maybe a pro baseball player out and about in street clothes.

It was rare for Gordo to look at him this way. Most of the time, Gordo
still thought of his partner as he was when they first met and became friends
in junior high school – a skinny kid with a crazy head of curly hair and basket-
ball shorts hanging down past his knees. They had known each other a long
time now – just about twenty years.

Gordo placed the beers on the table and slid on to his stool.

'You want some acetaminophen?' he said. 'I got some out in the car. Generic
store brand, but it works real good.'

Jonah shook his head. 'The stuff is poison, man. It kills the liver.'

Gordo saw right away that Jonah was in a mood. Well, then it was up to

Gordo to lighten the place up a little. 'Listen, it was poor planning,' he told Jonah. 'The fucking guy out-thunk me, that's all.'

'I don't want to talk about it,' Jonah said.

'We learned something today, that's what I'm trying to tell you. Planning is the key, all right? We just gotta look at all the angles. Cover all possible exits, no matter how crazy they seem.'

Jonah grimaced in response and stared down at the table. 'That's a long way to go to learn something.'

Gordo sipped his beer.

He was thirty-two years old, stood a shade under six feet tall, and weighed almost two hundred and fifty pounds. He thought he carried it pretty well, more like a strong, heavy thickness than fat. His massive belly was as hard as an iron skillet. His legs were like the trunks of California redwoods. His arms were like the big bass pipes on a giant church organ. And the nickname? He loved it. El Gordo. It reminded him of a superhero, or maybe a monster from the old Jap Godzilla movies. He had loved the girl down in Santo Domingo who thought it up, too. She was dark black with dyed-blond hair and a killer body. Chocolata, she called herself, though God knew her real name was probably something a little more conventional like Rosa, or Maria. In any case, Gordo did her good, in ten different ways and in the morning he gave her an extra tip for the nickname idea.

He had been around.

He sold cocaine for a while when he was coming up. He had a little route that took him all over the metro area three days a week. It turned him off pretty quick. He grew tired of listening to screaming babies in the back bedrooms of tiny houses while Mom and Dad had a taste in the kitchen before buying. How often had he seen that? Once or twice, but it seemed like every week. He also didn't like that paranoid, up-all-night feeling after too many lines, hours of time to think about the cops knocking down the door and coming through the walls one day soon. He got out before that could happen.

Later, he spent some time repossessing cars. It was back when the collapse started happening, the first phase. People had bought all kinds of junk on credit, and now they were out of money. Gas prices going through the roof, house values tanking, people losing jobs left and right – suddenly, paying the note on that Hummer or that Land Rover didn't seem so smart any more. Those were good times and Gordo made good money. It seemed like he could always make money, up or down, it didn't matter.

But the banks themselves started going belly up. There was a glut of consumer shit out there – cars, boats, jet skis – and nobody was paying on any of it, but the companies didn't want it back, either. It cost more to collect the stuff than the money they could get reselling it or unloading it at auction. Then the gasoline dried up, and no middle-class worker bee would take a powerboat or a jet ski if you tried to give them one. You might as well try to give them bubonic plague. It was a good lesson to learn – toys that had once cost ten thousand, twenty thousand, even thirty thousand dollars or more could become worth zero, or less than zero, practically overnight.

When that happened, Gordo drifted for a while. The occasional repo popped up from time to time, but it wasn't enough. During a brief period, maybe six months, he lost his confidence a little bit. He began to think that maybe he was going to go down with the ship, that he wasn't going to be able to turn this thing around.

Then he stumbled on an idea while watching television one night. They did a short piece on some fluff news show about guys who went around serving lawsuit papers and summonses to people who didn't want to be served said papers. The show said the guys worked for themselves, on their own, taking jobs from the courts and from law firms that operated around the court buildings. It could be a rough-and-tumble-type job, according to the announcer, good for snoops who weren't afraid when people got out of line. The news piece was over in about five minutes. Afterwards, Gordo sat on his couch and drank a beer, staring at whatever came on the television next. But what he was looking at was an image in his mind's eye, an image of the Bronx County Courthouse.

For as long as he could remember, Gordo had known about the court-house. It was that huge off-white ten-storey Art Deco monster looming in the distance beyond the white bunting and the bleachers at the old Yankee Stadium. It sat high above the elevated subway line and all the shops and fast food restaurants wedged together along the wide boulevard of 161st Street. It ate up a whole city block. It always caught his eye, and he would gaze at it between innings, but he never imagined himself going up the hill and walking inside. Then one day he found himself there, as if he had floated to it in a dream. He passed through the security checkpoint without incident. He asked some faceless person for directions, waded through the crowds, and stood in line at a window. He took a course, complete with a workbook and pencils and a buttoned-down instructor who told the twenty people gathered in the dusty classroom how it was all going to go down. Two weeks later Gordo was serving paper.

He liked it and was good at it. He could find people, even the people who didn't want to be found – especially those people. And once he found them, there was no mystery to serving them. His first test came early on.

One day, he had to serve a mechanic who was delinquent in his child-support payments. It was a typical set-up. As the economy went from bad to worse, a lot of women were chasing down a lot of deadbeat dads who claimed they had no money. And an auto mechanic would be a good candidate for deadbeat dadhood – cars were dropping off the road like houseflies had once dropped in the first chill of October.

It was 6.30 in the evening, and Gordo tracked his prey to a nudie bar a block away from the auto body shop. The bar had a steeple in front as though it had once been a church. The guy Gordo wanted was in there drinking dinner with two of his buddies, watching some blond-haired Bavarian sow in a lime-green thong gyrate to loud disco music back behind the bar. She liked the night life, she liked to boogie. Her huge pink nipples hung down almost to her waist. The thong carved into her love handles. The bartender, a creaky old Slav, looked so bored he was about to expire from the tedium.

Gordo had a copy of the mechanic's photo from a driver's licence, so he knew what the guy looked like. He walked up to the three of them at their table and sat down. The guy he needed to serve was the one in the middle, still wearing his grimy and oil-caked work overalls. He had slicked-back hair, a pock-marked face, and oversized hands. His two friends were a small round Mexican in a baseball cap and a skinny, dark West Indian. Gordo envied them their openness – here in the Bronx, the various cultures mostly steered clear of one another.

The three men eyed Gordo.

'Eddie?' Gordo said. 'Eddie Valence?' Gordo thought that somewhere in the past the family had Americanised its name from Valenzuela.

'Who wants to know?'

Gordo gave them all an apologetic grin. 'Hey, I hate to bother you, man, but I got a problem with my car outside. I think it's the carburettor. A guy told me to look in here for you, said you might be willing to make some extra money. It'll probably take somebody like you five minutes to fix it. Me, I don't know anything about cars.'

He paused, Valence looking at him, the other men staring past him now, eyes glued to the girl on stage. At the end of a long day, and after a few drinks, even a specimen like that could get a man going. Gordo knew how they felt. He was the same way.

Valence nodded. 'It's me. I'll look at it in a minute.'

'Tell you what,' Gordo said, taking the papers from the pocket inside his jacket and placing them on the table. 'Before you look at the car, why don't you go in and talk to the judge about all those child-support payments you missed?'

All three men were gaping at him again.

'What I'm saying is you've been served.'

Valence took it hard. Without a word, he stood and grabbed Gordo by the shirt. The West Indian also stood. A moment later, both men were splayed out under the table, with the Mexican standing ten feet away, wanting no part of the action. It happened so fast that Gordo had no memory of putting them down there, just a blur of throwing fists and knocking beers over. His hands were slimy from Valence's hair gel.

Gordo looked at the Mexican, but the Mexican shook his head. Gordo looked at the girl, who had paused in her dance routine. She made no sign, just stared at him. The ancient Slavic bartender held a sawed-off pool cue, but made no move forward with it. Just before he left, Gordo folded the papers and placed them in the breast pocket of Valence's overalls.

That sort of thing got around, and Gordo started to gain a reputation. Somebody who's gone to ground, with no forwarding address? Give it to Gordon Lamb. A hard-ass who popped the last process guy in the mouth? Lamb will take it.

Then, eighteen months ago, while hanging around the halls of justice one morning, he got to talking to a bail bondsman, a short guy named Leo who always wore a bowtie and pants held up by suspenders. Leo's thing was that the suspenders and bowtie always had themes – whales against a deep blue sea one day, the red hammer and sickle of the former Soviet Union the next day, green hundred-dollar bills the next. Leo's bald head glistened in the over-head fluorescents – if Gordo didn't know better, he'd guess that the little man polished it like a bowling ball. Leo was also hanging around that morning.

'If you're so good at finding people,' Leo said idly, 'then why don't you do the bounty hunter thing? Catch a couple of these assholes that've skipped out on me? I got criminals disappearing left and right. How am I supposed to make a living when nobody shows up for trial any more? You want money, that's where you can make some real money. Bring these fucking jerks back.'

'Tell me more,' Gordo said.

Inside Kelly's Bar, ten minutes had gone by since Gordo brought over the beers, and Jonah's headache had not improved at all. The sound system pounded out some bad rock tune. It was just after six o'clock, and almost nobody was in there. Three long hairs, skinny guys in black T-shirts and dirty jeans, crouched over in the corner getting loaded and shovelling dollars into the juke.

Jonah's head thumped along to the music. A few moments ago, he had gone in the bathroom and seen the angry red lump growing on his forehead. It stung where the skin was broken and it throbbed with every beat of his pulse.

He didn't want to touch it. Now he sat at their table and sulked while Gordo pored through a pile of mail he had found in Foerster's apartment.

'That fucking guy,' Jonah said. 'All these skips are crazy, man.'

Gordo seemed fixated on the letter he was reading. There were so many envelopes, it seemed that Foerster hadn't opened any of his mail in a month. 'You know,' Gordo said, 'this guy tells his landlord his name is Mark Foster, then goes ahead and tells half the world his real name. All his bills at that address came to Davis Foerster, not that he paid any of them. Isn't that dumb?'

Jonah said nothing.

Gordo peeled his eyes from the paper and peered at Jonah for a moment. 'Sure you didn't get any glass on your brain?'

'Fuck you,' Jonah said.

Gordo frowned. 'Relax. We missed one. Granted, it was the big fish, but that's the first one we missed in a month. And maybe we'll pick up his scent again. What more do you want?'

Jonah shook his head. 'I want some more money. How about that?'

Gordo smiled. 'The money's coming, brother. You just gotta stick with it a little while longer. We catch this guy and then we're talking about real money, right?' He picked up his beer glass and took a long sip. 'Listen, you need to think like me. I'm in the same boat as you. I'm just about flat busted. But I don't worry about it. As long as I'm still breathing, I'm cool, because I know something big is just around the next corner. Every dollar I get, I put it back into this business. I'm building for the future. See?'

'I got you,' Jonah said. 'Look at the money like it's no big deal.'

'That's right. If everybody's going broke, then the fact that you're going broke is no problem.'

There was some truth to that. Jonah wasn't the only one going under. The modern world — the world Jonah had grown up in — hadn't exactly rolled over and died. But it was going away and faster than anyone could have imagined. It was already a disintegrating remnant, a pale shadow of its former self. Economies had ground to a halt. Millions were out of work. Governments fell apart overnight. In the Third World, there was mass starvation and disease.

Earlier this year, for the first time, there were food shortages in the United States. Food shortages in the land of fat people? It was hard to accept.

Jonah remembered being comforted as a child by the fact that the grown-ups were in charge. Now, as a grown-up, he realised no one was in charge. In this new world, you had to make your own way and figure it out for yourself. Nobody was going to do the figuring for you.

Gordo was wrong. It was a problem. It was a fucking big problem. The year was three quarters over and Jonah had pulled down less than half his old salary. It wouldn't have turned out so bad, except he had lived a high-flying lifestyle in years past, and he still had the bills to prove it. Gordo might be busted or he might not, but one look at the man would tell you that he'd never spent money the way Jonah had.

Less than three years ago, Jonah had been driving a sleek white Jaguar XJ8 with a luxurious interior. He thought of that car as a high-water mark of sorts. At some point he had stopped making payments on it and one morning it just wasn't there any more. Goodbye to the leather bucket seats and goodbye to the lamb's-wool foot rugs. Goodbye to the walnut trim with the Peruvian boxwood inlays, and goodbye to the charging silver jungle cat on the hood. Jonah had heard that all the jaguars in the wild were dead – the only place they still existed was in the zoo and as hood ornaments on expensive cars. When he heard that, it made him kind of sad to keep driving it. So when the repo men took his fancy ride, Jonah didn't even bother to call anybody. It didn't matter anyway. He knew what they would say.

The weird thing about it was that every now and then Jonah would get the suspicion that Gordo himself had taken it. And why not? Gordo was a repo man – even now, he wasn't above a repo job if one came in. Gordo knew where the car was, and he knew how far behind Jonah was on the payments. He knew Jonah's personal habits and schedule. It wouldn't take much for Gordo to put out a feeler and see if the car was slated for repossession – probably no more than a few phone calls.

Jonah brought up the issue over drinks one night.

'What?' Gordo said. 'Are you crazy? Why would I repo your car?'

Jonah shrugged. 'Money. Why else?'

'Man, you are crazy. You've obviously lost your marbles. Listen, I'm not even going to dignify this by talking about it.'

Now Jonah owned a brown 1992 Toyota Corolla, which he rarely even drove. Jonah was just not the type of man who spent his days scrounging for gasoline. In any case, the car was a joke. The rear bumper was missing, although the black rubber covering of the bumper was still there. To the naked eye it seemed as if there was still a bumper, but there was no substance to it. If he ever got rear-ended, the other driver would be sitting in the front seat with him.

The cable TV was gone, and had been for months – no more watching the big booties shake it on BET, no more watching the white girls spank each other on the Playboy channel. He was months behind on the telephone bill, and every now and then the phone company sent him a threatening letter. When the letter came, and he knew the letter by the red envelope it came in, he would open it and send them a cheque for half of what he owed. Otherwise he didn't open their letters. Losing the phone wasn't on his mind. What needed to go was the apartment itself – it was the crib of a man who could blow money on Hudson River views. He was no longer that man, but he had renewed when the lease expired, more out of a misplaced sense of optimism than anything else.

He'd had a bad couple of years. Every time he thought he'd hit bottom, that things couldn't get much worse, life dropped him another notch. A few weeks ago, he would have thought this had to be it – flat broke, deep in debt, working with Gordo, wrestling crazies back into police custody for chump change – that had to be the bottom. But today was a new bottom. He had risked his life for nothing, no reason at all. Tomorrow he'd probably get killed for the same reason.

If he really wanted, he could remember the exact moment when things in his life first started going dark. It was the day Melinda met Elaine.

Melinda kept her pubic hair shaved clean.

Whenever Jonah thought of her, that bald mons was the first thing that

47

leapt to mind. She was a nice little white girl and Jonah often worried that he didn't deserve her. She worked that body till it was lean and tight and hard. She cut her brown hair in a short bob. She wore Donna Karan for nights out, with white gold from Fortunoff. For casual times, she picked the smallest clothes she could find at Eileen Fisher. Beneath everything, she wore only Victoria's Secret. When she slept she wore nothing.

She and Jonah looked good together, whether sitting at a table in Carmine's after taking in a Wednesday evening Broadway show, or cruising home in the Jag with the sunroof open, or wrestling nude on silk sheets later that night. She was fair and small and smelled like money, and he was brown, but not too brown. No, too brown wouldn't look right, but the kind of brown that came from his mother's honest blackness and his old man's rumpled, cigar-chomping whiteness, that was a good soft brown. Jonah thought Melinda liked them together, the look of it. She liked his money, although she had her own, more than he would ever have. She liked that he was strong. Above all, she liked his skin against hers. Yes. She had a taste for brown. It made for three years of damn fine rutting.

But Jonah had a problem. He was not a one-woman man.

It was the Sunday morning just after Thanksgiving. It was rainy and over-cast, and they had wasted the weekend and each other in bed. By Jonah's count, they had fornicated nineteen times since a good-morning romp on the kitchen table the day before.

He lay sprawled on his back in the bed, head resting on the pillows, watching himself in the mirror embedded in the ceiling, and listening to the sound of Melinda taking a shower in his bathroom. After a moment, the water stopped and he waited for her to come out. He felt sexy and pretty damn good about himself. The soreness, the physical emptiness was like a tingling throughout his body. Just seeing his body made him feel pretty good, too. It always did. Other men bought magazines and lotions and uppers and downers because they wanted a body like his. He worked out like they did, but not as hard and not as long. The body was just there for him, better than most of them would ever have. Washboard abdominals without the infomercial gimmicks.

48

Wide, round shoulders and a broad chest. And down below the waist . . . If he was half-black, it was the half that mattered. Little Melinda was fascinated by his size, obsessed with it, maybe addicted to it.

He ran a hand along his chest, played with his nipple ring, and rested his hand on his stomach. He didn't know why he'd got that ring. He just did it on impulse one day, walking past all the freak shops on St Mark's Place in the East Village. It was a small gold hoop like a pirate would wear in his ear.

Melinda came out of the bathroom holding something.

He knew she saw all of him from where she stood. She was already dressed. Dark tights clung to her legs. She wore a blue boiled-wool jacket, what he thought of as her fuzzy coat, against the chill of late fall she would face outside.

He figured if he played the next few minutes right, he could get something moving inside her body. If she watched him a few seconds too long, she would take all those clothes off again and they'd go for it one more time before she left for the day. Make it an even twenty.

'What are these?' she said.

He caught a note of alarm in her voice. It made him look at what she was holding. The first thing he noticed was a pair of black panties, too large for Melinda. His heart did a lazy belly flop as he responded.

'Looks like underwear.'

'I found them in the bathroom drawer,' she said. Now her voice began to shake and her chin began to tremble. She held the label in the waistband face out so he could get a good long look. 'They're La Perla.'

'OK.' His mind went dumb, searching for anything, any thought.

She shook her head so hard that her hair bounced back and forth. It returned to almost the same position from which it started. 'Wrong. Not OK. They weren't there the last time I went in that drawer. Neither were these.'

She offered her other hand for his inspection. That hand held big trouble. Jonah recognized the items, a tube of KY Jelly and a clear plastic applicator which resembled a toy syringe. They came as a kit and were designed for women who had a hard time maintaining lubrication during sex play, a problem Melinda just didn't have.

'Where did these things come from, Jonah?'

There was nowhere to hide. He saw this and he didn't run from it.

In his mind's eye, as though it were showing on a giant high-definition liquid-crystal television, Jonah watched his relationship with Melinda collapse and crash apart. It was an awesome thing to behold, like a chunk of ice the size of Rhode Island calving away from Antarctica and falling into the ocean.

'They belong to a woman named Elaine,' he said. 'She's my boss at work.'

Melinda nodded.

She left without another word, but that wasn't the last he saw of her.

'I make myself sick,' she said two weeks later.

She pulled on a thick wool sweater as she readied herself to leave. She checked her look in the full-length mirror. She was satisfied with what she saw. She turned to Jonah. As usual, he lay on the bed watching her dress.

Tonight had been a grudge match.

'You know that? I make myself sick by coming here again. Already I feel horrible about what I just did. I don't know what I ever saw in you. I don't know what *you* even see in you. On the surface, you seem so arrogant, so self-centred. But what you really are is weak and pathetic.'

'I'm weak?' he said. 'In what way?'

She laughed at him then. 'In what way aren't you weak? You're like a weak little white boy, an accountant maybe, in a nice body. Oh yeah, you have a nice body, not the best, believe me, but nice. But inside, you're weak and ugly, and when I think of you touching me tonight, it makes me sick.'

'Come on, Melinda,' he said. 'Be honest. It was good, wasn't it?'

She was dressed, had tousled her hair some, and was ready to go. 'I need a man, Jonah. I need a real man, not some Oreo cookie, not some pretty boy who never passed a mirror he didn't like, not some coward.'

She stood by the door, waiting for him to say something. When he didn't, she went on without waiting. 'You're hiding, Jonah. Big ladies' man. Flashes his money around. Smiles his pretty smile. Talks all that sincere bullshit. Gets whatever piece of ass he wants. Right?'

'Hey. You said it, not me.'

'But without all that, you're nothing. I can't believe I didn't see through you sooner. You always need a new one, right? A new little piece? Because without it, you're nothing and you know it. You're not a man, and you think maybe if you can fuck every woman in sight, that'll make you seem like a man. You're so weak. You keep acting this way, you'll be their slave forever.'

He laughed. 'Whose slave?'

'The people who own you.'

'Nobody owns me.'

She pointed at him. 'Wrong! They all own you. The job owns you. Your little boss lady owns you. She's using you, Jonah. You might think you get something out of it, but you don't. She uses you. And you let her do it. You're like the house slave. They dress you up nice, and they teach you to talk nice, but you're still a slave.'

She had something more to say, he was sure, and he couldn't think of anything. She had him, calling him a slave. It caught him off guard. It hurt, that word.

'Fuck you,' he said.

She laughed, not a sound of mirth but a burst of stale air from a deflated tyre. 'Yeah,' she said. 'That's the best you can do.'

With that, she went out.

He lay still for several minutes after she was gone, his mind dark and quiet. Then he got up, put his robe on, and went about making something to eat in the kitchen. He picked up the remote control off the counter, leaned back into the living room and started a compact disc going in the stereo.

He figured he would just put Melinda out of his mind, like he had all the others. But in the days that followed, Melinda stuck with him, more than he would care to admit. She was always simmering on a back burner of his mind and, too late, he realised he had ruined a good thing. What's more, the things she'd said stayed with him. He began to see how some of it made a certain amount of sense.

Jonah knew what people thought of him. He wore a pinstripe three-piece suit, Armani; a gold Seiko chronograph, stylish because it was shockproof — he also could wear it mountain biking if he wanted; silk tie, also Armani; alligator shoes; a smooth hundred-dollar fade that enhanced what one art director had called his 'delicately shaped' skull. He was a young executive now, working big advertising accounts. Two belated years of night school at the Westchester Business Institute got him in as a glorified secretary, but he moved up fast. He didn't handle the accounts, no, he was too brown for that, but he was in the meetings, eating the lunches, bouncing the ideas back and forth, selling the people yet another light bulb that lasted even longer. The honchos liked having him there, and not because he ever hit the home run. They liked him there because they needed a lapdog. They paid him well. In exchange, he smiled and looked good and smelled good and didn't cause trouble. He did what they wanted.

Sometimes what they wanted was sex.

Elaine was not the first well-kept middle-aged lady executive to bed Jonah, but she was the most giving. Even before Melinda found him out, Elaine's generosity had begun to make the whole thing look like a job, one that paid in sushi and nights out and new clothes.

Now, with Melinda gone, Jonah was free to spend more time with Elaine. Elaine must have sensed the change, because right away she took him for a weekend on the East End of Long Island. They stayed in a rental cottage hidden back in the scrub pine and sea grass along Old Montauk Highway, with Dom Perignon on ice, a Duraflame burning in the fireplace, and the surf crashing outside and just down the hill from the sliding glass doors.

When any bill came, he reached for his wallet.

'Oh please,' Elaine would say. 'Put it away. I enjoy paying for you.'

Later, after a nightcap, his bill would come. And he always paid in full. Elaine was divorced, and she made love in absolute darkness.

'Jonah,' she said as she drifted off to sleep on his chest. 'Don't let me fall in love with you.' As if such a thing could happen. For him, maybe it could. He often fell in love. Women were exotic and wonderful creatures to him, no matter what Melinda said. He felt it for them down deep. It might last for just a little while, but it was there, like the best music. When the music was right, when it was some smoky Miles, or some funky driving hip hop, he caught the line and felt it all over his body.

Love was like that.

But for Elaine, love was improbable at best. She had scraped and crawled and scratched people's eyes out to get her position, and it had cost her half a lifetime to get there. The wars had taken their toll. Even in her most human moments, even in passion, she was like a granite cliff face warmed by the sun. The heat was there, but then so was the stone.

Jonah grew weaker and less alive the more time he spent with her.

Show up, smile at the dumb jokes, fuck the expensive lady. He knew why he was moving up. He was the thinker who never had a decent idea. But behind the scenes, people pulled strings – Elaine was the chief string-puller right now.

Bending had become routine for him. He came in one morning and some comic genius had cut a picture of Step'n Fetchit out of a book and taped it to his computer. All he did was he pulled the picture down and threw it in the trash.

They were laughing at him.

Meanwhile, shopping had become his consolation. He bought so much expensive shit his apartment looked like the inside of *Home & Garden* magazine. In fact, he subscribed to *Home & Garden* and got his ideas from there.

He lived through his things: the car; some pricey Crate & Barrel knick-knacks gathering dust on his shelves; a couple of one-of-a-kind ironwood Nubian sculptures, one of a man and woman making love, the other of an old man's balding head, both of which were good at gathering dust; the cleaning lady from Romania who came in once a week to wipe the dust off everything; his hanging ferns and aloe plants, which the Romanian gave him a hard time for neglecting; a Trek mountain bike (which he sometimes rode on the streets near his apartment); his two-year-old Rossignol skis (he had gone skiing once since buying them); his bedroom set, his living-room set, his home entertainment centre; that river view, don't forget that, put that first on the list; his Ray Bans; his jacket from the Leather Factory . . .

He couldn't afford any of it. The pay was good, but not that good. He carried nearly forty grand in balances on four credit cards. Some days it made him want to cry. But the fun didn't stop there. As the economy went down the tubes, the firm started letting people go. The citizenry stopped buying things, the companies that sold things started going under, and there came a steep decline in the need to advertise things – especially in the need to have a whole creative group sitting around, throwing out ideas about how to advertise things. Jonah sensed that Elaine protected him as long as she could, but there came a day when even she couldn't do anything for him.

He remembered the day they pinked him, going on two years ago. He was in her office that day. He could tell from her tone that he was dismissed in every way. 'Baby doll,' she said. 'You're going to do great things one day. I know that about you. This downturn isn't going to last for ever, and when it ends, even before then, I'm sure you'll be doing better than ever before.'

Half an hour later he was out on the bright and cold evening streets of the city, the people a faceless swirl around him. Christmas coming – the shop windows were all dressed up for the holidays. Tourists ran around, all bundled up and carrying packages. Downtown, the spire on the Empire State Building shone green and red.

He went down into the subway and made the long ride up through the Bronx. He stood at the head of the first car, looking out the front window at the tracks ahead. It was a place he had stood many times as a child. The mystery of it, the vastness of the dark underground empire, never lost its hold on him. He stared and stared as the train roared through tunnels, lights zooming by on each side. The train changed tracks, never hesitating, as workmen with lanterns stood to the side in the gloom. The train passed through stations that were out of service, darkened corners, graffiti-stained walls, empty platforms long disused. Sometimes there'd be no lights at all out there, and he'd catch a glimpse of himself in the mirror of the black window. He stared back into his own eyes.

Who was he? Where had he gone?

Now, Jonah poked his head up and was almost surprised to find himself still in Kelly's Bar. He glanced around. The long hairs had gone. The juke box was silent, and the only sounds came from the television and a few people sitting along the bar and talking in low voices. Jonah's head had settled down to an almost pleasant thumping.

Three pints of beer hadn't hurt him any.

Thump.

Thump.

The pain beat slow and gentle, like the bass signature on a sad love song. He was already thinking better about the day's fiasco. At least one good thing had come out of it. He had sure flown across that alley. There were many days when he felt he wasn't cut out for this kind of work, but man, what a feeling today. He envied the birds. He was beginning to think he should take up hang-gliding.

Gordo nudged him. The big man sat with three piles of Foerster's open mail before him, one pile for possible leads, one for garbage, and one for mail he hadn't opened yet. That third pile had dwindled away to almost nothing.

'I found him,' Gordo said, waving the piece of paper in his hand. 'He's out on Staten Island. He's at his mother's house.'

3

They gave Gant a bedroom, and a girl to go with it.

The bedroom was very large, with a gigantic bed and the girl draped across it. Cool stone floors and windows facing the ocean. Evening was coming in. Peach-coloured curtains billowed in the light breeze. Wide double doors opened out on to a private balcony. Someone had left him a cart on rollers with a bottle of spirits, as well as a bottle each of red and white wine. Also, there were some finger sandwiches, a pitcher of water and a bucket of ice. He barely glanced at the wines or the sandwiches. The whisky was Glenfiddich thirty-year-old Scotch, so that was good news. He poured three fingers-worth into a glass, without ice or water, and sipped it, enjoying the taste and the feel of the fire entering his belly.

The girl was fair-skinned and young, just old enough to be out of high school. She was dressed in an electric blue sarong and a bikini top, and had a body with so many curves that it was almost an outlandish cartoon of the female form. She spoke English with a strong accent from somewhere. Her eyes were green, and while Gant stared out at the breakers marching towards land far below him, he felt those eyes on his back.

'Russia?' he said, still facing away from her.

'Moldova,' she answered.

He shrugged. Same difference to him. Commies. They lost, we won. It took a hell of a bite out of some of us, but we did win. He turned now, and took a long look at her. Good Lord, he remembered how they used to make you think Eastern Bloc women were huge, ugly ⊢ powerlifters in the Olympics. Of course, after the collapse it turned out nothing could be further from the truth. He thought of maps and how one day the Soviet Union was this big red smear across the top of the world, and the next day there were all these little countries you never heard of there instead, places like Tajikistan, and Belarus, and Moldova. He remembered air-raid sirens and how in junior high school, when the sirens sounded, the teachers used to make the kids go out in the hallway, kneel in front of the lockers, and cover their heads with their arms. Each kid had to kneel in front of his or her own locker. Gant figured that if the nukes ever came, whoever was left afterwards would know him as the pile of radioactive dust on the floor at the base of locker number 126.

Gant remembered other things as well, things that happened during his time as a soldier for the United States of America, but he pushed them aside for now. He sighed, just a little. This girl was probably too young to know the history, or even care. She didn't know she was a trophy taken from a defeated people. Well anyway, she was here, and he was here, so he might as well put her to her intended use. To the victor go the spoils, after all.

'Wine?' he said.

'Yes, please. Red, with ice.'

He grimaced at the thought of it, but uncorked the bottle and poured it for her. She drank it fast and he poured her another. She downed it and he poured yet another. If she needed to numb up, so be it. From her perspective, this could hardly be the ideal romantic encounter. She drank about half of her third glass then put it aside on the table. She removed her top and her sarong. Her body coming free reminded Gant of wild horses galloping on a high plateau. He sipped his Scotch.

'Who are you available to?' he said.

She stared at him, her head slightly to the side, her pretty mouth open just a bit. She didn't understand. For a moment, Gant tried to think of another delicate way to put it, then decided he couldn't be bothered.

'Do you have to fuck everybody?'

'Oh. No, only guests. You. The fat politician. People like that.'

'The gunmen?'

She shook her head. 'Uh-uh. I stay far away from them. They are animals.'

'Do you ever see a doctor?'

'Every month. The old man's doctor himself sees me.'

He joined her on the bed. She'd been with the fat politician, and recently – Harting, Hartley, whatever his name was – that wasn't great news, but it could have been worse. She could have been servicing the goon squad every day, too. Gant ran a hand along her leg, and soon forgot about the guards, and the good representative, and even Fielding himself. He took his time, even though he knew it was all about him, and not about her at all. Once, he looked into her face and saw that her mind was elsewhere, maybe running on that high green field with all those beautiful horses. Afterwards, they lay on top of the sheets, not tangled, not even touching. Gant picked up his drink again.

He looked at the girl and her sad face. An artist could make a painting of her – *Tragic Girl*. Gant was nothing if not curious – he could attribute his success to several factors, including luck, but certainly one of the factors was that he had a voracious appetite for knowing things.

'OK, Moldova, how did you wind up here?'

She polished off the last of her wine, then stood on unsteady legs and fixed herself another one. 'I was poor, but men always liked me from the time I am young.' She shrugged, probably at the self-evident truth of her statement. 'I was dancer in club. A woman came to my village and told me about good jobs abroad. I could be cleaner in hotel, or work as hostess. I sign up, pay some money, and they bring me here. I owe more money, of course. And so maybe I can never leave.'

Gant thought maybe the alcohol, combined with the travel and his tiredness, had given him a buzz. He wasn't sure he had the girl's responsibilities down pat just yet. 'Do you also clean up around here?' he said.

She gave him a baleful look. 'Island women come and clean. They have to be searched every time they come. I don't know how to clean. I fuck instead.'

'Do you hate it?'

'It bores me. I fuck, I eat, and I watch the satellite TV from America. Stupid reality shows, people shouting at each other, and then crying, and giving hugs. We read *The Great Gatsby* in school in Moldova. It is the best story. I owned a poster of F. Scott Fitzgerald, and I hung this on the wall in my room. The great American writer. But they don't show these things on the TV. The greatness is over. I think all Americans must be stupid now.'

She was on to something, but Gant didn't want to get into it. What to do or say about an entire nation of overweight, lazy people so addled by junk television and junk food and prescription drugs that they had only recently begun to notice they were systematically lied to, and robbed blind and left to sink in quicksand? Only now, long after the cheese had been moved, were some of the mice starting to wake up to that fact.

'Well,' he said, 'at least you probably don't have to fuck all that much. I mean, there can't be that many guests.'

'Howe. The assistant. I have to fuck him, too.'

Gant felt a knife twist in his heart. He didn't even have to examine the feeling – it was a visceral response. 'I wish you had mentioned that earlier. I don't like Howe.'

'I don't, either.'

'Is there anything you do like about this place?'

She didn't hesitate. 'The view.'

Gant nodded. 'It's a great view. Anything else?'

It took her a moment to come up with something more. 'Howe's wife and daughter live on the grounds here in guest house, so I never have to spend whole night with him.'

The conversation made Gant sleepy. He lay back with his glass propped on his chest and closed his eyes. He could sip his Scotch with only the slightest movement of his hand and his chin. His mind drifted from its moorings and began to scan through the past, settling here and there on various memories. It was a pleasant sensation. He smiled.

Gant was nobody to mess with.

It was back in Philadelphia where Gant wished he could still be. Young again, cruising the mean streets. Not the Philadelphia of Market and Broad Streets, the corporate towers, not the place the rich yuppies had once commuted to from the suburbs, not the weekday morning traffic jam brought to you by BMW and Mercedes and Lexus. Gant's part of town was North Philadelphia. It was the drug deals going down in the shadows of burnt-out row houses. It was the homeless men sleeping under highway overpasses. It was the emaciated crack whores plying their trade in the alleys and vacant lots. It was chalk outlines on bloody sidewalks. It was booming hip-hop from tricked-out lowriders and the night he caught two carjackers single-handed.

He savoured that night like he savoured fine whisky.

1990, or thereabouts – a long time ago now. A couple of gangbangers took a new Toyota at gunpoint near the bombed-out Amtrak station, but they didn't know there was an infant in the back seat. The daddy lost his car OK, but went hysterical when he realised he'd lost his baby too. It became a wild all units call. The bad boys broke a hundred miles an hour on the wide lanes of North Broad, hung a turn and disappeared like smoke. Gant in an unmarked car heard it on the radio and made a guess. He was four blocks away. He roared the wrong way down a one-way, headlights off through the low-slung housing projects, engine screaming, and here came a car burning up the street towards him. He guessed again – it had to be them. He hit the flashers and jammed the brakes, skidding sideways, blocking the whole street.

They plowed into a parked sedan, heavy metal crunch at high speed. He leapt out ahead of them, a gun in each hand, running crazy on fear and adrenaline. One move, one funny twitch, and he would kill them both.

'Freeze, motherfuckers! Out of the car! Down on the ground!'

He had guessed right both times. Back-up units showed a minute later, and Gant already had both suspects cuffed and in custody. The baby was fine, still strapped into the child restraint, goggling at all the curious onlookers.

Gant felt his heart beating at the memory. It was one of his favourites. He imagined pro athletes had memories like that – moments when, either through luck or experience or a little of both, they did everything right and for a brief time were unbeatable.

He opened his eyes and the girl had climbed on top of him again. He welcomed her there. It went on between them for a long while, and at some point he slept. When he woke, she was on the terrace, nude in the night air, leaning against the stone railing and smoking a cigarette. A bright quarter-moon hung low in the dark sky. When she finished her cigarette, she pitched the butt out into the night then came back inside. She saw Gant was awake.

'You work for him, right?' she said.

'I work for myself. He's a client of mine.'

'So you work for him.'

Gant nodded. 'Yes.'

'I hear things, from the cleaning ladies. They're going to kill him. The islanders. They think he wants to starve them to death, so they want to kill him first.'

'He doesn't want to starve them,' Gant said. 'Believe me.'

'I don't care. I hope they get him. He's a terrible, evil man. He can send me away from here any time he wants. One day, after he's used me up enough, and my youth is gone, he'll sell me to somebody worse and they'll make me a whore on the street.'

'Who told you that? Howe?'

'You don't listen. I said the cleaning ladies.'

Gant reached over and poured himself another drink. 'You know what? It's a strange world. You never know what's going to happen next. If I were you, I guess I wouldn't worry about things so much. And I'd stop listening to the cleaning ladies.'

Waves of pleasure rolled through Katie's body, one after another after another. She was on her stomach, her face in the pillow, her free hand gripping the bedsheet, pulling it loose from the mattress. She was a rich lady, on a weekend trip to a fancy desert spa. She had gone in for a hot oil massage, but when she was on the table, it turned out that three men, three masseurs, would work on her. They turned down the lights in the room, and she couldn't see their faces. At first they just rubbed her down, but soon they were saying things to her, things that embarrassed her. Then they were doing . . . things . . . to her, things she had never done before. She couldn't protest. She didn't want to.

It went on and on, and she went with it, higher and higher. She arched her back, eyes squeezed shut. At long last, one final, intense shudder went through her, and she collapsed on to the bed.

'Oh my God,' she said, and no one was there to hear it. She felt her heart-beat slowing down, her breathing coming deeper and slower. She opened her eyes. It was dark. The digital clock on the bedside table told her it was 3.15 in the morning.

The high was fading, and thoughts began to intrude, as they always did. In fact, they rushed in, like cascading water. The thoughts were never good.

She was a failure. It was amazing to think of herself this way. An outsider might say that she had many of the things people wanted from life – she was attractive, she was rich, she lived in this big house, and she was still young. But she had wanted, and still wanted, so much more. From her own perspective, her life was empty. She had failed at nearly everything.

She was a failed artist.

That was one of her greatest failures. She had been a working artist in various media, trying different things, for close to ten years. She thought – no, she knew – that she was good at it. Back in Dewey Beach, and since they moved down here to Charleston, she'd taken part in numerous shows. And in all that time, she'd sold only three paintings, for a grand total of less than $2,000. Even worse, she suspected that Tyler had secretly bought the paint-ings through intermediaries. When she confronted him, he denied it, but that didn't mean anything. That little conversation had taken place nearly two years ago – she hadn't sold a painting since then.

She consoled herself. Maybe she wasn't commercial, but so what? Or maybe she just wasn't a saleswoman. She knew that selling yourself was a big part of success, but she just wasn't that person.

She had also failed at love. The man she had finally married, she realised now, was like a more distant version of her father. Capable, supremely confident and in charge, very good-looking in a distinguished, hair-greying-at-the-sides sort of way. A man who, like her father, made a lot of money. A man whom people worked for and looked to for leadership. A man who knew what to do.

But he was cold and unemotional. He was distant, and increasingly so. It seemed that he no longer cared what she did. It seemed that all he'd ever really wanted her for was to show her off – a trophy wife – and to make a baby with him. A son. Which was yet another way that she had failed. There wasn't going to be a baby.

And that led to the final failure, ironically the one thing she had always succeeded at, had always been confident about. She had always prided herself on being great in bed, a wonderful lover. Of being able to make a man feel like a man, while at the same time feeling like a woman, incredibly so, and loving to feel that way. She knew she had a beautiful body. She'd had some amazing sex in her life, and some amazing men. She could have powerful orgasms, over and over again, for as long as her man's stamina could hold out. She'd read about all the problems women sometimes had in bed, she'd read about them in magazines like *Cosmopolitan* and *Mademoiselle*, and yet these were problems she'd never experienced, not till this past year.

After she'd lost a baby for the second time, Tyler had become ever more distant and consumed in his work. He didn't want to talk about the options available to them – weird science, he called it. He didn't want to talk about anything any more. He took no interest in what she did. It was like they were two room-mates in this lovely spacious home they shared, nearly strangers. They almost never had sex, and when they did – four months ago was the most recent time – it was perfunctory, a formality, maybe just a physical release for Tyler, but not for Katie. Katie needed more than a twenty-minute session every four months to get a release.

In recent months, a funny thing had occurred to her – maybe she could take a lover. Of course she wouldn't do anything to risk the marriage, but Tyler was away a lot. If it were the right person, someone who was discreet, and who wouldn't get too attached, it was just possible that she could do it. At first, she pushed the thought away, was almost embarrassed by it, even though no one could possibly know she was thinking it. But after a while, she would return to it, again and again, and it began to fuel her fantasies. Her marriage had turned barren, and she needed physical intimacy. Everybody did, but perhaps she more than most. It was a simple equation, after all.

An even funnier thing was how, now that she had an emotional and phys-ical distance from him, she began to see Tyler clearly for the first time. She realised that when Tyler had given her everything she needed, emotionally and physically, along with all the creature comforts that went with being his wife, she had never really looked at him with a critical eye. She had let him be the sugar daddy. Was she really that self-serving, that immature? It seemed now that she was.

But now that was she was looking at him with a clear eye, it turned out she didn't like what she saw. It was as if she had suddenly awakened from a long and deep sleep. About the only source of income he had that she knew about for sure was his pension from the Philadelphia Police Department. Other than that, Tyler was secretive. Certainly, he was some kind of a secur-ity contractor. His pension wasn't paying for this house in a gated, secure community, for the two cars they drove, for the black market gasoline, for the swimming pool they had put in, for the big dinner parties they some-times threw, for his personal trainer, and for all the rest.

But what kind of security did he provide? He was gone a lot, but where did he go? He would disappear in the middle of the night sometimes, a car picking him up outside at the front kerb. He would leave only a short note on the kitchen table, and then return a day or two days or a week later. It made her curious.

He had only brief telephone conversations in the house, and not very often. Tyler seemed to have plenty of workers and subcontractors, but the only one he allowed to come to the house was the big, grinning redneck named Vernon. Vernon had a hook nose and a huge jaw and tended to wear a Caterpillar baseball cap and T-shirts with the sleeves cut off, all the better to show off his massive, tattooed shoulders and arms. He had laughing eyes that seemed to size you up and find you wanting. Vernon struck Katie more as hired muscle than as some kind of security operative.

Katie would bite her tongue for long periods of time, but eventually she could remain quiet no longer. 'How's work?' she would say to Tyler, usually after one of his business trips, or after one of Vernon's appearances at the house.

'Work is going good. It's going OK. We've got something big we're cooking up. It could be a step forward for us.'

'Really? That's great. What's it all about?'

'Katie, it really doesn't concern you. You shouldn't worry about it.'

'Well, I'm not worried. I know you'll be successful, whatever you decide to do. I'm just interested.'

'Well, don't be. OK? Sometimes it's better if you just aren't interested. You know a lot of my work concerns national security issues. I'm not free to talk about it, not even with my wife, whom I love.'

National security issues? OK, that was one product she wasn't buying any more. It just didn't feel like Tyler worked for the Government. Tyler never seemed to look at any paperwork, and if Katie knew anything about the United States Government, she knew that government contracts meant gigantic mounds of paperwork – she knew this from being an assistant at a law firm that dealt with government contracts. The paperwork generated could be astonishing. Breathtaking. And Tyler never had anything like that kind of paperwork lying around. In fact, he didn't seem to have anything at all in writing. He was much more likely to sit in his study – which he kept locked from her when he wasn't home – poring over maps than to ever read a contract. He had a telephone wired in there, and she didn't have its number. Ten minutes ago, yes, in the middle of the night, it had started ringing and then had gone to voicemail.

66

What was it all about? Anyway, would the Government really hire an operation where the second in command was big, dumb Vernon? She thought not, and as she thought that, she realised she had reached a breaking point with Tyler. She would stay married to him, of course. It was hard times outside of this house, and she had no intention of being cast out there. But she didn't believe in him any more. And she would, within reason, snoop around to see what it was he was up to. She might even consider finding a way into that locked study — not tonight, but soon. He'd probably be back tomorrow, at least that's what his most recent note said, but it wouldn't be long before he was gone again.

'Tyler Gant,' she said aloud to the empty bedroom, and was just a little startled by her own voice. 'What do you do for a living?'

Foerster lay awake in bed, in the small room that had been his throughout his childhood. His bed was narrow, like a nun would sleep on, and the springs creaked whenever he moved. The mattress was lumpy. It was an uncomfortable goddamned bed. He probably didn't get a decent night's sleep the first eighteen years of his life, and it was no wonder why.

His door was open a crack, and down the hall he could hear his mother snoring. Good God, all his life, he had hated it in this house. He had half a mind to march down the hall and stifle those infernal snores for good.

The desk lamp next to the bed was on, casting a weak pyramid of yellow light, and Foerster, on his back, held up a business card where he could see it. He'd found the card in the desk — he must have left it behind the last time circumstances forced him to stay in this pit of despair. Foerster had been given this card at least two years ago. Now it was a little crumpled and faded, but you could still make it out fine. On the left side of it was a picture of a chess piece, a white knight. Running down the right side were the words *Executive Strategies — Security and Intelligence Solutions. Tyler Gant, President.* Then it gave an office address in Charleston, South Carolina, and a phone number. No website or email address listed, but there was another phone number scrawled in ink along the bottom, which Foerster had called only a few minutes ago from the ancient rotary dial phone on the desk.

He wasn't sure why he had waited until three in the morning to call the number, or why he had hung up without leaving a message, except that he wasn't sure if he should call it, and at the same time he was curious to see if it still worked. It did work – the same bland 'leave a message at the tone' recording that was on the machine two years ago was still there. Foerster knew that the phone rang in the upstairs den at Gant's house. Or at least that's where it used to ring. He also knew he was taking a chance by calling there. Gant had given him that card grudgingly, and had told him never to call the number except in a desperate emergency, and only from a payphone.

Well, this probably qualified as an emergency – he was hiding out from bounty hunters at his mom's house! Gant would probably pop a blood vessel if he knew where Foerster was calling from, but hey, payphones could be hard to come by in this day and age. Anyway, Foerster needed to get a message to Gant that he was no longer where he said he'd be, and that he needed to be picked up quick before he got put away again. The fastest way to do that seemed to be by telephone.

But it was a risk. Phone calls were easy to trace, and Gant had said in no uncertain terms that he didn't want the cops to have any way to connect them. Well, fuck it. If Gant wanted him to do the job, then he needed to know where Foerster was. If he sent one of his men over to Foerster's apartment, Foerster wasn't going to be there. And Foerster couldn't wait around here for ever, wondering when Gant would send somebody – he had fucking people on his trail, man.

Shit. Foerster could not understand why everything always got so fucked up. It seemed like the simplest thing would suddenly take a turn and head off down some trail towards disaster. It was the story of his life. By all accounts, he was a genius. From his earliest days, he had a tested IQ in the 150s. It was at the far right end of the bell curve, where fewer than one per cent of the population could be found. He could sleepwalk through school – without even trying, he was done with the sixth-grade curriculum before the end of fourth grade.

This wasn't good enough. His father had wanted an athlete, a football player, not some scrawny kid with a big brain. Foerster's drunken bum of a father had taken to calling him Nancy Boy, and beating him with a leather strap. When had that started? He wasn't even sure. It seemed like his first memory was of a huge, red-faced beast standing over him, the smell of mingled beer and whisky in Foerster's face, the smack of the leather loud in his ears, the sting of the whip on his skin, and his father saying, 'I'll make a fucking man out of you yet.' If there was a hell, Foerster hoped the old man was roasting there right this minute.

But his father had only been the start of his problems. It seemed that nobody in this entire world wanted a smart kid. Having intelligence made you some kind of a freak. Nobody ever liked Foerster. His school teachers hated him – probably because they knew he was smarter than they were, and were envious of him. The other kids? Forget about it. If they noticed him at all, it was to throw rocks at him, or chase him home, or hold him down and punch his legs till his muscles spasmed. He'd show up at the house bruised and battered, and his father would laugh and say, 'Serves you right for not fighting back.'

If Foerster had been dumb enough to believe in God, he'd say that God was testing him like He'd tested Job. Almost nothing had turned out right as far back as Foerster could remember. Till he met Tyler Gant. Although Gant's personality left something to be desired, and Gant's tough-guy authority act chafed on Foerster, the time he had worked for Gant had probably been the one thing that had gone well in more than twenty-five wasted years.

Gant had used Foerster's brains the way they were meant to be used, working him to his highest level. He had shown Foerster at least a dollop of respect, and had paid him what he was worth. Their project had come off without a hitch, and they had made history together. Foerster had watched the news coverage for days, silently bursting with pride, almost unable to contain himself. At the Illinois state house, politicians and their staff members – blood ticks sucking on the near-dead carcass of this diseased country – were dying of anthrax.

Foerster wanted to go to a bar and have a few drinks and say to someone, some stranger, 'See that? See what they did? That was me. I was on that team. I grew that stuff.' He wanted to call his mother and tell her all about it. He wanted to dig up his old man and rub it in his face. But, of course, he could never talk about it with anyone, ever, for the rest of his days. About the only person he could possibly talk about it with was Gant himself, but Gant had told him to stay out of communication. One day, Gant said, he would be the one to reinitiate contact.

Foerster never imagined two cruel years would pass before he heard from Gant again. The world had slid further into the abyss during that time, and Foerster had slid with it. He had nearly forgotten about Gant, about the feelings of achievement, of being a winner, that had come with working for him. Then a brief note, no return address, had appeared in Foerster's mailbox. Although Foerster had moved three times since last they spoke, Gant had found him. *Got some work for you (maybe). Same terms as before, times 2. Will send someone. Burn this letter. TG.*

Same terms, times two – that was awesome. Foerster had made $25,000 on that job, for two weeks of work. He had received ten per cent in cash before he ever did anything. That meant he would get $50,000 from this job, and $5,000 as an advance. Foerster had been in and out of jail in the months since that first note had arrived, but other notes had come since then. The time was getting close – Foerster could expect someone to pick him up any day.

Until yesterday, when those two clowns had crashed into the middle of Foerster's plans like a bulldozer, he hadn't realised how much he was looking forward to working for Gant again. As he slid the business card on to the table and closed his eyes, Foerster committed himself – he would do whatever was necessary to keep out of jail and get back to working with Gant.

Jonah felt exposed.

It was early the next morning. He and Gordo were parked in St George, a few blocks from the Staten Island Ferry Terminal. They sat at the corner of Richmond Terrace and a quiet side street of shabby homes. Traffic was busy on Richmond Terrace, a weird parade of bicycles, motor scooters belching exhaust, a few cars and many people, some pushing along carts of various kinds. Diagonally across from Jonah and Gordo was a convenience store. A hand-lettered sign in the window read 'CASHIER LEGALLY ARMED'. Jonah wasn't sure if that sign made life safer or more dangerous for the cashier.

From the passenger seat, Jonah pointed a big parabolic microphone at a house maybe fifty yards down the side street. The house was a ramshackle place, with light-blue aluminium siding that had seen too many winters. The microphone protruded from its base like a long black phallus, and was surrounded by a clear plastic half-dome. Jonah gripped it by its handle, which was rather like that of a gun. The mike was plugged into a tape cassette player sitting between them, which in turn was powered by the car's cigarette lighter. The whole rig looked somewhat like a satellite dish, or perhaps like a death-ray weapon from outer space. Gordo had picked it up at a second-hand sale.

For years, Jonah had noticed men on the sidelines at professional sporting events, holding the ultra-powerful mikes so that the television audience could get the benefit of every grunt, every scream, every high-speed collision between the finely tuned war machines out on the field. Later, he learned they were also used by nature lovers for listening to songbirds. The mikes were even sensitive enough to listen to those birds through walls, or while the birds carried on boring phone conversations near open windows half a block away. Yeah. Jonah was familiar with parabolic microphones.

Unfortunately, nobody else seemed to be. He was attracting a lot of hostile glances.

'Man, everybody's gawking at us.'

In the driver's seat, Gordo was reading the science pages of the *New York Times*. For once, he was dressed neatly, in a pressed shirt and slacks. He was clean-shaven. If things went their way, today he would be a man of God.

He glanced up from his newspaper. He gazed up and down the street.

'I say fuck 'em. Let them gawk.'

He snatched the binoculars off his lap and scanned the street.

Jonah watched the spy glasses move back and forth. The big man had brains – Jonah had to admit that. Among Foerster's mail had been a bill from North Bronx Central Hospital. It seemed Foerster had been admitted for a bleeding ulcer some months before and still hadn't paid. The dunning letter came with a copy of Foerster's admission form. The form contained the name, address and phone number of an emergency contact.

Foerster's mother.

'Nothing yet, huh?' Gordo said.

'No.'

'Don't worry, he'll come.'

'Oh, I won't worry,' Jonah said. 'Why should I worry? Here's a black man, probably from Mars, pointing a laser gun at somebody's house in broad daylight. Nothing unusual about that, right? We're lucky they haven't called out the National Guard. And meanwhile, Foerster would have to be an idiot to show up here.'

Gordo raised an eyebrow.

'Patience, my brother,' he said, scanning the paper again. 'He'll show up. I feel him in my bones, like some people feel the rain. A friendless bastard like that, he's got to come back to his mother eventually.'

And as if by magic, Foerster appeared.

Jonah stared at him for close to a full minute before he realised who it was. Skinny, unkempt Foerster stood at the bottom of the concrete steps of his mother's house, talking to a heavyset older guy. Foerster wore a grey wool cap like a sailor, probably to hide the scars on his head. It wasn't remotely cold enough out for wool. Jonah could hardly believe the state of the man. He looked . . . dingy, like a ring of soap scum left around the sink after washing the dishes. He appeared to weigh about twenty-seven pounds. It was hard to imagine that this specimen had fought Jonah off yesterday, then had outrun him and given him the slip. He must be highly motivated.

'Would you look at that,' Jonah said. 'He's right out on the street.'

Gordo held the binoculars to his eyes. 'Put the mike on them.'

Jonah turned the volume up and aimed the mike at the two men.

'Yeah, yeah, I may stick around awhile,' Foerster said. 'My project in

Cleveland just ended. It looks like I have something lined up down south, but after that job ends, I might just settle here in the old neighbourhood for a while.'

'What the hell is he talking about?' Jonah said. 'What job? Cleveland? I mean, come on already.'

Gordo shrugged. 'He lies like other people breathe.'

'Well, we're glad to have you back, Davey,' the oldster said. He clapped Foerster on his scrawny back and the mike picked up the slap. 'I'm sure your mother will be happy to have a man around the house again.'

'Sure, sure. I guess she gets lonely sometimes. It'll be good for her.'

'It'll be good for both of you. Nothing like Mom's home cooking to fatten a man up.'

'For Christ's sake,' Gordo said. 'They're gonna need a lot more than Mom to fatten Foerster up. The guy's a walking hunger crisis.'

They watched as Foerster went in the house.

The oldster crossed the street and walked off down the block.

'All right,' Gordo said. He took a deep breath. 'I guess it's time to go for it.'

He climbed out of the car and dropped the binoculars on the seat. In his hand he held a pile of religious tracts he hoped to discuss with Mrs Foerster. The top one, the one Jonah could see, was called THE COMING FIRE.

'Let's go over this one more time, OK? Just so we don't get crossed up out there. When I see an opening and decide I'm going in, what am I gonna say?'

'God is love,' Jonah said. 'I hear that, then I come running to back you up. Fifty-yard dash. I'll be there in about six or seven seconds. When I come through the front door, you'll be shouting out instructions – upstairs, or back door, or cellar, depending on where he's going. He's only been here one night, so he probably hasn't had a chance to come up with much of an escape route.'

'Sounds good, right? Workable?'

'Actually, it sounds about twice as half-assed as yesterday's plan,' Jonah said. 'But given the circumstances, I feel pretty confident about it. At least you're the one going in first.'

Gordo smiled. 'OK. As long as you feel good, I'm happy.'

Jonah watched Gordo amble up the block towards the house, tracts in hand. He trained the microphone on Gordo's wide back. Gordo started muttering under his breath as he walked along.

'Are you listening, Jonah? Lovely neighbourhood they got here. Looks like the tide went out on this place about twenty years ago.'

He arrived at the house. His breathing came a little heavier, a little more laboured. He seemed like maybe he was talking to himself now. It was hard to tell. 'Are you ready, kid? This is the test. This is the big test. This is for all the marbles right here.'

He climbed the short steps to the front door.

Inside, Davis Foerster went around in circles with his mother yet again.

She wasn't happy to see him. Hey, he wasn't happy to see her either. But when she had opened that front door last night and seen him standing there, she might have been auditioning as an extra in a low-grade horror movie. Her jaw had dropped, her eyes had widened, and her face looked as if a creature from the swamp, trailing gore and slime, had appeared at her home. But she had let him in. That she had. What else was she going to do? He was her only son, after all.

She wanted him out as soon as possible, and he wanted to go – more than anything. If it were up to him, he would walk out that door right now and make a beeline for Charleston. Hanging around here gave him the creeps in more ways than one. He kept expecting the angry ghost of his shit-for-brains father to pop out of a closet or from behind the mouldy shower curtain in the bathroom. Foerster wanted out before that or something worse happened. But he needed a grubstake to get him going, and she wouldn't part with the cash.

Oh, she would give him enough for a bus ride, maybe as far as Philadelphia, and for a Big Mac at a highway rest stop, but that was it. She wouldn't give him what he needed to get where he was going, to set himself up with a room for a couple of weeks in case the job didn't come through right away, and to eat like a human being during all that time. His mom was a major disappointment. Then again, he wasn't surprised at all. Why should he be? This was the way she had always been. You couldn't prise money out of her with a crowbar.

Now she was sitting across from him at the kitchen table in her goddamn house dress, a hair net on her head, the cordless phone at her elbow like a faithful dog. That was her big hobby, talking on the telephone. Any minute now, she would pick up that phone, dial a number and start her gabbing. She was a world champion talker and not much of anything else. To Foerster, she looked old and tired, like a hag. She didn't even bother to get dressed any more. For a moment, he studied the lines of her face. He decided she should have a wart on the end of her nose. That would complete the picture.

'But Davey, why don't you just get a job? I'd let you stay here if you were working.'

He reached for the hard pack of Camels he had placed next to her on the table. She didn't allow smoking in the house. He didn't care. He slid one out and lit up. 'No way, Ma.' He pointed the lit smoke at her. 'No way, you understand?' He laughed, and for a moment the depth and breadth of her stupidity, the sheer grandeur of it, delighted him. His mom was the Grand Canyon of dumb, and he could finally see the humour in it.

'What kind of job am I supposed to get? Everybody's out of work around here, the whole city's going out of business, and you tell me to get a job. That's a big help, Ma. A big, big help. Anyway, I have a job. I told you that already. It's a good job and it pays good money. OK? It's just that if I want the job, I have to get to South Carolina, and I need money to do that. What am I gonna do if I stay here, flip burgers for eight dollars an hour, if anybody's even hiring? How am I gonna live like that? Why would I want to?'

She seemed on the verge of crying. Again, no surprise there. Tears were her favourite weapon. 'For one thing, you'd be living here, eating my food. That way you could save your money. For another, you wouldn't be a criminal. I don't want a criminal in my family, Davey. I can't stand it any more.'

She looked up at him, looked into his eyes. 'Aren't you tired of dealing with the police? Aren't you tired of being afraid? I know I am.'

He smiled, a modern Jesse James. 'I'm not tired, Ma. I'm just getting started.'

With that, he left her. He went down the hall and began climbing the wooden stairs to the first floor. He remembered how those steps used to give him splinters when he was a kid. All these years later, and she had never done anything about them. The wood was still raw and rough. Well, at least he wasn't dumb enough to go around barefoot any more.

Halfway up the stairs, the doorbell rang. He turned and glanced back down at the door. Doorbells gave him a nervous feeling. They always had, but especially in the last twenty-four hours.

Below him, his mother shuffled into the foyer, and Foerster continued up the stairs.

His escape set-up here was good – not nearly as good as it had been at his apartment, but good. He had put the whole thing together years ago, and when he'd looked at it last night, he'd decided it could still hold water. His room was on the first floor and he had a twenty-foot fire ladder, called the Res-Q Ladder, coiled on the rug by his window. It was a chain-link ladder with metal slats. It hooked to the window sill with big iron hooks. If a fire started, you were supposed to throw the ladder out the window. It would uncoil itself on the way to the ground, ready for action in a couple of seconds. He had taken it out of the closet last night as soon as he came upstairs. He had even tested it, and it worked just as it always had.

Fire ladders weren't just good for fires. As a kid, he used to climb out to go smoke a joint without alerting the parents. Now, if the shit happened to hit the fan again, he would be ready. He hadn't yet worked out what his escape route on the streets would be, but he still had some time to put that together. He was thinking he would run for the vacant lots down by the waterfront esplanade, maybe even the ferry to Manhattan if a boat was in and the timing was right.

He reached the top of the landing. He listened. His mother was there at the front door now, just chatting away, probably with some crone from down the street.

He started towards his room, relaxing a bit.

Then the old bat screamed. 'Davey, help! Help me!'

'God is love!' a man shouted. 'God is love!'

Foerster bolted for his window.

Jonah ran towards the house. He went hard and covered the distance in no time, flying across the tiny front yard and vaulting up the three steps.

The door gaped wide and he flew through the opening.

The old woman sat on the floor, her back to the wall. Gordo must have knocked her down. Jonah noticed her thick legs, which had support hose pulled to just above the knees – she had the legs of an elephant. Her hands were splayed out on the floor. Her breath came in sporadic gasps. That worried him. The last thing they needed was a heart attack or a stroke victim on their hands.

'Ma'am, are you all right?'

'I'm OK,' she said, gazing back into the house. 'There's a man in here,' she started, but then turned to Jonah and screamed. He followed her eyes and was surprised to discover the microphone in his hand. He had forgotten about it and had torn it loose from the cassette recorder.

'Don't kill him,' she said. 'Please don't kill my son.'

'Jonah!' Gordo shouted from the top of the stairs. 'He's coming out! He's coming out the window.'

Jonah turned and darted back outside. The blood roared in his ears. He leapt down the steps and went around to his right, running down the narrow grassy space between houses. The grass was spare and brownish green. He looked up at the windows on the first floor, but saw no sign of Foerster. He stopped and glanced back out at the street – just in time to see Foerster chug past, arms and legs pumping up and down like the pistons of a steam engine.

'Shit.'

Jonah ran back up the alley to the street.

Foerster's slight figure dashed ahead towards Richmond Terrace. Jonah wouldn't underestimate him this time. Foerster had a head start and he knew the neighbourhood. All the same, there was nothing to do but chase him.

Gordo came out on to the front steps, but Jonah paid him no mind. He tore off after Foerster instead.

At the corner, Foerster turned right.

Please, Jonah thought, *please don't let him be gone when I reach the corner.*

He turned and Foerster was up ahead, bursting across the street through the traffic. Jonah followed, mike still in hand. He cut across the street, eyes pinned on his prey, too much so. A woman in front of Jonah stopped short. She wore a kerchief on her head and a long coat, and she had an old supermarket cart piled high with rags and aluminium cans and chunks of scrap metal. Jonah crashed into it, knocking it over, but stayed on his feet. A car screeched and a scooter zig-zagged around them. People yelled.

Jonah kept running.

Foerster weaved through the milling pedestrains. He turned left and headed along the walkway towards the Staten Island ferry terminal. Jonah saw his head bobbing and weaving through the crowds. Jonah made the turn five seconds behind him.

The ferry was there. Its horn gave a blast, signalling it was ready to leave. The last stragglers were getting on board.

Shit! Could he have the ferries timed too?

Foerster ran past a fat couple and disappeared into the crowd. Jonah kept moving, waiting for Foerster to resurface. A moment later, he passed the fat couple himself and entered the terminal building through a double doorway. He stopped running and walked through the dismal waiting room. Foerster must have come through here, but now he was nowhere in sight. Damn! He had lost him.

He couldn't have turned right or left, Jonah was sure of that. He must have got on the ferry. There was a bottleneck of people up by the ferry entrance. Jonah joined the line. A man did a double-take when he saw Jonah's microphone. Jonah flowed along behind him and climbed on board.

The ferry was the *Samuel I. Newhouse*, commissioned in 1982. Jonah shuffled past a plaque commemorating its namesake. Random thoughts flashed through his head. The boat was old, and still plying its trade. Was that good or bad?

He didn't know whether to go right or left. If he went the wrong way, and Foerster doubled back, they were sunk. No, he had to assume Gordo had followed them to the ferry terminal. If Foerster climbed off the boat, Gordo would get him. Unless Foerster had made himself invisible, which now seemed possible. The horn blasted again. The boat was leaving. Jonah went right, flowing along with the crowd. He moved slowly through a corridor with padded chairs arrayed along the big windows.

He felt the boat lurch, then begin to move.

He walked slowly to the end of the corridor. The ferry had left the terminal and now he was going to Manhattan. He glanced out the door at the end of the corridor. Another sitting room, filled with people. He turned around.

And spotted Foerster.

Thirty yards back, Foerster slid between people up a flight of stairs. Jonah had gone right by without noticing the stairs or Foerster. Now there was a thick knot of people, a crazy New York stew-pot of races, colours and creeds between Jonah and those stairs, between him and Foerster. The people were all trying to follow Jonah into the next compartment, but Jonah wasn't going that way any more. He was swimming against the tide.

He pushed a small Asian man out of his way.

The man pushed Jonah back with both hands, getting his body into it. He shouted something into Jonah's face. Jonah shoved him hard, knocking him towards the window. The man fell into a woman's lap. But the two men behind him were also Asians. They were together. All three started yelling now. One of them punched Jonah in the chest.

Jonah had no time for this.

'Gang way!' he shouted. 'Police!'

He blasted through the two remaining Asians, and the rest of the crowd parted in front of him. He burst up the stairs, went through some doors, and came to an outdoor deck. Foerster waited out there. His head swivelled, surveying the whole deck, but there was nowhere left for him to run. He stood and gaped at Jonah.

'Let's do this the easy way,' Jonah said.

But Foerster didn't do anything the easy way. He moved towards the edge of the deck. Suddenly he vaulted up on to the safety railing. A woman nearby gasped. Foerster squatted on top of the railing like an insect, watching Jonah carefully.

The railing was to Jonah's left. He looked over it, down to the water. The boat was really moving now. It had to be a three-storey jump to the harbour. The water was foaming down there as they motored along. The whole scene gave Jonah vertigo, but it didn't seem to bother Foerster. When he was young, Foerster should have run away and become a circus freak. It would have saved everybody a lot of trouble.

A breeze had kicked up. Jonah took a couple steps towards his quarry.

Foerster grinned. His face was sweaty and pale.

'Don't come any closer. Take one more step and I'm out of here.'

Foerster would jump. Jonah knew he would. And there was no way Jonah was going after him. Not from this height. Not into that water. He glanced down at the microphone in his hand, and an idea struck. Foerster was less than ten feet from him. Jonah brandished the microphone like a gun. He moved into a two-fisted crouch. He hoped Foerster didn't watch much football.

'Freeze, Foerster!'

'Get away from me!' Foerster shouted.

A crowd had gathered around them.

'You climb down off there or I'll let you have it with this.'

'I'm gonna jump. I swear it, I'm gonna jump if you don't get the fuck away.'

'This is a stun gun, motherfucker. I give you a pop, you'll be useless. You ever get a blast from one of these? This is a new one. It'll put you in shock. You don't want to go in the water like that. I promise you'll drown. You want to drown over this? Is that what you want?'

Foerster gazed down at the water below him, then back at Jonah's stun gun.

'Climb down RIGHT NOW. Let's go. Climb down. On the deck.'

Foerster eyed the stun gun.

He eyed the water.

The light went out of his face. His jaw sagged.

'That's not a gun,' somebody said. It was a man's voice, coming from just a few feet behind Jonah.

'What?' Foerster said. His eyes focused on a point just over Jonah's left shoulder.

'It's not a gun. It's a microphone. You never seen one of those before?'

Jonah glanced in the direction of the voice. Mr Know-It-All was chubby, maybe thirty years old; he had a heavy beard and was wearing a Yankees windbreaker jacket. Jonah heard his own voice, coming as if from someplace else. 'Foerster, you're gonna die, understand? This guy has no idea what the fuck he's talking about. In another second, I'm going to shoot you and you're going to die in that water.'

'Then I'll see you in hell.'

Foerster dove off the railing. Someone in the crowd – a man or a woman, Jonah couldn't tell – screamed as Foerster's skinny body carved a graceless, tumbling arc through the air, then splashed into the water below. Jonah rushed to the railing and saw Foerster disappear beneath the surging foam.

Jonah closed his eyes and took a deep breath.

He looked again.

Foerster's body appeared, bobbing off to the right and already well behind the boat. Jonah watched it closely, looking for signs of life. An arm moved. Then the other arm moved. A moment later Foerster was swimming, pulling hard, growing smaller and smaller in the distance. Soon he was a speck, then maybe he was there and maybe he wasn't – a tiny spark on the water, a ray of sunlight reflecting off a discarded beer can.

The *Samuel I. Newhouse* motored along, passing the Statue of Liberty.

Up ahead, the tall buildings of lower Manhattan drew nearer. They seemed to launch themselves heavenward, like bamboo shoots springing up out of the ground.

'Shit,' Jonah said. 'That's twice now.'

He turned and faced the guy who knew what a microphone looked like. Five feet away, the guy stared at him blandly.

'Was that any of your goddamn business?' Jonah said.

The guy shrugged. The beard looked like it came from a costume store and was just glued right on there. 'I made it my business. You have a problem with that?'

Jonah stepped into the punch, landing it solidly across the guy's chin. The guy's head swivelled to the right and he took two stumble-steps backwards before falling on his ass. His head bounced off the ironwork of the floor. He was down and his eyes said he would stay down. A woman from the crowd kneeled by him and glared up at Jonah, not saying anything. All around them, people murmured.

Jonah could feel it already – the dull ache in his hand and in his wrist that by tonight would travel the length of his arm up to his shoulder. Instant karma – you paid a price for hitting people in this world. Still, punching that loud-mouth felt good. It felt right. It felt like something Gordo would do.

'I don't know how it happened,' Foerster's mother said between heavy gasps for air. She had sobbed for a time and had only stopped a few minutes before.

'I don't know how Davey got so bad. I can't tell you how smart he was as a boy. He was the smartest boy in his whole school. Everybody said so. He won big prizes for science and math.' She shook her head. 'And now this. In and out of jail. Beat up by the police. Always on the run.' A long, world-weary sigh escaped her. 'You know, his poor father must be rolling over in his grave.'

Gordo put his big hands on top of hers and let them rest there a moment. They sat at her kitchen table. Jonah had come in a few minutes before and had shaken his head – missed him again. Now he hovered around, not saying anything, generally making Gordo nervous. Gordo was working here.

He glanced around the kitchen, really noticing it for the first time. The wallpaper was peeling away in several places. The ancient cabinets were half falling out of the wall. There was almost no counter space. The linoleum on the floor was scuffed and ripped. The plastic tablecloth was sticky with age. Through a doorway he could see into the living room. The furniture was old – *old*, and not in a good way – and covered in plastic. Hell, back here in the kitchen the refrigerator was five feet tall. Gordo hadn't seen one of those in ages. If he opened the icebox, he knew what he would find. Caked ice, five inches thick on every side, with a few frozen dinners stuffed into the dim tunnel remaining.

In the aftermath of the raid, he had managed to charm her. Even after bursting into her home, even after accidentally knocking her over – thankfully, she was a sturdy woman and hadn't broken a hip or some vertebrae when she went down – he had managed to win her over to his way of thinking. With a maniac like Foerster for a son, she must have been halfway there already.

He had helped her up, brought her here to the kitchen table, and told her that he worked for the courts. He deliberately kept it vague, allowing her to believe whatever she wanted to believe about that. It seemed she had come to the conclusion that he was a court officer of some kind, maybe a special detective who reported directly to the judges. That was a fine thing to believe. He had also told her that he was trying to help her son, not hurt him. He had told her that if the police got to Davey first, her son might not get off as easily. You could tell by the bruises and the stitches in his head that the police had very little compunction about the use of force, even deadly force. The court system was a great deal more humane than the police.

He had won her over so thoroughly that she had agreed not to call anyone right away. She had also agreed to let Gordo look around in Davey's room for a few minutes. There wasn't much to see. A twin bed that might cramp the style of a ten-year-old. Posters of obscure heavy metal bands still on the walls. An aluminium fire ladder attached to the window sill and hanging down to the alley – quite the escape artist was our little Davey. And one thing that might actually mean something, though at this moment Gordo couldn't imagine what: the business card of a security consulting firm located in Charleston, South Carolina. Gordo found it on the bedside table, which suggested to him that Foerster had it out for a reason. It was a very curious thing, that card.

'Well, it happens,' Gordo said now. 'People go bad. It's no reflection on how you raised him.'

Mrs Foerster looked up, and in her eyes Gordo detected the light of hope. 'Do you really believe that?'

'Of course I do. Jonah here can vouch for what I'm saying.'

Jonah nodded his head solemnly. 'Oh yes,' he said. 'Of course I can.' But it sounded empty, like the absent-minded blather of a man who wasn't listening and had no idea what he was agreeing to.

Gordo soldiered on with the lie. Jonah had already tuned the whole thing out, and Gordo himself was even growing a little bored with it. He wanted to keep Foerster's mom on the hook by projecting compassion, and he even wanted to feel compassion for her. But in reality some plenty warped shit must have gone on in this house during Foerster's upbringing, and no amount of hand-wringing was going to unmake that fact. In Gordo's experience, a career whacko like Foerster didn't get that way entirely on his own. He had help, and the help started early.

'In our line of work,' Gordo said, 'Jonah and I deal with some very bad men. Some of them – not Davey, mind you, but some others – are the worst men in our society. And we find over and over that many of them were raised in good homes. Maybe they have some kind of defect, a chemical imbalance in their brains, or maybe they get led down the wrong path by people they meet on the street. I don't know what it is.'

'I don't, either,' she said.

'Whatever the reason in this case, it's very important that Davey be taken off the street for a while. It's important that he gets help from professionals. And it's important that other people ... well ...'

'That he doesn't hurt anyone else,' she said.

'That's right.'

She nodded, as if finally coming to a difficult decision. 'I should have called someone as soon as he showed up here. But I wanted to protect him. I love my son, Mr Lamb.'

Gordo nodded. 'I know you do.' His hand moved to her shoulder. 'We can make things right for Davey. Will you help us do that?'

She began to cry again, silently this time. Her body shook all over. 'I'll do anything you want.'

Gordo held up the business card. 'Do you know anything about this? I found it upstairs. It could be a clue.'

She took the card in one hand. 'He told me he has a job lined up in South Carolina. I don't know if it's true or not. He's lied so much that I have no idea whether I'm coming or going sometimes. He wanted me to give him money so he could go down there, but I didn't believe that's what he wanted it for.'

'Did you give him any money?'

'I gave him forty dollars. He said it wasn't enough. I was actually afraid of him, what my son might do, to get more money from me.' She started crying some more at the thought of it, but not as forcefully as before. Silent tears rolled down her cheeks.

'Do you have any idea what kind of work he might do with a security firm?'

She shrugged. 'Something with computers, maybe. Like I said, he's very smart.'

'Can you do this for me? Can you call the phone company, right now, and find out if by any chance Davey called that number from this phone? I'd do it myself, but I'd have to go through channels and it might take a couple of days. We're really working against the clock here.'

'Well, he was only here one night, and he came quite late. I don't know when he would have called.'

'Mrs Foerster, a man like Davey can be quite resourceful.'

'Well, OK,' she said, but she sounded uncertain.

'Good. That's good. Here's the phone.'

Gordo and Jonah waited while she sat on hold. Jonah was pacing a little bit, and if he was going to do that, Gordo wished he would go out on the street where Mrs Foerster didn't have to look at him. But she was a good girl, a trooper. When she got someone on the phone, she did just as he told her – she asked them to outline all the calls made from her phone in the past twenty-four hours. As she listened, she jotted something down on a piece of scrap paper. She turned it around so that Gordo could read it.

3.07 a.m.

She looked deeply into his eyes. He noticed her eyes were bloodshot, and yellowing. He nodded. She nodded.

Jonah floated closer and looked at the note.

'OK, thank you,' Foerster's mom said into the phone just before hanging up. 'You know, I have some family visiting, and I just don't like the way they think my phone is their phone. Calling wherever they please, any time they want. I have to keep close tabs on them.'

Gordo liked the story. She was clearly a veteran liar. She had flowed into it just as smoothly as he would have.

'Well, you were right,' she said. 'He called there in the middle of the night while I was sleeping. But the call lasted less than a minute.'

'That's very interesting,' Gordo said. 'I wonder what it means.'

'It doesn't mean anything,' Jonah said as they walked back to the car. 'The guy called some random office in the middle of the night when he knew nobody would be there. He probably did it so he could lie to his mother a little more about some place that was supposed to hire him. I can't imagine anybody hiring that guy.'

'Sure, that could be,' Gordo allowed. 'Or he might have called there for a hundred other reasons. He's a crazy person, so he might actually think that some private security firm wants to hire him. For all I know, he's so delusional he thinks he works for the Government, or for some clandestine foreign spy agency.'

'Or the New World Order,' Jonah said.

'Right. He might go to South Carolina and walk in the office there, and they won't have the slightest idea what he's talking about. It could be bad for them because it might set him off.'

They were almost at the car. For some reason, it bothered Jonah that any firm, especially a security contractor, would want Foerster to work for them. It burned him up. He didn't want his mind to think it.

'Or, and I know this is a little hard to swallow,' Gordo said, 'Foerster might have some skill or combination of skills that makes this security company want to hire him. Hey, these guys might be people who hire rent-a-cops with tinfoil badges to hang around empty shopping malls and make sure nobody walks off with the sheetrock or the wiring. But we know one thing about Foerster – he thinks about two steps ahead, and he can be pretty fucking hard to catch. These might be enticing traits to somebody. And we know one thing about private security companies in this day and age – it's not always clear what they're really up to.'

'So you're saying?'

'I'm saying I'm going to do a little research on this company, see what I can find out. Then I might give them a call and try to talk to this guy Tyler Gant.'

'Are you going to tell him why you're calling?'

Gordo unlocked Jonah's door, then went around to the driver's side. 'That's the tricky thing. I want to find out if Foerster's headed there, if I can, but I really don't want to tip my hand and let this guy know we're looking for Foerster. I mean, fifty grand is fifty grand. Better we get it than he does.'

They slid into the car, and Gordo started it up. 'So let me get this straight,' Jonah said. 'You're thinking of going down there?'

Gordo gave Jonah a wide-eyed look as if they'd got their signals crossed somehow, as if something so simple a child could understand had, nonetheless, been misunderstood. 'Of course I am. Aren't you? I mean, if we find out that's where he's going. This is the biggest single score we've ever seen. We're not going to give it up that easy.'

Jonah said nothing.

'Are we?'

Jonah shrugged, hating the tight, petulant sound in his voice that he knew was coming. 'It's going to cost money.'

Gordo nosed into the traffic on Richmond Terrace. The new realities – the bikes, the scooters, the pedestrians, and all the rest – meant that if you were still driving a car it wasn't always clear when you were free to merge. 'Think of it as an investment,' he said. 'I mean, this is the big one. This is the white whale. We can't just walk away from this, right?'

Jonah wasn't sure. They had missed the guy twice already, even though the cops had caught him on more than one occasion. Foerster's slippery moves had Jonah thinking maybe he, and maybe even Gordo, weren't cut out for bounty hunting after all. Sure, they'd caught a couple of nickel and dime skips. But when they went for the real money, the guy juked them and jived them and faked them out of their shoes. Beyond that, what if the whole South Carolina thing was a decoy or some scam Foerster was playing? What if he headed west, or north, instead of south? They could go down there, spend at least a couple of thousand dollars they didn't have, go deeper into the hole, and it could all be a washout, a big nothing.

'Jonah, am I right?'

'I think we should wait a minute and think about this,' Jonah said, knowing his words were exactly what Gordo didn't want to hear. Already Gordo's face looked pinched, as if a painful cramp had seized his lower abdomen. Jonah plunged on anyway. He had an opinion, so he might as well express it. 'I think we should be a hundred per cent certain he's headed down there before we make a move that way.'

Gordo followed the flow of congested traffic towards the bridge into Brooklyn. It was amazing to see that on this monster span, one that went so high in the air and had such wicked crosswinds, an entire lane in each direction was now reserved for bicycles. What was next – a lane for oxen?

'Jonah, don't kill it, man. We'll never be one hundred per cent sure of anything.'

'OK, ninety-nine per cent. Ninety-eight per cent.'

Gordo sighed. 'I'll do whatever I can to put together enough evidence so you will know that going to South Carolina is the right move.'

'Well,' Jonah said, and again the sound of his voice irritated Gordo. 'I'll be waiting to see it.'

4

There was a delay with the plane.

The pilots were up front, dickering with some part of the instrumentation. At one point, Gant saw the younger of the two take out a screwdriver and remove a panel, then start poking among some wires inside. Rather than watch these guys fool around with things they probably didn't understand, things they would need to keep Gant alive and up in the air in the very near future, he went outside on to the tarmac.

It was just after eleven o'clock, and the sun was riding high and hot. Gant walked a little way from the plane and took out his cell phone. He had world service, so he could call Vernon from here. Three goons milled around over by the shed where Gant had stripped down yesterday, waiting for the plane to take off. A black SUV was parked there. The men eyed Gant with unfriendly stares. Did they have some way of listening in to his conversation? He thought not, but supposed it didn't matter anyway. He could keep it brief and to the point with Vernon.

The phone rang three times. 'Yessir,' came the sunny voice. 'I know it's gonna be a wonderful day when I see this number calling.'

'Vernon.'

'That would be me.'

Patrick Quinlan

'Where are you?'

'I'm walking down the street. I just had my breakfast at the Charlotte Inn, and man, what a breakfast it was.'

Gant smiled. Vernon often took his meals at the best hotels and restaurants in Charleston – he had the money to spend, and he enjoyed the jarring contrast between himself and the alarmed gentry who ended up sitting at tables near him. Gant could picture Vernon strutting through the historic district like a peacock. Six feet, four inches tall in bare feet, the top of his white Stetson hat adding another four inches, the heels of his snakeskin cowboy boots adding another two. Tight jeans, a black T-shirt painted to his broad chest and shoulders, a riot of tattoos reaching from the razor wire tattooed around his neck, all the way down his shoulders and arms to his big rawboned hands. He was a piece of work, all right – toothpick in his mouth, huge jaw jutting out, daring just about any hard man to go ahead and try his luck. There probably wouldn't be any takers today, or tomorrow, or any time this month.

'You ready to work?' Gant said.

'I'm always ready to work.'

Gant glanced up and saw the stewardess, flight attendant, waitress, or whatever from the plane. She clicked across the uneven paving in her high heels and skirt, waving to him. One passenger, one stewardess. Man, it was crazy.

'Listen, I don't have much time,' he said. 'I'm about to catch a plane here. That thing with the boat? The delivery? I need you to give the green light on that. It's a go. So tell our supplier we're ready and tell the boat it's coming at them.'

'Got it, boss.'

The woman came almost to within touching distance. 'Mr Gant, we're ready for you now. The plane is all set.'

'Thank you. I'll be just another minute.'

'Of course.' She turned and started back. Without much interest, he watched her big behind move away towards the plane.

'Also,' he said to Vernon. 'What's the story in New York?'

He sensed a hesitation on the other end of the line. It was uncharacteristic for Vernon, to say the least.

'Vernon?'

'There ain't no story in New York, I'm sorry to say.'

'What?'

'There's no story. At least, none that anybody would want to hear.'

'Vernon, I don't have time to dance around. Out with it. The plane's about to take off without me.'

'All right,' Vernon said, but his voice didn't sound like it was all right. 'Our man went to make the pick-up late last night, and nobody was there. Our boy wasn't home, even though he knew we'd be coming soon. Nobody was home, and there was no message left.'

Gant thought about it. He started walking towards the plane. 'Maybe he went out last night to a bar and picked up a girl or something. Tell the guy to wait around a while.'

'I already did. He's waiting in the apartment. See, it wasn't locked. In fact, the door wasn't even closed.'

Gant felt his breathing become just a tiny bit shallower. 'Shit.'

'Yeah.'

'All right. Keep on it. I'll be home in a few hours.'

'I'm on it.'

Gant rang off and trotted up the steps into the plane. He took his seat as the flight attendant pulled the door closed and locked it airtight. He cinched his seat belt as the woman took her fold-out seat near the door of the cockpit. The engines roared into life, and without further ado, the plane taxied into position for take-off. These guys were in a hurry to get out of here. Gant settled back, closed his eyes and relaxed himself as the plane accelerated down the bumpy runway and then left the ground. He took several deep breaths as they went into a steep ascent. Later, when they levelled off, he opened his eyes. Out the window he saw huge, white puffy clouds. Only then did he begin thinking again.

Jesus, that Foerster thing was bad news. This business was about knowing people. It was about relationships, and he was beginning to think the relation-ship with Foerster was not a good one to have. It wasn't the first time he'd had these thoughts. In fact, he had it on good authority that his relationship with Foerster should have ended after just a brief fling.

Gant had once known a man named Monty. Monty was restless, a mover, and an adventurer. He had his fingers in a lot of different pies. He was the only man Gant had ever met who wore a handlebar moustache – it gave him the effect of being a man out of time, a museum piece catapulted from the 1800s into the present day. Gant half expected Monty to pull up on a bicycle with an enormous front tyre, instead of the vintage Corvette he normally drove.

Monty was gone now, turned up dead in the Amazon more than a year ago, in the nearly lawless border region where Colombia, Peru and Brazil all met. They found his body in an alley behind a bar in Leticia, Colombia. What he was doing there was never explained by anybody. In fact, the only reason Gant knew he was dead was because one morning when he slid behind the wheel of his car, a small newspaper clipping to that effect from *The Toledo Blade* was taped to his dashboard. It turned out Montgomery Blaine was born and raised just outside Toledo, and still had parents there. A small handwritten note was taped to the dash along with the clipping.

He would have wanted you to know.

It gave Gant the creeps sometimes, to think of the people who must be watching him. Whoever they were, they must approve of, or at least not care about, Gant's more unsavoury activities. Still, it wasn't a good feeling to have those eyes following his moves.

In any case, Monty was the one who had given him Foerster. It was during the lead-up to the anthrax job, more than two years ago now. Certain people were feeling Gant out about it. Could it be done, take out two Illinois state senators at the same time, in a government office building in Chicago? The key here was that the two good liberal senators, a man and a woman, both very powerful in state politics, shouldn't look like they were specifically targeted. And whoever took them out either had to escape completely, or know nothing of the reason or the people behind the attack.

Taken as an intellectual exercise, Gant said yes, he thought maybe it could be done. There'd have to be collateral damage to cover up the purpose of the attack, and that meant innocent people would have to die. Also, a bomb wouldn't work because you'd never get it past security and into the building. But an airborne biological agent in the ventilation system – highly concentrated, highly virulent anthrax, for instance – that might do the trick.

OK, his audience said, but could he, Gant, pull it off?

He wasn't sure, even then, if the job was for real. Maybe it was just some people blowing off steam by fantasising about something they wanted to see done, or might want to see done. Maybe it was a set-up, a sting, someone somewhere had been turned by the Government, and the FBI was listening to every word. Gant didn't know. In fact, even now, he still wasn't sure. But at the time, despite the uncertainties, he decided to treat it as if it were real. If it were a sting, then he was looking at a lot of time, possibly the rest of his life, in prison. But he took the gamble anyway. Fortune favours the bold.

'I need a microbiologist,' he said to Monty one evening. They were walking, as they often did, among the Friday-night crowds in downtown Charleston. They moved along streets lined with multimillion-dollar pre-Civil War homes into Battery Park, where the breeze off the harbour and the chatter from the gawkers would surely thwart any attempt to listen to their conversation.

'A microbiologist?' Monty said. 'I didn't suspect Tyler Gant even possessed a word that long in his vocabulary. That's a six-syllable word. What, pray tell, do you need one of those for?'

'That's classified. But I need a good one. And I need him or her to have a certain, shall we say, moral flexibility.'

Monty became serious, as he always did when he realised that Gant wasn't kidding around, or that an opportunity had presented itself. 'It could cost you some money, finding a person like that.'

'I'm prepared to pay money.'

Monty nodded. 'Let me see what I can do.'

The next conversation took place a month later in the parking lot of a closed rest area off the Blue Ridge Mountain Parkway in West Virginia.

It seemed like a long way to go to have a chat, but Monty insisted on it. They parked their cars about fifty yards apart. Gant walked across the asphalt to the rental sedan Monty leaned against. The pavement was cracked and broken. The rest area itself was high up in the mountains. The view of the valley far below and to the west was wide open. You could forget to breathe while looking at it. The view south along the ridgeline was probably the purple mountain's majesty the children used to sing about. The wind howled incessantly, and immediately Gant knew why Monty had picked this place to talk.

Gant glanced only once at the rest area building – in some distant past it had been home to bathrooms and maybe a restaurant or gift shop. It was boarded up now. One of the wooden boards that covered the front doorway had been prised open a crack. Gant peered at the darkness between the board and wall – it wasn't out of the question that people were living in there. It wasn't out of the question that vampires lived in there. It looked like a place where they would hide out in the daytime.

Monty had a single sheet of paper in a manila folder. Neatly typed on the page was a name, an address and a telephone number. That was all.

'Davis Foerster,' Monty said, his voice just barely audible above the wind. 'The CIA has been watching him from the time he was fourteen. He won a prize from the National Science Foundation that year, for a project that demonstrated ways of accelerating the growth of cancer cells. The following year he jumped to computer science and won another national contest, this time for a paper arguing that in our lifetime, artificial intelligence would become smarter than man, and would bind all the networked computers in the world together into a single, hyper-intelligent entity that would quickly make humanity obsolete. This entity would then go on to use the available computing capacity on earth to unlock the secrets of the universe.'

'The CIA?' Gant said. 'You work for the CIA?'

'I work with all kinds of people.'

'For the job I'm thinking of, I'm not sure a CIA man will do.'

Monty shook his head. 'As far as I know, the CIA has never touched Foerster.

They were interested in him and that's all. They did a psychological assessment on him. What you have to understand is this guy is eight different kinds of bad news. He's unstable, from an abusive upbringing. He's considered deeply neurotic and possibly delusional. He's consumed by rage and feelings of power-lessness and persecution. He's been in and out of various facilities, juvenile detention and mental hospitals, for the past seven or eight years. His first stay in juvie came when he was sixteen – a group of ten-year-olds were outside his window taunting him, so he went outside and sliced one of them up with a razor blade.

'He seems to lack empathy for other living things, human or animal. He tortured stray cats as a child. He conducted experiments on them, like some kind of grammar school Josef Mengele. As an adult, he's believed to be a serial rapist, and his M.O. is most likely blitz attacks with blunt objects on defenceless victims, like old women or women who are asleep. In fact, it's likely that at one time or another he's killed a woman in the initial attack and then had sex with the corpse. Of course, by now he may have graduated to more sophisticated methods.'

'If they know all this about him,' Gant said, 'why is he still on the street?'

Monty shrugged. 'You're the ex-cop war hero. Go and arrest him if you want. But I suggest you hire him for the job. He can do whatever science you need, and he has the moral flexibility you described. Keep him close while the operation is ongoing. Afterwards, I think you should dispose of him. He's not the kind of person you want out there knowing your secrets.'

Monty smiled then, his white teeth gleaming. 'And, as I'm sure you realise, the world will probably be a little better off without him.'

In the end, Gant took half of Monty's advice. He hired Foerster. Afterwards, he paid him handsomely and sent him on his way. Why had he done that? For one, Foerster seemed a lot more stable in person than Monty made him out to be. He was a jerk, of course, almost unbearably obnoxious at times. But he was no drooling psycho. He worked long hours without complaint, living on take-out food and very little sleep, and when it came to the science he knew exactly what he was doing. There was trial and error, sure – he had never grown anthrax before, weaponised or not – but he mastered the intricacies of it in short order.

There was something creepy about Foerster, but the operation was a huge success, and he was part of that success. It might have been bad judgement, it might even have been short-sighted selfishness, but Gant figured that if he ever needed a microbiologist again, Foerster was his man, so it was better to keep him alive. And it was even more than that. Gant recognised something in Foerster. In a sense, they had some things in common, were almost kindred spirits.

They both kept secrets.

'You can't hide out here for ever.'

It was her mother talking. That morning, Katie had evacuated to her mother's tidy house in Beaufort, about an hour away by car. Now, in the late afternoon, she was still there. She had no immediate plans of leaving.

She'd eaten lunch with her mom, and as the sun waned they were enjoying a few Margaritas on her mom's back patio. It was pleasant enough, sitting at the table and putting a buzz on. The patio looked out on her mom's backyard and garden. They were more modest, certainly, than Katie's, but still pretty nice. It had rained a lot down here this summer and even now, in November, the whole backyard – the trees, the bushes, the hanging vines – were as dense and lush as a rainforest. It seemed to Katie like a magical place out of a fairy tale. And the strong drinks didn't hurt either. They put a filter between Katie and her mom's more annoying commentary.

It was good to be there in one important sense – Tyler had arrived home and found her gone. In fact, he had called about an hour ago, wondering where she was and what he ought to thaw out for dinner. Of course, he knew exactly where she was – both their cars were outfitted with GPS units mounted inside the dashboard, which he could monitor from his laptop computer. It was very convenient. If the cars were ever stolen, he could find them again with just a few clicks. And if Katie ever used her car to run away from home, he could find her again the same way.

98

Tyler also knew what he ought to make himself for dinner. He was a big boy and had lived on his own for many years before they met. He had called her to send a message. Although their conversation was brief, and polite, he was in effect telling her: *I'm home now and you should be, too.*

But she wasn't home and she wasn't coming home. Not tonight. See, two could play at this game of being absent without leave. He thought he could come and go as he pleased and she was supposed to stay home and play wifey, but she was done with that. It was over. Certainly, she would make it look good for public consumption – for instance, she was organising their annual Halloween party as she always did – but privately, she would make him feel how she felt.

Katie's mother went on. 'I mean, it seems like every few days you're sleeping over here, and I doubt it's for my benefit. If you're having these sorts of problems, maybe you should go into counselling together.'

She looked at her mother, really soaking her in. She was a woman in her late fifties. She was careful about sun exposure. She drank eight glasses of pure spring water a day. She followed a mainly vegetarian diet, though she wasn't a fanatic about it. At Katie's insistence, she had taken up yoga about ten years ago, and had retained some of her youthful flexibility and strength. Her eyes were bright and alert, even after a few drinks. About the only obvious clue to her age were the crow's feet around her eyes, and the wrinkles on her forehead and neck – she refused to consider plastic surgery, though many women she knew had already gone for it two or three times.

Still, Katie's father had died five years earlier and his death had taken its toll. Her mom wasn't as vigorous as before, wasn't quite the queen of the ball she had once been. She had diminished without him, and had become thinner and more fragile. She was still passionate about gardening, and about her charity work. She still lived life and gave herself to it. If anything about her had outwardly changed, it was that she no longer travelled the way she and Katie's father had loved to do together. But that was par for the course now anyway – few people were travelling like they once had. Even so, her mother was getting older, and it was happening right in front of Katie's eyes. She could almost picture her mother in another ten years, and she didn't like what she saw.

'Mom, would Dad have ever gone to marital counselling?'

'Well, we never needed counselling, as far as I know.'

'That's not really my point. My point is, would he have gone?'

Her mother gave a gentle shake of her head. 'I don't think certain men of your father's generation would go in for that kind of thing. Many did, but some men were holdovers from an earlier time. They weren't very touchy-feely. They held their pain inside and didn't talk much about it.'

Katie took a sip of her Margarita. It was fruity and delicious. She was about to score one on her mother and took the time to savour it. 'Exactly my point. Tyler is a man from Dad's generation, and I'd say he qualifies as a holdover from an earlier time. Like maybe the Great Depression.'

Her mother made a pained expression. 'I'm not the one who told you to marry a man your father's age.'

'Nobody told me to do it. He's the man I fell in love with.'

'Well, for God's sake, Katie. A younger man, a more modern man, would be better able to deal emotionally with the problem you've had. A younger man would be more open about it, would be more willing to talk about it, and then maybe the two of you could move on from being stuck in this place.'

'Mom . . .'

Her mother held up a slim hand. To Katie, this was the first indication that her Mom had crossed the line from tipsy to drunk. 'No, I'm going to say it. Tyler wanted to have children, his own children. He wanted to have them with you. But you can't have children, and what's worse, you can't have them because of your own flagrant behaviour. OK, you were young, but that doesn't change the facts. You ruined your body by sleeping around.'

'Jesus, Mom,' Katie said. What she thought was: *Fuck you, Mom.*

'It's true, isn't it? How is an old-fashioned person like Tyler supposed to deal with that? He can't talk about it. He probably can't even think about it without getting upset. Personally, I think your marriage is doomed.'

With that, she stood on unsteady legs and gathered their glasses. 'Are you having another drink?' It came out ferociously, almost an accusation.

'Sure, why not?' Katie said. 'I'm not going anywhere.'

Her mother went inside and Katie sat, watching the light begin to fade from the sky. She never watched the news, but even she knew that many people thought the world was ending. The weather was changing. The economy was collapsing and millions of people were out of work, or had lost their homes. None of these hardships had touched her life, but somehow she felt them, as though they were all around her, in the air she breathed, on the empty highways, in the gated communities where she and her mother both lived.

And she had her own hardships, hadn't she? It was a painful thing, not being able to bear a child. She had lost that ability years ago, at the age of twenty-five, without even knowing it. Back in her Dewey Beach days she had picked up a case of gonorrhoea. Worse yet, apparently she had had it for months before any symptoms appeared. Even worse, she got it during a time when she was particularly active, partying too much, and she wasn't even sure whom it came from. She was horrified by it, of course. Who wouldn't be horrified by a foul-smelling, painful discharge coming from their body, especially that part of their body? But she had gone to a medical clinic and a round of antibiotics had knocked it out in a few days. Katie was good at forgetting unpleasant facts, and a short time later it seemed that the whole episode had happened to somebody else.

Then, two years ago, she had miscarried a baby. It was early into the pregnancy, less than two months. These things happened. Then, last year, it had happened again. A battery of tests quickly revealed something she hadn't even suspected. Her uterus had been scarred by the gonorrhoea. As a result, her pregnancies were ectopic – meaning the foetus lodged each time in one of her fallopian tubes, and grew there for a little while. But the tubes were too narrow. They weren't designed for growing a baby, so her body expelled the foetus in self-defence. This was one impromptu anatomy lesson that she hadn't wanted to learn.

The good news was that there was no threat to her overall health, and she could enjoy a normal, active sex life with a willing partner. The bad news was that she could never carry a baby to term. The worst news was that there was no way to explain her past to Tyler in a way that would make sense to him, or that he could accept. She had never felt like a whore before – not till the day they found out why she couldn't have a baby, and not till she looked into her husband's eyes.

She remembered how some weeks afterwards he wasn't home one night, and she'd wandered through the big house, thinking that she might start cleaning. Instead, she'd poured herself a glass of wine and gone into the living room. She'd sat on the leather sofa across from Tyler's chair. She could see the indentations his body had made. It was like he was sitting there, invisible. When the grandfather clock had chimed nine, she'd begun to cry. There wasn't much force behind the tears, and she'd regained her composure. Maybe she was reaching the point where she was all cried out. She hoped so.

She remembered another time when he had left the bed in the middle of the night. She'd padded down the stairs, looking for him. She found him in the living room, slouched in his chair, whiskey glass in hand. His eyes were open, staring straight ahead. He looked up when she came to the doorway. Those eyes were hard. She saw no caring there, no warmth, just cold intelligence measuring her. He could have been a creature from an alien race, come to take specimens back home. He stared at her a long time.

'Go ahead,' he said. 'Tell me how much you love me.'

There was nothing she could do, nothing she could say. Things were never OK between them. They had moments when they were easy together, like they used to be, but those moments became increasingly rare. It was quiet in the house, and she felt his anger most of the time, rather than saw it. He shut her out. She suspected that when the time was right for him, he would put an end to the marriage. Right now, Katie, flawed as she was in his eyes, fit his purposes. Appearances were important to Tyler, and in their community they still seemed the perfect couple – a wealthy, successful and very fit older man with a stunning young wife. But she imagined a day would come when his purposes changed, and then he would make her go away. Maybe he would find himself another young woman. For all she knew, maybe he already had.

He blamed her, of course. He blamed her for those men who came before him. She had always been vague about her past love life. But that luxury was gone. He extracted confessions from her regarding each and every man who came before him. When she told him about Ray, she could swear she saw Tyler's heart break. He got drunk and slapped her that night, for the first time ever. It didn't hurt, but it surprised her and she cried.

Good for you, she told him in her mind as the tears rolled down her cheeks. You should be the one with the broken heart for a change.

Now, her mother came out the sliding glass doors with the next round of drinks. 'Mom,' Katie said, 'I just don't know what I'm going to do. I can't live like this any more.'

Foerster was dead tired.

He stood at a payphone on the street in downtown Myrtle Beach, South Carolina. It was night, just after ten o'clock, and he was half a block from the beach. He could hear the water lapping at the sand. High-rise hotels and low-rise motels lined the strip here. A lot of them were closed and boarded up. Foerster didn't care. He had exactly nineteen dollars left of the money his mother had given him, and he would avoid paying for a room if he could.

A handful of honky-tonk bars were open right near here. Neon lights blinked, country music blasted, and people milled around and smoked cigarettes in the night air. A lot of military types in olive T-shirts and crew-cut hair. A lot of biker types wearing leather and denim jackets and showing gang colours. A lot of sun-kissed, big-haired blondes wearing shorts, bikini tops and high-heels. Once in a while, a police cruiser rolled slowly by. To Foerster's eyes, these were the only people who seemed to be out.

He seemed to have no energy left – like someone had inserted a tube and drained the vitality right out of him. The payphone kiosk was practically holding him up. His head was congested and he felt a bit feverish. No surprise there. By his own estimate, he'd travelled about seven hundred miles in a little over thirteen hours. Luck had been with him. After swimming to shore from the ferry, he'd limped to the highway entrance ramp, stuck his thumb out and inside of ten minutes got picked up by a long-haul trucker headed for Maryland. Half-drowned and bedraggled, the barest trickle of traffic on the roads, and he'd still managed to get a ride. Foerster was almost willing to say that something more than luck was at work here.

Maybe it was meant to be.

Of course that was silly. Nothing was meant to be. The universe unfolded in random fashion and people were the helpless playthings of enormous forces beyond their control. But then again . . .

If mere luck had sent that first ride, it couldn't have worked out much better than it had. The driver was young, with a three-day growth of beard. He had been arrested half a dozen times, hated cops, and sympathised completely with Foerster's story. He even gave Foerster a flannel shirt and jeans to wear, plus a towel to dry himself off with. The clothes were a size or so too big, but it was better to be dry than wet.

'How do you even keep this thing on the road?' Foerster said after they'd travelled a while. They were rolling down the New Jersey Turnpike by then, headed for Delaware. 'I mean, it must cost a fortune. Most of the independents are already out of business, aren't they?'

'Want the truth?' the young guy said, a mischievous gleam in his eye.

'Of course.'

'I'm carrying a load of dry goods for a discount chain. Buried here and there in the boxes with the ladies' nightgowns and bed linens is a load of cocaine headed for the Midwest. There's more than a million bucks worth of coke inside this truck right now.'

Foerster was impressed. 'Yours?'

The trucker shook his head. 'The guys who own the chain store. It's how they stay in business. Drugs, my friend, are good for America. It's how my employers stay in business, how I stay in business, how everybody stays in business.'

Foerster had hoped to go all the way to Charleston tonight, but he hadn't made it there. The ride he'd gotten out of Virginia, a middle-aged salesman named Mort, was coming here to Myrtle Beach. Mort would have been happy to drop Foerster off along the interstate. But the place where Mort exited the highway to come here, some seventy-five miles inland, was the same exit where an old rundown roadside attraction called South of the Border had once been. Foerster had been there once as a kid – a bunch of rinky-dink rides, an observation tower that looked out on nothing but the highway, a bad restaurant and a gift shop selling cheap crap and T-shirts with funny slogans. South of the Border's major claim to fame, a dubious one, had been the billboards advertising the place, posted every mile or so for more than sixty miles before you ever arrived.

South of the Border was still there at the highway exit, but it had changed. It was closed, and some bomzhies had taken it over. When Foerster and Mort had arrived after dark, much of the place was on fire. Silhouettes raced back and forth in the light cast by the flames. Traffic raced by on the highway. No sirens sounded, and no firemen worked to put the fire out. The amusement park just burned and burned, the crackling of the flames punctuated by the screams and the laughter of the drunken nutjobs who had torched it.

Mort had pulled over a little way from the inferno. 'Sure you don't want to try your luck in Myrtle Beach?'

Foerster didn't want to, but what choice did he have? No one was going to stop for him – not in the dark, not with that blaze going. Finding another ride was going to be a bust, and Foerster sure as hell didn't want to stay over in that nightmare stop. So Myrtle Beach was his only option.

Now, at the payphone, with the night's action unfolding all around him, he dialled his mother collect. It was a little late, but she wasn't famous for her early to bed, early to rise work ethic. She was famous for her loud snoring and her late-night TV watching. He wouldn't be surprised if she answered.

As the phone rang, he took a look around. He was getting a few funny looks from people on the street, and why not? Here was a pale, skinny guy with a carved-up scalp, wearing a flannel shirt and jeans that hung off of him. Tanned beach bunnies and muscle-bound, vein-popping steroid freaks, all in skin-tight clothing, would see him as a member of an alien race. But none of the looks they gave him were too threatening, so he took no immediate action.

On the other end of the line, his mother accepted the reversed charges.

'Davey?' she said. 'My God, where are you?'

'Don't worry about that right now. I'm OK, and I'm in a safe place. That's all you need to know. What happened today after I left?'

'What happened? Those two men chased you down the block. Later, they came back and asked me all kinds of questions.'

'What did you tell them?'

'Nothing. What could I tell them? They wanted to search the house. I told them to see a judge and get a search warrant. Till then, I couldn't help them. I know how these things work. The police can't just barge in here any time they want.'

Foerster shook his head. 'They're not the police.'

'What?'

'They're not the police, Ma. They can't search the house. They can't get a search warrant because they're not cops. They're private goons.'

'Well, they left anyway.'

'OK. Good, Ma. You did the right thing. That was good. Now I need you to do something for me. Upstairs, on the bedside table, I left a business card. It's the business card I showed you. It's from a friend of mine, like I told you. He wants me to do some work for him. The number I need is the hand-written one. It's his private, unlisted number.'

'Davey, I don't have that card any more.'

'What? What do you mean?' Foerster felt his heart do a jerky little dance in his chest. If she had given those clowns Gant's card ... No. His mind rebelled against going down that road.

'I didn't want those men to see the card. So when they chased you I went upstairs, tore up the card, and flushed the pieces down the toilet.'

Foerster rubbed his head with his free hand. His fingers moved along the railroad line of scar tissue and stitches. OK, he'd live through the night without calling Gant. He'd make it down to Charleston tomorrow, the same way he'd made it this far. He'd have to find some kind of sleeping arrangement, maybe on the beach, maybe in an alley, but that was OK. Hell, maybe he'd find a chick to take him home, right? Stranger things had happened in this world. It was better that she had destroyed the card than that it had fallen into the hands of those bounty hunters. And it showed him something, too. Maybe, just maybe, she was on his side for a change.

'You did the right thing, Ma. Thank you.'

'Davey, are you OK? You sound like you're on drugs. Where are you? This is your mother talking.'

Foerster rolled his eyes. 'I'm fine. I'm on my way to Charleston, like I said.'

'I don't believe you.'

Jesus. He wished someone else could listen in sometimes, just so people would know what a psycho bitch his mother was. 'Ma, I'm in Myrtle Beach right now, about a hundred miles from Charleston, calling you from a payphone. That's where I am. I hitchhiked all this way. I'm gonna go down to Charleston in the morning and see that guy about the job. I was thinking I'd give him a try tonight if you still had the card, but it's not a problem. I'll meet up with him tomorrow.'

Her tone said she still didn't buy it. 'OK, Davey. If you say so. I'm glad you're all right.'

'Thanks. I'm glad you're all right, too. I'm glad they didn't . . . do anything to you. Listen, Ma, I'm almost out of money. I'm tired and I need a place to stay. Maybe some food. Is there any chance you could Western Union me some more money down here tomorrow morning? If I know the money's coming I can probably convince somebody to give me a room for the night.'

His mother hesitated. Foerster already knew what was coming. 'Davey, I'd feel funny about it. I just gave you money this morning. After everything that happened with those men, I'd just feel funny about it, that's all.'

'OK,' he said. 'I understand.'

'Davey?' came his mother's voice, but Foerster hung up the phone. He glanced around. The nearest bar was a place across the street called Bottoms Up, with a blinking neon sign of a cowgirl in a short skirt, bending over.

A buzz of music and raised voices came from the place. Foerster stepped into the street and headed towards the front door. He took the money from his pocket and looked at it – a ten, a five, and four ones.

It was going to be a hell of a night.

Tyler Gant lay in the grip of a nightmare.

He knew he was dreaming, but that didn't help. He couldn't seem to wake himself up. It made everything worse because he had already lived the nightmare, and knew what would occur at each moment. He lay impaled, waiting for what he knew must come.

It was springtime and Gant's unit was operating thirty miles north of Saigon. Above him the pale blue sky stretched away to forever. In the distance rugged hillsides loomed, their steep slopes dark green with foliage. Gant crouched near a jagged hole in the ground, eating C-rations and praying for Winner to come back. He liked Winner. But with each passing moment Gant lost hope.

It was hot out, close to a hundred degrees hot, with heavy, moist air. The sun beat down, making Gant lightheaded. Earlier, a grunt named Morgan had popped a gook mine and blown off the bottom of his left leg. From the knee down, he was fucking gone. The morphine didn't take hold right away and Morgan screamed and cried the whole time while they waited for the chopper. More than half an hour had gone by since they lifted him out but somehow Gant still heard him screaming.

Worse than Morgan: the mine had blasted the scrub cover away from a hole, a dink tunnel, and now Gant was sitting at the mouth of the thing, smelling that nasty dank funk from there, waiting to see if Winner came back out or not. Lopez had told Winner five minutes, just check the fucking thing out, that's all; come back and we'll blow it.

Gant finished the rations and lit up a cigarette.

Winner's eyes had gone fear-wide when Lopez gave him the news. Into the hole, Winner. Winner's big Adam's apple bobbed, his hands trembled. But good old Winner, he played it by the book, and down he went.

Hah, Gant thought. Dave Winner, how's that for a name? He had gone down fifteen minutes ago. Maybe twenty. He wasn't coming back.

A shadow crossed Gant's face. Gant didn't even look up to see who it was. He already knew.

'Gant.'

Gant took a long drag from the cigarette. 'No way, Lieutenant.'

'Come again, soldier?'

'No fucking way am I going in that hole.'

Lieutenant Lopez was small and dark, some kind of second-generation wetback from Arizona. He could fit in the hole just as well as Gant. He wanted somebody to go in there? He should go.

'I need you to go in there and get Winner. Tell him I said five minutes.'

'Winner's dead.'

'Gant?'

He jumped up, almost in Lopez's face. 'Winner is fucking dead, sir. You sent him in there, the dinks got him and he's dead. You want me to go in there and be dead too? Is that what you want?'

'If he's dead, then bring back the body.'

'You bring it back. I say we leave him there.'

But then Campbell was with them, the big black platoon sergeant. Lopez's enforcer. From the Deep South somewhere, Gant thought Alabama. Campbell with his unlit cigars all the time, chewing them till the ends were like mulch. He had a hard-on over segregation or slavery or whatever. His calling in life was making sure white boys got a rough ride.

Campbell had a deep voice. 'Gant, what do we look like, gooks? We don't leave personnel behind. Do what the man told you and get in that hole.'

Gant went chest to chest with Campbell, Campbell five inches taller and much broader. They glared into each other's eyes.

'Slim, you could die up here just as easy as down there,' Campbell said, 'you keep looking at me like that.'

The time wasn't right to take on Campbell. Gant wrapped a bandana around his face like a bandit, to help cut the stink in the tunnel. He got his gear together – a flashlight, a bayonet and his pistol. He kneeled before the dark mouth, peering in. A few feet down, it turned to the left. He couldn't see any further. Images of vermin came to mind. Black spiders, thousands of them, crawling all over each other in a seething mass. Scorpions. Snakes. Centipedes half a foot long. They were all down there with the bats and the rats and the Viet Cong.

They were trying to kill him by sending him down there. Lopez was trying to kill him. Gant paused for a moment. He was breathing too fast, too shallow. He had to calm down first. He felt like crying. He didn't want them to see that.

'Don't worry, Gant,' Campbell said. 'I'll write to your mama.'

'Fuck you,' he almost said, but didn't.

He climbed down, took the first turn and plunged into the darkness. It was a different world down here, Charlie's world. It smelled like wet shit. He almost gagged, the smell was so strong. He flicked on the flashlight and grasped it at the bottom, holding the light as high and as far away from his body as he could manage. If the gooks fired, they would aim for the light – that's what guys told him. This was his fifth time down in the tunnels, and so far he hadn't run into any gooks. Please God, not today.

The tunnel followed a long, gradual bend to the left. He inched forward on his knees, getting as low as he could, hugging the wall.

Roots scraped him like fingers. Each one made him jump.

He crept along, pistol drawn, following the dim shaft of light. In the underground silence, his breath sounded monstrous to his ears. The passage was so cramped now he could just about squeeze through. He went on and on – fifty yards, he thought, then maybe a seventy-five. Too far. Dirt crumbled down on him, got in his eyes and hair and inside his shirt. A cave-in, wouldn't that be nice? All he wanted was to turn around. He would have to crawl backwards a long way to even manage that. He stopped.

He held his breath to listen and in the quiet there was another sound.

Cluck. Cluck. Cluck.

Impossible to tell how far away it was.

There was a wall right up ahead where the tunnel made another sharp turn. To the left or the right, he wasn't sure yet. It couldn't just end right there, could it? Where the fuck was Winner?

The clucking sound was louder now. He was sure of it.

Wake up.

It was a left turn up ahead. The wall cornered, opened to another passageway. He could just make out the corner's glistening edge.

Had he missed another tunnel somewhere back there? Had Winner come this far? Why had he come this far?

Cluck. Cluck.

Gant pressed himself right up to the edge of the corner. He pointed the light at the ceiling. Deep, slow breath. Ready with the light? Ready with the gun?

Cluck.

WAKE UP.

He turned the corner.

Winner was there. Dave Winner, who at age nineteen still kept a collection of Spider-Man comic books in his pack, was there in the narrow passage. Gant's light caught Winner in the eyes. The eyes were open and aware. Owl eyes, even wider than before. Like big twin strobe lights. Winner saw Gant there, knew Gant. His eyes said everything.

It should have been you.

A sharpened stake extended across the tunnel, wedged into each wall, passing straight through Winner's long neck from front to back. Winner had tripped a booby-trap wire and gotten skewered. But the stake had missed the big blood vessels so Winner was still alive. He hung on the stake like a goddamn kebab, trying to hold his head up. The clucking sound was his breathing.

Gant felt the scream welling up from deep inside him. He couldn't let it happen, not down here, not down here with the gooks and Winner all by himself for twenty minutes with a stake through his throat and clucking like a fucking Christmas turkey.

He didn't want to scream, but here it came.

He opened his eyes.

It was dark in the room. For a moment, a small Asian boy about nine years old seemed to be at the foot of the bed, watching him. His head was cocked slightly to the side, and his face and upper body were pock-marked with bullet holes, and there was a question in his eyes. Then he was gone and what had been him became shadows from the elm tree outside, reaching through the window like grasping hands.

The digital clock on the bureau read 3.51. Gant lay on his back in his well-appointed, deep-carpeted master bedroom, listening. The house was silent except for the low drone of the air-conditioning. He was sixty-one years old and he owned this big house in a nice quiet neighbourhood with twenty-four-hour security, where his kids, if he had ever had any, could ride their bikes right out on the street.

He rolled over and of course his wife wasn't there. His beautiful wife, the hunting trophy of a wealthy man, twenty-eight years his junior, but not as young as she used to be, was getting itchy feet. She was wondering what kind of man she had married. He tried that thought on for a while, but didn't like the way it hung.

He was done sleeping for the night.

They woke Big Mama in the blackness just before the first light of dawn.

She was asleep in the small bedroom cabin of the houseboat, the *Sea Dog*, a protective arm around Gabrielle, when they came. Her first sense that they were coming was when Versace, the tiny Yorkshire terrier that Gabby insisted bringing on this trip, started yapping. Versace yapped at anything. He was one annoying dog. Big Mama was nothing if not completely indulgent of Gabby. If it had been anyone else's dog, she would have shot it by now. But Gabby was her sexy little girl. If she wanted the dog, they would have the dog. This morning, Mama heard the yapping, but kept her eyes closed against it.

Then she heard the rumble of a large engine powering down. A boat scraped the side of the *Sea Dog*, jostling it a bit. Voices spoke in low tones as someone tied up to the back deck. Mama picked her watch up off the side table built into the wall. She pressed the button, illuminating the time. 5.15 a.m. Shit. They were here. Who else but them? Vernon had called her yesterday and told her to expect them, but she hadn't figured they would come this soon.

She sat up in the gloom and swung her legs out so that her feet touched the cold floor. The weight of reality settled in, as it always did. She was Big Mama – that's how she thought of herself, and just about everyone else agreed. Her ID card said she was Marjorie White, but she couldn't remember the last time someone had called her Marjorie, or Margie, or Ms White. She'd been around for what seemed like a long time now, nearly half a century. People might say she was still young, but she felt old. She felt the years, and the struggles, in her bones.

Outside, the dog was growling now.

'Hello?' a man's voice called, not loud, little more than a whisper, really. There were neighbours here. No sense waking them. 'Hello?'

Big Mama sat there on the side of the bed. She said nothing in return.

She'd always been big. As a girl, she played football and ice hockey with the boys. She liked the contact, and she was better than most of them. She liked to fight. She also liked to read. From an early age, her heroes had been women. Not models, not Barbie dolls, but real women, strong women. Eleanor Roosevelt. Babe Didrickson. Joan of Arc. When she was twelve, she read how they had stripped Joan of Arc naked before burning her alive – they were so convinced that this leader of men had to be a man, and not a teenage girl, that they wanted to see her penis. Turned out she didn't have one. Didn't need one. Margie White learned something that day.

Now, she pulled on a bra, T-shirt, and a pair of jeans. Her body was heavy, much heavier than in the past. These days she was carrying the most weight she'd ever carried – nearly two hundred pounds. Oh well, fuck it. She quickly tied her hair back into a ponytail. She reached under her pillow and came out with a nine-millimetre. It was a big thing to have stuffed under a pillow, and sometimes Mama banged her head on it when she lay herself down. She put the gun on the table. She gave Gabby a gentle nudge then ran a rough, callused hand along the curve of Gabby's body.

'They're here, baby. You need to wake up and put some clothes on.'

Gabby's voice was thick with sleep. Indolent, lazy Gabby. Everything about her broke Mama's heart. 'Who's here?'

Big Mama stood and tucked the gun into her waistband. 'The delivery boys. The bad men we've been waiting for.'

She left the cabin and padded down the narrow hallway in her bare feet, past the galley, the control console and through the sitting room, towards the back deck. A tall man stood in the doorway. As Mama approached, the man took shape – wide shoulders, a broad chest, fair skin, blond hair. Your typical Aryan superman. She came closer. Sure, he even had blue eyes. His cheeks looked like they had never seen, nor needed to see, a razor. A lock of hair hung down in front of his forehead.

He smirked. 'Big Mama, I presume?'

She shooed him outside and followed him on to the deck. Here was another man similar to the first, except his blond hair was long, and he was wearing a baseball cap. Another man stood at the steering wheel of the speedboat tied up to the back of the *Sea Dog*. High above them, the stars were fading out as the darkness slowly turned to light. All around them, Mama could just begin to make out the derelict cruising yachts, sailboats, and even the ancient green tanker that constituted the neighbourhood. The tanker was probably an old container ship that had been designed for medium-range coastal runs, rusting out now with what seemed like twenty bomzhies living on board, anchored here in shallow water a couple of miles from land with the rest of the flotsam.

Mama liked it out here. A loose-knit community of deadbeats, junkies and a handful of felons lived on the water a fifteen-minute dinghy run from their jobs as prostitutes, pushers and panhandlers in the tourist haven of Key West. Key West was dying like every other vacation destination. Its condition was terminal, but it was going out slower than many places. In the meantime, hide in plain sight was a pretty good motto for Big Mama's operation, and the neighbours here tended to mind their own business.

The coast guard rousted this area every few months, pretty much like clock-work. They confiscated all the controlled substances and weapons they could find, they took known fugitives into custody, and they towed in any boats that they no longer deemed seaworthy. All of this was a good thing – the last raid was two weeks before Mama showed up with the *Sea Dog*, and the next raid wasn't expected for about another eight weeks, long after the *Sea Dog* would be gone. If Mama worked diligently and kept everybody on task, by the time the coast guard showed up again the *Sea Dog* would be a vague memory in the drug-addled minds of the locals.

Yeah, there might have been a houseboat over there for a while. Couple of lesbians living on there, maybe. I don't know when that was.

Yes, Mama liked it here just fine.

'Hello, ladies,' Mama said to the men. 'I'm guessing you have a delivery for me, yes? Well, we don't have a lot of time before folks around here start their day. So let's get busy, shall we?'

The stuff was packed in air-tight boxes made of hard plastic. The boxes each looked big enough to hold maybe a hundred tea bags. The Aryans had the boxes stuffed in the storage compartments of the speedboat, buried willy-nilly beneath life jackets, a gas can, an inflatable life raft, extra rope, a second anchor, some snorkelling gear and various other equipment.

The men made an assembly line, passing the stuff from the speedboat to the back deck of the clunky *Sea Dog*. The work proceeded quickly, forty green containers piling up in just a few minutes. Mama picked up one of the boxes. It was light, lighter than she expected. Some wit had affixed a self-adhesive label to each package – it read: *Freeze-Dried Taster's Choice*.

'Well, well, well. What do we have here?'

Mama looked up and now Gabrielle was on the deck with them. She was almost unbearably sexy, with her boobs that defied gravity and her round apple bottom and the long brown hair hanging down and half covering her pretty nineteen-year-old face. She wore a thin, oversized baby-blue T-shirt and nothing else. It was an old shirt of Mama's, and after ten years of wear was practically see-through. Gabby, unfortunately, wasn't that big in the brains department. She'd spent so much time on this boat wearing nothing at all that when Mama told her to get dressed, she must have figured next to nothing would suffice. And of course she liked to flirt. And oh yes, she liked to see the effect she had on men. She liked to get their testosterone pumping.

She must have heard them piling up the boxes and decided to see what kind of rise she could get out of them. Poor Gabby – she hadn't yet figured it out that not everything a woman did or was had to be in relation to men. Mama was a willing teacher, but Gabby was a goddamned slow learner.

'What do you say?' Mama said, suddenly feeling vulnerable and distracted by Gabby's presence. 'Can you boys move these packages inside? That way I won't have to do it. Down the hall there, the last door, the one that's locked. Just pile them up by the door, and I'll do the rest later.'

The big, broad-shouldered guy, the one who had first called inside, ignored her. He moved towards Gabby, put his hands on her hips and pressed her up against the wall. Mama came fully and suddenly awake, and focused on the guy's size for the first time. Before, her half-awake mind had categorised him and dismissed him – big guy. Now she really saw him. He positively dwarfed Gabby – the top of her head didn't quite reach to his chin. His shoulders must be nearly four feet across.

'Hello, little one,' he said. 'What is your name?'

Mama raised her voice, just a touch. 'Hey! Adolf. I asked you to do something there. So do it. That girl isn't for you to touch.'

The man slowly swivelled his head. Mama was aware of his partner, only slightly smaller than him, behind her and to her right. He was very close and she could feel the intensity in his body language without even having to look at him. Gabby had excited him too, and he was like a coiled snake ready to spring.

Mama was strong, but not as strong as she once was. These two men could easily overpower her. She didn't like the thought of it. A lightheaded feeling came to her, like her mind was starting to float away.

The big man, Adolf, smiled at her. He was missing a couple of teeth along the bottom. 'We're just having a little fun, Big Mama. Don't be jealous of us.' He raised Gabby's shirt up over her waist. Gabby squirmed and squealed, tried to pull her shirt down, but he held her, and her shirt, tightly in his big stone hands.

OK. That was it. Mama'd had enough. She pulled the nine-millimetre, chambered a round and pointed it at the man's head. 'OK, Adolf, that's plenty. Forget the packages. Get the fuck off my boat.'

Adolf stopped smirking. He turned away from her and back to the sexy little girl in his hands. 'Will she shoot?'

Gabby shrugged, her eyes wide and round and just a little afraid. She might even have a little remorse in there. 'I don't know. But back home nobody fucks with Mama.'

Mama put the muzzle of the gun one inch from Adolf's head. 'I don't think I'll miss from this distance.' She felt, rather than saw, the man behind her move closer. 'Hey, back there,' she said, directing her speech over her right shoulder. 'If you come one inch further, I swear to God I'll put your friend's brains in the ocean. You got me?'

'I got you, Big Mama.' This guy also spoke with an accent. What were these guys, Germans? Dutch?

Adolf backed away, hands up, knees bent, his eyes round and staring, his jaw hanging slightly agape. That was a better look for him. Still, he smiled.

'Mama—'

'You motherfucker,' she said. 'You see what you made me do? You made me draw my gun. Now get off my boat.'

He inched past her and she turned as he did so, bringing all three of the men into her sights in a broad sweep. For a few seconds, she put the gun on the man standing at the helm of the speedboat. He put his hands up and his eyes opened a touch wider. 'I'm the driver, Miss. Just the driver.'

She turned back and now Adolf and his partner lumbered across the gap between boats. Behind them, the boat driver quickly untied from the *Sea Dog*. She watched as he pushed a button on his dashboard and his big engines roared into life. He reversed away. Adolf, standing at the bow, blew a kiss, whether to her or to Gabrielle, Big Mama couldn't tell. A moment later, the speedboat had turned around and was bouncing across swells, dwindling in the distance.

Mama noticed another sound now. It was Gabby, and she was standing against the wall and crying a little bit.

Big Mama had pulled a gun, and easily could have killed some men delivering an outlawed biological agent to her boat. Tyler Gant would not be pleased, and that would have been the least of her problems. It would be daylight soon, and she would have had to get rid of the dead men before the neighbours saw them. Minding your own business only went so far. All of this had happened because Gabby had decided to come out and show them her body, and now Gabby was crying. Mama should be the one crying.

'Gabby! Please stop that.'

'What?'

'The crying. I mean, why are you crying?'

Gabby's hands balled into tiny fists and she rubbed her wet eyes with them. 'Are you mad at me?'

Mama took a deep breath. The girl looked so beautiful standing there. Eyes downcast, tears on her cheeks, she was just like a little girl. Mama went over and gave her a hug. Gabby melted into her embrace. God, that felt so good.

After a short time, Mama backed away a tiny bit and lifted Gabby's chin. 'How could I be mad at you? Just, when people come aboard and I ask you to put some clothes on, really put some clothes on, all right? We're not dealing with the nicest people in the world here. OK?'

'OK, Mama.'

'Good. Now give me a hand with these boxes.'

Gant sat with an unloaded Smith & Wesson .357 Magnum in his lap.

He was downstairs in his living-room easy chair, lights off, as the weak light of dawn just began to enter the sky outside. Here in the house, it was still dark, with looming shadows. At his elbow, Gant had a box of rounds for the gun and a bottle of Jack Daniel's. An empty glass sat next to the bottle – Gant had just finished his fourth whiskey. He poured another.

It was yet another long night alone. He was a man who shouldn't pass through the hours of darkness by himself. When he was with someone, like the girl from Moldova, he felt fine. He even felt good. When he was alone the dreams came. And often enough, when the dreams woke him, he couldn't get back to sleep. That was the bad time – alone with his thoughts in the middle of the night.

He had a prescription for sleeping pills. The pills helped kill the dreams, but Gant wouldn't take the pills more than a couple of nights in a row. Gant wasn't a pill-popper. He would be dead before he allowed himself to depend on a crutch like sleeping pills. So tonight was a night off from the pills and he just had to suffer through it. That was OK. That was good. He could make it through, and he'd be a better man for it. In the meantime, he had exactly what he didn't want – uninterrupted time to reflect on things.

She was annoying him now. She needed a talking to. His wife. His companion.

This living room, hell, this entire house was her masterpiece. For instance, Gant was now sitting in a leather, barrel-backed, reproduction Empire armchair. Katie had been offered a deal on it that she couldn't refuse. No doubt the chair was comfortable, but together with the incredible deals she had got on the matching leather ottoman and the leather sofa with hand-rubbed finish, the whole thing had knocked Gant back more than five thousand dollars. The furniture set worked together with the dark hanging drapes, the huge and ornate candle holders on the walls, and the baroque wallpaper style. Katie claimed their living room wasn't a living room at all. In fact, it was more of an Italianate drawing room.

Gant thought it looked like the waiting room at a morgue.

He didn't care about decorations. He didn't care much about the money she spent either, because he made a lot of it, more than Katie even knew. Gant had already clocked the biggest payday of his life on this current job, just for agreeing to take it on. He'd received the first half upfront, nonrefundable. He'd get the second half if they managed to pull the job off. Boy, if that happened, Gant would be all set. He might consider leaving the country then, and retiring for good. Leaving the wife, too. Maybe Fielding would give ol'

Gant a guest house on the island there. Maybe even give him little Moldova for his nightly pleasure.

Gant took a long slug of his whiskey.

He was a fraud — that was the thing. He had no idea what he was doing, and yet had somehow managed to convince everybody otherwise. He wasn't really a security contractor. Sure, he did some security jobs to keep the whole thing looking legitimate. But the jobs were penny ante stuff. They bored him, and nobody felt compelled to hire him for anything bigger or more exciting.

Till two years ago, he had made most of his money since retiring from the cops through his partnership with Big Mama. She set up crystal meth labs on boats moored in places like Hilton Head and Daytona Beach, and he helped her distribute the stuff to the biker gangs that roamed up and down the east coast. They made big money in short bursts, two months here, three months there, and then Mama would scuttle the latest boat and disappear for a while. Sometimes she disappeared for six months at a time — the truth was Mama didn't really like to work.

Then came the epic job two years ago, and now Gant was known, in a small and select underworld, for a very different kind of contracting. Some of the skills from the earlier work translated well. Setting up and operating floating laboratories, for instance. Moving people and materials around in a clandestine fashion, often in the middle of the night. Acting ruthlessly and without hesitation, when necessary.

Still, he felt like a fake.

Gant picked up the .357 Magnum, one of two guns he kept around the house. It was a big gun, more than ten inches long overall, and heavy. It weighed more than forty ounces. It was stainless steel and felt solid in his hand, a good pistol-whipper. A revolver, it was also a good Russian roulette gun. The other gun, also a Smith & Wesson, was a green and black nine-millimetre semi-automatic. It was almost twice as light as the Magnum, and smaller. He liked the Magnum better, but the semi-auto, with ten rounds in the magazine, would be better in a gun fight. If anybody asked, he would say he felt the two complemented each other, and that's why he kept both. Nobody asked.

He slid a round into one of the chambers of the Magnum, then gave it a spin. He pressed it to his head, forefinger away from the trigger and riding along the edge of the barrel like he was taught a lifetime ago. The gun settled in there, muzzle pressed to his temple. The dark grandfather clock in the hallway tick-tocked, tick-tocked, waiting for him to do it. A few long moments passed. He closed his eyes.

He kept the gun to his temple a moment longer. His forefinger brushed the trigger then settled against it. He waited, eyes on the clock, watching the silver pendulum swing back and forth. Despite the air-conditioner, a bead of sweat formed between his eyes and rolled along the ridge of his nose.

He couldn't do it. He couldn't pull the trigger. He brought the gun down and checked the chambers. The round was away from the firing pin. He would've won that time. OK. He wasn't ready. He couldn't play this game till he was ready, that's all. He took a long slow sip of the whiskey. Tennessee sippin' whiskey, yessir. The liquid warmed him all the way down.

He tried to put his wife out of his mind. He tried to put all his troubles away. That was his problem, though. Gant couldn't stop thinking. The minute he pushed one thing out of his mind, something else came right on in – usually something he'd rather not think about.

He remembered the week or two after the Winner incident back in Vietnam. Gant stayed high all the time and the days blurred one into the next. He felt something bad coming, and he wanted to insulate himself from it when it arrived. It was in the air all around them, like static electricity. It was a monstrous presence, something big, like a tidal wave. It was impossible to get out of its way. Gant thought of how wild animals often went berserk just before an earthquake. They sensed it coming, much like Gant sensed this.

He lifted his glass, saw it was empty, and took a long slug straight from the bottle. Did he really sense it coming all those years ago, or was he rewriting history with the benefit of hindsight? He wasn't sure. But things definitely went wrong.

More guys got torn up by mines. Toe poppers, they called them. Gant didn't care. He would stand there and look down at the guy and not feel anything. The guy could be screaming, blood everywhere, making that agony terror face. Gant would think oh well, fuck it, then go off and smoke some more pot.

They had fucking good pot over there.

Some of the other guys got pissed off. They wanted a stand-up fight, something they could win, some way they could show the gooks what Americans were made of. But they never made contact with the enemy. They'd get a report of VC in a village, and by the time they got there, Charlie would have faded away like a ghost. Time and again, the unit entered villages filled with nobody but nervous peasants going about their nineteenth-century activities. The villagers helped hide the VC. They helped feed them. Then they smiled and pretended they didn't know anything about it. They were fucking liars – that much was clear.

Frustration wormed its way to the surface. The guys slapped a few villagers around once or twice. Soon it started happening every day. One day Church and his buddy Van Horne rounded up a few of the village girls for later that night, and knocked their crying, grasping, begging mothers to the dirt. Another time Church ran a bayonet through somebody. He said he wanted to show the fuckers he meant business. After that one, Gant got up close and read the bad news in Church's eyes.

Nobody home. Church had gone psycho.

One day seven guys died in a vast, well-hidden minefield. A bunch more got ripped up, but lived. Gant was fifty yards away when the first mines went off. Guys panicked and started running, but not him. He stood still. BOOM, there goes another one. BOOM, another. It was almost funny, the way they all started running and getting blown up. More screaming. Gant thought it unnecessary, all that screaming. He thought if he stepped on a mine he wouldn't scream like that.

He saw Lopez break down and cry later that night. *Good for you, you fucker.* A lot of guys cried that night. Some of them punched the ground and cursed the fucking gooks. Gant didn't care. They could all die, the gooks, the guys in the unit, everybody. As long as he was still standing afterwards, the rest of them could go straight to hell.

He was higher than high the next morning. The air was heavy. Lightning flashed off in the lush green hills. Rain was coming. He was so high that everything glowed and shimmered, like the whole world was wrapped in gauze. Beautiful. They entered a hamlet, the platoon walking in line.

Then the killing started.

A woman crossed in front of them, almost running, a baby in her arms. Gant saw her as if she was highlighted in yellow magic marker. There was rifle fire to his left. He looked and it was Church and Van Horne, firing together. Everybody stopped and the scene went quiet. Gant glanced back at the woman and baby. They were dead on the ground, a few feet apart.

Gant checked Lopez. Lopez didn't say a thing. The line moved on.

The Zippo lighters came out and the thatched roofs of the huts began going up in flames. Villagers ran out of the huts and the guys started rounding the people up. Casey and Kingman rounded up twenty or thirty of them. Gant stood right there with Casey and Kingman, about fifteen feet away from the villagers. They were all women and children, a couple of old men thrown in for good luck. The people were crying.

Kingman turned to Gant. 'You want 'em?'

'Nah, I don't want 'em,' Gant said.

'I don't want 'em either.'

Kingman opened fire into the crowd. Casey joined him. Gant stood and watched. Afterwards, a couple of the bodies in the bloody pile were still moving, just sort of arms and legs moving like they were trying to crawl somewhere. Casey went over and shot them from a foot away.

Gant moved on. Gunfire went off all around him. The whole hamlet was on fire. Some people tried to get away and were gunned down as they ran. Campbell and Smith had a bunch of them rounded up by a drainage ditch. Spotting Gant, Campbell smiled and waved him over.

'You too, Gant.'

Gant shrugged and unshouldered his rifle.

'That an order?'

Campbell just stood there, hands on his hips, unlit cigar stuffed in his mouth. 'That's a direct order, slim.'

Gant checked his weapon. The people huddled together, crying and hugging one another. Gant sighted and moved from face to terrified face. Here was a withered old man, as knobby and twisted as a tree trunk. Here was an old woman, shaking, eyes closed. Here was a little boy, maybe nine years old, the only calm one in the group, staring right at Gant, a question in his eyes.

Why don't they run?

There were no men of military age in the group. Gant didn't think he'd seen a single military-age male in the whole countryside so far. All the men lived underground. Gant began to think he should count the group so he had an accurate number for later. It looked like eight or nine. Maybe it was eleven. Did old people count?

'Gant! You know how to fire that weapon, don't you?'

'Of course.'

'Then do what you came to this country to do.'

Gant fired.

Now, decades later, he reached for his whiskey bottle and saw it was empty. He stood and the Magnum slid to the floor. He tottered over to the bar and fixed himself another drink. Pour the Jack into the glass and *voilà*. Gant liked to keep things simple.

Later, after he got back to the States, Gant became a student of atrocities. That was how he thought of it, and it helped him make sense of everything. It was a huge subject, one he couldn't hope to exhaust if he studied it for a lifetime. Hey, some guys liked to follow sports. He liked sports too, but he liked atrocities more. He read about the big ones, the little ones, everything he could get his hands on. He covered them in no particular order, just jumping from one to another, whatever caught his eye, whatever piled the bodies up.

In Indonesia, the Suharto regime put to death half a million suspected Communists. Gant liked that phrase, *suspected Communists*. In Europe, six million

Jews were dead at the hands of the Nazis. From Russia, the barest hints leaked out that Stalin had killed a lot of people, maybe twenty million. Nobody knew and nobody would ever know for sure. The Allies bombed the civilian population at Dresden. The Italians tore up Ethiopia. Of course, the Americans were doing it in Vietnam. Then he looked at the Japanese doing the Rape of Nanking and the Bataan Death March. There was no end in sight. The African slave trade came next. Then the Spanish conquests. The Trail of Tears. The Irish Famine.

A pattern emerged.

Atrocities were as common as rainwater. It didn't take a genius to realise that they were the rule, rather than the exception. They were woven into the very fabric of things. Maybe forest fires were a better example than rainwater. A lot of people thought forest fires were all bad. But the fires were good for the forest. They were necessary. They cleared the dead wood and fertilised the soil.

Atrocities were like steam escaping from a valve. If the steam didn't get out once in a while, it would build up under there and pretty soon the whole thing would blow.

The theory made sense. It kept things clean and simple.

Gant looked out the window and saw the first rays of sun. Wisps of mist clung to the lawn. It was time to shower up. He polished off the two fingers left in the glass. Shower up? Hell, maybe he could sleep now that the sun was up.

The phone rang. It was his cell phone, lying there on the table. He hated people calling that phone, or any phone. The thing about it, though, was only a handful of people in the world had the number. If it rang, there was a good chance it was something important, especially this time of the morning. He looked at the little caller ID window.

Out of Area.

That wasn't much help. He opened the phone.

'Hello?'

A voice came on the line. Calling from South Africa. The voice was angry.

Patrick Quinlan

Gant listened for a while, trying to make sense of it. A delivery, sure, sure, to a boat. That was as it should be. But something went wrong. Gant's person pulled a gun. That didn't sound good. Had anything else happened? Anybody get shot? No, just the gun pulled on them. OK, not too bad.

Gant went into charm mode. He worked to assuage the concerns of the man on the other end of the line. A misunderstanding, that's all. Gant had just got up but he would handle it right away. He could say with confidence that nothing like this had happened before, or would happen again. After about five minutes of this, feeling better, feeling heard, the man hung up.

Gant stared at the phone for a minute. He dialled a number. After several seconds, a voice came on the line.

'Yeah?' Big Mama said.

Gant looked out the window. It was becoming full daylight now. 'Mama, tell me something, if you don't mind.'

'OK, Tyler. Shoot.'

'What the hell is wrong with you?'

5

Foerster woke up on the beach.

He was sick. His head and body ached. He felt like a dead thing lying there. Soon the gulls and the crabs would come and feed on his flesh. No rest for the weary. He opened his eyes. Out on the ocean, he saw the first pale light of day touching the sky beyond the horizon.

They had beaten the shit out of him last night. He had no idea why. Four guys. He was in the bar, drunk in a corner, hunkered down, spending the last of his money. He wasn't bothering anybody. He had decided to get good and zonked, the better to sleep in uncomfortable surroundings. Suddenly these guys were all around him, and they started punching him. They dragged him outside to the alley, amid hoots and hollers from the crowd. The lights were crazy. The music pounded. He fought them, God knew. He always fought them. But it was too much, the punches and then the kicks were too much. He fell to the ground and lay amongst broken bottles and cardboard boxes. He didn't care. Let them kick him to death. Instead, they picked him up, carried him out to the beach and dumped him there.

He stood slowly and started walking. As the sun rose, he trudged north along the sands of Myrtle Beach. To his right, tiny waves lapped at the shoreline. To his left, behind the dunes, were some private beachfront houses owned by rich people. The high-rise hotels and condos and the big amusement park of downtown towered behind him now. There was nobody on the beach, and he was glad to be alone.

He noticed he had started collecting things he found on the sand. He had a jagged length of broken green glass. He had a strip of thick cardboard. He had an oily rag that might once have been a T-shirt. These were random items, but as he walked he worked, and in his hands they quickly became something specific and intentional. He folded the cardboard around one end of the broken glass, leaving the sharper end of the glass protruding. Then he wrapped the rag around the cardboard and tied it tight. Now he had a knife – if he chose to cut someone with the glass, the cardboard and the rag would provide him with a good grip and would protect his hand.

He'd been walking for a little while. He glanced at the big beach houses. A couple of them had Confederate flags flying outside on flagpoles. It was a great town if you liked the Confederate flag. Last night he'd seen it painted on motorcycles, and T-shirts, and the walls of buildings. He'd seen it etched into people's skin.

Foerster sighed. He hated the South. Even the rich were ignorant rubes. The Confederate flag. That one was so old it was new. Now that the big bad federal government was on the ropes, and was having trouble projecting its mighty power outward from Washington DC, the sneaky little southern states were starting to make a noise about seceding again. Shit, they would probably reinstate slavery if they could.

The funniest part was that the people behind this wanted their national capital to be Atlanta – a city so parched for water that thousands of people were departing there each month, leaving their homes and their lives behind. You'd be lucky to give away a house in Atlanta. Who would want it? The population decline was so pronounced that the main artery out of the city, Interstate 75, was now known as the Exodus Highway.

The whole thing was laughable. It had started as a fringe movement, but in some places, people with these ideas were getting elected to public office. Well, that was fine with Foerster. Let them secede. Let the whole fucking country explode into a million pieces. He'd enjoy that, though it didn't make him hate these morons any less.

They made Foerster sick.

He walked along close to the dunes and the sea grass which grew on top of them. Here and there, someone had left a catamaran or a rowing boat up against the dunes.

Up ahead, someone was walking towards him.

It would be something just to fuck somebody up right here on the beach at dawn, some stupid Southern-fried hick. He glanced behind him. Nobody that way, as far as the eye could see. Even better, there was a light haze in the air now, some kind of ground fog coming off the water. It made things look fuzzy and indistinct. He glanced up at the darkened windows of the nearest home. No way to tell if anybody was there. Probably not, he guessed.

'You're guessing,' he said. 'You're just guessing.'

As the figure approached it began to take shape. Sure, it was getting clearer. It was a woman, grey hair, late middle age, in a black nylon jumpsuit, walking along the beach, perhaps enjoying the sunrise. Her body was formless under the jumpsuit.

Foerster slipped his homemade knife behind his back.

She was about to pass ten yards to his right, closer to the water. She gazed at her bare feet as she walked, as though she were deep in thought.

He stopped walking.

'Excuse me,' he said.

She looked up, surprised to see him there, but not alarmed, not at first. Her face was pleasantly mild. No trouble had ever come to her here on the beach, and her eyes said no trouble ever would. After all, this was a good neighbourhood, pretty far outside town. That's what she probably told herself. She was stupid, Foerster realised, stupid to be walking out here all alone this time of day.

'Yes?'

'Do you have the time? I'm afraid I left my watch at home.'

'Of course.' She lifted her arm and pushed back the nylon sleeve to expose her watch. 'It's just after five-thirty.' Now she looked at him more closely. 'Are you all right?' she said. 'Your face looks injured.'

Foerster took three quick steps towards her, bringing out the knife as he did so. He was upon her before she even made another move. She gasped as he touched the sharp edge of the glass to her neck.

'Don't make a sound. Don't even speak. If you say anything, I'll cut your throat.'

She nodded, eyes agape.

'Give me your hand.' She did as she was told. He held her hand with his bad hand, his two broken fingers protruding in their cast. 'OK, now we're going to walk off into those dunes over there, hand in hand like we're best friends. Understand?'

She nodded again. It was just that easy.

As they entered the dunes, Foerster felt the excitement grow within him. They settled down in the valley between two dunes together, hidden by the tall grass. He thought one move ahead. Her pants made a handy bind for her hands. Her shirt made a handy gag when stuffed in her mouth. As he tied her, he noticed the diamond on her finger. Somebody around here loved her. As her clothes came off, Foerster realised she couldn't live through this morning. He would never get away if she was alive.

He thought how in other circumstances, she might think this was romantic. For a moment he wondered about her name. He looked at her. Her eyes were tightly shut. Tears had formed at the edges and rolled down her cheeks. Foerster thought idly about her husband, what he looked like, where he was. He imagined the guy was lying in bed, waiting for her to come back from her walk. That excited him so much, he rushed up the peak and finished before he was ready.

Afterwards, he felt calm. He was getting better and better at this. It was like anything, he reflected. If you get enough practice, you start to get better.

The sun was full bright now. Across the dunes, seagulls called to one another as if to announce the start of another work day. The woman opened her eyes and turned her head away from him. She looked instead at the sand.

Foerster reached for the knife. Clean, he thought to himself, make it clean. He wasn't even sure what he meant by that. He sighed and glanced up at the pale blue stretching away above him.

It was about time he blew out of this town.

Late that morning, Gordo got a phone call he didn't expect.

He was at home in the living room of his two-bedroom apartment, the nerve centre of his operation, thinking quietly and very carefully about nothing. Things were slow. Having missed Foerster twice, now there was nothing on his plate. That was OK. The rent was paid. There was food and beer in the refrigerator. He could afford a couple of days of doing nothing, just sitting. If he wanted to, later in the week he could start serving paper again.

All the same, he didn't want to go backwards. This Foerster job was a monster – it was the Holy Grail. It couldn't be that they had lost him. It couldn't be that he was gone. There had to be some way to get him back.

Gordo was waiting for a strike of lightning to hit him, some insight that would hand him his next move on a platter. In front of him, the computer showed him the newspaper stories available about Executive Strategies and Mr Tyler Gant, President. There was no company website, there wasn't much else to go on, and most of the information was a few years old.

The City of Charleston had contracted Executive Strategies to set up video monitoring equipment on street corners downtown. In lean economic times, it was important that the city's tourists felt safe and comfortable – they could always spend their travel dollars in another city. The South Carolina National Guard had hired them to audit and recommend changes to coastal evacuation procedures in the case of a hurricane or other high-water event – which were projected to occur with increasing regularity and severity in the years ahead. A visiting South African businessman had hired them to provide an advance security team while he toured farmland for sale in the region. The businessman had his own bodyguards – Gant's people just travelled ahead and swept each location for possible threats before the South African got there.

It was pretty dry stuff.

Tyler Gant himself was a decorated former cop from Philadelphia, and a veteran of the Vietnam War. He had received a tax break to buy a small office building in a run-down part of Charleston and use it as his headquarters – in doing so, he planned to help revitalise the neighbourhood. Photos showed him in his police-dress blues, in a three-piece-suit meeting with members of the Charleston City Council, and in business casual slacks and open-collared shirt at a breakfast sponsored by the local Chamber of Commerce. He looked like the quintessential All-American – crew cut, handsome face lined with age and experience, and the slim, fit body of a triathlete. Gordo had trouble imagining what a straight arrow like this guy could possibly want with someone like Foerster.

Across the living room from Gordo, the TV news was playing – something stupid going on. Gordo was barely paying attention, but his brain had absorbed some part of it by osmosis. A white woman had been found raped and murdered on a secluded stretch of beach somewhere in the Deep South early that morning. Or at least, a lot of people believed this had happened, or might have happened, although there hadn't been any confirmation from law enforcement. Acting on the rumour, a local white supremacist militia had decided that a black guy or guys had done it. About a dozen white males in combat fatigues, armed with automatic and semi-automatic weapons, pulled two black guys out of a BMW – How dare they have a car! How dare they have gas! – and hung them from a telephone pole. One of the black guys was a 63-year-old grandfather.

Not satisfied, the militia had then gone on a rampage through a black neighbourhood of what looked on the TV like tarpaper shacks. Within half an hour, they'd been overwhelmed by at least thirty members of what the announcers were calling a local affiliate of the nationwide Bloods gang. It seemed that all of the militiamen were killed, and in some cases, their bodies dragged through the streets by an angry mob. Elements of the National Guard and the State Police had gone in to restore order, and now the gang and the Government were in a pitched battle for control of the area. At least two dozen homes were on fire.

Earlier in the day, a cameraman from a local TV station had been shot and killed. His camera was still on. It was lying on the ground somewhere, giving a bizarre and disturbing worm's-eye view of one of the burning houses, dark black smoke rising from the blaze, people running here and there, oblivious to the filming. The network kept returning to the real-time feed from the camera. Some producer must have thought the camera, still running even though its operator was dead, was a metaphor for something.

Gordo sighed. Where was this going on? Every so often, just when he began to think maybe things would return to normal one day, they'd put on this footage that looked like something out of Liberia or Chechnya, and he'd think: *Wait a minute. This is America they're showing.*

He looked out the window. Down the block, on the corner, some teenage boys were hanging out. He drifted back in his mind – when he was that age, it had seemed like there was always something to look forward to, some way to make it happen. But it had turned into a cruel joke. What kind of future did those kids have? Every year, things got a little meaner, the basic necessities got more expensive, and things fell apart a little more. Mostly it was a slow grind, like the way garbage collection had gone from twice a week a few years ago to once a month now. But sometimes it happened fast, like this thing on the TV – simmering tensions suddenly exploding into a full-scale riot.

The phone rang and Gordo picked it up. It was Foerster's mother.

'Mr Lamb? Have you seen the news? About all the fighting in South Carolina?'

'Sure, Mrs Foerster. I have it on right now. Is that South Carolina? It's a terrible thing. Just terrible.'

'I don't know how to say this, Mr Lamb . . .'

'Well, probably the best way to say it is to just say it.'

'Davis is there. He called me last night from. Myrtle Beach. He said he was on his way to Charleston. He was hoping I still had the business card I gave you. He wanted to call the man on that card.' Foerster's mother started crying. Gordo could hear his own breath catching as she sobbed.

'That poor woman.'

Gordo stared at the flames on TV. *Myrtle Beach, South Carolina*, said the caption at the bottom of the screen. Till that moment, he hadn't given the woman on the beach much thought. If anything, he had dismissed her as a rumour, a lie. She had probably never been alive in the first place. These shoot-buts, especially these crazy race wars in the South, could start over anything. Half the time they started over things that later turned out to be mistakes. Now he looked at the TV and in his mind's eye he saw Foerster down there, a demon, moving across the land, killing, raping, starting infernos wherever he went.

'Mrs Foerster? What did you tell him? About the business card?'

'I told him I tore it up and flushed it down the toilet.'

'You did the right thing. That was the exact right thing. Now, I'm going to call you back in a just a few minutes, OK?'

She began to say something more, but Gordo clicked off. He looked at the phone for several seconds, then dialled Jonah's number. As the phone rang, he looked once more at the TV.

You son of a bitch. I'm coming for you.

'I need some chloroform,' Gordo said into the phone that afternoon.

'Chloroform? What do you need it for?' came the voice on the other end.

'I'm working a job, and it looks like I have to knock the guy out.'

The voice hesitated. 'Well, chloroform will do it.'

'I also need some gas. Thirty gallons, if you have it. The guy ran away and I'm going on a trip to bring him back. And I need something else as well. I need two of them, in fact.'

'Gasoline, check. Chloroform, check. I can probably put that together for you. But something else? I thought you didn't go in for that.'

'The job could get heavy,' Gordo said. 'The guy has friends.'

'That troubles me. I've never heard this sort of thing from you before. I wish I could un-hear it.'

'Sorry.'

'That's OK. I imagine I'll live. What kind of something else do you need?'

'Any kind. As long as they work and I can carry them around. Nothing too big, in other words.'

'When do you need all this?'

'Today.'

'Today? Jesus, Gordie. How am I gonna round up all this shit today?'

Gordo was talking to an old friend – Wendel – who was a sometime customer from back in the cocaine days. They kept in touch, and years later Gordo worked for him again. Wendel's sister had married a man who left her alone with two kids and no money. The deadbeat dropped off the face of the planet.

'Just find the fucking guy,' Wendel had said. 'Whatever it costs and whatever it takes. It will give me infinite pleasure to see this guy's paycheque attached by the courts, and to watch these kids suck him dry for the next twenty years or so. Hell, I don't even care if the kids get the money – I give my sister a thousand bucks a month and don't miss it. It's the principle of the thing, you know? I just want to watch this maggot bleed.'

It took Gordo ten phone calls to find the guy. He was living in a boarding house in Youngstown, Ohio and working in a machine shop there. Soon, the family court and the man's employers were notified of each other's existence. Every now and then, when the guy dropped out of sight again, Gordo found him again.

Now it was Wendel's chance to return at least some small part of the favour. He lived in a ramshackle house in a neighbourhood of ramshackle houses just over the city line in Mount Vernon. Three hours after calling, Gordo was there.

It was a bad neighbourhood, but people didn't mess with Wendel. The neighbours, the gangs, the stick-up men, everybody left him alone. Even the beat cops steered clear of him. He was doing business, and he made his pay-offs further up the line. He had a couple of grim-faced, bald-headed steroid monsters hanging out on the porch to handle any enquiries and to clear away the riff-raff, and that was the shape of things.

An old-school Cadillac Escalade and a Range Rover, both polished and gleaming, were parked out by the front kerb. These were people who just didn't care about cost, about scarcity, about anything. Whatever Wendel and his buddies were doing inside this place, and Wendel wasn't talking, they did pretty well at it.

'Geek stuff,' Wendel would say. 'I don't want to bore you with the details.'

Gordo leaned on the battered red Honda and waited. The thing about the car was its gas mileage – thirty miles to the gallon in the city, almost forty on the highway, and pretty good in the zip department. It had an aftermarket reserve fuel tank mounted inside the hatchback, which held twenty gallons of gas in addition to the stock tank that came with the car, which held eleven gallons. Thirty-one gallons in total – a $600 fill-up, if you could even find that much gas in one place. Fuel-efficient cars like this could be hard to hold on to – since the assembly lines shut down a few years back, the thieves were doing a brisk business stealing them.

It didn't take long for Wendel himself to appear, right on time as always. Gordo watched him from across the street and, as always, couldn't muster a straight face at the sight of the man. His hair was untamed. Salt and pepper at late forty-something, it ran wild in loops and swirls across the top of his head. It hadn't seen a comb in years, and maybe not a drop of water in days. Wendel wore glasses so wide and thick his eyes seemed like fish swimming in an aquarium. He was thin except for a rotund belly where all the Mountain Dews and late-evening pizzas went. Right now he was wearing a white V-neck undershirt, the kind Gordo might wear to mop up sweat stains beneath a shirt and tie, or maybe a beer spill off the couch. The shirt was too tight, so it accentuated the belly even further. Tufts of thick chest hair poked out of the V-neck. To go with the unfortunate shirt, Wendel wore khaki pants at least a size too short for him. He wore blue tube socks and sandals on his feet. To sum it up, and putting it kindly, Wendel was a mess.

Wendel said something to the two men on the porch and they laughed. Sure. It was always a good day at Wendel's house.

He swaggered on over, striking a nonchalant pose, as self-conscious as the nerdish child he had probably been, as confident as only the men whose minds generate large amounts of money can be. Gordo smiled as he watched the whole shambling, shuffling wreck of a sideshow approach.

'What do you say, buddy?' Wendel said.

'Wendel, you're always a sight for sore eyes.'

The two men shook hands and Wendel put an arm around Gordo's shoulder.

'Got some stuff for you,' Wendel said. He glanced around at the houses of his neighbours. 'But we can't do it out here. This your car? Nice. Do me a favour. Bring it up the driveway and around back. We can take a look at everything there, away from any prying eyes. Got a lot going on inside, and I don't need any more attention than I already have.'

As Wendel crossed the street again, Gordo got in and drove the Honda up the dirt driveway between houses and parked it in the back. Wendel's house looked worse from the back than from the front – paint peeling, siding falling off, various steel drums and boxes piled up. There was an old discarded refrigerator back here, its door removed.

Wendel climbed out from the basement through a set of double storm doors. He opened a battered tool shed and wheeled out a fifty-five-gallon drum.

'You got everything I ordered?' Gordo said.

'Of course. More or less.' He ran a hose into the drum and began to squeeze a small rubber hand pump attached to the hose. 'This is the car you want to put the gas in?'

'Yes, sir.'

Wendel removed the Honda's gas cap and began pumping the liquid into the tank. After a few more pumps, the gasoline began running by itself.

'It holds thirty gallons,' Gordo said. 'But there's probably a few in there.'

'That's all right. I trust you. Let's call it twenty-five.'

'Deal.'

Gordo took the hose and Wendel went back inside the house. In a moment he came out, this time with a gun in each hand. 'When you told me you wanted something else, I wasn't sure I was talking to the right person.'

Gordo shrugged, said nothing.

Wendel indicated the guns. The first one was a smallish revolver. 'This is a thirty-eight calibre police special. I don't know why they call it that, because I haven't seen a cop carrying one of these things in years. It only holds six rounds. You put them in one at a time. I have a speedloader here, and you can have it for free, but unless you've used one before, I wouldn't bother with it.' He held up the other gun, a semi-automatic. 'This is a nine-millimetre semi-auto. It holds fifteen rounds in the magazine. I have an extra magazine for it. It's a lot faster and easier to reload because you can just load up the extra one ahead of time and pop it in there. If you plan on having a shoot-out, this is the one you want to use for that. Both guns are easily concealable. Neither one has a serial number. If you get caught with them, you have no idea where they came from.'

Gordo handed Wendel the gasoline hose and took both the guns. They felt heavy in his hands. 'Do they work?'

'Of course they work. Would I sell them if they didn't? Of course, as in any sale of this kind, no warranty is stated or implied.'

'Which means?'

'Which means when you get out of town, pull over in a field somewhere and fire them a few times. The wrong time to find out one of them jams is after the shooting has already started.'

'I see.'

Wendel eyed Gordo closely. He indicated the guns. 'You sure you want to carry those around?'

Gordo nodded. 'I'm sure.'

'It's just that, you know, it's not my favourite thing, selling guns. They have a tendency to go off, and not always in the right direction. To be honest, I've sold a couple of guns to people who later turned up dead. You're a good kid, Gordie, and I like you. What were you, just out of high school when we met? I've always thought you had a good head on you. But I'll tell you, once you start a gunfight, you don't always get to decide when and how it ends.'

'I'm not a kid any more, Wendel.'

'OK, if you say so. It's your neck. Anyway, here's one last thing.' From his pocket Wendel produced an amber glass bottle with some liquid in it. He held it up for Gordo to see. To Gordo, if the container weren't dark yellow, it would look like an old airline wine bottle. He reached for it, but Wendel moved it away.

'Wait a minute. You have to listen to me first.'

'Are you gonna give me my super-spy instructions?' Gordo said.

'What I have to say is important. I couldn't get the chloroform.'

'No?' Gordo said. 'Then what is that?'

'It's ether.'

Gordo snapped his fingers at Wendel. It made no difference to Gordo what it was, as long as it worked. 'Yeah, that's just as good, huh?'

'Oh, it'll knock somebody out pretty good. Just soak a rag with this stuff, cover their nose and mouth, and it'll do the job. Give them just a little and they'll be out on their feet. Also, it'll make their eyes burn. Be careful not to get any of it in your own face because it works real well.'

'OK, Dad.'

Wendel raised a stubby forefinger. 'But here's the bigger problem. This stuff is flammable and highly explosive. If you held a cigarette lighter on this bottle for less than a minute, it would cause a flash fire that would probably incinerate us both. Right now, the bottle is sealed. If you break the seal and expose this stuff to sunlight and air, it'll start to destabilise, making it more likely that any little spark will blow even this little bit sky high. So don't open it until you're ready to use it. And when you're done with it, dump whatever's left over in the ocean. I mean it. This shit is dangerous. It worries me just giving it to you.'

Wendel paused and the two men stared at each other for a moment.

'What do you have to say to all that?' Wendel said.

Gordo smiled. 'I say cool. Hand it over, brother. I like danger.'

When the doorbell rang, echoing through the entire house, Gant himself answered it. He shouted for Katie a couple of times – she had arrived home early that morning – but then noticed from his study window that she was out puttering in the garden. Either she hadn't heard the bell ring, or she had decided to ignore it.

A security guard from the housing development stood on Gant's front steps. A golf cart they used to patrol the place was parked at the kerb, with another guard sitting in the front seat, and what looked like a vagrant hand-cuffed in the rear-facing back seat. The guard here on the steps was a young guy, largish, with a good-sized chest and a weird cow-lick. Gant fancied that it really did look like a cow had come along and licked the front of the kid's hair with its big, sticky tongue. The kid wore a blue uniform, vaguely similar to what a cop would wear. He had a pepper spray dispenser hanging from his belt, but no gun. The guards, Gant knew, had some birdshot guns locked up at the gatehouse. Anyway, this kid had missed his calling – he should have joined the cops. Maybe they wouldn't take him because of the cow-lick.

'Mr Gant?'

'Yes.'

'We apprehended this individual by the west gate, attempting to sneak into the community. In fact, he was already trespassing on community grounds, and when we approached, he tried to escape from us.'

'But you caught him?'

'Yes sir, we did.'

'Good work. That's what we pay you for.'

'Yes, sir. Thank you. The thing is, the man claims to be an associate of yours.' Now the guard looked at a piece of paper he held in his hand. 'He says his name is Mark Foster, but he doesn't have any identification on him. Do you happen to know anyone by that name?'

Gant took another look at the golf cart. Jesus. Could it be? Yes, it could. Disappears from New York, out of contact, and then reappears on Gant's doorstep in broad daylight, in the custody of two rent-a-cops. Gant's mind raced forward, inventing a story on the fly.

'I know him. He's a homeless man who lives on the street near my office downtown. I hire him sometimes to do odd jobs for me. He's harmless.'

'What would you like us to do with him?'

'Give him to me. I'll talk to him. He shouldn't be out here, bothering you guys. I'll have one of my men come out and pick him up, bring him back downtown.'

The kid seemed disturbed by that prospect. 'Are you sure, sir? He's very dirty, and a little bit aggressive. It took both of us to get the cuffs on him. If you prefer, we can hold him at the gatehouse till your man arrives. Or we can give him over to the police.'

'I appreciate the offer, but I'm sure I can handle him.'

A moment later, Davis Foerster stood there on the front steps between the two security guards, the cow-licked guard unlocking his plastic handcuffs. Gant felt a weird little flutter in his heart when he saw Foerster – it had been nearly two years. He looked a lot worse for wear.

The last time Gant had seen him, Foerster had been well-rested, well-fed and Gant was sending him back to New York with more than twenty thousand dollars in his pocket. Now, Foerster was a dishevelled wreck in a ripped flannel shirt and jeans. His clothes were too big for him. He wasn't dirty – he was filthy. He smelled like stale beer. His hair stood up in weird tufts around what looked like at least two dozen stitches making a railroad line across his head. Both his eyes were bloodshot, and the area around his right eye was black and blue. One of his hands had a yellowing cast on two of the fingers.

He lit a cigarette. He smiled, showing yellow teeth. In fact, the word with Foerster today was yellow. Even his skin looked yellow. 'Nice neighbourhood, Gant. Looks like a nice house ya got here, too. And a nice Gestapo squad to keep out the undesirables.'

'Mark,' Gant said, using the alias Foerster had given the guards. 'You're the last person I expected to see. You should know better than to come here.'

'Is this going to be OK, Mr Gant?' the guard said.

'It's fine, guys. Thanks. It's no problem.'

'OK. You know how to reach us if you need us.'

'Yes, I do. I'll be sure to do that – if I need you.'

The guards walked down the steps and then down the path to their golf cart.

One of them glanced back to make sure all hell hadn't broken loose in their fifteen-second absence.

Foerster ran a hand over his crazy hair. 'Listen, I know what you're thinking. But these guys were harassing me, a couple of bounty hunters, and I had to get out of New York. I couldn't wait any longer for your guy to show up. They were gonna put me back in jail. I've been on the road for thirty-six hours straight. I need a shower and some rest. I'm about to keel over from exhaustion.'

Gant looked around the neighbourhood. There was no one out. No telling what was going on behind the windows of the big, handsome homes. No telling what the respectable folks thought of Gant's sudden house guest. There was no controlling the situation – the guards would talk even if nobody had noticed them pull up to the house. Gant had to do what he said he was going to do, and get Foerster out of here in a hurry.

'How did you get here?' he said.

'Hitchhiked. I couldn't take the bus or the train – I'm a wanted man. So I took to the roads.'

'Come inside.'

Gant led Foerster across hardwood floors through the living room, past the baby grand piano, and into the kitchen. From the corner of his eye, Gant noticed Foerster checking the place out. Foerster went to the sliding glass door and looked out at the yard, at the lawn, at the shimmering in-ground pool, at the gardens. He whistled.

'This is some spread, Gant. And in these meagre times. I guess I see where the big money goes on these little jobs that we do.'

Gant was already dialling a phone number. 'You've done one job with me so far. One. And that was two years ago. I do jobs all the time. Almost non-stop. That's why the big money comes to me.'

On the other end of the line, Vernon picked up. 'Yessir.'

'Vernon, he's here. I need you to swing by and pick him up.'

Vernon's confident drawl, usually reassuring, was annoying in the current circumstances. 'He's there? How the fuck did he get there?'

'Don't ask a lot of questions, OK? Just come by.'

'You got it, boss man.'

Gant hung up. He looked out the window. Katie had disappeared. She was out there somewhere, or in here somewhere. The last thing he really wanted was to explain the presence of this scruffy drifter to his wife.

'A guy is coming to pick you up. He'll take you someplace where you can get a shower and a nap. He'll fill you in on the job – not the details, but a general overview. Then tomorrow morning, first light, the two of you will leave for Key West. The shipment is already there, and we need to make this happen fast. If you leave here by six in the morning, you should be there tomorrow night sometime, maybe by dinnertime.'

'Shit, Gant. I don't know. Like I said, I've been on the road for a while already. Some rednecks beat me up in Myrtle Beach last night, don't ask me why. I'm fucking tired.'

Just then, something occurred to Gant. It was something in the way Foerster said Myrtle Beach, an emphasis that he put on it, like he was sending Gant a message. It was almost like Foerster had just hung a neon Myrtle Beach sign around his own neck. Gant got a picture in his mind, and he didn't like the look of it.

'Myrtle Beach?'

Foerster smiled. 'Yeah. Last night. I slept on the beach there. Why? What's wrong with Myrtle Beach?'

Gant fired a punch into Foerster's face. It happened almost before he knew he was going to do it. He'd been lazy. He should have killed this bastard last time; it was just as he'd suspected, just as Monty had told him. The man was crazy, running loose, and doing sensitive jobs for Tyler Gant. Well, Gant wouldn't make the same mistake twice.

Foerster held his hand to his face. 'What's the matter with you?'

Gant seethed. He was aware of trying to keep his voice down, but his anger was rising so quickly, in another minute he wouldn't be responsible for his actions. 'It was you, wasn't it? You son of a bitch, you were the one.'

Foerster smiled. 'I was what one?' he said, every word pregnant with hidden meaning.

'You fucking idiot. Nobody gets raped and murdered in Myrtle Beach. It's all over the news. The place is on fire. Every hard-on cop in the state wants the piece of shit who did it, and wants to torture him, and slowly chop him up, and feed him to the dogs. If you led them here, I promise I will kill you myself before I let them have you.'

'What are you worried about, Gant? I'm slippery as a snake. I made it out of there. They didn't follow me. They're not gonna get me.' Foerster's voice began to rise. 'Hey, you know what? Even if they did, it wouldn't matter. I was in jail a week ago. I was looking at serious time. I needed a way out. But did I give you up? Did I talk about the little anthrax scare two years ago? No, I didn't, and I could have. I could have given them Tyler Gant, prominent businessman, living in his fancy house on the hill, all the while secretly organising terrorist attacks on American soil. I'm sure they'd rather have you instead of little old me. But no, I didn't give you up, and then you left me sitting in my apartment for a week, waiting for somebody to come get me, who never showed, and I almost went back to jail because of it. You know what? If I had gone back to jail, the first words out of my mouth would have been Tyler Gant.'

Jesus. Gant was done. He went to the cupboard and reached high above it, on his tiptoes. He came down with the .357 Magnum.

Foerster grunted. 'Huh. What're you gonna do with that?'

Gant was dimly aware that he might actually do it, right here, in his own house. He would have to clean up the mess later. Cooler heads were not necessarily going to prevail.

He grabbed Foerster by the throat. That got his attention. Foerster's face turned red and his hands went up to Gant's hand. Gant grabbed the gun by the muzzle and slammed the handle down on to Foerster's head. Then he did it again.

'Listen, you piece of shit. Don't you ever suggest that you would give me up. Don't you ever even think it. You're alive because I want you alive, and no other reason. The minute I don't want you alive any more, then you're dead. If you say my name to anybody, you won't live another forty-eight hours. Understand?'

A shadow moved near the doorway. Gant looked over and Katie was coming in with a bucket and some pruning shears. She wore a flower-pattern sundress and a floppy hat. She looked good, consumed by her own thoughts. She stopped at the threshold and glanced up, surprised to see them there.

In his mind's eye, Gant saw it from her point of view. Her husband, standing in the huge, gleaming and spotless kitchen, holding some dirty homeless man by the throat, pistol-whipping him with a large gun. Had she heard what they were just saying? Gant couldn't tell. Her face gave away nothing.

'Tyler, I . . . I'm sorry to interrupt.'

'It's OK. It's OK, hon. We're just having a little bit of a misunderstanding.'

A narrow stream of blood ran down Foerster's face. His eyelids fluttered, like he was about to pass out. But his weasel smile returned, on full beam. It had retreated into a wince, just for a second, when the gun had slammed into his temple.

'That's your wife, Gant? She looks pretty good.'

'You shouldn't piss him off like that. Next time he might actually kill you.'

Foerster sat on the edge of the double bed, drinking beer from a can. They were in a drab second-storey room in a no-name motel along some anonymous highway. Foerster had a hand towel from the bathroom, filled with ice from the machine out in the hallway. He held it to his face and head where Gant had battered him with the gun. The ice felt good. Sometimes he just rubbed the towel all over his face and got that cool feeling on his skin. He didn't remember leaving Gant's house – after he made the crack about Gant's wife, Gant had pistol-whipped him into unconsciousness.

Now he was here, nowhere, in a room with this gigantic tattooed cowboy named Vernon. Vernon had picked them up a twelve-pack of cold Budweiser and some take-out Chinese food. Vernon had even brought Foerster a bottle of Tylenol for the pain. Foerster didn't have much appetite after the beating he'd taken, but he hadn't eaten a decent meal in two days, so he forced himself to choke down some of the food. The noodles were greasy. The chicken made him think of dead cats in alleyways.

He looked at Vernon. Vernon was sprawled in a chair near the TV set. Everything about him was long. His legs and muscular arms were long. He had a long torso. His feet, in a pair of red pointy-toe boots, were huge. His long hair was pulled back into a ponytail. He had a nose like a bird's beak.

'How tall are you?' Foerster said. 'About six-six?'

Vernon took his big hands and laced his long fingers on top of his head. 'Nah, six-four, maybe four and a half. But the boots add another inch or two, depending on which boots I'm wearing.' He gestured at the white Stetson hat sitting on the table beside him. 'And the hat adds another four or five, depending on the hat. The whole set-up makes me look bigger than I really am.'

'Does it bother you to be so much bigger than other people?'

Vernon smiled, flashing a missing canine. 'It bothers other people, not me. I tend to like it.'

Foerster remembered him from before. He had only met Vernon once or twice, a big cowboy who came out to the lab, running errands for Gant, but he'd left an impression. At the time, Foerster figured him for hired muscle, an easily replaceable goon that Gant would probably swap out at some future date. But here it was, two years later, and Vernon was still around, still in Gant's good graces. Foerster, meanwhile, had been left on his own for two years and had taken a savage beating just for showing up.

'He shouldn't hit me like that. This is supposed to be a respectful working relationship. I went through hell to get here. If he doesn't want me to work for him, that's one thing . . .'

'Oh, he wants you to work for him. In a day or so, he'll remember he's glad you're here. But you've been a bad boy, and that complicates things. He's been worried about you, worried that you're a weak link, and this . . . problem . . . up in Myrtle Beach doesn't exactly increase his confidence any.'

'Well, I'm sorry about that. I don't know what came over me.'

Vernon sat up and eyed Foerster closely. 'Are you sick? Is that the issue?

You got like, some sort of mental derangement? I mean, you look like shit right now, but a young boy like you, clean yourself up some, you don't have to engage in that kind of behaviour. You're smart, too. You know we've kept our eye on you, on and off? And I always wonder what in the hell is wrong with you. You got all these special skills. You could be making lots of money. Meanwhile, you live in places where I wouldn't leave my dogs, the cops are up your ass, you're always flat busted, and you got this problem with women. It doesn't add up, if you ask me.'

The Tylenol was starting to kick in – Foerster's pain had receded from a sharp spike driven through his skull, to a heavy thump coming through the wall from next door. He shovelled another lump of the Chinese noodles into his mouth. The texture made him think of eating worms.

'I guess I should straighten up, huh? Be thankful for what I have and become a regular Joe?' Foerster actually couldn't imagine what that would be like. It didn't interest him – even if it were possible. But he sensed that simple-minded Vernon wouldn't pick up on those subtleties.

'You need to do something, cousin. You're embarking on a big operation, bigger than last time, and meanwhile we have to hide your ass. You should see how I'm taking you down to Florida tomorrow. Not pretty. And it didn't have to be this way.'

Foerster didn't want to know about how he was getting to Florida. If he knew about it, and it was bad enough, he might decide to run. He couldn't run, though. His freedom, and at this point probably his life, depended on the kindness of these strangers. It would be another day of rough travel, that's all. He'd try to get a good night's sleep tonight and tomorrow he would just accept whatever was in store for him. In the meantime, he would focus on other things.

'What is the job?' he said. 'Gant still hasn't told me.'

Vernon reached into the shoulder bag near his feet and pulled a large book from it. He tossed it into Foerster's lap. It was a wide, heavy, dog-eared paperback, the same microbiology text that Foerster had referred to on the last job. A little out-of-date, and with no specific mentions of working with weapons-grade technology, but the general principles were all there.

'Cholera,' Vernon said, and his eyes gleamed. 'As far as we know, the first lab-grown cholera attack the world has ever seen. We're gonna take out a whole island.'

'Amazing,' Foerster said, and meant it.

Vernon shook his head. 'More than just amazing.'

Foerster searched for a phrase that fit. 'Mind-blowing.'

'At the very least.'

'Totally fucked-up.'

Vernon smiled. 'Cousin, now you're getting there.'

6

By dawn, Gordo and Jonah had gone nearly four hundred miles.

They had left New York at midnight and driven through the night. South of Washington DC, near Richmond, they had exited the highway and headed south and west along a two-lane secondary road. The road was in bad shape. Keeping the interstate open was a higher priority than worrying about side roads.

As the sky brightened, there wasn't another car in sight. Gordo was at the wheel. He never slowed down on the winding road, pounding over the occasional pothole and crumbling asphalt at high speed. They passed through far-flung, no-name towns. Here and there, they went by a bicyclist or a pedestrian moving slowly along the road. To their left, the sun was yellow behind a haze of clouds. The radio was on, as it had been all night, a constant stream of nonsense about the dead woman in Myrtle Beach, and the fighting there, and the police response.

'Hey, man. You awake?' Gordo said.

It had been quiet in the car a long time, no sound except the chatter on the radio, the road rolling past, and the emptiness of it unnerved him. He thought Jonah had drifted off to sleep. He turned and found his co-pilot, eyes open and staring straight ahead as the green Virginia countryside passed by through the window beside him.

'Yeah,' Jonah said. 'I'm awake. You?'

'More or less. Anyway, we should be there soon.'

He opened his window so the breeze would keep him alert. There was nothing out here now except rolling hills and as the light grew stronger, the occasional car going the other way, headlights on against the mist and the new day. The grass on the hills grew tall. Man-high grass, it looked like. Gordo imagined diving into all that grass like it was a swimming pool. Up ahead, the road was so straight, it was like the car could drive itself the rest of the way. They passed an old barn that might have been red once. The colour had faded to a dull brown. The barn didn't know which way to fall. Its rear wall faced the roadway.

Painted on the wall in white letters six feet tall: JESUS SAVES.

That bothered Gordo.

He snorted. 'Let's face it, Jonah. We're alone out here. We're insignificant. We're a bunch of apes banging on coconuts. We just gotta take what we can get. Anybody who thinks different is kidding himself.'

Jonah turned from the window and stared at him. The look in Jonah's eyes said he didn't understand, or he hadn't heard.

'Science, man. Survival of the fittest. We live in a world where the strong eat the weak. It's the way things are. It's the way they've always been. There's a good chance that it's the natural order of things.'

'You would say that,' Jonah said. 'Since you're one of the strong.'

Gordo shrugged. 'So be it.'

Ten minutes later, driving from memory, he turned off the road and cruised through a residential area. It had been a few years since Gordo had seen Ronny's home. The whole neighbourhood had been built on farmland maybe six years before, and Ronny had moved the family down about a year later. They were selling the American Dream here – a big house in a new development for a price they called affordable – and to pay for his piece of the pie, Ronny had planned to drive forty miles each way to work in Richmond.

'Windswept Lane,' Gordo said. 'Here it is.'

The place had changed. The homes were large and set back from the road, hiding behind weeping willows and massive oaks with thick hanging moss. The streets were all curved and there were no sidewalks. That much was still the same. But several of the houses they passed were empty. In a couple of cases, they sat like huge skulls, windows gone, doors missing. On one lot, a pile of rubble stood where there might once have been a house. In a dozen places, bushes and shrubs grew furry and out of control. Lawns were a foot high.

Gordo pulled up to the house, your typical raised ranch. He was glad to see that this one hadn't changed too much – the grass was cut and the front yard was littered with bikes, skateboards and plastic toys of all kinds. It was a warm day, and the buzzing of insects was loud all around them. There was no car but Gordo's in the driveway.

Gordo opened his door. 'I guess we'll have to stay the night.'

'I thought we were leaving right after dinner.'

'You must have been asleep when I had the radio on. They put up check-points on the highways into and out of South Carolina. Local cops, state police, and the Marines out of Camp Lejeune. They want to stop Foerster from getting out of state, and they want to stop any crazies from coming in with guns to start the fighting up again. We don't want them finding guns in our car.'

Jonah looked sharply at Gordo. 'They said Foerster's name?'

'No, but we know it was him. Listen, the entryways open again at six tomorrow morning, so we can leave here as early as four, if you want. I just want to avoid getting searched, that's all I'm saying.'

When they rang the bell, the door opened and it was Annabelle. Gordo stepped back and took her in all at once. She was short and round, wearing glasses and a fuzzy blue robe. She had done a wonderful thing by taking his brother and making an honest man out of him. Ronny had always been the crazy one, and she had saved him from himself. She had also squeezed five puppies out of that body for him. It was too much for words. She held Gordo's heart in her hands, that's what it was.

'Gordon, it's so great to see you.' She smiled and hugged him.

'It's been too long,' he said.

Then she was saying something else, and hugging Jonah too. She brought them through the house and sat them on the back patio. It was a brick patio with a round white table in the centre, surrounded by six white chairs. She put out some doughnuts and coffee, but Gordo was too tired to touch them.

Jonah gave the two littlest children, Amy and Terrence, piggy-back rides on his broad shoulders. The kids laughed and laughed, begging for more till it looked like it might go on all day. But then Annabelle said enough was enough. She put the kids together in an inflatable pool ten yards away. Amy was so small she wore inflatable water wings around her tiny biceps in the two-foot deep Mr Turtle. The family dog, a grizzled white mongrel Ronny had named Blizzard, panted and looked at the water with a kind of canine longing. Blizzard wasn't allowed in the pool.

Gordo watched the action unfold from somewhere inside himself. He had trouble keeping his eyes open. He didn't want to go to sleep, because if he did, he might sleep for ever. He had been awake almost twenty-four hours. Jonah was slumped in his chair now, eyelids drooping. He hadn't said anything in about ten minutes.

Annabelle smoked a cigarette, one eye on the kids. 'You boys look dead. Let me put you to sleep for a little while.'

She led them into a room for children. Blue cartoon whales swam on the walls. Within minutes, Jonah was passed out on one of the small beds. His heavy snoring was atrocious, like a wild animal growling over food. Gordo couldn't imagine a more un-Jonah-like sound.

He put his own hands behind his head, and stared up at the ceiling. There were baby dolls in this room, most of them sitting in a crowd on top of the dresser. Every few seconds he caught some motion out of the corner of his eye, as though the dolls were moving. He turned to look, but never caught them. Then, one by one, their glass eyes opened. They stood and began to dance around his bed. Then he knew he was dreaming.

*   *   *

It was dark inside the funeral casket.

Foerster lay there, feeling the soft lining of the coffin against him, the vibration of the truck as it rolled down the highway, and the occasional jolt as it hit a pothole or bump in the road. He could hear the other coffins above him, shifting from time to time because of the motion, straining against the straps that held them in place.

He was inside a coffin, like a dead person.

He'd had trouble breathing when he first climbed inside. Vernon assured him that he had drilled more than two dozen holes in the sides of the coffin, small enough and spaced out enough to pass a cursory inspection from the cops or military personnel, but big enough to give Foerster the air he needed to stay alive. But when Vernon shut the lid on him, and the deep blackness came down, Foerster panicked. The dark was so total, it didn't matter if he opened or shut his eyes. As soon as he heard Vernon close the clasps, effectively locking him inside, Foerster started screaming and banging on the walls of his tomb.

'Relax,' Vernon said, and his voice already sounded far away. 'You can breathe. Just slow down and take some deep breaths. You're gonna be fine. We got the hard part to do out here.'

Vernon and a big bald-headed guy named Max began piling more coffins on top of and around the one Foerster was in. Max was shorter than Vernon, but he was thicker and his muscles were bigger. In fact, Max looked like he inflated his muscles with air. Foerster could hear them out there, grunting and swearing and pushing the boxes into place. He could picture the veins bulging on Max's giant biceps. They were burying Foerster alive.

Foerster kept banging, but Vernon kept ignoring him. Foerster ripped through the frilly insides of the casket, then clawed at the hard wood, to no avail. Sure, this was the kind of treatment he'd come to expect. No one understood him, and since they were glorified monkeys anyway, hardly smarter than chimps, they tried to destroy him. But he would not be destroyed. He would survive.

In the darkness, he saw his parents. Fucking troglodytes. If he'd had smart or somehow enlightened parents, they would have recognised his gifts as something precious and tried to protect him and encourage him. He might have ended up at Harvard or MIT if that had been the case, rather than inside this coffin. But no such luck – he was cursed with parents who had barely emerged from the caves. How was it possible? How could two morons spawn a child with abilities on the level of . . . well, probably not an Einstein, but almost certainly a Pasteur or a Marconi?

Time passed in the coffin, and Foerster must have fallen asleep at some point. He knew it was later now because he couldn't hear Vernon or Max any more, and he could feel the truck moving. As they rolled along, Foerster noticed some things about his surroundings. He could breathe easily, and fresh air was getting in through the holes Vernon had drilled. In fact, a bit of a draught blew in. He could also see. If he held up his hand, he could just make out the lines of it – he wasn't in utter darkness.

Calmer now, Foerster began to run preliminary information about the job through his head. He had taken a couple of hours last night to read about cholera from the microbiology text. Vernon had also let him see a one-page description of the weapons-grade version he would be working with. Its makers called it Cholera B. Just thinking about it began to bring Foerster alive. It was like he'd been living in a fog for two years, and now the fog was burning off, showing him a wide open view from the top of a high mountain. The past was the past, and the future had no limits.

He smiled at the cruelty of Gant's mind. Cholera was a nasty little bug. It gave people diarrhoea so severe that the victims died of dehydration, sometimes within hours. Some people lost so much fluid that before they died, they seemed to age decades overnight. Whomever Gant had been hired to kill, and apparently it was a whole island full of people, would basically shit themselves to death.

That is, if the stuff worked. Normally, it would be hit or miss. Cholera occurred naturally in zooplankton, and outbreaks usually happened after zooplankton blooms. People needed to ingest the water the cholera was in to get the disease, so the infected water had to find its way into the drinking supply. Outbreaks became epidemics in backward places where sewer water mingled with drinking water – people dying of cholera shit the disease back into the drinking water, infecting more people. Modern water system tended to keep suspect water out of the drinking supply, stopping the disease before it could get started.

This operation would take the guesswork out of the equation. The Cholera B multiplied faster than normal cholera. It was much more virulent, meaning it was easier to catch, and it was much more deadly. A number that had jumped off the page at Foerster was the 95 per cent death rate. Nineteen out of every twenty people who caught it would die from it, and Gant planned to pour it directly into their drinking water.

Foerster's job was to take the delivery of Cholera B already on the boat and culture it, growing colonies from each individual organism. As the colonies multiplied, there'd be a lot of bacteria around the lab – hundreds of gallons of infected water, in all likelihood. Moving it and delivering it to the target wouldn't be easy, but those were logistics, and logistics were Gant's problem. If anybody could pull this off, Gant could. He probably already had it figured out.

As Foerster lay like a corpse in the darkness, he realised that the latest developments – the money, the food and beer, the night's sleep on a real bed, and the sheer audacity of the plan – had him thinking well of Gant again.

Despite a few rough patches, he and Gant did make a pretty good team.

'We're going to have to kill Foerster,' Gant said. 'We just can't have him around once this is over. The situation is too sensitive.'

He sat in a beach chair on the roof of the *Sea Dog*, gazing west into the wide open Gulf of Mexico. All around, decrepit boats bobbed on the gentle swells. The sun beat down, its reflection sparkling off the green water. On the roof with him sat Big Mama in another beach chair. Gant was indulging her by helping her drink a pitcher of whiskey sours, her own recipe. He took a sip from his glass. He had to admit, it wasn't bad. Mama knew how to mix a drink.

'When do we do it?' Mama said. 'And who does it? I only ask because it seems fitting that a woman be the one. On this job, that's me.'

Sexy young Gabrielle lay on her stomach nearby, in a strapless jungle-pattern bikini, sunning herself on a white chaise lounge. Gant didn't look too closely at her. She was Mama's girl and Mama's problem, and doing or saying anything about her would only upset the applecart. He spoke openly about the job, as if Gabrielle wasn't even there. In fact, she might as well not be there – Gant had watched her swallow two or three tranquillisers, chasing them with two large tumblers of the whiskey drink. She appeared to be sleeping. With that mixture of drugs and alcohol in her system, a person her size should probably be dead.

Gant had known Mama for twenty years now – ever since he got wind she was selling designer drugs out of her hole-in-the-wall dyke bar in Philadelphia, and he started shaking her down for a percentage of the action. It had been the start of a beautiful friendship, one that long outlasted Gant's retirement from the police force. In their time together, Gant had seen a lot of Gabrielles go by. They were waifs and throwaways, finding moment-ary safety in Mama's loving arms. They tended to live fast and die before their time. They usually broke Mama's heart. It was understood, and had been from the beginning, that Mama always told them what kind of work she was doing.

Gant had flown down early that morning, paying three thousand dollars to sit in a Lear jet with three other business travellers. During the past month, he had come to this boat, this little floating paradise Big Mama had built, again and again. He was impressed by the tiny laboratory she had put together inside the place. Detail-oriented was Mama, right down to the three hand grenades tucked away in the bulkhead of the main cabin. They were an insurance policy of sorts. If the law ever came knocking, Mama could blow the place up before they got hold of it.

But these things were a given with her – she always did good work. It was more the location and the vibe that pleased Gant – the open air, the light, the movement of the water, and the easy, alcohol-induced buzz Mama and Gabrielle kept going day after day. Life at sea agreed with Gant so much, he sometimes thought he'd like to stay here for good.

He was done with his marriage. The end was long overdue, but he'd been busy. When this job was finished, he'd have enough money to live on for as long as he wanted. As soon as that happened, he planned to pull up stakes and ditch Katie – he'd been transferring money to offshore accounts for a year. She'd be in the house for a while after he left, but soon she'd realise she had no way to pay the bills. That would be one rude awakening. Meanwhile, he might move down here to Key West, but it was more likely he'd go to one of the islands. He could easily run his business from anywhere.

Of course, tomorrow he'd be on the plane back to Charleston. Every year for the past five years, he and Katie had thrown a big Halloween bash. It was becoming something of a tradition, and Gant thought that was just fine. Right up till the day he disappeared, it was important to keep up appearances.

It had been Katie's idea to move to the Lowcountry, as she liked to call it. She'd grown up in that stretch of coast between Charleston and Savannah, and Gant had learned all about the Lowcountry in his time there. Tidal flooding. Marshlands with alligators, and mosquitoes the size of his hand. The mindless, gung-ho patriotism of Parris Island. The empty pageantry of the Citadel. Modern-day good old boys whooping it up and rebel-yelling at February oyster roasts. The glorious slave economy, long dead, still cherished in everybody's mind, but marked by just a few plantation houses rotting away up dirt roads off the highways, and in the ten-million dollar antebellum mansions along the waterfront in Charleston.

Gant knew about the Lowcountry. It made him think of heat, oppressive humid heat, like in Vietnam. And of course, all that delightful southern hospitality and courtesy.

'Fuck your courtesy,' he muttered under his breath, feeling a little buzz from Mama's brew.

'What's that, Tyler?' Big Mama said. 'I didn't hear you.'

'I'll kill Foerster – or you can, if you want. Doesn't matter to me. But whoever does it, it won't be right away. We'll wait to see if the operation is a success or not. If everything goes according to plan, then we'll take care of him right away. If the guys deliver the stuff OK, but for some reason nothing happens, we might want to try again. We'll need Foerster for that. Since we're scuttling the boat before the stuff even flies out of here, that means we'll have to keep him alive on dry land somewhere, at least for a little while. That's a problem. He's slippery. We'll have to watch him all the time.'

'Morphine poppers,' Gabrielle said over her naked brown shoulder. Her voice was little more than a husky whisper. She sounded dazed, thick with sleep, languorous in the bright sunshine.

Gant looked at Mama. She shrugged her beefy shoulders. 'Sure. That would work. You know those little one-hit morphine syringes? The military designed them for use on the battlefield. Somebody gets wounded, and you just put them to sleep. It kills the pain and they stop screaming.'

'Yes,' Gant said. 'I know them.'

'Well, they're easy to get. As soon as Foerster finishes up, and Vernon and his pals start offloading the stuff, one of us comes up to Foerster and says, "Hey, great job, kid." We pat him on the back and give him a little morphine pop. Or we do it as he's going to sleep. Whenever. Now he's doped up and we can keep him that way as long as we want. Bring him to a motel room, tie him to the bed, put the TV on, and he'll be fine. Whenever he starts to come down, we give him another little hit.'

Gant liked it. He probably would have thought of it himself eventually, but that's what he had a team for. 'Sounds good.'

'It is good,' Mama said. 'It's humane, too. When we decide to get rid of him, he won't even notice. He'll be a lot better off than the women he killed, or those poor bastards on the island.'

'Dead is . . . mmm . . . dead,' Gabrielle said. It came out slowly, as though her tongue were swollen and the words had to squeeze their way around and along its bloated length. She never lifted or even moved her head.

Gant smiled. 'Smart girl,' he said to Mama. He raised his glass in the air. 'Cheers to that. Dead is definitely dead.'

* * *

Vernon sat alone up front, listening to the engine rumble, and watching the light fade to the west as the highway narrowed and the last of metropolitan Miami receded behind him. He was on the long approach to the Keys now. A warm breeze, heavy with moisture, blew through the open window. He fancied he could smell the ocean in the air.

It was a perfect evening.

He focused on the last of the sun setting to the west, behind the southern edge of the Everglades. It was nice to be here, the truck poking along, the wind blowing through the window, cooling the hot night air.

He felt pretty good. He'd had a little nervous thing happen at the highway checkpoint between South Carolina and Georgia, but he'd handled it the right way. The cops had the crossing locked down. They were young, in full gear – body armour, helmets and visors, the whole nine yards – as if they expected a shooting war to erupt right there at the border. They had the dogs out, and that was bad. Worse, they had hand-held heat sensors. All that one of these snot-noses had to do was run the sensor along the outside of the truck, pick up Foerster's body heat in there, and this day would suddenly become long indeed.

When he pulled up to the stop, before they even started the twenty questions game (Where's you headed? What's in the truck?), Vernon handed the helmeted cop his national ID card. It noted his military service right on there. Cops liked the military. A lot of them were ex-military themselves.

'Where were you stationed?' the kid said. It was a good path to head down, much better than a conversation about interstate funeral casket deliveries.

'Mexico,' Vernon said.

'I was in Mexico,' said the kid. 'When were you there?'

'Three and a half years ago.'

'Three and a half years? Man, that was a bad time. Were you at—'

'Chicontepec,' Vernon said, finishing the thought for him. He looked the kid in the eye, showing him it was real. 'The oil fields. Yeah, I was there. The day the Mexies blew it up. I was one of the guys carrying bodies out. The flames were three hundred feet in the air. The smoke was so thick it turned day into night. At the end of the first day, I was so black from the soot it looked like I'd been dipped in shit.'

'Christ.'

Vernon gave him a short bark of laughter. 'Yeah.'

He hadn't thought of these things in a long time. He never thought he'd use them as a ploy to sneak a fugitive past a checkpoint. Maybe that was a good sign.

The kid looked at the ID again before handing it back. 'Vernon? It's a pleasure to meet you, man.'

'Likewise.'

'Roll out. Have a good day.'

'Thanks.'

He glanced in his rearview as he guided the truck on to the empty highway. The next car in line pulled up to the checkpoint. The kid would probably bring the hammer down to make up for letting Vernon and his coffin truck slide.

Once he was on the road again, the memories came back, and came back for real. For a little while, in northern Florida, he started getting the jitters. He thought he might have to pull over and find a motel, buy a bottle, and give it up for the day. Instead, he pushed through it and kept going.

He was at Chicontepec for three weeks after it happened. The place was on fire the whole time. A lot of the bodies were charred black, twisted into grotesque shapes, like monsters. These were Americans – American soldiers.

By the time they rotated him out, Vernon was a mess. They put him on a detail sandbagging along a hundred miles of the Ohio River. It was hot and sticky loading up sandbags, and there were all kinds of mosquitoes and biting flies. Water breached all up and down the line, and people got swept away, entire families got sucked downriver right in their trailers, and Vernon just didn't care. He was happy to be there.

The Ohio River was a Roman fucking holiday after Chicontepec. He saw a guy get his eyes melted right out of his head at Chicontepec, and that wasn't the worst of it. He saw guys who were bright red like steamed lobsters, their skin cooked right off them, and who were somehow still alive. And all for a few more lousy barrels of oil. Come to think of it, it was all for nothing since they never did get the oil.

He took a deep breath.

Now the truck moved through the low-slung strip malls of Key Largo. Some things were still open, but many weren't. Dive shops, roadside motels, restaurants, all boarded up as if a hurricane were coming, the storefronts without boards sporting broken windows like missing teeth. He pulled the truck into an empty parking lot. The asphalt was cracked and rutted and the store itself was gone – just a concrete foundation and a jangle of pipes sticking out of the ground. Ahead of him on the Overseas Highway, the sun was going down in a spectacular blaze of red and orange.

Gant had said that once Vernon made the Keys, it was OK to let Foerster come up front. But you know what? Just because it was OK, didn't mean it was necessary. Now that he was here, Vernon saw the pitfalls in that idea. He would have to open the back of the truck and hump a bunch of heavy coffins around by himself, all just to have Foerster climb up here in the cab and spew rapid-fire, meaningless bullshit at him for the next hundred miles.

You know what? No thanks. Things were going just fine with Foerster right where he was. Why fix something that wasn't broken? Vernon would listen to music instead. He turned the radio on and dialled around for a decent song. Then he put the truck in gear and rumbled out on to the road, headed into the sunset.

Katie intended to find out exactly what was going on. She strode down the hallway of the first floor to the locked room at the end of the hall. She hadn't been inside that room in years. Walking behind her was a local handyman and locksmith she'd found in the phone book.

'The minute I don't want you alive any more, then you're dead. If you say my name to anybody, you won't live another forty-eight hours.'

The words had replayed over and over again in Katie's mind. Tyler had said these words yesterday, nearly shouted them, in the three seconds before she had walked into the kitchen and seen him with that man. The man was scruffy, dirty, maybe a homeless man, a bomzhie. Blood streamed down his face. The whole thing was so out of place that for the first few seconds Katie wasn't even sure she was seeing it. Here was her wide-open kitchen, a kitchen that caterers told her rivalled their professional kitchens. Here was ample granite-topped counter space, a double refrigerator, the island with an extra sink and more counter space. Large pots and pans hung from pegs. Sunlight streamed through the large windows. And here was Tyler, gripping a much younger man by the throat, with a gun poised above the man's head.

They both looked in her direction as she walked in. They were startled, as though they'd been discovered doing something intimate, something only for them. For a few seconds, they seemed frozen in place, like a hyper-realistic sculpture, like the victims of Mount Vesuvius turned instantly to stone by the flowing lava. Then Tyler said something Katie couldn't remember now. But she remembered exactly what the beaten man had said. He looked her up and down, his eyes roaming her body, something inside those eyes enjoying this moment, and said: 'That's your wife, Gant? She looks pretty good.'

Then Tyler had smashed him with the butt end of the gun, over and over, till the man was unconscious on the floor. She had never seen anything like that in real life. She'd barely seen anything like it at all – she avoided watching violent movies or TV. She had almost no frame of reference for it. The viciousness of it was amazing, like watching a wild animal tear apart its prey. No hesitation, no questions, no concern for another life. The kitchen floor was wet with the man's blood.

Katie had run away then, up to the bedroom, and locked herself inside. She lay on the bed, her face pressed into the pillows. It was quiet in the house, so quiet that she became aware of all the sounds: the loud ticking of the grandfather clock downstairs, the buzz of the digital clock here in the room, the chirping of birds outside. Running water as Tyler probably washed the blood from his hands. Later, a car pulled up and the doorbell rang. Vernon came in – there was no mistaking his voice. She heard Vernon and Tyler speaking, but couldn't make out what they said. Sometime later, Tyler had come upstairs to her.

Of course, he had a key to the bedroom and he let himself in. He stood by the door, watching her on the bed. She wouldn't face him.

'You're probably wondering what's going on,' he said to her back.

'No.'

'OK, well, I just want to remind you that I deal with difficult people in my line of work, and that man is one of them. You know I was a police officer for many years. Sometimes I have to use force on people. I'm comfortable with the use of force.'

'Did you kill that man?'

He laughed. 'Katie, no. Of course not. I taught him a lesson, that's all.'

She turned and looked at his face. 'Is Vernon going to kill him?'

'No, Vernon's going to take him and get him a comfortable bed, a hot shower and a meal. Look, the guy is someone who needed the facts of life explained to him, and now that they have been, everything is fine. He works for me. I wish I could tell you more than that, but I really can't. Suffice it to say that he's going to be fine. We don't kill people.'

Tyler was lying. Katie could see it in his eyes. She didn't know what part of it was a lie, or if all of it was, but no doubt Tyler was lying. She'd had enough of it, either way. She slept in one of the spare bedrooms last night and early this morning, listened as Tyler packed up and left again. Gone away on business.

Now, Katie felt a small burst of exhilaration having the handyman there, a thrill running through her entire body. Tyler would know – he would find out – that this man had been in the house. At the very least, the guards would give him the visitor log when he got home. Katie would tell him the man was one of the workers coming to set up for the party. That was the plan, anyway.

'This is the door,' she said. 'It's embarrassing to admit, but we just don't know where the key is to this lock. If you can just take the door off, it'd be a big help.'

The handyman was sexy in a sweaty, toolbelt-hanging-on-his-hip kind of way. He needed a shave. He needed a shower. He needed a new T-shirt to wear. His hands were dirty from jobs he'd done earlier in the day.

'You know, I could just drill the lock out and replace it with a new one. It wouldn't take long. Then I'd just give you a few extra sets of keys. It's a little more expensive than taking the door off the frame, but I think you can afford it.'

'Yes, but I don't want a new lock.'

The man ran a hand through his hair. 'If I take the door off, what are you going to do, just leave it like that?'

Katie smiled. It felt awkward on her face. 'Let me ask you a question. Do you make house calls outside of normal business hours? Late at night, or in the wee hours of the morning?'

The man smiled now, too. His smile seemed a lot more genuine than hers. His mind had run off down its own path. She could practically see his wheels spinning. Was it possible, he was thinking, that this woman didn't want any work done? Was it possible she wanted something else? 'Sometimes I do. I could come by here any time. If it's an emergency.'

Katie indicated the door. 'This is an emergency. The room is locked. Understand? What I need you to do is take the door off the frame. Then I need you to come back very early tomorrow morning, when I call you, and put it back on again just like it is now. Locked.'

The smile died on the man's face. 'Oh. It's like that, then.'

'Yes,' Katie said. 'It's like that.'

'You know,' Ronny said to Jonah, 'that's one hell of a physique you got there.'

Jonah, Ronny and Gordo sat on lawn chairs in Ronny's backyard, feet resting in the inflatable pool, drinking beer from cans. Jonah had grown comfortable during the day. He wore only a pair of swim trunks as day melted into evening. The three men were enjoying the night air.

'Thanks,' Jonah said to Ronny. 'Even if you are a man.'

The years had changed Ronny. Long ago, he had stood tall and straight, with his sharp chin thrust out. He wore glasses now, and the once jagged face had grown jowls. His hairline was receding, and there was a solid bald spot on top of his dome. His gut, while no match for his brother's, also hung out over his waist. When he had come in from work around six, wearing a wrinkled suit with his tie already taken off, he seemed to walk hunched over, as though he carried a boulder strapped to his back.

'Oh, I ain't hitting on you, partner. I just wish I could lose a little of this.' Ronny pulled up his T-shirt and grabbed his belly, which was big. 'I used to look something like you, maybe never quite that good, but I'd love to get even halfway back there.'

Jonah held his beer up. 'You keep drinking these, it's gonna make it hard.'

'Old boy,' Ronny said, 'life is a series of trade-offs.'

They all laughed.

Time went by. Ronny went in and brought out a bottle of Old Grand-Dad. It made the rounds. Jonah could hardly drink any, a sip here and a sip there. He drank another beer instead. He noticed he was putting a buzz on. It always happened that way when he spent a lot of time with Gordo. While Jonah watched, Gordo and Ronny had a chugging contest. Ronny chugged a beer about two seconds faster than his brother. The whiskey came around again. Jonah took a bigger swig of it this time. It was getting easier. More time passed. Jonah drank another beer.

Full darkness settled in and Ronny lit some yellow citronella candles to keep the bugs away. A few moments later, someone started a fire about three backyards over from Ronny's house. It went up quickly – one minute it was deep black over there, and the next minute flames reached towards the sky, embers flying and blowing around on the breeze. Someone over there cheered. Jonah could make out a handful of silhouettes – maybe four, maybe five – against the flames. It was a big fire, as if lumber or furniture were piled up. Jonah hadn't noticed any kind of pile there in the daytime.

'They only come out at night,' Ronny said.

'Crazy neighbours,' Gordo said.

'No. Bomzhies.'

'Shit. Really?'

Patrick Quinlan

'Yeah. That house was empty for six months. The bomzhies took it over maybe three weeks or a month ago. At least a dozen different people have been living there at various times. I've seen three different rustbucket cars parked in the driveway. Annabelle says it's more than three. I don't know how many people are in there right now, but I do know they light fires sometimes.' Ronny took a long, slow sip of the Old Grand-Dad. 'Ever notice how much bomzhies light fires? It's like a special thing with them. They love to set shit on fire.'

'Fucking bomzhies,' Jonah said, and now he knew for sure he was buzzed. 'They're like zombies, man – they turn up everywhere. My mother found one in her cellar. It's like a bad movie.'

Jonah rolled his eyes. A couple of years ago, just as things were starting to go very wrong, some squatters had started a squatters' rights campaign. They didn't want to be called squatters any more. They wanted to be called bomzhies – the name had something to do with the collapse of the Soviet Union twenty-five years ago. They thought it conferred more dignity on people who had lost their homes. They also wanted the right to legally occupy abandoned suburban houses and businesses. They wanted the right to burn open fires to stay warm. They wanted the right to farm and graze sheep in closed office parks. They wanted to gather in tent cities.

There were a lot of things they wanted, but as far as Jonah could tell, the only thing they had actually received was the name change – people did call them bomzhies. Otherwise, all they had was the right to keep moving. Probably fifteen million people by now, almost universally hounded and upended wherever they took root – their settlements rousted and torn down, any empty house they took over razed to the ground, their livestock confiscated, including dogs. The fucking bomzhies, man – they were raising dogs as food.

'Doesn't that bother you having them there?' Gordo said. 'I mean, you got kids living here, and your wife. You're out at work all day.'

'Yeah. It bothers me.'

'Did you call the cops? The cops'll clear 'em out of there. Cops like nothing better than clearing bomzhies out.'

166

Ronny stared at the bottle in his hand. 'I've been reluctant to do that.'

'Why? What's the matter with you? I sympathise with them, but you know what? You gotta live. Your family has to be safe. The people over there have the right to be bomzhies and do their thing, but they need to do it somewhere else.'

'I don't want to call the cops,' Ronny said. 'What goes around comes around. And I don't want somebody calling the cops when it happens to us.'

Gordo made a face of exaggerated disgust. 'What? Come off it.'

'Gordie, you're my brother and I love you. I even like you. But a lot of times you don't know what the fuck you're talking about. I sell advertising space on highway billboards. Don't you realise that? I work on commission, and it's the only fucking job I've been able to get. I'm making pennies. I barely earn enough to feed the kids, put clothes on their backs, and keep some gas in the car. The gas is getting harder and harder to find and it costs more every time I do find it. I have no money. I haven't made a mortgage payment in eleven months.'

'Jesus, Ronny.'

'Yeah,' Ronny said. 'Jesus. Maybe he's gonna come down here and save us, but I doubt it.'

'What are you going to do?'

'What does it look like I'm going to do? I'm going to stay right here till the bank comes and kicks me out. With a little luck, it might still be a while. Then I'm gonna load up the car with the kids and as much stuff as we can carry, and go house to house like those people over there.' He gestured with his chin at the flames dancing in the near distance. 'We're gonna be a whole family of bomzhies.'

Jonah watched Ronny's face in the weak yellow light from the candles. The big man was working hard not to show emotion. He stared at the shimmering water in the crappy plastic turtle pool. His eyes were doing something – they were blinking a lot. But he wasn't crying.

'Listen, Ronny . . .'

'Save it, Gordie. You're not going to help me. No offence, but you can barely help yourself. What are you gonna do, carry a family of seven on your back? For how long? Till I get back on my feet? When's that going to happen?'

Ronny put the bottle on the ground near Jonah's feet and carefully stood up. 'OK, look. Forget it. I drank too much. Everything's gonna be fine, but I have to work in the morning, so I'm going to bed.' He gestured at the bottle. 'Finish the booze. Stay as long as you guys want. If you're here tomorrow night, I'll see you then.'

He went in, leaving Jonah and Gordo alone. They passed the bottle back and forth, Jonah taking nips, Gordo taking full slugs. For a long while, the only sound was the crackling of the flames from the bonfire. Then someone started beating on a bongo drum. It started gradually at first, a few beats here and there. Then it became louder, stronger, more consistent. The drummer picked a rhythm and started to work with it. A man shouted, and then started to chant. A woman's voice joined in and picked up the chant. It sounded vaguely like Native American chants Jonah had heard and seen performed on television. It sounded haunting. It sounded ridiculous. It went on and on, rising and falling.

'You know,' Gordo said. 'He could have told me this was going on.'

'Yeah,' Jonah said. 'He could have.'

'You know what else? I'm sick of listening to this shit.'

Gordo stood and disappeared into the darkened house. A moment later, he came back out. He had something in his hand. He showed it to Jonah. It was a gun, a semi-automatic. Gordo's eyes were flat and hard. His jaw was set. 'Wendel told me to make sure these things work.'

'Gordo . . .'

He pointed the gun at an angle over the heads of the people across the way. Jonah covered his ears as Gordo fired three times, the blasts loud, the muzzle flashes burning fiery angels into Jonah's retinas. Afterwards, the flames crackled against deep silence. The drumming had stopped. The chanting had stopped. There were no bomzhies in the shadows of the fire.

Gordo handed Jonah the gun. Jonah could smell the burnt gunpowder from it. 'You can have that one,' Gordo said. 'We know it works.'

* * *

Foerster felt weird.

The coffin where he'd lain all day had deprived him of his senses. Very little light. Very little sound except the rumble of the truck. Nothing to look at. Nothing to eat or drink. No one to talk to. To escape his surroundings, he'd gone deep into his own mind. He slept, he woke up, he slept again – asleep and awake were almost the same to him. When Vernon opened the casket, the weak overhead light of an empty warehouse surged in like the blinding glare of the sun.

'Welcome back,' Vernon said. 'Happy to see you're still alive.'

He gave Foerster a banana and a chocolate bar. Foerster sat on a folding chair in the empty cavernous warehouse, eating his food as Vernon very slowly and deliberately removed his huge red boots and changed into a pair of flip-flops. A cab was waiting outside the front door of the warehouse, and they took a twenty-minute taxi ride here to the waterfront. The warehouse was out of town, past the airport, maybe even on another island. It seemed to Foerster they had crossed a bridge getting here.

Now, they were out among the crowds of Key West. The sights, the sounds and the smells were almost too much to bear. Neon lights strobed in the darkness. Music pounded from the bars, with a steady background hum of chatter and laughter. A breeze blew off the water, bringing the stench of rotting fish. Well-dressed tourists and scruffy locals streamed by, their heads seeming large and oddly misshapen. They didn't appear human at all – they looked like imposters wearing masks.

'What do you say, boss?' Vernon said. 'What about a quick drink for me and the kid here? I don't know about him, but I had a long day.'

Somehow, Gant had arrived in Key West ahead of them. Foerster and Vernon met him at the docks near a big outdoor bar called the Schooner Wharf. The bar was crowded with laughing drunks. Gant was in good spirits, maybe even a little drunk. He wore khaki shorts, a black T-shirt and sandals. He looked like a guy away on a pleasure trip. When they got out of the cab in front of the bar, Gant was already waiting. He smiled and clapped Vernon on the back. He shook Foerster's hand as though all was forgiven, and yesterday's violent assault was a little misunderstanding that had happened years before.

'I hate to break this to you,' he said to Vernon, 'but we've still got work to do. Getting here isn't the end, it's the beginning. But I'll tell you what. Let's go out to the boat and you can both drink if you want. We won't start in with the heavy lifting till tomorrow.'

They motored out in a small inflatable dinghy, Gant at the rear running the engine and steering, Vernon up at the front holding a flashlight. Once they got a little way out from the city, Gant opened the throttle full-bore, and the little boat accelerated into the empty night. They rode some large swells, water breaking over the side, splashing into Foerster's face, a brisk wake-up call. Foerster held on to a canvas strap. He didn't like blasting through the dark like this. He didn't like the way the silhouettes of boats loomed up, then flowed silently past like ghost ships.

The last time they had done a job like this, the boat wasn't at sea – it was parked at a huge dock, one of dozens of anonymous boats, in a marina at Hilton Head. Foerster could get out of the lab and walk around if he wanted. He could take a short break from his work and stroll around the docks in the sunshine, looking at the mega-yachts. This going way out on the ocean, he didn't know what it was all about. It felt a little like being trapped.

After what seemed like a long time on the water, they pulled up to a houseboat. Gant eased off the throttle just as they approached. The boat was dark except for a couple of lights – one inside the cabin and one on the roof. Vernon expertly stepped across the gap from the dinghy, pulled the dinghy close with the rope, and tied it up to the cleat on the back of the houseboat. Only then did he extend a hand across to Foerster.

Gant stepped across and put a hand around Foerster's shoulders. 'I know you're probably itching to see your lab, and I'll show you it in a little while. I think you're going to like it. But first let's meet the family, shall we?'

Foerster liked that, the way Gant gave him ownership of the lab. It was a subtle touch, and no doubt Gant was doing it to manipulate him, but he liked it all the same. It was his lab, after all. He followed Gant around the side of the boat, and walked a couple of steps out on to a narrow ledge that extended the boat's entire length. A ladder was mounted on the wall just a few feet from the back deck. Gant climbed it and Foerster followed suit, Vernon bringing up the rear.

Only upon reaching the top of the ladder, his shirt and pants wet and clinging to him from the ride out, did Foerster realise how tired he was. Exhausted. It had been three days of almost non-stop travel – none of it comfortable – getting to this place.

He stepped out on to the roof, the boat rocking gently from the swells, the wind kicking up a little. There were two people here, lying squashed together on a lounge chair in the dim light from a burning hurricane lamp. Curled up near them on the floor was a little dog. It started to growl as the men came up and stepped off the ladder.

'Big Mama!' Vernon said when he reached the top. 'There's my girl. How long has it been?'

'Vernon, you lazy redneck motherfucker.'

'Folks, she's got me pegged.'

With some effort, the woman moved her bulk off the chair. Big Mama, dressed in a T-shirt and jeans. She looked bigger than Foerster remembered her. Two years will put weight on a person. She opened a cooler at her feet. 'Have a beer, big man. You deserve it.'

Vernon looked at Gant and Foerster in the gloom. He smiled. 'Gentlemen, that's what I've been waiting on all day, a cold adult beverage and a jump in that big beautiful ocean. I'm gonna wash this long day off of me, and maybe wrestle a few sharks while I'm under there.'

'Do your worst,' Gant said. He put his hand on Foerster's back and brought him forward. It felt oddly paternal, having Gant's hand there. Gant was certainly old enough to be Foerster's father. 'Mama, you remember Davis Foerster? He helped us with a little project back a couple of years ago.'

The heavy woman came closer. 'Of course I remember. How you doing, Davis? Welcome home. My house is your house. You want a beer?'

Foerster smiled. 'Sure.' A moment later, the cold can hit his hands. He popped it open and took a sip. There was no word for what it tasted like, and how it felt, going down his throat. Delicious didn't nearly get there. As he drank it, the little dog started to bark and yap madly.

'Don't worry about Versace there,' Mama said. 'He's a Yorkie and they're very, very territorial. That's why they make such good guard dogs.'

'Yorkie?' Foerster said, pretending interest. He didn't really care about the dog, but everybody was playing friendly, so he thought he'd go along for the ride. He felt pretty good. They were buttering him up, and it was working. But in other circumstances, he'd just as soon gut the dog.

'Yorkshire Terrier. The best breed of dog in the world. Versace is actually just a little too big to be a pure-bred Yorkie. Somebody snuck into the blood-line there somewhere. But he's a real friendly dog, a great little guy to have around out here. He'll warm up to you once he gets to know you. Then he'll be your best friend and you won't be able to get rid of him even if you want to. Isn't that what friends are for?'

Next to Foerster, Vernon had pulled his shirt off and was shrugging out of his jeans. He stood, gigantic, a long strand of lean muscle mass, in tiny dark underwear, and downed his entire can of beer. His underwear looked like something a guy on the high-school swim team might wear, or maybe a guy from France. A crazed imbroglio of tattoos covered his shoulders, his arms, and his chest almost down to his belly button. In the darkness, Foerster couldn't make out any of it.

'That was good,' Vernon said, and belched. 'Now who do we have here?'

Another woman came up to them out of the darkness. In the glow from the lamp, Foerster could see her – young, long hair, great body, wearing a bright orange fleece jacket covering only a bikini.

'Davis, this is my girl Gabby. She's Versace's owner, and she's living here on the boat with us. It's tight quarters around here, so we'll all have to learn to be friends. But don't try to get too friendly – I'm armed and dangerous.'

The girl extended her small hand and Foerster pumped it once. He decided to play it shy around her. Hell, he felt shy around her. It occurred to him now that Mama must know his history, and must know what had just happened in Myrtle Beach. The girl must know, too. Vernon knew and, come to think of it, he made his living as Gant's enforcer. He was probably here to watch Foerster and keep him on his best behaviour. In fact, they'd all be watching him. Foerster felt a twinge of something, and a few seconds later recognised it as embarrassment.

'Nice to meet you.'

'Aren't you going to introduce me?' Vernon said.

'Gabby, don't mind Vernon in his little man panties there. Don't even look at him.' The whole group had a good laugh over that.

'That's right,' Vernon said. 'Nobody look at me. Nobody look at me do this.' He got a running start, took three big steps, and dove off the side of the boat into the dark water below. For a second, he had seemed suspended in air, a great gangling bird in flight. Foerster watched Vernon, but he also watched the girl's eyes – she was looking at Vernon, all right. Her pretty eyes followed Vernon's body the whole way.

Gant's hand landed gently on Foerster's back again. 'Davis, let's go check out that lab, shall we?'

7

Vernon had spent the night alone.

He sat slumped on the couch in the main cabin, sipping a beer. Outside, the first weak light of day broke in the sky. It was Halloween morning and he could barely keep his eyes open. He'd been sitting on this couch for the past several hours. Gant, who kept a hotel room in town, had left in the middle of the night. But he had this idea that someone – either Vernon or Mama – should be awake at all times to keep an eye on Foerster. Vernon was willing to play along, but the idea was starting to look silly. Foerster had taken to that laboratory like a tadpole to water.

He was in there right now, as he had been more or less since they'd got here, in his white lab coat, his goggles and his mask, endlessly putting drops of this or that in little glass dishes, endlessly gazing at plastic slides under the microscope, and endlessly moving what he described as 'colonies' into glass jars of specially prepared water. He was in a race against time – their opposite numbers from the island were supposed to get here in three days to pick up the stuff. Foerster claimed the work was going well, better than he'd expected, and Vernon imagined it was true. He had hardly come out of there in the past fourteen hours except to eat, shit, shower, or change his clothes. Maybe once every couple of hours he'd go outside and sit on the back deck

Patrick Quinlan

for a while and have a smoke. He drank coffee by the gallon – another responsibility of the Foerster watcher was to make sure there was always fresh coffee. The man already had black rings under his eyes from lack of sleep.

Vernon was starting to wonder why he, Vernon, was here. His job was supposedly to make sure Foerster didn't escape, and to keep him in line. Making sure he didn't escape was a ridiculous task. Foerster didn't know how to start or operate a dinghy, it was a long damn swim to Key West, and in any case, Foerster liked it here. All he wanted to do was play with his toys. At the same time, keeping him in line, as Vernon understood it, meant keeping the women safe from him. Big Mama was safe from Foerster by virtue of being Big Mama. Gabrielle was safe from him by virtue of being Big Mama's girlfriend.

'Oh, I'm not worried about having Davis around,' Mama had said to Vernon last night. 'If he tries to do anything to Gabby, I'll cut his balls off. I'm sure he knows that.'

Vernon was confident this was true. Mama was so confident of it that after Gant left, she and Gabby went straight to bed. It looked an awful lot like Mama felt that since she had put the boat together, her work was done. And with Gant flying out for Charleston today, she'd probably slack off even more. That left big dumb Vernon, as usual, stupidly sticking to the plan, holed up here with nothing to do but sit around and drink. Oh yeah, and listen to the radio. The Weather Service was monitoring a small tropical storm coming up through the islands – that was the big news. Vernon shook his head. He should have told Gant he wanted to get on that plane with him. He could have come back here the next time Gant did.

Well, a job was a job and money was money.

He finished the beer in his hand, and thought about going to the icebox for one more. He heard a sound to his left, *click*, very quiet. You'd almost say it was stealthy. He looked up and who was there but Gabby, maybe fifteen feet away, stepping out of the small cabin she shared with Mama. She stared at Vernon for a long moment. Vernon stared back at her. The staring contest went on for another full minute. Gabby wasn't wearing a stitch of clothing.

In fact, now probably would be a good time to get another beer. Vernon stood and took the three large steps that brought him to the icebox. It cut the distance between himself and Gabby in half. Gabby took two tentative steps forward, halving the distance again. She pushed the long hair out of her face.

Vernon smiled. 'Girl, can I help—'

Gabby raised a finger to her lips. Then she shook her head. She stepped close to him and looked up into his face. He was a lot taller than she was. He took her waist in his big hands. She put her hands on his chest. Hello, this was interesting. She mouthed something without making a sound, a long, slow sentence.

'She's going to be awake soon.'

This was a little girl who liked to play games. OK, Vernon could swing with that. Nothing was going to happen right now, but maybe later it would. He nodded. She nodded. He ran a hand along her curves and let her go. She smiled, turned around, and went into the bathroom – what a sailor might call the head. He opened the icebox and grabbed himself his last beer of the night.

Wide awake now, he brought the beer over to the couch and proceeded to have a think about this latest development. By the time he heard that stealthy *click* again, which signalled to him that Gabby had slipped back into Mama's cabin, he'd come around to the opinion that this job might not be too bad after all.

'That's the office,' Gordo said, climbing in behind the wheel of the car. 'Executive Strategies. I remember it from the news clipping. He actually owns the whole building. He was gonna revitalise the neighbourhood, but it doesn't seem like he gets here much these days.'

It was just after noon. Jonah and Gordo had awakened early and left Ronny's and Annabelle's house. Thick white mists had hung over everything as they drove across southern Virginia, North Carolina, and into South Carolina. It was a long ride and Gordo hardly spoke a word. Dark hours crawled by and the road stretched on and on and they never seemed to get anywhere. But now they were idling in a parking lot along a dismal strip of downtown Charleston. Many of the nearby homes and businesses had burned out some time ago. It looked like it had happened all at once, like a bomb or an earthquake had taken down several city blocks. To Jonah, it also looked like no one was in any hurry to rebuild.

The building in question was a brown-brick two-storey office plaza. The locked building sat next to a former Piggly Wiggly supermarket with smashed windows. People appeared to be living in the old supermarket. As Jonah watched, a heavy black woman in pink shorts, T-shirt and flip-flops pushed a shopping cart full of rags and cast-off clothing across the parking lot. She backed into the supermarket, forcing the heavy door open with her body.

'Let's go out to the house,' Gordo said. 'Maybe Mr Gant will talk to us there. And maybe we'll find Mr Foerster in.'

The home address Gordo had found for Gant was a twenty-five-minute drive into the suburbs. The run-down houses of the city gave way to half-built housing developments, empty shopping plazas and barren parking lots. These gave way to open country. They followed a winding road over some hills and past a horse farm. The horses cantered in a vast penned-in area of bright green grass. They looked strong and healthy. Their coats gleamed.

'Pretty horses,' Jonah said.

Gant lived in a gated community along the narrow two-lane road. It wasn't just gated – security guards were stationed at the gate. Across from the gatehouse were some dense woods. There was nowhere to stop and just watch the gate to see who came in and out of the complex. They took a slow circle tour to see the full set-up. A chain-link fence topped with looping razor wire ran the perimeter of the place. The fence was tastefully set back in the bushes. The bushes themselves had thorns. Every fifty yards or so, two cameras were mounted on the fence – each taking a sweep in opposite directions.

'Looks like you'd get cut to ribbons breaking through there,' Jonah said. 'And by the time you made it in, the guards would be waiting to escort you right back out again.'

'Yeah,' Gordo said. 'Or hand you over to the cops.'

'Maybe we should just go to the gate and announce ourselves. Maybe the man will see us.'

Gordo shrugged. 'It's worth a shot. Maybe the guards will let us in. Stranger things have happened.'

They pulled up to the gatehouse. The guards were young guys – big, clean-cut, eager-beaver types in blue uniforms, almost like cops. The one who came to the window had a sort of weird cow-lick thing happening with the front of his hair. He gave Gordo's half-dead car the once-over and smirked. These weren't the kind of wheels that rolled in and out of this place on a regular basis. The guy's eyes said he was someone who would enjoy denying them entry.

Inwardly, Jonah smiled. Nobody enjoyed denying Gordo anything, not if he didn't want them to.

'Can I help you, gentlemen?' the Cow-lick said.

Gordo's voice was flat. He pulled out the badge and flashed it, doing it smoothly, like it was something he'd done a thousand times before. 'Detective Robert Darker, New York City Police Department. Homicide. This is Mr Maxwell, a consultant with the department. We're here to see Tyler Gant.'

The Cow-lick's smirk faltered a tiny bit. The other guard inside the office looked up from his desk. The Cow-lick glanced back at a large board inside the office.

'Mr Gant is away at this time.'

'Where'd he go?'

The smirk evaporated. 'I'm sorry, Mr . . .'

'Darker.'

'Yes, Mr Darker. Did you have an appointment to see him?'

'I did. I was supposed to see him at his office, but he didn't show up.' Gordo reached into the back seat of the car and came back with a manila file folder. He slid the mugshot of Foerster from the file. It was a big, glossy, five by seven. He handed the photo to the guard. 'I wanted to talk to him about the man in this photo. Have you seen this man on these premises?'

The Cow-lick frowned now. He held the photo gingerly, between two fingers, like it might pass on an infection. A long moment passed. The guard's eyes gave everything away. He'd seen the man. He wanted to do the right thing here, but he wasn't exactly sure what the right thing was. His job, first and foremost, was to protect the interests of the resident. But his passion was law enforcement. He probably listened to a police radio at home.

'He's a vagrant that hangs around downtown,' he said, handing the glossy back. But Gordo didn't take it. He left the Cow-lick's hand floating there, holding the photo out in the space between the guardhouse and the car window.

'No,' Gordo said, sinking his teeth in. 'He's not a vagrant. He's an escaped convict wanted for multiple rapes and murders in New York City.'

The Cow-lick's eyes did a funny thing. Jonah would say they darted. Sure, that was it. They darted down to the photo in his hand. Then they darted up again. Behind the Cow-lick, the other guard stood up from his desk. Now he hovered there, unsure whether to come forward or not.

'I can't speak to that opinion,' the Cow-lick said.

'It's not an opinion. It's a fact. This man's name is Davis Foerster. He finds old women who are alone in their apartments, he rapes them, and then he kills them. He's a known associate of Tyler Gant. You may not know what kind of people live in your little' – Gordo made an exasperated gesture at the gatehouse, at the surrounding property, at the young guard himself – 'community here, but I do. Listen. No bullshit now. We're looking for Davis Foerster. We've driven a long way, we're tired, and we're starting to get irritated. Has Foerster been here, let's say, during the past forty-eight hours? He has, right?'

The Cow-lick had moved into new emotional territory. He was a good kid – somehow, he had never learned how to lie. Gordo had struck the bull's-eye, and the Cow-lick was impaled now, blank face staring straight ahead. Behind him in the tiny space, his friend paced back and forth, hands in pockets.

'I don't know what you're talking about,' the Cow-lick said.

'Buddy, let me tell you this. If I find out Foerster was here, I am personally going to arrest you and charge you with obstructing a criminal investigation, conspiracy to obstruct, aiding and abetting a known fugitive, conspiracy to aid and abet, and every other appropriate felony my friend the District Attorney can dream up. Then I'm going to extradite you to New York, where you're going to sit in a holding cell for two days with twenty of the most violent subhumans on earth. If you survive long enough to make bail, I'll be waiting outside on the courthouse steps, where I will personally rip your nuts off and ram them down your throat.'

The other guard stepped forward now. He nudged the Cow-lick out of his way. 'Mrs Gant is home today. Mr Gant's wife. She's preparing for a party. Maybe you should talk to her about all this.'

'That sounds like a good idea,' Gordo said. 'Open the gate, please, and we'll go talk to Mrs Gant. And when we're done, we'll come back and see if you boys have changed your minds about whether Foerster was here.'

'Do you want your photo back?' the second guard said.

'That's OK. You go ahead and study it. I have more.'

As the gate slid open, Jonah watched the two young guards. He could see it in their stricken faces – they would spend the next fifteen minutes in a fevered argument, trying to get their stories straight. They probably wouldn't even be there when Jonah and Gordo came back from Gant's house.

It was almost a shame, Jonah reflected, that Gordo wasn't actually a cop.

Katie hadn't slept. She had lain awake all night, staring into darkness. She didn't know when she might sleep again.

She stood on the stone terrace, watching a couple of workmen assemble the low wooden platform where, in a few hours, the band could set up its equipment. Down in the backyard, a few people from the party supplier were using noisy air-blowers to put up the giant inflatable monsters. As she watched, a nine-foot tall Frankenstein monster quickly took shape. Nearby, a huge orange Jack-o'-Lantern was already up and grinning malevolently. Inside the kitchen, two women from the caterer were preparing hors d'oeuvres. In a little while, the caterer herself would be here to do the walk-through, to determine how many roving servers they would need, how many stationary servers, and where to set up the beer and wine bar.

On the surface, these were the things happening. On a deeper level, something else was going on, something terrifying.

She had spent four hours in Tyler's study last night. Mostly, there was nothing much in there. In fact, it seemed like he rarely used the place. Two small, identical metal filing cabinets sat in a corner – one empty, one full. The full one had files dating back nearly a decade, insurance papers, brief contracts to carry out this or that security role. The empty one? She didn't know. Maybe he'd bought them at the same time, thinking he'd have more paperwork to file than he ended up having.

Some framed photos hung on the walls. A very young Tyler, maybe twelve years old, photographed with his father. They were dressed in flannel shirts, wool pants and boots, and were crouched in the woods somewhere, facing the camera with big smiles. Each of them held a rifle. Between them on the ground, flat on its stomach was a large black bear, dead, also facing the camera. The bear was larger than both of them combined. Other photos showed Tyler with members of his unit in Vietnam; at a graduation ceremony of some kind; in a police dress uniform shaking hands with the man who was Vice-President of the United States when Katie was in junior high school – she remembered the face but couldn't think of the name. People on television used to crack jokes about how dumb the man was. They were nice photos, she supposed, though she noticed with a sting that there weren't any of her and Tyler.

A slim blue telephone sat on the polished cherrywood desk – the mysterious landline phone that she heard ringing from time to time. She picked up the receiver and it beeped several times before offering a dial tone, indicating there were unchecked voice mail messages on there. The only other item on the desk was a wire inbox, empty.

The desk itself was mostly empty. A few pens and pencils rolled around inside the centre drawer. The shallow drawer on the right side contained some piles of magazines – *Soldier of Fortune, Guns and Ammo* – all more than a year old. The deep drawer below it was locked, but the key was in the centre drawer with the pens and pencils. Inside the deep drawer she found a pile of stuff – a manual on gun maintenance, a warranty and instruction booklet for Tyler's laptop computer, half a sheaf of blank paper, some random wiring and an old digital pager, among other things. Buried at the bottom was a scrapbook, of sorts.

Even now, as Katie watched two men come down along the side yard and into the back, she tried to erase the horror of that book from her mind. She remembered something – some image of herself and Tyler holding hands and walking on the beach in the early days, some remnant of what they once had between them. It was good at first, and Katie would even go so far as to say it was beautiful. Tyler had only recently retired, and he had moved down from Philadelphia to a condo on the Delaware coast. In some ways, he seemed so young for a man in his fifties – almost like a child, riding his Styrofoam boogie board in the ocean, doing handstands and cartwheels on the sand. But then there were the dinners out, and nights lying by the fire in his living room. When she was with him, she felt loved, and she felt safe. The truth was she felt like she was home again. If the scrapbook meant what she suspected it meant, the beauty of that time was destroyed now. In fact, it had always been a lie.

The two men entering the yard were big, one black and one white, in dress shirts, slacks and shoes. She noticed the black man first. He was tall and muscular, with the inverted triangle shape – narrow at the feet and ankles, powerful legs, broad at the chest and shoulders – that would make him a beautiful artist's model if he were able to hold a pose long enough. He was also stylish, with clothes cut to his body and close-cropped hair. A diamond stud glinted in his left ear. He moved fluidly, like an athlete, and with just the hint of a swagger.

The white guy was thick from top to bottom. His clothes hung loosely, like he'd picked them off the close-out rack without bothering to try them on. He could use a haircut. Although it was only early afternoon, his face sported a five o'clock shadow. Either he needed to move one step closer to the razor, or he had facial hair that grew at time-lapse pace. He seemed to stomp when he walked, and she imagined that if she went down there she would find his heavy footprints in the grass. The two men stopped and talked with the man inflating the Frankenstein. The man pointed up at the house, and all three of them looked her way. They would probably tell her she needed a permit of some kind after last year's noise complaints. More party business – she could deal with it.

Tyler called his scrapbook *Items of Interest*. He'd written the phrase on a piece of white surgical tape, and affixed the tape to the top of the front cover. It was the kind of book people saved old photographs in. Each page had clingy, see-through plastic matting you could peel up and press down again. The first page held a copy of the photo showing Tyler and his dad with the dead bear. The handwritten caption beneath it read: *Black Bear/Maine Woods/Sept 1961*.

The next few pages held old press clippings referring to an incident during the Vietnam War. *Possible Massacre Investigated*, read one headline. *Infantry Commander Denies Atrocity*, read another. The same grainy black-and-white photo accompanied each article, showing the remains of a burned-out village.

Katie flipped forward a few pages. Till that moment, she had stood by the desk with the book open in her arms. After seeing what was next, she slid into the desk chair. There were a series of clippings here, from the 1980s and into the early 1990s. Each clipping was a news story about a murdered prostitute, five in Philadelphia, one each in Camden, New Jersey and Chester, Pennsylvania. A few pages later, clippings about murdered gang members began. The murders took place over several years. All of them were unsolved. This was bad enough. But what accompanied the clippings was the stuff of nightmares.

Next to each clipping was taped an instant photograph. Katie remembered photos like these – the cameras were called Polaroids, and they would spit out a blank card after you pressed the button. The picture would appear like a miracle on the blank card just a few minutes later. In Tyler's book, all the Polaroid photos were of dead people.

She couldn't look at them. All she was left with were impressions – staring eyes, bloodied faces. *The photos are trophies. This is a trophy book.*

She flipped pages randomly then, skimming across more news clippings, looking for some reason why this book was OK. These weren't trophies. These were cases Tyler had worked on, cases that had never closed and that he still wondered about, that he still wanted to solve. Of course, that was it. Headlines jumped out at her, each more recent than the ones before: *Outspoken*

Ohio Congressman, Family, Die in Campaign Plane Crash. Billionaire Dallas Oilman Found Dead in Florida Motel. Anthrax Suspected in Illinois Attack that Killed Eighteen. The anthrax clippings went on for several pages. Some of the clippings were from newspapers in other countries. Some were in other languages.

She shook away the memory. The two men, black and white, climbed the stone terrace steps and walked towards her. Their eyes focused on her and she caught an image of a wounded gazelle on the savannah, two lions approaching, hunger in their eyes. Something told her these men weren't here about the party. She had a moment, no more than an instant, when she wondered how they had got past the guards.

'Mrs Gant,' the heavyset man said. He introduced himself as someone with the New York City Police Department. He introduced his partner as someone else with the same department. She didn't catch all of it. The heavy man held out a glossy photograph to her and she took it. It was a mugshot, even she could see that. The man in the picture had sandy blond hair. His face was bruised, one eye was nearly shut. His mouth hung partly open. The lines on the wall behind him suggested he was about five feet, eight inches tall. He was the man Tyler had beaten half to death in the kitchen just two days ago.

'Did you happen to see this man?' the handsome black man said. He spoke softly. He gave her a half-smile. She got the impression it didn't really matter whether she'd seen the man in the picture or not. Either way was OK.

She moved to hand the photo back, but neither man would take it from her. 'Who is he?' she heard herself say. 'Officer . . .'

'Maxwell,' the black man said. 'Please call me Jonah.' This close to him, he was nearly a full head taller than she was. He had white teeth. His skin was very smooth and clear. 'The man in the picture is an escaped felon. He's wanted for multiple homicides and rapes in New York City. We have reason to believe he's been here to your house.' He hesitated for a few seconds, as if what he was about to say embarrassed him.

'We think he's a friend of your husband.'

* * *

The woman was out on her feet. Gordo watched her weave and stumble, like a punch-drunk palooka. If she were a boxer, she'd barely even have her hands up any more. The referee would have to stop the fight.

She'd seen Foerster, all right, and it was recently. She was going to deny it, and that was OK. The information was all over her pretty face. It was in her body language. She had tried to hand the mugshot back like it burned her skin. She hugged herself, the photo rolled up like a bugle in one hand, her body closed off from them and facing away at an angle. She looked up into Jonah's eyes, then down at the tiled stone of the terrace, then out at the crazy rubber lawn ornaments the worker bees were busy putting up. She hardly glanced at Gordo.

That was OK, too. She was in a fragile state and there were a bunch of people around. It felt like a good idea to let Jonah work his magic on her, charm her, try to win her over to their side. It was probably no good to try to break her right now, in front of everyone, even though she seemed ripe for the breaking.

'You see, it's just that I'm very busy today.'

'I see that,' Jonah said. 'It looks like you're about to throw a Halloween party.'

'Yes, that's right. I am. Tonight. We throw one every year. It's just been getting bigger and bigger.'

'The logistics of something like this must be . . .'

'They are. Incredible. I'm pulling my hair out.'

Gordo ignored the bullshit talk and took a moment to survey his surroundings. Giant brick house, with a rolling, tree-lined back lawn and a big in-ground pool. The size of the chimney suggested a massive stone hearth in the living room, with smaller fireplaces in other rooms. They could lease the backyard as a practice range for weekend golfers. Everything was well maintained – the grass healthy and newly cut, the brickwork recently re-faced, the windows modern, the paint fresh. The water in the pool was blue and sparkling. He and Jonah had passed several beautiful homes after they'd bluffed past the guards, but this one was the winner.

Gordo had forgotten, or maybe he simply hadn't known, that people still lived like this. His thoughts went to his brother. He recognised, without dwelling on it for too long, that if he could take this house away from the Gants and give it to Ronny, he would do so.

'I know this is a sensitive matter,' Jonah said. 'Perhaps we could go inside for a few minutes.' He indicated the hovering workers with his eyes and gestured with an open palm towards the sliding glass doors.

'I'm not sure what good that would do,' the woman said. 'I don't think I've seen this man you're looking for.' She held up Foerster's picture and seemed surprised to see what she had done to it. 'I'm sorry. It looks like I crushed your photograph.'

'Mrs Gant, can I call you . . .'

'Katie. Yes, that's fine.'

Jonah spoke in soothing tones. He moved closer to her, invading her space just a little. If he were using other words, Gordo could almost imagine Jonah was trying to pick the woman up. 'Katie, don't worry about the photo. We have more. But I really feel that just a few minutes of your time, and a few questions, will resolve any lingering concerns we have about your husband. We've travelled a long way to catch the man in the photo. He's a rapist and he's a murderer. We're worried that he's been inside your home. Please, let's talk privately, inside.'

She shook her head. 'Well, it's just that my husband is away on business right now. I have all these people here. The caterer is coming in a few minutes. I'm really over my head at the moment, and then, you know, you hit me with this. Is it possible you can come back at another time?'

'Katie, I'm not sure you understand your situation. We're with the police. We can take you in right now.'

'Take me in? Take me in for what?' Her eyes were very large. Her lower lip quivered a tiny amount.

'Questioning,' Gordo said.

'How about tomorrow? Can you come back tomorrow? It'll just give me a little time to . . . I mean, the party's tonight, you know? I have a lot to do. Tomorrow would be better.'

Gordo gave her a serious frown. 'This isn't up for debate.'

'Listen,' she said. 'I have an idea. Come back for the party. Why not? Tyler will be home from his trip later this afternoon.'

Jonah shrugged and looked at Gordo. 'That might work.'

Work? Gordo couldn't picture anything working better. If the woman wanted to offer them free rein to wander around her house while it was crowded with people, Gordo thought that was just fine. What she really wanted was for them to leave. She didn't seem to care about, or hadn't thought through, the price she would pay in the future to make that happen right now.

'I don't know,' Gordo said. 'I'm not sure that's what we had in mind.'

'Please. Be my guests. You can talk to Tyler and you'll see there's nothing at all to this. I'm sure he doesn't even know that man.'

'Is it a masquerade?' Jonah said.

'The party? Yes, it is. Probably ninety per cent of the guests will wear a costume. A few stick-in-the-muds won't, but nearly everybody else will.'

Gordo took a long moment. He didn't want to appear too eager. 'How will we get in? I mean, there's a gatehouse. I doubt the guards will just let anybody wearing a costume on to the grounds.'

Her eyes spoke directly to Gordo, telling him that somewhere deep down, maybe so deep she wasn't consciously aware of it, she'd hoped he wouldn't think of that. 'Oh. Yeah, you'll need invitations. I have some extra ones inside. They have a computer chip embedded in them. The guards will scan the invitation and let you in.'

'High tech,' Jonah said, flashing a winning smile. 'I like it.' His smile suggested that the ugly business from before, talk about rapes and murders and coming in for questioning, was over. They were all going to be friends now, good friends who were just having a party.

Foerster's brain was on fire.

He could feel the synapses in there, crackling and firing, processing information, growing new connections all the time. It made his scalp itch. He checked his watch and it was already late afternoon. He had sat down and started working almost as soon as Gant had shown him the lab. Except for a couple of naps and a couple of smoke breaks, he'd been working ever since. An entire night and most of a day had flown by.

Mama had outdone herself with the lab. Being in there was like going to fucking Disneyland. It must have cost a lot of money to set this up. First off, Foerster's lab took up half the boat. That wasn't immediately obvious when you were in the main cabin – what was obvious was that the boat was cramped and a little cluttered. But pass through that door, and the whole feeling changed. It was like entering another world.

In here, Foerster had space to move around. He had a large, well-lit work table against one wall with two workstations and a splash guard running the length of it. He had a high-powered microscope, two incubators, a refrigerator and an autoclave. He had an electric agitator, a microwave oven, an egg timer, and a sink with a dedicated water supply. He had two Bunsen burners, a fire extinguisher, some liquid droppers with digital readouts for measuring precise amounts, digital thermometers, and stacks and stacks of consumable supplies – Petri dishes, rubber gloves, masks, beakers, and everything else.

There was a walk-in storeroom with hundreds of litres of alkaline peptone water, the perfect medium to promote the growth of the cholera, while killing off any unwanted bacteria. That's where the massive colonies of Cholera B would live. The culturing media were also in the storeroom – blood agar, TCBS – as well as thirty or forty hundred-litre carboys. The whole lab was run on a huge, dedicated battery behind a panel in one of the walls. A wall-mounted meter told Foerster how much juice was left in the battery, and if it got low, he had to get Vernon or Mama to run the engine for a few hours to power it up again. There were solar panels mounted towards the back of the roof, which, during the daytime, were constantly rejuicing the battery – Foerster doubted he was getting much more than a trickle from that. Finally, there was a diesel generator, also in the storeroom, in case the boat engine failed for any reason.

When it came down to it, the boat existed to support the lab. That had probably been true two years ago, but he'd never thought of it that way.

Now that he saw the truth, he finally understood his own importance. He was one of the keys to the operation – at least this part of it. The other key was the cholera itself.

It was some scary shit. According to its makers, Cholera B's virulence was more than ten times higher than normal. A person usually needed to ingest about a million individual organisms of cholera to reliably get the disease. With Cholera B, it might take less than a hundred thousand. Normally, most of the bacteria got killed off by the acids in a person's stomach. But Cholera B was resistant to human stomach acids. And that wasn't all. When people knew of a local cholera outbreak, usually they avoided getting it by boiling the drinking water, and killing off the cholera that way. Cholera B was resistant to heat.

When Foerster read that, he called bullshit. Stomach acids, OK. But heat? So he took some of the small early colonies and boiled them. He boiled the first one for five minutes, timing it from the moment the roiling boil started. He figured five minutes of waiting for a little water would exhaust the average chimp's patience. No good. The colony was still alive. He boiled the next one for seven minutes. Then he went to ten, and twelve, and finally fifteen minutes. At fifteen minutes, the water had basically boiled off. In the bit remaining, he still found a few organisms alive.

At that moment, how he handled himself in the lab changed. Foerster was a little lazy – he knew that. He hadn't worn his lab coat, his protective glasses, a mask, or even gloves at first. He started wearing them all the time.

Vernon had come in earlier and watched him work for a little while. It took some time before Foerster noticed what Vernon had on. The big ape was wearing a T-shirt, cut-off shorts, and flip-flops.

'Man, I don't think you want to be in here dressed like that.'

Vernon was leaning up against the doorway. 'Why?'

'Because this shit is dangerous, that's why. I don't really need you in here if I'm gonna have to worry about some of it spilling on you.'

Vernon shrugged and left. After that, Foerster kept the door closed and locked. What kind of security procedures had it so somebody who had no fucking idea what they were doing could just wander in at any time? Keeping the door locked was for Vernon's, and everybody's, own good. They didn't want to be in here. The Cholera B was so deadly that it would kill as many as ninety-five per cent of the people infected with it, usually within twenty-four hours. And dying of cholera was no way to go. A whole bunch of people were about to find that out.

Given the water towers Gant had described to him, Foerster guessed that ten, or more likely fifteen, hundred-litre carboys of the stuff, per water tower, at the right concentration, would lead to the outbreak they were looking for. It would happen so fast that most of the people involved would be dead or dying before the outside world knew there was a problem. By the time any kind of rescue effort got going, the only people still alive would be the listless five per cent who survived the infection, and any person lucky enough to have avoided drinking the water, or being exposed to people who did, the previous day.

Amazing.

Even more amazing was how soon it could happen. At the rate normal cholera multiplied, and with some trial and error in the process, it might take Foerster a few weeks or a month to grow the right amount. But Cholera B also multiplied faster than normal – a lot faster. Less than twenty-four hours into this, he was astounded at how fast the shit was multiplying. He'd never seen anything like it. How could it happen so fast? It scared him. In fact, it scared him even more than the heat resistance. Be that as it may, the accelerated reproduction, combined with the high virulence, meant that Foerster could have the necessary amount ready in just a couple of days.

That left only one issue still nagging at him. Did it really work? Would it in fact kill anybody? Gant didn't seem too worried, but it weighed on Foerster a little. They could never be sure, right up to the point when they put the stuff in the water towers, whether anything would even happen. All this effort could wind up being for nothing.

It would be nice, Foerster realised, to have a test subject to try it on.

* * *

They showed up fashionably late to the party. In fact, they had never quite left. Jonah hung around the grounds at the house while Gordo took the car, ran out and bought costumes. There was so much going on, and so many workers wandering around, that nobody – except Katie Gant – seemed to notice Jonah at all. She marched here and there, with this or that clipboard-wielding woman in tow, making all of the last-minute preparations. Occasionally her and Jonah's eyes met. She didn't say anything or make him try to leave. She didn't look like she was trying to warn anyone away, and she didn't seem about to flee herself. What she seemed was very, very nervous. Meanwhile, Jonah did his best to act natural. At one point, he went into the huge, gleaming kitchen, got a bottle of beer from one of the refrigerators, and drank it on the back deck, looking out at all of the activity.

At some point, Gordo called him on his cell phone, and Jonah went out to the car. It was mid-afternoon and the sun was already setting. Gordo, already dressed as a hobo, pulled maybe a hundred yards from the bottom of the driveway, and Jonah slipped into his own costume – the Lone Ranger. Then they sat and watched the guests pull in. At one point, early on, a sleek black limo came. A man climbed out with a couple of travel bags – Tyler Gant had arrived home.

Now, at least fifty cars were parked in the Gants' sloping, circular driveway. They parked at the bottom, and Jonah dug the makes and models as he and Gordo walked up the hill towards the house. Some old-style luxury cars were here – Porsche, Mercedes, Lexus – but they were in the minority. The new thing was concept cars. Tiny, egg-shaped two-seaters, gas-electric hybrids that got more than a hundred miles to a gallon of gas. High-performance electric cars. Even a few eccentric retro-fits – like a red Alpha Romeo with solar photovoltaic mesh embedded on every square-inch of its exterior.

'We can just play this cool,' Gordo said. His hobo costume included a crazy, oversized patchwork jacket, baggy pants, a crushed velvet hat pulled down over his eyes and a cigar plastered in his mouth. He hadn't shaved in twenty-four hours, so his thick beard was coming out. The jacket and pants had extra pockets – deep inside his costume, Gordo carried a pair of handcuffs, a gun, a small bottle of ether and a rag. He also had his detective's badge.

Jonah had a small black mask covering his eyes. He also had handcuffs on him and a small bottle of pepper spray. A real gun, the semi-auto Gordo had fired at the bomzhies, dangled from his costume gun belt.

'We don't really need to talk to Gant right away,' Gordo said. 'And we don't need to show ourselves to Mrs Gant. She'll be busy hosting, so we'll let her do her thing. The one to keep an eye out for is Foerster. If he pops up, we knock him out and cuff him. That simple. I'll pull the badge, we tell everybody we're police officers, and then we're out of here. If we have to draw guns, we do it, but hopefully it won't come to that.'

They walked along the side of the house, as they had earlier in the day. Jonah heard a three-piece band as they approached – guitar, bass and drums doing a little something, maybe just getting warmed up. Out on the back lawn, the inflatable monsters loomed. They were lit up from the inside. Frankenstein was there, a vampire, a ghoul of some kind, and that giant Jack-o'-Lantern. On the pool, lily pads floated, each with a lit candle at its centre. Maybe a hundred people milled around beneath the monsters, drinking and talking and laughing.

'What if we don't see Foerster?' Jonah said.

Gordo shrugged. 'Play it by ear. Have a couple of drinks. Wait around and see what happens. People are probably starting to liquor up. We let the party get hopping, and maybe Foerster suddenly turns up. Maybe he doesn't. If that happens, maybe we let everybody leave, we corner Gant, soften him up a little, and get him to tell us what he knows.'

'You give the signal. I'll be ready.'

They climbed the steps to the terrace. The band was up here, but so was the bar. Jonah waited a moment in line behind Gordo, and got a glass of red wine. The wine glass was made of clear plastic. He took a moment to look around at the crowd. Monsters, gangsters, and 1920s flappers moved to and fro. A caveman walked by with a big club over his shoulder. Gordo had already attached himself to a knot of chatting people.

Katie Gant came up the steps wearing a black catwoman suit. It came complete with utility belt, hood and high-heeled boots. She had the body for it. Her blond hair was tucked away somewhere under the hood, she had painted her face with whiskers, and had used some mascara to give herself cat's eyes. Damn, she was pretty. She saw Jonah there, recognised him, gave him a small wave and a shallow party smile, but then kept on going into the house. She didn't want to talk right now, he supposed. He watched her go – body twisting and sashaying through the crowd.

Jonah ambled over to the group Gordo had joined. The five people broke into laughter just as Jonah arrived.

'OK, Tyler,' an enormously overweight woman said. 'I guess you know where the bodies are buried.' The woman was dressed, as far as Jonah could tell, as Cleopatra. She wore a shimmering gold robe that hugged the folds of her body, and a headpiece with a bright red plastic ruby in the centre of it.

'What're you drinking there, Tyler?' a man in a court jester outfit said. 'I didn't see them serving those at the bar.'

The man named Tyler in question stood maybe five foot ten, maybe less, slim but with good, round shoulders. He wore slacks and a tight, horizontally striped red and white T-shirt. Boat shoes covered his bare feet, and a white sailor's cap sat perched on top of his head. He had grey hair, cut almost to his scalp, and his skin was brown and red, tan bordering on sunburned. Crow's feet around the eyes and lines around his mouth betrayed his age. He had the body of a guy who had wrestled in college and had worked hard at keeping it together. He held himself straight and tall. The torso beneath that T-shirt was still sculpted, giving no quarter to the passing decades. Jonah had seen photos of this man on Gordo's computer screen. In person, Tyler Gant looked pretty strong.

Gant considered the amber liquid in his glass. 'I'm drinking straight whiskey,' he said with a shrug. 'I guess it helps if you own the place.' The little group laughed, including Gordo. Gant smiled, really putting it on. Jonah didn't believe that smile for even one second.

'Everybody,' Gant said, 'have a good time. It's great to see you, but the boss says I have to keep mingling.'

'Nice guy,' Gordo said to the group after Gant had left. 'I wonder what he does for a living.'

Katie was ready to vomit.

She slipped through the crowds on autopilot. She jumped from group to group, she laughed at the jokes, and she feigned interest in the gossip. But she was living in a nightmare. She could barely hear what the people were saying.

A woman dressed as a dairy cow – one of Katie's good friends – pulled her aside. 'Katie, this is the best one yet.' A woman dressed as a baseball player said, 'Katie, how do you keep that body?' A drunken man dressed in a red Satan costume, complete with tail and horns, swerved into her path. He had a pot belly. Katie had never seen him before, but he took one of her hands and tried to pull her towards him. She slipped out of his grasp with a grin.

'Better luck next time,' she said, but her skin broke out in gooseflesh at the thought of Tyler seeing him do that.

Tyler had come home late from his business trip. All day, she had dreaded his return, and the delay had made it worse. By the time he came in, it was early evening and dark outside. She had already squeezed into her skin-tight cat suit. The servers were putting their trays together in the kitchen. The bartender was opening a couple of wine bottles. The band had set up its equipment and told her they were ready any time. The first guests had even begun to arrive. She drank a glass of wine to calm her nerves, and paced back and forth on the terrace, looking at the glowing monsters in the backyard. Her body trembled a tiny amount.

'It's going to be fine,' the bartender told her. He was young and good-looking, in a white shirt and bow tie, his hair greased back from his forehead. He could have passed for an actor. He smiled broadly. 'I worked this party last year, remember? Everybody had a great time.'

'You're right,' she said. 'I know. Everything's going to be just fine.'

It was easy to say, but hard to believe. The tall, good-looking cop had stayed at the house for more than an hour. He didn't ask – he just did it. He stood around, watching her every move. She felt his eyes on her even when he was nowhere in sight. She began to worry that he would still be standing there when Tyler came home. Thankfully, he was gone by then, but not by any effort on her part. She didn't ask him to leave. She didn't say anything to him, even when she saw him drinking a beer from her refrigerator. He acted like he owned the place.

When Tyler finally came in, he seemed fine. Distant, as usual. A little tired, maybe, because his flight had been delayed several hours. *His flight from where?* She didn't know. But that was OK. He might also have been a little drunk already – maybe he'd had some drinks on the plane, or in the car from the airport. He stopped and looked her over before carrying his bags upstairs. Then he gave a tight little smile and indicated her costume with a slight bob of his head. 'You sure you want to wear that?'

She glanced down at herself. She was proud of her body, and she thought justifiably so. 'I'm comfortable with it.'

He shrugged. 'If you got it, you might as well flaunt it.'

He didn't come back downstairs for forty-five minutes. When he did, he wore a very basic sailor's outfit. That was fine. At least it was something. He was playing along, and he looked good. He ignored the bar on the terrace, went into his own liquor cabinet and poured himself a glass of whiskey. That was less good, but she wasn't going to argue with him about it.

She stood alone at the sliding glass doors to the terrace when he sidled up to her. The party was unfolding in the backyard. People were here – the cream of Charleston society. Business leaders, politicians, old money, new money. They were drinking, they were mingling, and more cars arrived in the driveway all the time. Normally, this was when she would begin to relax. Tyler put an arm around her, something he hadn't done in a very long time. Her heart knocked on her chest a couple of times.

'The guard at the gate told me something funny,' he said.

'Oh? What was that?' Her voice sounded stiff and unconvincing to her own ears.

'He told me the police were here today, looking to talk to me.'

'That's true.'

'I find it odd that you didn't mention it.'

She shrugged. She had prepared herself for this one. 'I was busy today. People were coming and going all day. A couple of detectives came, and I told them you weren't home. I asked them to come back another time and they said they would. I just figured it had something to do with your work.' She turned her head and looked into his eyes. Something strange was in those eyes, but she kept to her script. 'I didn't think of it when you came in. I've got other things on my mind right now.'

His eyes never wavered from hers. His mouth moved and he said something she hadn't prepared for. 'I know you were in my office.'

His arm tightened around her waist. He pulled her closer. A guest at the party might think they were sharing an intimate moment. She focused on his mouth. His teeth were very close to her face. The whiskey was already on his breath. His grip was almost painful.

'I'm not stupid, Katie. I had ten different security traps set up in that room, and you tripped all of them. You took the door off, right? And then put it back on. You'd never gone in there before, right? Not since I locked the place up. See? I know. You went in my file cabinet. You went in my desk. You looked at my book.'

The knowledge of what was in that book floated there between them. She had allowed herself a last strand of hope that the book was something besides what it appeared to be. Now that hope was crushed. She was looking into the eyes of a monster. How could she not have known?

He sighed. 'These things, by themselves, aren't the end of the world. I wish you hadn't gone in there in the first place, but I think we can overcome it. Hell, I probably wanted you to see the book, or else I never would have left it in that drawer, right? But the police were here, and that raises some difficult questions. Did you bring them in there? Did you show them the book?'

She didn't even try to lie. She didn't try to pretend he was wrong about her. She was exposed now, everything was out in the open, and the important thing was for him to see she was telling the truth. 'No. I didn't.'

He nodded. 'You're absolutely sure of that?'

'Positive. It was just a coincidence that the police came. I didn't show them anything. They were here for five minutes.'

'OK, I'm willing to buy that. But then why did you go in my room? Why now, after all this time? Why all of a sudden?'

She shook her head. 'I was curious, that's all. I was just curious. You hurt that man and—'

'What man?'

'The man who was here the other day.'

His grip tightened again. His fingers were like talons. 'Katie, get one thing straight in your mind. This is the only thing you need to know.' He spoke slowly now, enunciating every syllable. 'You didn't see any man here the other day. There might have been a man, there might not have been, but you don't know because you didn't see anyone. OK?'

She could not look at her husband's face. She stared instead at his red-and-white-striped chest. 'OK.'

'Good. Now I'm going to go enjoy the party and I suggest you do the same. We'll talk about everything else later, after our guests go home.'

He left her then and moved through the growing crowd, fluid, charming, the lord of the manor. She caught a glimpse of him from time to time, holding court at various small groups, laughing, accepting compliments and returning them. She made the rounds feeling stale and brittle. When anyone touched her, she had to stifle a shriek. She got herself a plastic tumbler from the kitchen, went behind the bar and poured herself a big one. A while later, she saw it was empty and poured another.

At some point, she noticed the policemen had come back. She watched them from the corner of her eye. The heavy one had come as a hobo. The good-looking one – Jonah was his name – was dressed as the Lone Ranger. Neither one made any attempt to talk to her. They mixed among the guests, they drank beer and wine, and the heavy one even went out on the dance floor in the backyard. It was like they hadn't come here to see Tyler, or Katie, at all. Instead, they seemed to have come for the party itself. If Tyler knew they were cops, he gave no sign.

Even through a haze of alcohol, she knew she was in trouble. She'd made a terrible mistake opening that door. There was no telling what Tyler would do when this party was over. Would he kill her? No. She was sure he wouldn't. Not tonight. He was too crafty for that – he only killed people when he knew he could get away with it. But she realised now that she was afraid of him – very, very afraid.

Maybe there was some way, without Tyler noticing, that she could get a message to these policemen. But even if she could, what would she tell them?

Time passed, and Jonah had grown tired of the party. It had been a long goddamned day.

People were drunk now, and bordering on stupid. A mob of people were out on the dance floor, moving badly to the band, bumping and grinding. The band itself was drunk, and had lost its edge. Their sound was all over the place. A man in a gorilla suit had jumped into the swimming pool.

Jonah had downed a few glasses of wine and then started in on beer. He drank four bottles of beer. He was seriously buzzed, and he made a pledge to slow down. A few people had left. More were beginning to. He looked around for Gordo and spotted him down on the back lawn, dancing. He was one of the worst dancers out there.

Was this how they were supposed to catch Foerster? No matter, because the bastard hadn't shown up anyway. It made sense – Gant would never allow someone like Foerster near all these rich people.

Jonah went through the sliding glass doors and into the kitchen. More drunk people were milling around in there. He took a look around. It was a big white gleaming kitchen, as large as a restaurant's kitchen, a showpiece. There was a long island running down the middle, where someone had laid out crackers and cheese and grapes and carved-up roast beef on open-face bread, along with a host of other food selections. Maybe the servers had gone home.

Jonah took some crackers and a small cut of the sandwich. Katie Gant was there, talking to several people. She looked good. Better than good. She looked like dessert. He decided now might be the time to talk to her. She saw him – she couldn't miss him since he was the one black man in the room – but she made no move to acknowledge his presence. He shrugged and waited. Still no move. She didn't even glance his way again.

The overweight Cleopatra from earlier in the night squeezed past him on her way to say hello to someone. 'Hey, big boy. What's all this standing around for? Mingle, dammit!'

Jonah wandered deeper into the house. He stopped at the bathroom, but it wouldn't open. A voice from inside said something, but he couldn't hear what. A woman dressed in the uniform of an auto racer, plastered with corporate logos but without a helmet, passed by and said, 'There's another one upstairs if you're in a hurry.'

'I didn't know upstairs was open to guests.'

She smiled and flipped her long black hair. 'I'm sure no one will mind.'

The stairs were down the hall from the bathroom door. Jonah went on up. They were wide and curved to the left. The first floor was high ceilings, big windows and hardwood floors. Whatever Gant did, he was making money at it.

Jonah found the bathroom. The colour scheme was cream and white, with recessed lighting in the ceiling and two triangular skylights that must have let in natural light during the day. There was a glassed-in shower stall and a tub that could hold two people. All of the surfaces, the floor, the sink basin and countertop, even the tub deck, were made of dark polished marble that seemed to have fossilised shells and tiny sea creatures embedded in it. A second door led out of the bathroom and into a darkened bedroom.

He pulled both doors shut, opened the toilet, steadied himself with a hand against the wall, and did his thing. Afterwards, he went to the sink and washed his hands. He took his mask off and splashed some cold water on his face. *Time to sober up*. Maybe they could still pigeonhole Gant tonight. It wasn't out of the question, though Jonah didn't really feel up to it. Maybe they'd just go back to the motel and figure out something else in the morning.

Jonah sighed as he dried his face on the plush white hand towel. He'd have to peel Gordo away from the dance floor. That sounded like fun. He glanced at himself in the large round mirror over the sink.

Like a ghost, Gant's wife hovered in the bedroom doorway behind him.

8

'Mrs Gant? Katie?'

She waved her hands – don't speak. She pulled the door silently shut behind her and locked it. She went to the other door, the one that led to the hallway, and locked that one, too.

Jonah lowered his voice. 'There was a lady downstairs. She told me it would be OK to use this bathroom.'

She came towards him. Good Lord, she brought that body with her, packed into the clingy cat suit. This close, he could see she was actually shivering. It wasn't that cold in here. Her wide eyes told Jonah the fear was on her.

She spoke in a whisper and paused between each sentence. 'The man. In the photograph you showed me. He was here.'

'When? Tonight?'

She shook her head. 'Two days ago. He's gone now. I don't know where.' Her breath hitched, and she started to tremble. 'Tyler beat him with a gun. There was a lot of blood. I think he might be dead.' Her face broke up now, she hugged herself, but she didn't cry.

Jonah didn't think – he acted. He went to her and put his arms around her shoulders. She was shorter than he was, maybe by half a foot. She stiffened

203

at his embrace, then slowly relaxed into it. She let out a forceful exhalation, as if she'd been holding her breath for a very long time.

'It's OK,' he said. 'We're gonna take care of it.'

'I don't know what to do. I think Tyler's a murderer.'

She was trying to tell him Foerster was dead, and that Gant had killed him. That was too bad, but it was also for later. Jonah had an instinct for things, much in the way Gordo did, but Jonah's instincts were about different things. From the time he was young, he'd known when the time was ripe. It might turn out later that the decision to go forward was wrong – it was a mistake for him or a mistake for her, or both. But he was hardly ever wrong about the timing. He'd only just met this woman, he'd been attracted to her, and had thought that maybe she'd felt the same way about him. Now his internal alarms were going off – the woman was ready. She might not even know it yet, not consciously, but he knew it. She was shaking all over. She reached her arms around his back and pulled herself even closer. They squeezed together, body to body.

'I wanted you,' he heard himself say. 'From the first moment I met you.' The words amazed even him.

'I don't know,' she said.

Jonah didn't know either. But his hands did. They moved along the skin of her costume. They went slow. Jonah knew how to draw it out, and he knew it was important to do so – the knowledge was in his hands. He felt her body, let her feel his. He was patient and he could let it all unwind on its own. She cried quietly against his chest. As she did so, he began to wonder if he was ready. The question made him wince. She started to move her body against him.

Someone knocked on the door. A man's voice came through.

'Is anybody in there?'

That was Tyler's voice.

Her heart galloped. Had she lost her mind? In the bathroom with a man she had only met that morning. She was drunk, that was the problem. She had almost got carried away there for a second. She turned and saw the panic written on Jonah's face. The handsome police detective. His eyes were wide, his mouth a comical O. Katie almost laughed.

'It's just me,' she said. 'I'm not feeling so good. I'll be out in a minute.'

She and her new friend stood still. To Katie, he looked like he might never move again, just remain there, turned to stone.

'Are you all right?' came the voice through the door. 'People are leaving and want to say goodbye. They're wondering where you went.'

'I'm fine. Just please tell them I'm coming.'

Tyler didn't answer. He was gone and there was no sound on the other side of the door. A moment later, he tried the knob on the door from the bedroom. She watched it jiggle but not open. Thank God she had thought to lock it.

'Katie? Open up a second.'

'Tyler, I'm on the toilet. I'm not going to open up. Please, go on downstairs. I'll be out in a few minutes.'

The voice made a noise like a snort, then went away.

Katie stepped away from the Lone Ranger. She had wanted to talk to him about the man in the photograph, and she had wanted to say that she was afraid of her husband. She might have even wanted to tell him about the scrapbook she'd found. She wasn't sure. Instead, he had tried to seduce her, and had done a pretty smooth job of it. If Tyler hadn't shown up ... But there was nothing she could do about any of this now. It would all have to wait till later.

'Tyler?' she called, but no answer came.

A million questions hung in her mind. What if he was standing out there, waiting for her? What if he had seen this man come upstairs first? She thought of Tyler's guns, and somehow, that thought calmed her. Till a couple of days ago, she had never seen him be anything but completely responsible with his guns. He was hardly about to wave one around now, not with a house full of people. She brightened, and realised her brain was still working. She might as well use it. The first order of business was to get this big policeman out of here.

'Tyler?' she said again.

Again there was no answer.

Gant stood motionless inside the big walk-in closet.

On either side of him, a row of coats and dresses and suits wrapped in plastic hung on wooden poles and marched away towards the back of the closet. It was all stuff neither of them wore any more, packed into a closet in a spare bedroom they never used. Ridiculous. Just above his head was a shelf where Katie kept about a dozen pairs of shoes she hadn't looked at in years.

He was drunk. It had been one hell of a day and night. He'd been pouring it on tonight, trying to insulate himself from all the bad news. The cops had been here looking for him. He'd asked the guard what cops these were, but the kid said he wasn't on duty when they came, it was just something he'd heard. Good kid, letting Gant know he was the subject of gossip in the community. And now Katie knew about his book. She said she hadn't shown the cops the book, and he believed her. But her knowing about the book made life complicated all of a sudden.

He was going to have to think long and hard about his next move. If the cops knew Foerster had come here, he'd have to think about ending the operation. Call Vernon, tell him to pull the plug and disappear the mad scientist. Even then, Gant would probably have to undergo questioning, and Katie might, too. It could be a tricky situation. If Katie seemed the least bit squirrelly . . . well, he could leave that for later.

The closet door was open just a crack, affording him a clear view across the darkened bedroom to the bathroom door. He didn't know exactly why he was doing this. It was just a hunch. He'd been watching her, and her sudden exit from the party seemed strange. One minute she was in the kitchen chatting with friends, acting naturally, the next she was making a beeline for the stairs as if she suddenly remembered she had something terribly important to do. When he found her up here in the bathroom, it wasn't so unusual that she wouldn't let him in. No. It was her voice, which seemed high and startled, and the total lack of movement he heard on the other side of the door that bothered him. People usually stopped moving when they were caught doing something they'd rather you didn't know about.

God help her, he thought. God help her if she's been running out on me. And God help the guy, for that matter.

The bathroom door opened a crack.

Gant held his breath.

She made a hand motion, as if to shoo him out.

Jonah stood poised, his hand on the knob. He glanced at Katie one last time. Her face was pinched. She nodded. OK, he thought, here goes nothing. Heart beating, he opened the door and went out through the bedroom.

It was dark in the room, but Jonah saw nobody in the shadows, and he worked his way back around to the hall. The hallway was wide open and empty, so he went downstairs, already feeling better. He'd caught a break and found out Foerster had been here. And the thing with Gant's wife . . . well, they'd see. In the kitchen, he passed among a few guests. An open bottle of wine sat on the counter, so he poured himself a glass. He stood sipping the wine, as if lost in thought. Long moments passed and he waited to see what would happen next.

Through the kitchen doorway, he could see into the dining room. Katie had appeared there. She was talking with two other women. Big Cleopatra was one of them. Then Gant entered the room and went to her.

Somebody tapped Jonah on the shoulder.

Gordo stood behind him. 'Where've you been, man? I've been looking all over for you. The party's ending. Everybody's leaving.'

'Does that include us?'

Gordo shook his head. 'I don't know. I think we should talk to Gant while we have him. Two of us have a go at him, maybe shove his head into the toilet; he might tell us what he knows. What do you think?'

Jonah glanced back at the dining room. Gant and his wife were gone. Cleopatra and the other woman stood by themselves, chatting on.

'Foerster was here,' Jonah said. 'A couple of days ago.'

'Awesome. How did you find that out?'

'Gant's wife told me. She said Gant beat him over the head with a gun. There was a lot of blood. After that, Foerster was gone. It sounds like Gant killed him. That's probably where he was yesterday – getting rid of the body.'

'Really? Shit.'

Jonah looked at Gordo. 'Does it matter? I mean, do they care if we bring him in dead or alive?'

Gordo shrugged. 'Yes, it matters. The reward is for his capture. If he's dead, they're not going to give us any money – they don't like to encourage that sort of thing.' Gordo eyed Jonah closely. 'Listen, how'd you get her to tell you?'

'I don't know. I think she must be drunk.'

'Well, this changes things.'

'Does it?'

'Sure. If he killed Foerster, he's never going to tell us that just because we rough him up a little. He's got too much to lose. He'll also never believe we're cops. He's a former cop himself. And we definitely don't want him to know his wife is giving us information. If Foerster's really dead, maybe she can find out what Gant did with the body and we can still salvage something out of this. *Two bounty hunters break open a murder case* – it could be good advertising for us. If he's not dead, and I hope he's not, maybe she can find out where he is. Listen, if you haven't done it already, slip Gant's wife your phone number and our address at the motel. Tell her we want to meet her away from the house. Get her phone number, too. Then let's get out of here.'

'Got it,' Jonah said. 'Give me a couple of minutes.'

'All right. But let's not take all night.' Gordo backed away and passed through the sliding glass doors to the outside.

Jonah lingered. He took out the motel's business card from his Lone Ranger breast pocket, found a pen in a drawer, and wrote his name and cell phone number along the bottom of the card. He counted to thirty, then headed back through the house.

'Pssst,' somebody said to his right. He turned and there she was again, standing in a doorway. She looked better, less scared than she had in the bathroom. 'Were you going to leave without saying goodbye?' she said. Jonah had trouble with the question. Her face was still serious, but it seemed like a playful thing to say.

'No. I was looking for you. We still need to talk. Are you going to be all right?'

'I think so. There's more that I haven't told you.'

Jonah handed her the card. 'This is where I'm staying. That's my phone number. I can meet you tomorrow.' He paused. He noticed he had burned off the entire night's alcohol consumption in just a few minutes of excitement. 'If you think it isn't safe for you to stay here, you can leave with us right now.'

'No, I think it's fine. I talked with my husband. He seems normal.'

'Either way, can I get your phone number? In case I don't hear from you.'

She handed him a slip of paper. 'Here. I already wrote it down.'

'OK. Thank you.' He put the paper in his pocket. They touched hands, but that was it. Then he went out.

In the driveway, most of the cars were already gone. Gordo sat slumped in the passenger seat of the Honda, his eyes half-closed. He looked like a man ready for a nice long sleep. Jonah put the car in gear and cruised out of the driveway, then a few minutes later, past the gatehouse. The gate on the exit side was open. The overnight guard waved as they passed.

'Who was that man?'

Katie watched the Sullivans roll to the bottom of the long driveway as Tyler spoke. The Sullivans were the last to leave the party. Katie and Tyler stood on the front porch waving to them as the car pulled out on to the street. She turned to him. He held a drink in his hand, another straight whiskey. He didn't smile.

She was still buzzing from the drinks, from the exhaustion, and from the fear. Her head felt like it was wrapped in packing tape. She wasn't sure she had heard him correctly. She hoped she hadn't. The fear came back like a high-speed train. Tyler stared at her.

The porch around them was littered with the detritus of the party: empty plastic cups, dirty paper plates, wet napkins. A couple of candles still burned in their translucent plastic wind guards. The neighbourhood was dark. The nearest house was a hundred yards away.

Tyler's eyes burned red in the gloom. He was drunk, she could see that. In the dim light of the candles, he looked like a demon.

'I'm sorry?' she said.

'The big black man, in the Lone Ranger costume, who you were sneaking around in the locked bathroom with. Who was he?'

Tyler had caught her again. He would always catch her. The truth of that hit her like a punch in the stomach. Whatever it was Tyler did for a living, it involved sneaking around, keeping secrets, telling lies and catching people at lies. If things were how they seemed to be, he'd been killing people for years and getting away with it. There was no sense trying to lie to him. It might actually be safer to tell him the truth.

'He was one of the police detectives,' she said.

He threw his drink in her face. She wasn't expecting it and didn't even have time to flinch. The whiskey stung her eyes and the sharp smell of the alcohol made her gag. She backed away a step. Her hands went to her face and rubbed away the liquid. She was afraid and she was was right to be afraid. Of course Tyler knew about Jonah. How could he not have known? She opened her eyes again, tears streaming down her cheeks.

Then he slapped her.

Flesh struck flesh with the sound of a whip crack. The impact made her ears ring. Her head spun sideways towards the house. A second later, the rest of her body followed. She felt the sting of the slap on her cheek below her left eye.

Things moved fast.

She turned back to him, hand to her face, just in time to see the back of his hand coming for the other cheek. The impact spun her away from the house and towards the stairs. She was flying now, it seemed, everything spinning around her and out of control. She caught the iron railing on the side of the porch and leaned over it.

There were cigarette butts and empty cups in the grass down below, inconsiderate guests throwing their garbage over the side. The strength went out of her legs. Her mind raced. What to do? What to do?

'You must think I'm pretty fucking stupid, huh?'

Make a break for it. Run down the driveway.

She still clung to the railing. She wasn't sure if she could stand without it. She gathered her strength for a burst of speed.

'Right? You think I don't know shit, right?'

She turned to the left, and as fast as she could, she broke for the stairs. For a second, she thought she would make it. She reached the top step. She even put a foot on the step below. Then a strong hand gripped her from behind. The hand pulled the hood of her catwoman suit down. The hood choked her and yanked her backwards.

'Where do you think you're going?'

'Tyler, please,' she heard a voice say. It was her own voice.

'Please, I like that. Now we're getting somewhere.'

He pulled her up the stairs, one hand on her hood and one hand under her arm. Then he spun her around and shoved her – he was surprisingly strong. She lost her balance and stumbled across the porch. She crashed into the heavy oak front door. The door rattled in its frame. She slid down its face like blood running down a wall. She finished on her knees, hands pressed to the wood.

'Tyler!' she screamed. 'Stop it!'

He came up next to her. His hand gripped her hair this time. His face was close to hers, and he whispered with such ferocity that spittle flew from his mouth on to her cheeks. His teeth were bare inches from her. She thought he might bite her.

'You'd better just shut up,' he said. 'Just keep that big mouth shut. We don't want to bother the neighbours, now do we?'

She turned to him.

Patrick Quinlan

His eyes were there, glowing with his madness. She saw it now, saw it as clear as crystal for the first time. How had she never seen it before? It had always been there, hadn't it, lurking just below the surface? Now that she saw it, she realised the truth. Her husband was insane.

'You're going to listen to me,' he said. His face was flushed, maybe from the alcohol, maybe from the exertion. His mouth, so close to her eyes, was all sharp teeth, like razors. It grew larger and larger till it was an abyss. His eyes became slits. She saw him transforming, and her heart pounded beneath her breasts. She felt a surge of something, of some strange power, coursing through her arms and legs.

'You understand me?' he said. 'You understand me?'

His hands gripping her hair, his strong fingers hard against her scalp, he forced her head to nod up and down.

'I understand,' he said. 'I understand.' He smiled. 'Now you say it.' He waited but she said nothing, her mouth clamped tight. 'Come on, say it. I understand.' His hands tightened on her head, one on each side. He pressed hard, as if he were trying to squeeze her head till it exploded. She saw the veins standing out on his forearms. A thick vein throbbed across his forehead. His face was bright red, his eyes wild. The force against her head was like water pressure at the bottom of a deep pool.

'Say it, goddamn you.'

She scratched him.

She did it before she knew she was going to, before she could telegraph it to him with her eyes. She did it before she even knew she was capable of it. Some primal gear, long unused, kicked into action. Then Katie Gant went back to the jungle. She reached for his face and raked the claws of one hand down his cheek. The blood welled up in four even lines, like the rows of a cornfield.

He grunted and now his hands clasped his own face.

'You bitch.'

But she was up and moving by the time he spoke. She made talons of her hands and slapped him with the left, then the right, her nails – she'd painted

212

them black for the party – ripping into him. He backed away. She turned, tore the door open, passed through it and slammed it shut behind her.

She fidgeted with the metal deadbolt. His face appeared in the small window at the top of the door, inches from her own, just on the other side of the glass. She screamed when she saw him. The blood was flowing down his cheek.

Still, he smiled. He wrenched the door open, ripping it from her grasp. She screamed again and backed away. She should have gone for the eyes. She wouldn't make that mistake twice.

'Is all that screaming necessary?' he said as he entered the house. 'I've seen men die with less noise.'

Katie backed down the hallway, then turned and ran. She could hear him, just a few steps behind her. She made a right then burst into the kitchen. Pots and pans dangled above her head. She considered grabbing one, but rejected the idea. A wooden knife block rested on the counter. That caught her eye. Amidst all the leftover plates and glasses and food from the party, the knife block signalled to her like a homing beacon. The handles of four carving knives protruded from the block. She reached and pulled the largest one. A long smooth blade followed the handle out.

She brandished the knife at him.

Still he came, sliding along the edge of the counter. He grimaced at the sight of the knife. He had a lot of blood on him – it was on his face, on his neck, and staining the white stripes of his shirt. But he seemed calmer now. His features softened. He no longer seemed angry at all. Just concerned, a little breathless, and maybe in some pain.

'Katie, put the knife away.'

'Tyler, I'll kill you if you come near me. I swear to God I'll kill you.'

He held his empty hands out to her.

'Look, I don't have a weapon, OK? It was all a big misunderstanding. I'm not going to hurt you. I was out of my mind there for a minute, but it's over now.' He took a step closer. 'I just want to talk, OK? I just want to find out what's going on. Come on, put the knife down.'

'Tyler . . .'

'Katie, come on now.' He came even closer, and she backed up another step, moving behind the island.

'Tyler, stay the fuck away from me!'

He swept his arm across the island, launching a pile of garbage towards her. A wooden bowl, half filled with some kind of dip, struck her arm. He darted at her. As he did so, he yanked a copper stew pot down from the overhead rack. It had a thick, heavy bottom for high heat.

She jabbed the knife at him but missed.

He lunged, then backed away.

She jabbed again.

'TYLER!'

He swung the pot, bringing it over the top like a sledgehammer. It struck her hand, making a sharp smacking sound. She felt a shooting pain and then her fingers went numb. She looked at the hand and the knife was gone.

Now there was another sound. Tyler Gant, blood streaming down his face and neck, was laughing.

He stepped forward with the pot.

For Katie, the knives were out of reach. There was a half-full bottle of wine next to the sink. It was a strawberry dessert wine. Thick and rich, a little too sweet, almost like syrup. She picked it up. She turned the bottle over and held it like a club. The wine poured out, soaking the front of her costume. It was a good thing the costume was black.

'Katie, look at what you're doing to yourself.'

'Come on and fight, you bastard.'

He marched straight towards her, no hesitation at all. He swung the pot again. She swung the bottle. The two weapons connected between them. For an instant – it seemed like for ever – they froze in combat.

Then the bottle smashed, spraying glass across the room.

Katie was left holding the neck.

Gant swung the pot again. Katie saw it coming and lifted her hands to block it. Too late. The pot banged into the side of her head. It made a hollow metallic

BONG against her skull. Her vision blurred. It didn't hurt, though. That thought made an impression on her. That big heavy pot struck her head and it didn't hurt. She reeled around the room. Time passed in shattered fragments. She came to a doorway and went through it. Here was the dining-room table. She leaned against it. Her hand squashed a piece of chocolate cake that had been left behind on a paper plate. She gazed at the cake stuck to her palm. She fought an urge to lick it off.

She shook her head, trying to clear it. Where was Tyler? Things seemed to have quietened down.

'Katie?'

She turned and there was Tyler. He didn't have the pot any more. She tried to run but lost her balance and fell over a chair. She half turned, and had the sense of falling backwards into a deep pool.

When she looked up, she saw an overhead fan. But the overhead fan wasn't in the dining room. Somehow she was in the living room now. She was on her back. OK. Tyler kneeled over her. Maybe she had passed out and he had dragged her here.

She didn't know what she looked like, but those scratches on his face were nasty. *Good for you, you son of a bitch.*

She spat in his face. The spit hung there on the side of his nose. It was pink, and so she knew the inside of her mouth was cut. He wiped it away with his hand and smiled. She decided not to give up. She would never give up. The stairs were nearby. She rolled over and began to crawl. But it was too much. She was too dizzy. She sprawled out on her stomach, her cheek against the carpet.

Tyler loomed above her.

'Where do you think you're going?' he said.

Gant came down the stairs with a Polaroid photograph of a corpse in his hand. He placed the photo on the coffee table and stood over the prone figure of his wife. She lay on the dark living-room carpet. Despite everything, including the sharp pain of the scratches on his face, he felt calm. Things had got a little out of control, but now they were back in order. He had to find out some things, and then he could decide what he needed to do tonight, and in the coming days.

He stepped out into the kitchen and picked up a knife from the counter. When he returned, he rolled Katie over on to her back again. Her eyes fluttered. Her face was going to swell up a little tomorrow. It was already starting to. That would be embarrassing for her, what with the workers coming in to clean up after the party.

He shook her. 'Katie, wake up.'

Now the eyes opened and saw him there.

'Tyler, listen . . .'

'No, it's your turn to listen.' He brandished the knife, putting its point against her face. He ran it lightly along her skin. That got her attention. The blade stopped a quarter of an inch from her left eye.

'There's no reason why I couldn't just pop your eyes out with this right now. There's no reason why I shouldn't kill you, OK? But I'm not going to, not if you tell me the absolute truth. I need to know what's been happening here. Who was that man?'

'I told you. He's a cop. He's from New York City.'

He stared into her eyes, looking for the lie. It wasn't there. She honestly thought the man was a cop. OK. Gant was OK with that. They were getting somewhere here. 'Did you have sex with him?'

'Tyler, no!'

She said it emphatically, and Gant could see that it was also probably true. But then what was she doing in there with him? 'Katie, I want to tell you something. I was a police officer for thirty years. That man might be from New York, but he's not a cop. I don't know what he's doing or thinks he's doing, but if you told me he was a fashion model, I'd be more inclined to believe that.'

'He said he's a cop. I don't know what to tell you. He and his partner are looking for the man who was here the other day. The man you told me to forget about.'

'Who is his partner, please?'

'He's a big husky guy. He was at the party. He was dressed as a hobo.'

Gant remembered him. The wise guy who wanted whiskey instead of beer, practically advertising his presence here in Gant's home. 'You thought these men were the police and you invited them into our house?'

Tears began to well up in her eyes. Her chin began to quiver. 'Yes.'

'And what did you tell them?'

'Nothing. Please, I didn't tell them anything.'

'Katie, what did you tell them?'

The tears started in earnest now. They rolled down her cheeks. She squeezed her eyes shut. Her whole face spasmed.

'Katie?'

'I told them the man they want was here. I said you beat him with a gun and that I think he's dead now.'

It took Gant an effort of will not to drive the blade through her eye. But he managed it. See, it wasn't her fault. Not really. Their marriage had been dead a long time and to keep up appearances, he had left her here at home, bored, with nothing to do. Was it any big surprise that she had got herself in trouble? Was it any big surprise that she had betrayed him?

'Did you tell them about my book?'

She shook her head, exhausted, Gant would say defeated. 'No. I didn't.'

'OK, that's good. Now, I saw the man give you a card. What was on it? His telephone number, maybe his address? I want it.'

'I lost it.'

'Katie, don't lie. I'm not feeling very well disposed towards you right now.'

She sighed, and reached down to the tiny pocket on the front of her costume. She pulled out the folded-up card. He took it from her.

'Those men haven't done anything to you, Tyler.'

He raised a hand to cut off conversation. She had talked enough. 'OK. Here's what we're going to do. I'm going to leave here tonight. I'll be back, but I don't know when. There'll be people watching you while I'm gone. You're to act as if everything's normal. In fact, everything is normal, so don't call the police. Don't talk to anybody about this, especially not your mother. Just put it out of your mind. If you can't do that . . . what do you want me to say? I can't have you running around, stabbing me in the back. If you do it again, I'll have to retaliate. There'll be nowhere you can hide, and no one who can protect you.'

He looked deeply into her eyes. 'Do you understand?'

She indicated that she did.

He pressed the knife against her skin, applying pressure till just a drop of blood appeared. She squeezed her eyes tight. She began to shake again.

'Look at me,' he said, and she obeyed. 'Good. Now, when I get back, we can talk. If you want to stay married, OK. If you want to get a divorce, I'll consider it.'

'What if those two men call me?'

'Don't worry. They won't.'

Gant rose slowly to his feet. He had to get ready for his trip. He was tired, but he could buy some coffee on the road. It should only take him a few minutes to pack, but he had to do something about his face, and he already wanted to get gone from this place.

There was one thing left to do. He went to the table and picked up the Polaroid. It showed a crack whore lying dead in an alley, the blood still running from her head on to the concrete. Her eyes were open, gazing out in what seemed like confusion. It was a good crime-scene photo. Gant had taken it himself. He placed it on his wife's stomach.

'Don't underestimate me, Katie. It's the worst mistake you can ever make.'

They called him Max Impact.

He kept his head shaved perfectly bald. People used to call him Mr Clean, because he looked so much like the bald-headed cartoon character that sold the floor wax on TV. For a long time, he didn't mind the comparison. He was big and muscular like Mr Clean, too. But he wanted his own name, his own persona.

He'd thought of the name while living in Atlanta. He had a little gig down there for a while where he and these three guys would stick up hip-hoppers and pro athletes out partying and getting fucked up at night. Depending on the size of the entourage and who else was around, Max and two of the boys would just walk up to the targets in the parking lot after hours, put the heavy metal to their skulls and take the money away.

'One move and I blow your fucking head off. Ain't worth it, is it?'

It happened that fast. The third guy was the getaway driver.

Max's three partners were all Christian Identity creeps, some kind of three-way car crash between holy rollers, neo-Nazis and the Ku Klux Klan. They talked constantly about mud people and the Jewish conspiracy and the impending return of the Saviour. That was OK with Max, because when it came to taking people off, those three guys were fucking rock stars. Their reward was in heaven. Nothing down here could scare them.

Even now, a couple of years later, Max still couldn't believe the amount of cash some of these pro ballers would be carrying around – one time, they hit a guy with a hundred grand. Some big jerk's just out, at a crowded night-club, with a hundred thousand dollars in cash in a gym bag. A hundred grand split four ways wasn't a bad dime for hanging around and watching a bunch of strippers till closing time. There was more to it than that, of course, but not much more.

All the same, it was a dangerous business and Max stopped enjoying it like he once had. He began to yearn for a change of scenery. One thing about Max: he had a knack for walking at the right time. A month after he left Atlanta, his three partners went to meet Jesus over a gunfight with some rap mogul's bodyguards. Didn't matter, Max supposed – the business would have dried up eventually. The rich weren't as rich as they used to be, and nobody really partied much in Atlanta any more.

He was thinking about these things and not quite sleeping when the phone next to his bed rang. He glanced at the phone's read-out – it was a number he didn't recognise. He looked at the clock. Nearly 3 a.m. Nothing but wrong numbers and trouble at that hour. He let the machine pick it up. In the other room, he heard Tyler Gant's voice on the answerphone.

'Max. Pick it up.'

'Shit.'

Max picked up the phone. 'Trouble,' he said.

'Yeah.'

'Where are you calling from?'

'I'm at a payphone.'

'You need me to come down there? I thought it wasn't gonna be for another little while. That's what your buddy said.' Max was always careful not to use names, especially on a phone like this, his home phone. Vernon had said they didn't need Max in Key West for a few more days. Now it looked like the plans had changed.

'I'm not there. I'm here.'

'Here, meaning—'

'Yes. Here.'

'OK. Shoot.'

'Twenty minutes ago I slipped a job under your door. I need it taken care of. It's not just one. It's two, but the name I gave you is the only one I have. I need the whole thing to disappear. I need it like it never existed.'

Max began to rub the sleep out of his eyes. 'What does it look like?'

'Black and white. Thin and fat.'

'Hmmm. When do you need this done by?'

'By sun up.'

'By sun up? Shit, man. It's three o'clock now.'

'That gives you about two hours, maybe two and a half.'

Max's shoulders sagged. Fucking Tyler Gant, calling him in the middle of the night to get up and waste some cocksuckers by dawn. The guy was fucking crazy. But he knew Max would do it. Money was money, after all.

'Standard rate. Me and my two guys.'

'Fine.'

'Where are you gonna be?'

'I'm leaving right now. I can't be anywhere near this. I'm going down. I'll make it there by tomorrow afternoon sometime. You can call me when everything's taken care of. No need for a big discussion. Just keep it short and sweet. Then follow me down. I'll let you know where to meet me. Everything is a go.'

Max stood and padded to the front door to check out the message Gant had left for him. It was a motel card. He knew the motel. It was about fifteen minutes from here. Someone had scribbled a name, a phone number, and a room number across the bottom. The name was *Jonah*.

'All right,' Max said. 'Don't worry about it. Leave everything to me.'

'Really, Max, what do you think of it?'

An hour later, Max strode across the parking lot of a cheap highway motel with the two guys in his crew, Eggie and Dave. The motel was down in the heels, a dead end perched on a grassy knoll, looking out at a highway that hardly anybody drove. Here and there, tufts of grass poked up through the tarmac. There were exactly three cars in a parking lot that could hold forty.

Eggie and Dave were good guys – he'd had them with him for more than a year now. It felt like he had the whole thing settled. Two guys who liked to work, liked to make money, and could keep their mouths shut.

Dave had a sense of style that Max could live without. That was the only problem. He went in for these weird pieces of personal flair. For instance, right now. Sometime in the past forty-eight hours, Dave had gone out and got some earrings put in, but not exactly earrings: they were like small round pieces of blue wood. He'd had his earlobes cut and then stretched, so that these wooden pieces could be inserted. Now his earlobes dangled way down, each with these chunks of wood embedded in there, and he was hoping that people liked it. Aside from the fact that it would make him stand out in a crowd, which was bad enough, it also looked ridiculous.

'You really want to know what I think?' Max said.

'Yeah. That's why I asked.'

'Well, I think you look like a fucking Ubangi.'

They reached the door to Room 11. Nobody was around. Max drew his gun. A long silencer poked out at the end. Eggie and Dave drew their guns in unison. Both had silencers. All three men wore black gloves. Was this a good fucking crew, or what? It was just going to be wham, bam, and see you later. Bring the car around and drop the bodies in the trunk. Grab the guys' cell phone on the way out and smash it to bits a couple of miles down the road. There was an old gravel pit, long out of business, about ten miles away. They had a bucket of lye in the car. Dig a small ditch, pour the lye on the corpses, shovel some gravel on there, and let nature run its course.

Max took a deep breath and looked out at the night. About a hundred yards away, a single car went by on the highway. He pulled the flashlight from his belt. It was a powerful fucking flashlight. When he put it on them, they'd think it was the light from a thousand suns in their eyes. He put his ear close to the door of the room.

'Call the number.'

Eggie pulled out a stolen phone and dialled the number. Eggie stole a cell phone at least once a week – in bars, he'd reach into women's handbags and walk off with their phones. Then he'd use the phone till the service died. It was a habit. Some people smoked. Some people chewed gum. Eggie stole cell phones – his habit was more useful than other people's.

A moment passed. On the other side of the door, a phone started ringing. It rang twice. Someone moved around a little in there – it sounded like a body rolling on a squeaky bed. A sleepy voice said, 'H'lo?' A split second later, the same voice, tinnier now and smaller, came out of Eggie's phone. 'H'lo?'

'Jonah?' Eggie said.

'Yeah. Who is this?'

Eggie hung up.

Max looked at Dave. A lit cigarette dangled from Dave's lips. Dave always went in with a smoke in his mouth. It kept him calm. Dave might have weird tastes, but he also had good strong legs. He could squat four hundred pounds in the gym.

'Kick it.'

Dave reached up and ploughed a steel-toed boot into the door. The frame half dislodged from the wall. He kicked it again and a crack appeared down the centre of the door. He kicked it again and the whole thing came off.

Max hit the flashlight and went in first. He felt Dave and Eggie half a step behind him. Max started firing the instant he got a clear sighting on the beds.

Gordo woke up the moment the phone rang. His antennae started twitching. No one called at almost four in the morning – Gant's wife must be in trouble.

In the darkness, he looked at Jonah across the space between the two double beds. Jonah picked up the phone. He was half-asleep. 'H'lo?'

'Yeah. Who is this?'

Jonah blinked and looked over at Gordo. 'He hung up,' he said, the grog still in his voice. 'But he knew my name.'

Suddenly a commotion started on the other side of the door. BOOM, and the door came halfway off its frame. Cracks of light poked in from the parking lot. Jonah's eyes grew two sizes in one second. BOOM, as somebody hit the door again.

Jonah got the message right away. Someone, not friendly, was coming in. He rolled away from Gordo, disappearing on to the floor. An instant later Gordo took the hint and rolled the other way. He hit the hard floor. His costume! His gun was in the jacket pocket. It was on the floor here somewhere. He reached for it, found it, starting groping for the pockets.

The door burst in and the room filled with blinding light.

Sounds came; low, silenced guns firing, drywall exploding, the blunt thuds of bullets ripping through mattresses, metal scraping wood as a box-spring got destroyed, like a dead piano being hacked apart with an axe.

Gordo found the gun. He took it into his shaking hand. Jesus, the revolver! Why had he picked the revolver? It only had six shots. He screamed, pointed the gun at the bright light, at the muzzle flashes behind it, and pulled the trigger. Nothing happened. He couldn't depress it all the way. Was it locked? Was it jammed?

'Fuck!'

Just then, the room erupted in real gunfire. Muzzle flashes from the floor, on the other side of the room. BLAM! BLAM! BLAM! The explosions were loud, shocking, disorienting, like monstrous thunder claps in an enclosed space. Jonah must have found his gun, and it must have worked.

Gordo couldn't see from all the light. He blinked his eyes – bursts of flame were etched into his retinas. He had to do something. They would get a bead on Jonah and he'd be dead. Any second now.

Charge them? No way. They'd rip him apart. One of his hands was still in the jacket pocket, and now it came out with a glass bottle of something. He looked at it. What the fuck was it?

Wendel couldn't get the chloroform. Instead he got . . .

Ether.

Gordo threw the bottle at the gunmen in the doorway.

Please work, he thought, but he had no idea what that meant. He heard the tinkle of the glass breaking amidst all the shooting, and seconds later the room was on fire.

Max ran back across the parking lot towards the car.

His leather jacket was burning, and he still had it on. He stopped running, shrugged the jacket off and stomped it on the ground. It was a smoking ruin. Fuck the jacket. He started walking now, at a fast pace, but not a run. There was no sense in running. His boots weren't made for it.

Eggie got shot full of holes. Max saw it. Lucky shots from somebody on the ground just about took Eggie's head off. Dave got set on fire. Max had no fucking idea how that happened. One minute they were all there, shooting, looking for the targets; the next minute the place was in flames and Dave went up like a torch, starting at the tip of his cigarette.

Max reached the car, an old-school gas-guzzling Camaro, with an engine that could burn nitroglycerin. Max's theory was you got the money, you know where to get the fuel, so do it up. It was probably one of the fastest cars left on the roads. The cops barely even had cars like this any more. Once he got inside this machine, he would put this whole bad scene behind him.

He glanced back and here came a guy running from Room 11. The room already seemed to have burned itself out – a few licks of flame in the doorway and that was about it. The guy was a black guy, pretty good size, running in boxer shorts, bare feet and nothing else. He had a gun in his hand. That was OK. Max still had his gun, and the guy was running hell-bent, not even trying to protect himself. Max raised his gun, drew a bead on the guy, and fired.

Click. Empty. He'd wasted all his bullets inside the room. Ten shots, huh? OK. That was OK, too. He could still bluff the guy, maybe.

'Stop right there,' he said, projecting his voice. 'Or I'm gonna have to blow your brains out.'

'I'm gonna blow your brains out, motherfucker!' the black guy shrieked. He raised his gun and jumped up and down. Max could see he was crying. The guy was flipping out, an excitable type. He probably didn't like gunfights. It looked like they made him nervous. But his crazy energy would make this thing complicated. And if his buddy had got smoked back there, that would make it even more so.

'Take it easy, man.' Max kept his empty gun trained on the guy's head. 'We can both walk away from this.'

'What the fuck's the matter with you?' the guy screamed.

'Jonah? Are you Jonah?' Max watched the muzzle at the end of the guy's gun. It was a big semi-auto. It would make ugly holes in Max's body.

'I'm Jonah. That's right. I'm fucking Jonah. I'm the one who's gonna kill your ass right now.'

'Jonah, you gotta take it down a notch. I want to live, and you want to live. Isn't that right?' Behind Jonah, Max spotted another guy coming out of the motel room. This guy was a heavy white guy, also in boxers and bare feet. The guy was so hairy he looked like a giant Brillo pad. He walked across the parking lot like he wanted to stomp holes in it. Bad luck tonight. Both of these guys lived, and both of my guys died. Max shrugged. It could happen to anybody.

The guy walked up behind Jonah, then walked right past him. He just kept right on coming.

'Hey, hold up there, big man. We got a stand-off here. One more step and me and Jonah are gonna end up shooting each other.'

The guy never stopped. He came right around Max's side of the car, his hands balled into fists, his teeth gritted like a pissed-off ten-year-old boy.

'Hey, man,' Max shouted. 'Hey!'

The big guy swung. His first punch rang Max's bell. The second one snapped his head back. Max didn't even feel the third one. The fourth one was just a filmstrip of a large fist, oncoming like a commuter train. Then Max was on the cracked pavement by the door to the Camaro, staring up at the black sky. The big guy reached down and took first the gun, then the car keys from Max's hands.

'Jonah, help me with this guy. We gotta go, but we're taking him with us.'

'I think I'm going to vomit,' Jonah said.

Max felt one man grab him by the arms, and one by the legs. He felt himself lifted into the air. He looked below and saw the open maw of the trunk of his car. The big black tarpaulin, the one he had planned to roll the bodies in, waited to receive him. He thought of all the things beneath it. Spare tyre in there. Tyre iron. Jack. A few other things. He lay on the lumpy tarp, then the lid came down and closed him in perfect darkness.

9

An hour had passed. Soon it would be daylight, but not yet.

Jonah felt sick. He had killed a man tonight and he'd never done that before. He'd seen it all as though it had happened in slow motion – his bullets hitting the guy, punching holes in his head and body. He never wanted to see anything like that again. The man had been trying to kill him, without warning, without reason, and yet Jonah had a terrible feeling in the pit of his stomach. The thing he felt most was guilt. It made no sense, but he felt ashamed.

They'd driven the Camaro through the city and over a bridge to an island community of beachfront shacks. Gordo had been here years before and knew what he was looking for. It was off-season now and the island was deserted. The homes sat empty in the darkness, many of them boarded up. They parked the car on a street that dead-ended at the grassy dunes.

'You ready in there?' Gordo said. He stood with the steel handcuffs, about to open the trunk of the red Camaro. 'One funny move and you get to die in the trunk of your own car. Sound good?'

'Sounds good,' came the muffled reply.

'No shit,' Gordo said to Jonah, loud enough for the guy in the car to overhear. 'This guy gives me any resistance at all, just kill him. I'm in no mood for any bullshit.'

'You don't have to tell me twice,' Jonah said. He held the gun ready, pointed at the trunk. He hated this, but he would carry it through. He would kill the guy if necessary.

Gordo opened the trunk. The bald guy was there, cramped in and doubled up on a black tarp amid a bunch of junk. He peered up at them.

'OK, roll over,' Gordo said. 'Hands behind your back.'

The man did as he was told, struggling to turn in the cramped space, and Gordo cuffed him. Then together, Gordo and Jonah yanked him out of the trunk and stood him on his feet. He was muscular, with big shoulders. He wore a white T-shirt that clung to his upper body, a pair of blue jeans and boots. Gordo guided him up the sandy path that went over the dunes and came down to the beach. Jonah followed a few steps behind with the gun. The narrow beach was fogged in for its entire length. Between the dark and the fog, Jonah could barely see out there. But he knew the surf was rough – the waves boomed against the shoreline.

'What are we doing here?' the man said.

'You got a name?' Gordo said.

'They call me Max.'

'Well, Max, I'll tell you. You're going to walk a few feet out into that surf. When you get about waist high, Jonah here is going to shoot you in the back of the head. This whole island is deserted, so nobody will see or hear you die. Your body will slosh around for a few days till somebody finds it. Or maybe it'll wash out to sea when the tide goes out and nobody will find it. We don't really care.'

'Hey, guys . . . Do you really want to do that?'

Jonah didn't feel much like talking to this creep, so he didn't say anything. Gordo went on in a detached, humorous tone that Jonah didn't feel at all. He didn't see anything funny about this. If he were speaking, it would be hard not to start screaming at the guy.

'Max,' Gordo said. 'You came barging into our room in the middle of the night and tried to kill us. We're very busy and you ruined any chance of us getting a decent night's sleep. As a result, we've already killed two guys tonight. I say, what's one more? Yeah, we want to kill you.'

'What would it take,' Max said evenly, 'for you to change your mind?'

'What do you have?'

'Well, there's five grand stashed in the front passenger door panel of the car. It's all yours if you want it.'

'That's a start,' Gordo said. 'And we'll take you up on it. But what we really want is information. We want to know how you got our phone number. We want to know why you tried to kill us. If somebody hired you, we want to know the name.'

'Sorry. That I can't do.'

Gordo shoved him. 'OK, get walking.' He walked Max right down into the shallows, about knee-high. 'There you go, into the water.' A final rude thrust and Max fell face first into the next wave. He came up sputtering and gasping on to his knees. Jonah waited at the water's edge, gun trained on Max's back. Another wave came and hit Max chest high.

'You ready, Jonah?'

'Yeah.'

'Do him.'

'Wait!' Max shouted. 'Wait a minute.'

'Wait for what?'

'Can't we just talk? Just for a minute?'

'Fuck that. Jonah, kill this piece of shit.'

'Tyler Gant! Is that what you wanted to hear? Tyler Gant sent me to kill you. I don't know why.'

Gordo waded out into the surf and yanked Max to his feet. Then he dragged him back to the beach and threw him face down on to the sand. The sand clung to Max's wet clothes, to his chest, to his legs, to his face and to the top of his bald head. Gordo rolled him over. Max looked weird, like the mud sculpture of a mad artist. Gordo pulled out a mug shot of Foerster and pushed it into Max's sand-covered face.

'Have you seen this man?'

'I don't know.'

'Jonah, can I see that?'

Jonah handed Gordo the gun. Gordo put the muzzle to Max's forehead. 'Max, you could live or die right now. The choice is up to you. Personally, I don't give a fuck.'

Max shivered. For a moment, he didn't say anything.

Gordo jabbed Max's head with the gun. Hard.

'Max . . .'

Max shrugged. 'He looks like a guy I helped pack into a coffin the other day.'

Jonah and Gordo exchanged a look.

'I didn't kill him, if that's what you're thinking. The guy's alive. He's a scientist. He's wanted by the cops and we were smuggling him out of state. Gant has an operation going on down near Key West, on a boat out at sea. This guy is going to make something for him.'

'What's he making?'

Max hesitated. Then he smiled. 'What do people make? Drugs, probably. Crystal meth, I'd bet.'

With his free left hand, Gordo punched Max in the face. The punch drove Max backwards into the sand. Gordo climbed heavily to his feet, took a deep breath, and kicked Max in the ribs. Then he stepped on Max's face, rubbing Max's cheek against the sharp, cold granules.

'Don't fucking lie to me, Max. It makes me angry.'

'I'm not lying!'

Gordo started kicking Max savagely, again and again. Max's muscular body undulated from the force of the blows. Blood mingled with the sand on his face. Blood mingled with the sand on the beach. For a moment, Jonah thought the questioning was over. Gordo was going to kick Max to death right here, and Jonah was going to watch him do it. Jonah had a sudden qualm about cold-blooded murder, but it seemed to pass like a summer breeze. Then again . . .

'Gordo,' Jonah said.

Gordo stopped kicking and dropped to his knees. He put a hand behind Max's neck and pulled his head up. He jammed the barrel of the gun into Max's mouth. Max's eyes went very wide.

'You think I'm dumb, right?' Gordo said. 'You're telling me Gant risked hiring a fugitive from New York, a fucking maniac rapist who set half the state of South Carolina on fire by his very presence. Gant brought this lunatic all the way down here to his own house, then smuggled him to Florida just to make a batch of crystal meth. Think carefully. Is that what you're saying? That Gant couldn't find anyone local to make a drug that thousands of people know how to make? Then he hired you to kill us because we want to arrest the one guy on earth he could find to make the drug? Max, I'm about to terminate this interview, do you understand me? It's becoming too fucking absurd to continue.'

Jonah thought he saw something change in Max's eyes. His shoulders slumped. A resignation came over him – Max had made a decision. He wanted to live and he saw one way he might get there.

Gordo must have seen it too. He pulled the gun from Max's mouth.

'It's a disease,' Max said.

'Go on. What's a disease?'

'Gant has the scientist making a disease. Cholera, to be exact. And he's not really making it – he's just growing more of some that already exists. Gant bought it from some South Africans. He's going to use it to kill a bunch of people on a Caribbean island.'

'A bunch? How many is a bunch?'

'A lot. He's going to kill a lot of people. Most of the people on the island.'

Jonah heard his own voice speaking, and was surprised by the sound. 'Why would he do that?'

Max spoke slowly, choosing his words with care. 'Because that's what somebody is willing to pay for.'

'Which island?' Gordo said.

Max was staring at the sand. 'I don't know.'

'Max, I will torture you all day.'

'No, I mean it. Gant would never tell me something like that. He didn't even tell me what they were doing. His second-in-command, Vernon, was the one who told me.'

'OK,' Gordo said. 'I believe you. See how simple that was? You could have just started with the truth and made things easy on everybody.' He switched his gun to his left hand, then reared back with his right and punched Max in the face. Then he did it again. The impacts made a hard smacking sound. The first punch rocked Max's world. The second punch brought the curtain down.

'Have a nice sleep, asshole,' Gordo said, shaking his hand out from the wrist.

Watching Gordo work sparked an image in Jonah's mind. Gordo – an operator, devastating, remorseless, cold . . . and sitting behind the wheel of a white Jaguar XJ8. Gordo was in his element dealing with these people. He didn't feel sick or guilty or dirty like Jonah did. He liked this kind of thing. He had enjoyed beating the right answer out of Max.

'You did it, didn't you? You repo-ed my Jag.'

Gordo nodded. His eyes looked bleary. 'Yeah. I'm really sorry I did that. If we live through this, when we get back to New York I'll give you half the money I made from it. It wasn't much.'

'What about the money in this guy's car, if it's really there?'

Gordo shrugged. 'I'm hoping you'll agree I should mail that money to my brother.' He put his hands under Max's arms. He looked at Jonah and gestured at Max's legs.

Jonah grabbed the unconscious Max by his knees.

'They're making a disease.'

Gordo didn't even look up. 'I know. I can't think about it right now. I'm too tired and it's too fucking horrible.' He tightened his grip around Max's chest. 'You ready, man? We got a long drive and a lot of work ahead of us.'

Normally, the thought of driving another twelve or fifteen hours would have given Jonah pause. But Gant had tried to kill him tonight, all for messing with his plan to give an unknown number of people a deadly disease. Jonah's body began to shake. He wanted the money, yes. And he wanted to put Foerster in jail. But more than anything, he wanted to take Gant down.

'I'm ready.'

Max woke up at home, in his own bed.

For a second, it seemed to him that it had all been a bad dream – the call from Gant in the middle of the night, the shootout, the beat-down on the beach. But then he realised he was in a lot of pain. Maybe more pain than ever before. His head, his face, his jaw and his neck all ached from the punches he'd taken. His torso was sore from the kicks – he might have some broken ribs. And he was still cold from his early morning dip in the ocean, chilled to the core of his body.

Worse, his ankles and one of his wrists were handcuffed to the bedposts. Ol' Max wasn't going anywhere.

'How did we get here?' he said straight up at the ceiling. It hurt too much to turn his head and look around.

The two men came into view. The black guy held the gun. 'Your car is registered to this address. We found the papers in the glove box. The key fit the door, so we came on in and made ourselves at home.'

'What do we do now?'

The big guy held out the receiver of the bedside telephone. 'We make a phone call.'

They propped Max up on some pillows and told him what they wanted him to say. Max held the phone in his free hand – it almost seemed natural. The black guy put the gun to Max's head. Through the doorway, Max could see the big guy listening in on the other line.

This would be a brief conversation, short and not-so-sweet. A moment passed, the phone rang several times, and then Gant came on the line. Max pictured Gant, sitting in that strange bubble of a car he drove – it reminded Max of an octopus.

'Yeah?' Gant said.

'It's Max.'

'I know who it is. I expected to hear from you a little earlier than this. What'd you do, go back to sleep after I called?'

'No, I got up.' Max heard his own voice. It sounded flat.

'How'd it go?'

'Tough. I've seen them go better.'

'OK. What's that supposed to mean?'

'We won. They lost. But I lost my entire team in the process.'

'Jesus.'

'Yeah.'

Gant hesitated. 'But everything's OK, right? There's no . . .'

'Everything's been erased, just like I said it would be.'

'Good. That's good. So what took you so long to get back to me?'

Max sighed. 'Well, I was in bad shape, to put it mildly. Just woke up a little while ago. Found myself sitting on a fence, if you take my meaning. Thinking about retirement.'

'Max, listen to me. What's done is done. I'm sorry this happened, but we can still work it out. Why don't you just come down this way? We can use your help.'

'Yeah? Just like that?'

'Just like that. Things get fucked up sometimes, Max. You know that. Look, I'll throw in something for you, all right? I'll pay you the full amount for all three guys last night, plus a little extra. Call it a hardship bonus.'

'I'll think about it.'

'Come on, Max. How soon can you get here?'

'I had a tough night. I need some more sleep before I do anything. I could probably be there tomorrow afternoon. Say about five?'

'We'll look for you then.'

'Where am I going? To the boat?'

'No. Meet me at the Schooner Wharf bar, down by the docks, and I'll take you out to the boat. And I know I don't need to tell you this, but make sure nobody follows you, all right?'

The line went dead. In the living room, the big guy hung up the extension.

The black guy – Jonah, that was his name – took the receiver from Max, then pulled the entire phone out of the wall. The big guy came stalking back into the room. Max looked at him.

'How'd I do?'

'You're still alive for the moment, so you must have done OK.'

Katie sat in a chair on the terrace in a dark stupor, taking sips from a strong Bloody Mary. She wore big round sunglasses to cover the bruises around her eyes. She wore a turtleneck and slacks to cover the bruises on her body. Luckily, it was a reasonably cool day.

The workers moved quickly. The catering people had come and taken the bar and the leftover serving trays. The bandstand was gone. The monsters were gooey piles of vinyl being packed in crates, and a small clean-up crew went around the yard picking up plastic cups and plates, half-empty beer bottles, napkins and discarded cigarettes. Someone would have to clean out the pool, but Katie figured that was a phone call for another day.

She was in pain. Her head hurt from the hangover. Her body hurt from the beating her husband had given her. Her heart hurt because the love she felt for him, which had been dying, was completely dead now. It was gone. She felt nothing for Tyler. Above all, her mind hurt. Hurt wasn't even the right word. Her mind reeled from too much sudden knowledge. It recoiled from the horror of who she had married. As she gazed out at her backyard, in her mind she surveyed the wreckage of her life.

Parts of last night were a blur. She was drunk, she was afraid, she was lonely. She had shared an embrace with a handsome stranger, and as a result, that man was probably dead now. Maybe he was lying about being a policeman. She wasn't sure and it didn't really matter. It was no good reason for him to die.

But, in fact, he wasn't dead. As she watched, he and his partner appeared in the backyard again, just as they had twice before. They climbed the stairs to her, and she watched them come. She didn't rise from her chair.

Jonah seemed to hesitate. 'Katie? Are you all right?'

'I'm OK.'

'Where's your husband?'

'He's gone.'

'Mrs Gant?' the heavyset one said. 'May we talk inside?'

'You guys aren't really cops, are you?'

'Not exactly. No.'

Jonah smiled, but there was no joy in it. It was the awkward smile of someone caught in a lie. And there was pain there, a sadness that Katie didn't recognise. 'Katie, this is my partner Gordon. As you've probably guessed, his name's not Robert Darker, but my name really is Jonah Maxwell. Gordon, this is my friend Katie Gant.'

They went inside and she poured them coffee. She topped up her drink. They might feel the need to be alert. She felt the need to be numb. Tyler had threatened to kill her if she talked to anybody – at least, it seemed like he had. He'd also said people would be watching her. Right now, she didn't care. He could kill her if he wanted. The drinks were doing their job.

She and her two guests sat in the small glass atrium off the living room. She didn't take off her sunglasses, even though the sky was overcast and the light from outside wasn't very bright. She found that it comforted her some-what to be surrounded by the hanging plants in the room – they were living things, and they knew nothing about her problems.

'Your husband beat you last night, after the party ended,' Gordon said. It wasn't a question. 'He made you give him the card with the name of the motel where we were staying at and Jonah's phone number.'

'Yes.'

'He sent three men to kill us. We were lucky to survive.'

'OK.' She let it all wash over her like a gentle wave. She found that she didn't want to know about it. It didn't interest her. She didn't want to know where the hired killers were now, or what had happened to them. It was almost like music, or a short essay about other people's lives in the newspaper – a fluff piece. Here and gone.

'Your husband has an illegal drug operation on a boat in Key West. The man we're trying to find, Foerster, works for your husband. It seems that Foerster is the one who's making the drugs.'

Drug dealers weren't very exciting, and she had a hard time imagining Tyler as one of them. Even now – especially now – it seemed beneath him. But come to think of it, one thing about all this did suddenly interest her. 'Listen, who are you guys? Why are you looking for this man?'

'We told you the truth. He's a rapist and a murderer, and we're trying to put him back in jail. I'm going to be completely honest with you. We're bounty hunters. If we catch him, we stand to make a lot of money.'

'How much is a lot of money?'

'Fifty thousand dollars.'

'Each?'

'No.'

Good Lord. When all the bills were totalled, she'd probably spent close to twenty thousand dollars on the party last night. The fee just to live in this community ran to more than four thousand a month, not including membership at the golf and tennis club. She had no idea how much it had cost to put the pool in, or how much it cost to keep it sparkling clean on an ongoing basis, or to make sure the grass in the backyard got mown. She had no idea what the house itself had cost, or the cars, but she guessed it was a lot. These men were risking their lives for lunch money.

'What do you want from me?'

'Want from you?'

She nodded. 'Yes. You keep coming back here. That tells me you want something.'

'We need a car,' Gordon said. 'The police may be looking for the car we're driving right now. Our own car is registered at a motel room that blew up with two men inside of it last night. So the police might be looking for us, too. They might even want to charge us with murder, even though all we did was defend ourselves. We're happy to talk to the police another time, but not now.'

Jonah held his hand up to stop his friend from going on. He really was a physically beautiful man. 'We want you to help us,' he said. 'However you can help is fine. Also, it may not be safe for you to be here alone, and we can't risk your husband finding out that we're on to him. So we want you to go into hiding for a little while. That's all we want. Are you willing to do that?'

She answered quickly, before she could change her mind. Tyler was a dangerous man and he frightened her. But he also made her resentful. She didn't enjoy being afraid. He had no right to do this to her. And he had no right to kill people.

'I'll help you,' she said. 'I'll do whatever you want.'

'There's a storm coming,' Vernon said from the doorway. He leaned there behind Foerster, drinking a can of beer and checking out all the high seas action with a small pair of binoculars.

Foerster felt a weird mixture of emotions. On the one hand, he was a little uneasy. No, it was more than that. He was afraid. The cholera were multiplying so fast now, so explosively, that there almost seemed to be a personality to it – that of a raging psychotic. Watching it under the microscope sent a tingle along Foerster's spine. It wasn't natural, what was happening in those colonies. At times, he began to worry the organism would somehow get out – but that was the whole point of the exercise, wasn't it? They were going to let it out. Just not around him, thank you.

On the other hand, he felt good. It was a nice day, and he was an important man doing important work – work that would make history. He sat on the bench bolted to the back deck of the houseboat and peeled an orange. He gazed out at the late-morning sunshine. Nearby, other boats bobbed on the water. He was starting to like it out here. As he watched, naked long-haired people, male and female, jumped into the ocean from the top deck of the old green freighter. Others stood around on the deck and cheered as each new jumper hit the water. Three went off at once, a man and two women, not a stitch of clothing on, all holding hands. They must be having themselves quite an orgy over there.

An image flashed in his mind – piles of naked dead bodies, being shovelled into pits by bulldozers. It was something from the Holocaust, film footage the Nazis took, if he had to guess. He blinked and the image was gone. Sure, no orgies for Foerster. Mass murder, but no orgies.

He'd been working almost non-stop since they'd arrived. Hours seemed to fly by, and then he'd be tired, and hungry, and he'd need some time to regroup. When he took his little breaks, it wasn't bad to sit out here and admire the sky and the sea. He had the run of the place. He ate the food. He smoked the cigarettes. He drank a couple of beers now and then. Nobody even seemed to be watching him too closely. Gant had gone home, and everybody relaxed a little when Gant wasn't around.

It was good to be on top.

The little dog was on deck with them, curled up in the corner near the edge. It growled at Foerster for no reason. It tended to do that. He kicked at it with his bare foot, but the dog was beyond his reach. So he threw a chunk of orange and pegged it in the head. It growled again, but came no closer. Foerster wouldn't mind getting up and kicking it right into the water.

'Go away, you little shit.'

'Listen man,' came the voice from the doorway behind him.

Foerster turned and smiled at Vernon. Vernon was tall, that much was true. He wore only a pair of cut-off shorts and his torso seemed unnaturally long. Did he have extra vertebrae in there? That crazy tangle of ink covered his upper body.

'Don't fuck with the dog, all right?' Vernon said. 'The girl sees you doing shit like that, Mama's gonna hear about it. Mama hears about it, then I have to hear about it. I don't want to hear about it.'

Foerster felt free to ignore Vernon's advice about the dog. Gant needed Foerster on this boat, more than he needed some silly show dog, more than he needed Vernon or Big Mama. Foerster was the key variable in this equation. If Foerster wanted to, he could probably ignore Vernon altogether. But he wasn't sure he wanted to – not yet, anyway.

'What's the deal with the storm?'

Patrick Quinlan

As if to confirm Foerster's suspicions, Vernon chose not to pursue the dog issue any further.

Of course not. I own this fucking place.

Instead, Vernon shrugged and took another slug of his beer. 'Tropical storm. About two days out. It may hit us and it may turn. It may strengthen and it may weaken. Nobody knows at the moment, but some of the weaker constitutions are already heading to higher ground. I guess they don't want to wait around and find out.'

Something about the news left Foerster feeling cold. An actual chill went through his body. They were on a boat, at sea, with a tropical storm coming. The boat was home to what was probably one of the deadliest bacteria known to man. What was wrong with this picture?

'That's pretty sudden. Why is this the first time I'm hearing about it?'

Vernon grunted. 'People get information around here on a need to know basis, and you didn't need to know. It was a tropical depression yesterday. Today it's a storm. Tomorrow it could be a hurricane, or it could fall apart. We'll see.'

Foerster heard his own voice as bitchy and high-strung, and wondered what it must sound like to Vernon. 'Are we going to get off the boat? I mean, if it becomes a hurricane? I've already got a bunch of shit growing, man. It's an isolated environment in there. If we're gonna get off the boat, we need to start making arrangements to do that. I don't want to lose the work I've already done. And I damn sure don't want to end up swimming in it.'

Vernon was calm. He raised a big hand in a STOP gesture. 'Hold on there, cousin. Nobody said anything about getting off the boat. Mama don't seem concerned. She says if it's anything but a direct hit we'll be fine. And Gant hasn't said anything at all. As far as I know, we're going to ride out any weather right here. I only told you about it to make conversation. So till you hear different, I'd say just keep working. If we get to rocking and rolling a little bit, you'll know why.'

'I'll take comfort in knowing that,' Foerster said.

240

'Take comfort in this,' Vernon said. 'Nobody has ever died around us, not by accident, anyway.'

Half a bottle of Tylenol later, and Max Impact's head and body still ached.

He'd lost five thousand dollars, his car and his crew, all in one bad night, and yet he counted himself lucky. He even felt pretty good. Those guys hadn't killed him after all. They'd just left him there, gagged and hand-cuffed to his own bed. He guessed they figured it would take him a while to get free, or that maybe he would just lay there till he died. They had underestimated him. It took him a little over two hours to pull the wooden bedposts and headboard apart with just the strength of his upper body. The metal of the handcuffs had torn the flesh of his wrists to shit, but he had done it.

Now, he parked his motorcycle, a low-slung Harley Davidson Fatboy, in the visitor lot on the campus of a junior college. He had it loaded down with a couple of leather saddlebags. Everything he needed fit in those bags. It was early afternoon, and he was already nearly a hundred miles west of Charleston. He walked into the student union and strode to the bank of two pay tele-phones. In this day and age, it wasn't always easy to find a payphone. Colleges were still a good place to start looking.

Max glanced around at the confines of the student union. College, a place he'd never been. Not much here to interest him. Maybe he'd stop in the bath-room and take a piss before he left. Maybe he'd just do it out in the parking lot in the fresh air.

The building was drab on the inside, and poorly lit. Here and there, a few kids were sprawled out on couches or on the carpeted floor with books open. A few others sat at tables in the middle of the large open room. None of the kids seemed to look at their books – instead, they seemed to be sleeping, or caught up in intensely intimate conversations with members of the opposite sex.

Max shovelled a few coins into the phone, and then hesitated. His idea was to call Gant's car again. He'd been on the highway, and had come down with a case of the guilties. Something was telling him that he should at least call Gant to let him know the earlier phone call was bullshit.

And then what?

Max had trouble picturing it, just chatting with Gant and giving him the news about how he'd punked on him. He'd heard rumours of Gant killing people who had done a good job, just to be rid of them. People who had failed? People who had rolled over to save their own necks? Gant would put out an all-points bulletin. It was better to be far away before that happened.

Max put down the phone and walked back out the glass front doors of the building. He would get on the bike and keep riding west, see how far he got before he ran low on gas. They wouldn't even begin to wonder where he was for another twenty-four hours – not till Gant walked into that bar and ran smack into the two heavies that Max had enjoyed so much recent quality time with. Gant would be pissed off when that happened, but from Max's perspective, it would probably be worth it. Gant had long tentacles, and getting out a full day ahead was a nice head start.

If there was one thing about Max Impact, he knew when – and how – to disappear.

The strange thing happened soon after Gant reached his hotel room.

It was three o'clock in the afternoon, already getting dark, when he entered the room on Garrison Bight in Key West. He didn't need to check in – he'd kept the room from before he'd gone back to Charleston – and that was a good thing. The place was nice enough – big king-sized bed, widescreen TV, and a view of the water along the wharf if he bothered to pull the shades.

He'd been awake about forty-five hours straight. He was so tired he didn't know how he'd kept his eyes open. He dimly recalled his fight with Katie, more than twelve hours ago now. He barely remembered the last four or five hours of the drive. About all he could picture was the road in front of him, and a long line of people going the other way. He remembered bright sun for most of his drive down – if a storm was coming, where were the clouds?

He remembered stopping somewhere and buying a bottle of Chivas Regal.

That was good. He dug it out of the paper bag right now and opened it. He poured some into one of the empty coffee cups on his desk, and took a mouthful. It burned going down.

God, that was good.

He only remembered the gist of his conversation with Max. He focused on that now. Max had taken out the clowns from New York, two of his own guys had been killed, and Max was on his way down here. OK, that was OK. Max was a good kid. Gant would make it up to him somehow, give him a little bonus or whatever.

Gant sat on the bed and opened his laptop computer to check the satellite weather images. The storm was still a tropical storm, not a hurricane. It was out there over eastern Cuba, but tracking north and west at seventeen miles per hour. It could pass this way. It could stall over Cuba. It could miss to the south but send some rain and wind. Gant lost interest in the storm pretty quickly. They'd have to keep an eye on it, that's all. They had at least twenty-four hours before the real weather hit, if it ever did. Tomorrow morning, if things looked bad, he could call Vernon and Mama and tell them to bring the boat in.

The thing that interested Gant – the strange thing that really grabbed his attention – was something other than the storm. It was the Bloodhound tracking system. The system's transmitter was factory-mounted in both of his matching cars – the one he drove and the one Katie drove – embedded deep behind the dashboard. The transmitter sent information to Global Positioning System satellites every eight seconds. As long as the transmitter could reach two satellites at the same time – and in good weather the periods when it couldn't only lasted a few seconds – the satellites could get a read on where the information was coming from. The satellites then described that location in terms of longitude and latitude to within sixteen yards of the transmitter.

The Bloodhound was originally designed for the owners of trucking and limo companies who wanted to make sure their drivers weren't off fucking around on company time. The satellites broadcast the vehicle location information to the Bloodhound corporate headquarters outside Richmond, Virginia.

Bloodhound computers then plotted the information on a map, and put the information online, updated every few seconds. The transmitter ran off the car's battery, so there was never any down time. As a result, Gant could monitor the location of his cars any time he wanted. If a car were ever stolen, unless the thieves knew where the GPS transmitter was and how to disable it, Gant could find the car again simply by going online.

In the past six months, Gant had developed the habit of checking Katie's car several times a day. He'd been on the move all day today, and hadn't gone online. So after looking at the weather, Gant reflexively went to the Bloodhound website and got a fix on Katie's position.

That was the funny thing.

According to this, she was driving through Florida. She was pretty far north, up near Daytona Beach, but heading south, coming this way. He refreshed the page again and again, thinking there must be something wrong with it, but each time it reloaded, it showed that damnable car, driving south, right towards him.

Gant picked up the phone and called the car.

The car was like a giant egg, or maybe a soap bubble on wheels.

Jonah and Gordo sat in leather bucket seats down inside a clear plastic dome, the top of which would slide backwards along a track when it was time to open the car and get out. Almost no sound from the outside world came into the dome, but inside the dome itself, there was stereo surround-sound. The car was its own little environment, its own little world – and a potentially dangerous world at that. The very top stood barely four feet off the ground. On the plus side, the car got more than a hundred miles to the gallon and had ten gallons in the tank.

They'd had an awkward moment when Jonah and Gordo were about to leave. Gordo had climbed into the driver's seat of the egg. Katie and Jonah stood facing each other, and Jonah could tell she wanted something from him. Was it a promise of some kind? That he'd come back to see her? That he'd bring her the car back? He wasn't sure. Finally, he pulled her to him and put his arms around her. Her arms snaked around his back. The embrace felt different this time – they weren't drunk, they were outside in her driveway, and Gordo was right there. There wasn't as much heat to this moment.

They stayed that way for several seconds, not long at all, and then it was time to leave. Gordo was way down in the egg, rolling his eyes. Jonah pulled away a little bit, and Katie Gant let him go. He looked into her eyes. She seemed OK. Shaken, but still on her feet. Then again, they had lied to her about what her husband was really up to. What would she look like if she knew?

'I'll call you,' she said.

He shook his head. 'I lost my phone last night. I think it got destroyed.'

'That's OK. The car is also a phone.'

Gordo and Jonah exchanged glances.

'When I call you, first it'll ring, and then my name will come up on the dashboard. Just hit the TALK button and you'll hear me. If you're not in the car, or for some reason you don't want to talk right at that moment, just let it ring and the car will pick it up.'

'It's some car,' Gordo said from inside.

'It is. But the downside is there's a GPS unit inside of there somewhere. You can't disable it. If he wants to, Tyler will be able to watch you the whole way.'

Gordo grinned at that. 'Lady, I can't think of anything that would make me laugh harder than your husband watching us come straight at him.'

Now, somewhere in Florida, Jonah watched the nearly empty highway roll past as the light faded from the sky. It was a long drive and they had a long way still to go – hundreds of miles. He'd been drinking coffee all day, but it wasn't working any more. He did his best not to think about Gant and Foerster, and the crime they were about to commit. Instead, he tried to focus on what he and Gordo were trying to do. He closed his eyes and became lost in a pleasant memory, something vague from early childhood, where he was in the old apartment and his mother was there, singing in the next room.

The phone rang, coming through the car's stereo system. It was programmed to mimic the sound of an old-style ringing telephone – before voicemail, before answering machines, a rotary-dial phone that just rang and rang till someone answered it or the person on the other end hung up. For a moment, Jonah thought he was still back in those earlier days. He reached for the handset, but there was none.

A name appeared in red on the dashboard's digital read-out. The name was *TYLER*.

'You know,' Gordo said, hands gripping the steering wheel, blinking and bleary-eyed as though the phone had awakened him, too, 'it never occurred to me that the guy would actually call the car. This should be interesting.'

The phone rang a moment longer, then the car's voicemail answered. 'Katie isn't here right now,' said a disembodied female voice all around them. 'Please leave a message.'

Gant's voice came on. 'Katie, what the fuck are you doing? Katie, this is ridiculous. I know you're there, so answer the phone. Katie? Katie! Jesus fucking Christ, will you please pick up the goddamn phone?'

Jonah and Gordo looked at each other. Jonah smiled. Gordo's breath burst out like steam from a high-pressure pipe. They both started to giggle like mischievous schoolchildren.

Gant paced the confines of his hotel room, wearing out a footpath in the carpet.

A couple of hours had passed since he'd first noticed the car, and in that time he had polished off nearly half the bottle of Chivas. At this rate, he might have to go out later for another. He looked at the computer again – even now, Katie came inexorably along.

He'd called the car twice and he'd called her cell phone twice. No answer. Then he'd called the house and he'd even called her mother's house. No answer anywhere. Was she crazy? That must be it. Katie had gone nuts. Somehow, she must have overheard him talking about business in Key West, and despite everything that had happened, she had decided to join the party. He didn't know what he would do when he saw her. He didn't want to face it.

On the desk, his cell phone rang.

He went over and checked the number – not Katie. A call was coming in from Elliott Howe, the well-known Moldova-fucker and personal assistant to the stars. Gant took the phone and the whisky bottle, and sat down on the bed.

He opened his receiver. 'Mr Howe.'

'Mr Gant?'

'Yes.'

'Thank you for taking my call right away. I was eager to reach you. Mr Fielding is very concerned and asked me to contact you.'

Gant rubbed his temple. 'What is his concern, please?'

'There are several. The first is that a tropical storm, now poised to touch down in Florida as a hurricane, passed through our area yesterday and last night. Mr Fielding feels this was a missed opportunity. It would have been an excellent time for the operation to go forward. Power is still out on most of the island, and probably will be for at least another forty-eight hours.'

Gant poured some more Chivas into the black coffee cup. He took a gulp, and then added even more. 'Mr Howe, please tell Mr Fielding that there will be other storms. And even if there aren't, if we're patient, there are ways we can manufacture opportunities.'

'Mr Fielding feels that time is not on our side. There have been some recent, somewhat alarming, developments here.'

Gant sipped the whisky. 'I'm listening.'

'In the aftermath of the storm, several of the dogs died.'

'The dogs?'

'There are trained guard dogs,' Howe said. 'Rottweilers. They patrol the perimeter of the grounds.'

'Yes. I remember them.'

'Half a dozen of them are dead. It turns out they were poisoned. And that's not everything. I have some other, shocking news. This morning, a cache of machetes and two handguns were found in one of the basement storage rooms of the main house. Someone, probably one of the washerwomen, has been sneaking in weapons. Mr Gant, there is real concern here that we are now, or will soon be, under attack. We want to get the operation underway as soon as possible. We want to dispatch some men to your location to make the pick-up – immediately, if that will work for you.'

Gant stared out the window. It was full dark now. He watched as a garbage can, blown by the wind, rolled off the wharf and into the water. The seas were picking up a little. The garbage can bobbed violently about five yards out from the dock.

The whisky, combined with his lack of sleep, began to put a comfortable distance between Gant's mind and the urgency in Howe's voice. Once Gant noticed that, he realised it had even started to take some of the bite out of the Katie situation.

'Mr Howe, I assure you we're working as fast as we can. Hold the fort and let me call you back in a few moments. I'll check with my team. It may only be another day or so before the material is ready.'

'Sir, I hope we have the luxury of another day or so.'

'I hope you do, too.'

Enough was enough. It was time for Foerster to get off the boat.

It was night, and in the past few hours, the sky had clouded up. Then the wind had started, a warm, heavy breeze that gusted now and then. Vernon had gone upstairs and brought the lounge chairs down off the roof. It wasn't raining – not yet – but the winds were kicking up some big swells out on the water.

Foerster had kept working for a while, but then it all became too much. The boat moved up and down, and rolled sideways and back. Once in a while, a heavy wave would hit the side with a bang, or a gust of wind would rip some piece of the boat off and carry it away like a triumphant child. He couldn't concentrate any more. Was the movement really that bad? No, but the movement was the least of his problems.

The real issue was the fucking cholera. It was like something out of a nightmare. In the past few hours, the rate of growth had become frenzied – for

248

some of the mature colonies it had doubled, and then doubled again. It was still accelerating, even for colonies he had removed from any growth medium. In essence, he was starving the little bastards, and they were still multiplying. Nowhere in the scant paperwork on Cholera B had its inventors made any reference to this.

Foerster sat in the lab, head in his hands. Hundred-litre carboys brimming with death were piling up around him. In some of those containers, the bacteria were becoming as thick as soup. An hour ago, he had exceeded the amount required for the attack on the island. By sometime later tonight, if this kept going on, he'd have twice as much as he needed. And once the newer colonies started to accelerate, he'd have so much so fast that he wouldn't know what to do with it all.

In a normal lab, the whole thing would be alarming, but manageable. Eventually, with no food supply, the colonies would have to collapse and die off. The only question would be when. But this was no normal lab. This was a fucking houseboat. The idea of being trapped out here in a hurricane with this shit made it impossible to think straight. To make matters worse, nobody would listen to him.

He had started in first with Big Mama. He stood in the doorway of her small cabin. She was on the bed with the girl Gabby, the two of them under the covers, wrapped up in each other's arms like pretzels.

'Mama, we gotta get off this boat.'

She shook her head. 'Sorry, Davis. You just gotta tough it out. I've seen a lot worse weather than this, and in less seaworthy boats than this. If things get bad, we have dock space rented at a marina and we can bring the boat in. But we're staying here unless it becomes an absolute emergency, so I suggest you go back to work. It'll take your mind off the storm.'

'We have dock space? Then what the . . . excuse my language . . . what the fuck are we doing out here in the first place?'

Mama shrugged. 'The feds aren't as dumb as they used to be. They've been raiding boat labs at marinas all up and down the coast. Any little thing can set them off. Unusual activity on the dock, boats registered to dummy companies, whatever. We lost a boat like that last year – it was for a different project, a drug lab, and I wasn't even done setting it up. This boat? It was a lot more complicated to put together than some meth lab. I'd rather lose it to the ocean than to the Government. I'd rather see it blown to smithereens than to let them have it.'

Foerster heard her – he heard the words, but didn't necessarily catch the meaning of them. It all sounded too rational, too nonchalant. He began speaking slowly, trying to help her see the gravity of the situation. 'Mama, you don't understand. In that lab back there is a deadly disease. It's growing a lot faster than anybody told me it would. Now there's a storm coming in. We don't want to be out here with that stuff if the boat goes down. We have to get out of here.' He took a step into the room, not sure what he would do. If she wouldn't listen, he might strangle her.

Still, she was calm. 'Davis, I do understand. I understand plenty. You know I have a gun under here, right? Don't make me pull it on you. And don't make me tell Gant you're becoming a problem.'

Next he tried Vernon. Vernon had just come in from a night swim. As usual, he was down to his famous man panties, showing off his long arms and legs, jagged with muscles and tattoos. He was still towelling off his big body when his cell phone rang.

'Vernon, I really need to talk to you, man.'

'OK, just a minute. This is Gant calling.' Vernon picked the phone up off the desk in the main cabin.

Foerster bounced from foot to foot, like a little kid who had to go to the bathroom, while Vernon gabbed with Gant. To Foerster, Vernon's breezy side of the conversation sounded like a couple of guys making a date to go bowling.

'Really? Holy shit. That's too bad.'

Vernon paused. He picked up a pen from the desk and started scribbling on the little notepad there. 'Bloodhound, got it. What's the account number? All right, I'll check it out. No problem. When she gets here, I'll deal with it. The storm? Yeah, we're keeping an eye out. It seems OK right now. I was just swimming in it.'

He looked at Foerster and pointed with one long finger. 'Gant wants to know your best estimate of when the shit's gonna be ready.'

'You mean the bacteria? It's ready now. That's what I need to talk to you about.'

'He says it's ready now. Yeah.' Vernon shook his head and looked at Foerster again. He smiled. 'Gant wants to know if you're sure it's ready now?'

'Yes. Right now. It's growing out of control in there. Vernon—'

Vernon went back to his phone conversation. 'Yeah. He's sure. I don't know. I guess he's good at it. That's why you hired him, right? So anyway, if they want to come in tomorrow night after Max gets here, that'll probably be fine. We'll be ready for them.'

He rolled his eyes at something Gant said. 'Yessir, I'll remember, and I will take care of it. If I get it done early enough, I'll meet you and Max afterwards. OK. No worries. Good night.' He pressed a button on his phone then closed it. He looked at Foerster for a long moment, as if he saw something curious there.

'You'll never believe what Gant just told me. Hey, Mama!'

Mama's voice came from down the short hall. 'Yes?'

'You probably want to hear this, too.'

They stood in the low-ceilinged main cabin, Vernon's head practically touching the ceiling, and both the ladies came out – Mama and Gabby. The girl wore just a small T-shirt and a pair of bikini bottoms tied at the side. Mama wore a big flannel nightgown.

'You'll never believe what's going on. All kinds of news. A couple of guys came down from New York looking for our buddy Foerster here. They crashed the party at Gant's house. They were posing as cops. He sent Max to get rid of them, but in the process they killed two of Max's guys.'

That tripped Foerster up a little. Those two dickheads had faded into a bad memory. In fact, he'd almost forgotten about them altogether.

Vernon smiled at him. 'You knew these guys, right? A black guy and a white guy? Relax. They're toast, probably rotting under a pile of lye at an old stone quarry, if I know Max.'

'And Max is coming down?' Mama said.

'Tomorrow, but he's not the only one. The client wants to speed up the job, so he's sending a crew, maybe as early as tomorrow night. So we gotta be ready to make the handover. But even that's not all. One more person is coming to town. A surprise guest. Gant's wife.'

Mama frowned. 'His wife?'

Vernon's smile became a big lopsided grin. 'Yes, ma'am. Gant's wife must have listened in on one of his conversations. She's on her way. Gant gave me a website where I can track the GPS unit in her car from the laptop here. When she gets to town, I'm supposed to go and put her out of commission for a little while. Lock her in a closet or whatever. Gant's so pissed off that he's not sure what he would do if he actually had to see her.'

'Sounds like a wonderful marriage.'

To Foerster's ears, it sounded like Vernon and Mama both took some perverse pleasure in Gant's domestic suffering. Foerster himself didn't mind hearing it. It was always nice to see people like Gant taken down a peg. And he didn't mind hearing that the two goons from New York were dead. But in the meantime, none of these were the major concern. The main thing was this boat, and when Foerster could get off it.

'Did you talk to Gant about the storm?'

Vernon stared at Foerster. Foerster got the sense he might look at an insect the same way. 'Yeah, briefly. We decided things were still OK, and we'd check on it again in the morning.'

'Yeah, but we really can't wait till then,' Foerster said. He touched Vernon on the arm. It was almost a grab, but not quite. 'We can't wait for the storm to get worse. We need to get out of here now.'

Vernon punched him. It happened so quickly that Foerster wasn't ready for it. The punch caught him hard in the left eye and he sprawled backwards to the floor. He hit his head as he landed. For a moment, he was more surprised than hurt. Then the left side of his face began to throb and Vernon scooped him up by the shirt with both hands. Vernon's big face loomed, with the long nose and angular jaw.

'Don't ever touch me. I've been patient with you so far, but if you touch me like that again, you'll see a side of me you won't like. We're not leaving the boat. Get that through your head. Now go back in the lab, and get to work. The client's guys are gonna be here in twenty-four hours, and you need to make sure you have everything ready for the transfer.' He shoved Foerster down the narrow hallway. Foerster lost his balance and fell down again.

'OK, Mama,' Vernon said. He went to the icebox and pulled out a can of beer. 'You can take a nap or get drunk, or read a book, or whatever you want to do. I'll keep an eye on the golden boy there.'

'Sounds good to me,' Mama said. 'Wake me up around midnight and I'll do the overnight hours.'

Foerster went back to the lab. He sat at his worktable and did nothing. He just stared into space. In containers all over the lab, the bacteria grew and grew. For the first time, he fully understood that Mama and Vernon were taking turns watching him. In other circumstances, that would be annoying, and maybe a little scary. But right now it was much more than scary. Not only was he trapped on this death ship – he was actually their prisoner.

'It feels so good to be held by you,' Katie said.

'Good. I feel the same way.'

She put her head against his chest. 'I've been alone and afraid.'

'I know.'

Katie opened her eyes. She lay awake in bed at her mother's house, her clean hair spread out around her on the pillow. This was the spare bedroom, a welcoming space with a queen-sized bed and light blue colour scheme. It was a corner room with a big window set in each perpendicular wall. Katie had never lived in this house – her parents had moved there after she'd grown up and moved out on her own – so the room had no associations for her, positive or negative. It was just a big, pleasant room with a comfortable bed that she slept in from time to time. She lay in that bed imagining what she might have said, *should have said*, to Jonah today, and how that little inter-action could have gone better.

the depths of her unconscious. It came slowly, like a messenger forced to climb a long spiral stairway. A rumour of bad news on its way reached her first, causing her growing unease. When the thought itself came, it arrived with the force of a punch.

She sat up. Fear gripped her heart. She had to warn Jonah before it was too late. It wasn't love, or lust, or warmth she felt for him at this moment. It was an icy feeling of dread. She didn't want to be responsible for his death. And she would be responsible, wouldn't she? She thought back to the conversations she'd had with Jonah and his friend Gordon – three so far. She'd told them the man they called Foerster had been to her house, that Tyler had beaten him and that she thought Tyler might even have killed him. She hadn't told them or even hinted that Tyler had probably killed a lot of people. She hadn't hinted that he kept a scrapbook filled with news clippings of murders and atrocities he'd committed.

Today was the worst dishonesty. Even after she knew everything, she withheld information. She didn't suggest that Tyler had placed a photograph of a murdered woman on her chest, or that he knew she and Jonah were in the bathroom together. She neglected to mention that Tyler had suspected they were in the bathroom having sex. Sure, she'd been half-drunk when they came to the house. But she hadn't done or said anything that might protect them.

Instead, she had lent them her car and sent them on their merry way. They thought Foerster was alive. They thought Tyler had sent some hoodlums after them who had botched the job. They thought Tyler was angry because they were interfering with some business arrangement of his. They didn't suspect that Tyler was a psychopath who had been killing people for decades, probably for money, but also for no reason at all. They had no idea of the danger they were in.

Katie did. Katie knew. Tyler had called her cell phone twice this afternoon. She didn't answer the calls, but she listened to the messages he left. He'd noticed the car was on its way to him. He sounded drunk, seething, barely containing himself.

'Katie, listen to me. You've made me very angry and I'm not sure what I'm going to do about it. If I were you, I would turn around and drive very far away. I suggest you take your mother with you, too. And change your name when you get there.'

Katie's breath caught in her throat. He was threatening her mother now? His second message was somehow worse. 'You know,' he began without preamble, 'there was a time when I thought I could be happy growing old with you as my wife. But then you know what happened?' He paused for a moment before going on. 'You happened, you whore, that's what. You fucking happened.'

Then he hung up.

After listening to his calls, she didn't know if she even had the strength to stand up again. The past twenty-four hours had taken much from her. She put a hand to her head. Strands of her hair were still matted to her scalp with dried blood. She wanted to vomit. She wanted to pass out. Instead she went upstairs and showered.

No one knew how dangerous Tyler could be. It had taken Katie two hours of begging, cajoling and finally crying before her mother would agree to fly up to Kentucky tomorrow to see family. Despite the evidence of Katie's bruised face, she just wouldn't believe that Tyler could be a threat to her as well. Katie finally couched it as a sudden gift – she wanted to pay for Mom to see her brother, it would be a neat surprise, and Mom went along with that.

Katie would have the same trouble with Jonah and Gordon. There was no way she could make them believe her over the phone, and maybe not even in person. She couldn't adequately describe the horror of the scrapbook, and the book itself was gone – when she had awakened that morning, Tyler's office door was wide open for the first time in years, and the desk drawer was empty. But she would have to do something.

For a little while, she'd thought of going to Kentucky with her Mom. Jonah could fend for himself, right? And so could his friend Gordon.

Sure, just like the dead woman in the photo.

256

She could save them, she decided. She could fly down to Key West, meet them, and show them the photograph that she had. She could explain everything that had happened. She could beg them to leave Tyler alone and forget about the money. She could pay them to leave him alone. Tyler was wrong – she did have a little money of her own stashed away. Hell, she could even cry if that's what it took. Whatever she would have to do to convince them, she could do it.

The thought of going to Key West, of landing where Tyler would be, sent shivers through her body. She wouldn't call it fear, exactly. It was more like terror. But she would go anyway. If only to talk to them once, and give them the chance to save themselves, she would go down there.

Night had turned to day, and Vernon was finally in.

The girl, Gabby. He'd spent days watching her parade around. They'd spent a couple of days and nights glancing at each other, flirting, making faces. Now they were together, and it was so good. She was against the wall of the main cabin, legs wrapped around his torso. He watched her face. It had changed from cool and bored to . . . beautiful.

He'd known the time was right – it was now or never. Mama was napping in her cabin. She had to sleep sometime. The storm was coming, and it had changed in the past few hours. It was a hurricane now, headed straight for them. The VHF was abuzz with people taking about it. The radio stations said retreat to higher ground. Already the boat had started to move, riding bigger and bigger swells. Foerster was in the lab – God only knew what he was doing in there. Vernon hadn't checked on him in a while and didn't see how anybody could concentrate with all the movement. This boat was no good for open water – it had been designed for use on lakes and inland waterways. They had to bring the boat into the marina soon, maybe even right now. Then again, it couldn't happen now; it had to wait till after this.

Vernon had been half-awake, sitting in the main cabin, skimming through the newspapers on the Internet and listening to the open chatter on the VHF – people clearing out, people wondering what to do. He'd slept on the couch for several hours, then switched shifts again with Mama around 6 a.m., maybe three hours ago. Down the narrow hall, he could hear her snoring behind the door of her cabin. He'd known it was time to wake her and tell her about the storm. He would need her help to steer the boat in. He'd known all this but still he waited.

The girl had come in from outside. She wore a pair of bikini bottoms and a T-shirt. Jesus. The dog was at her heels. It had begun to spit rain outside, just a little bit. Vernon could tell because the girl's clothes were damp. She stopped a few feet away and looked at him. Then she smiled. He could tell something else about her, even though she didn't say a word.

He stood, and he just . . . took her. Right there and then. Like a magic trick, his shorts came down and her bottoms came off almost before he knew it was happening. They'd been waiting long enough as it was. He eased her up against the wall. He lifted her, and she was lighter than air. He slipped inside of her and then they were together. They were silent for a few moments, going at it, looking into each other's eyes. She started to shake and moan.

'Oh my God, I'm already gonna—'

He covered her mouth with one hand. Her face turned red, she closed her eyes and her whole body trembled as she pushed against him. The dog yapped and Vernon kicked it away.

Good Lord, it was good. It was good. It was—

Vernon heard a sound. Big Mama had chambered a round right by the side of his head. From the corner of his eye, he saw the dark hole of the gun's muzzle. He looked down at her other hand, her right. In it, she held a large pair of metal scissors. She opened and closed them. They made that metal, click-clicking sound. Click-click, snip-snip. It reminded him of the barber shop when he was a young boy.

'Vernon, you son of a bitch, I'm going to cut your precious dick off.'

Vernon took a deep, slow breath. He and the girl had stopped moving. They were frozen against the wall, her legs still around him, an instant erotic statue. He looked into her eyes, but he saw nothing there. Maybe some fear, but not even that. Call it chagrin.

'Mama,' Vernon said. 'It takes two to tango. Are you familiar with that little saying?'

'Go ahead. Take it out of there so I can cut it off.'

Vernon turned his head just enough to see her face. Unlike the girl's face, Mama's was easy to read. It was a volcano of emotions. Rage, hatred, betrayal, heartbreak, sadness. They were all there, and she needed a place to put them. Poor Mama. Vernon felt for her, he really did, but she was gonna need to get all that under control. They were still on the job here. There was no way he would let her take her problems out on him – not by cutting his dick off, and not by shooting him in the head. Just wasn't going to happen, not today.

He looked at the girl again. Now he could read her face. She was gone. No fast-talk explanations, no calling off her big dyke girlfriend. She simply wasn't even there any more. Well, if anybody was going to defuse this situation, it would have to be him.

'Mama, we need to bring the boat in.'

The gun never wavered. The scissors waited at the ready. 'After we finish this.'

He nodded. 'OK.'

He ducked his head and swung backhand, slapping Mama's gun away. She fired it as he swung, the report loud and hot in his right ear. He went deaf instantly in that ear – no sound at all.

Holy shit, she nearly blew my brains out.

The gun flew across the cabin, thumped against the wall, and clunked to the floor. It was a big heavy gun and he felt the sting of its metal against the back of his hand. The pain barely registered – there wasn't time.

He turned and grabbed Mama's other wrist just as it came around with the scissors. She snipped and snipped, but missed him. She tried to stab him with the sharp point. He was stronger – he turned the scissors back towards her stomach. They stood toe to toe now, he with both her wrists in his hands, his shorts wrapped around his ankles, the boat moving too much, his balance bad. Beside him, he heard the girl screaming. She was screaming into his left ear, the only good ear he had left. Over Mama's shoulder, he saw skinny Foerster hovering there now, big red fire extinguisher in hand. Oh, there was an emergency out here, but it wasn't a fire.

'Mama!' Vernon said. 'Cut the shit.'

She pushed him backwards and she was strong – strong enough. His tangled feet went out from under him and he fell on his back, pulling her down on top of him. He heard a sound then, a sort of wet sound, and Mama lay heavy on top of him. She groaned and moved just a little bit, nothing but the smallest tremble.

If Vernon thought back a few seconds, he could remember what it felt like when the scissors punched through Mama's chest. The chestplate was hard and the sharp point of the scissors had gone in rather like a spike driven through thick wood. But Vernon didn't want to think back to that.

'Shit, man. Shit.'

With some effort, he rolled her body off him. He turned over on to all fours above her. Her face was slack now, the tumult of emotions gone. The silver handle of the scissors protruded from her chest right about where her heart should be. It was one hell of an unlucky shot. If she'd taken it in the stomach, maybe they could have rushed her in the dinghy to the docks, called ahead and had an ambulance waiting. A medic might have stabilised her during a fast-forward run through city streets to the hospital. She might have had some slim hope of survival.

But stabbed in the heart? Shit. She was already dead.

From all fours, Vernon looked up into Gabby's blank eyes.

'I didn't mean to do that.'

Foerster bashed Vernon in the back of the head with the fire extinguisher. He reared up – he had one chance to get this right – and put everything he had into it. The blow hardly made a sound, a dull thud, but a satisfying tremor went from the extinguisher up Foerster's arms to his shoulders.

Vernon collapsed to the floor, and Foerster hit him in the head again. And again. And again. He didn't stop till Vernon's skull cracked open and a small fountain of blood sprayed into the air. The blood fanned out on the floor around Vernon's head, first a puddle, then a pool, and growing all the time.

The VHF radio shrieked static then, startling Foerster. He jumped up and smashed it to pieces, hitting it three, four, five times. He looked at the bottom of the extinguisher – all those impacts and not even a dent.

He turned and looked at the girl. She was right there, against the wall, with nothing on but a damp baby-blue T-shirt. Her young body didn't interest him in the least, not at this moment. He'd heard them out here, she and Vernon, and he'd heard Mama sneak out and confront them, and he'd heard the gun go off. He'd been sitting in the lab, gazing down at his table and pretending to work.

Meanwhile, the boat had rocked and swayed, side to side, up and down, equipment falling off Foerster's worktable, Foerster's hands shaking, water that was alive – teeming with weaponised cholera and multiplying all the time – sloshing around in big drums right behind him. Why were they keeping him here? Because they were crazy as fuck and they were all going to die. That was fine, but count him out. That gun going off was freedom calling.

Foerster threw the fire extinguisher aside. 'This isn't funny any more,' he said to Gabby. 'I gotta get the fuck out of here. Do you know how to drive this boat?'

She just looked at him. Foerster shook his head. Of course she didn't know how to drive this thing. It was too fucking big. He thought of something else. 'The dinghy,' he said. 'Do you know how to drive that dinghy tied up out there?'

She was in the trauma zone – wide, staring eyes gazing down at those two dead bodies, silent tears running down her face. 'They were going to kill you,' she said, and her voice was small and far away. 'As soon as you were finished making the disease. I heard them talking about it.'

So what else was new? It didn't surprise Foerster in the least. Of course they were going to kill him. Everybody was always going to kill him or catch him or do some damn thing to him, but here he was alive and on the loose and there they were dead on the floor.

'Was Gant in on it?'

'Yes.'

OK. He'd get Gant too, if he could. He came around the bodies and grabbed the girl by the shoulders.

'I was going to tell you,' she said.

He shook her so hard her head made a crazy, bobblehead motion. 'Listen to me, bitch. We gotta get off the boat. There's a fucking hurricane coming. Can you drive the dinghy?'

She came alert and looked into his eyes. She seemed almost surprised. 'The dinghy? Sure I can drive it. I go back and forth for groceries and stuff sometimes, whenever Mama needs something in town. She's the one who taught me.'

'Good. Put some clothes on. We're getting out of here.'

Foerster released her, walked over to the wall where Mama's gun had landed and picked it up. It was a lot heavier than he expected – like picking up a brick. Guns had never been his thing, but maybe it was time to start a new habit. He spotted Vernon's binoculars on the desk and grabbed those, too. What else? The flashlight? Sure, he might need that. Then the notepad Vernon had scribbled on caught his eye. *Bloodhound*, it said, along with a website address and an account number. Gant's wife, coming to town – Vernon was supposed to track her down by GPS. Well, well, well. That might be something. He'd have to bring the laptop along, too.

He took two steps down the hall towards the lab – as much as he wanted to put Cholera B in the past, he figured a couple of small carboys of the growing bacteria and a package of the freeze-dried stuff would be enough evidence to take Gant down, should the need ever arise. But Foerster would only give the cops Gant if he himself got busted. It'd be his ticket out.

'Can I bring Versace?' the girl said.

He stopped and looked at her. 'What?'

'My dog. Can I bring my dog?'

The dog. Foerster hadn't noticed it in all the commotion. It cowered and growled under the seat by the radio. He hated dogs. This one, especially, was like a glorified rat. 'No. Forget the dog.'

She started crying again. 'Please let me bring my dog.'

He pointed the gun at the dog. The girl cringed and something about that made Foerster smile. 'Say it one more time and I'll shoot the fucking dog. Now hurry up and get dressed.'

10

Jonah drove the egg south through the Keys, the road one long, narrow and empty ribbon ahead of them, crossing small green islands and open water.

On the opposite side, bumper-to-bumper traffic snaked north, thousands of people getting out before the storm hit. The traffic was a motley collection of cars, buses, trucks, motorcycles and walkers – hundreds of walkers moving along the side of the road, carrying backpacks, pushing shopping carts, most of them going faster than the vehicles now. A dark helicopter gunship flew low overhead, poised against the gunmetal sky, moving along the line. The scene reminded Jonah of footage he'd seen from World War Two, with refugees fleeing ahead of the advancing armies.

Moisture in the air gave the illusion of the road ending just up ahead. On this side of the highway, it disappeared into the distance as though it had fallen through a trapdoor and into the ocean several storeys below. On the other side of the highway, the traffic appeared from out of the shimmer as though conjured up by a magician. It was just that narrow strip of road ahead, water on both sides and sky above. The sky was cloudy, and darkening with the impending storm.

Jonah felt a little better today. They'd stopped and taken a few hours' sleep in a roadside motel. They'd had breakfast, with plenty of coffee. He had energy, and was ready to face whatever came. The only thing he didn't feel good about were the words coming out of Gordo's mouth.

'No way, man,' Gordo said. 'There's no fucking way we can bring the cops in on this. I promise you that. They'll bust us for the shoot-out up in Charleston. We'll sit in a lock-up for two days before they even talk to us. Then what? Oh, by the way, we think this ex-cop is about to commit a terrorist attack? Would you believe that? I wouldn't. Anyway, we don't even know ourselves if it's real or not. My worst-case scenario is they do believe us, but then the terror thing turns out to be something that guy Max made up, and we lose the Foerster collar to the cops. I don't have to tell you if we don't make the collar, we don't get the money.'

Jonah drummed his fingers on the steering wheel. 'You know what my worst-case scenario is? We fuck around because we don't want to lose the money, and these assholes kill thousands of people on some island.'

Gordo sighed. 'And I'm saying that bringing the cops in is the same as fucking around. They will knock us off our game. We'll lose the collar, Gant will slip away, and those people on the island will be up shit's creek anyway.'

They drove on in silence for a long moment. Jonah glanced at the logjam of refugees streaming by on his left. Ahead of him, the road was wide open. Nobody was going this way. Light rain began to patter against the windshield and he turned on the wipers.

'Listen, Jonah, we can do this ourselves. We don't need the cops, OK? Here's the plan. We hit Gant at the bar. We get him to take us to the boat. If Max was right, the boat is out at sea.'

'What if he won't take us?'

Gordo smiled. 'He'll take us. I'll make him take us. Don't worry about that. So when we get out there, we grab Foerster and take a look around. If there's some kind of disease factory going on, we call it in on the shipboard radio, the VHF. We turn on an Epirb to mark the location, and we scoot out of there with Foerster before any cops or coast Guard show up.'

'An Epirb?'

'Yeah, an Epirb. It's this little emergency radio beacon. Works kind of like GPS. If you go in the water, or your ship is sinking, it turns on and sends a distress signal so they know where to find you. You can also turn it on manually. The social contract may be shredded, but for now, the Coast Guard still rescues people. I was hoping we'd find a marine store open anyway, because I want to buy a couple of life jackets. We can get one of these Epirbs while we're there. How does all that sound?'

Jonah shook his head. 'It sounds pretty half-assed, to tell you the truth.'

Gordo frowned. 'You got a better idea? One that doesn't involve cops?'

It was a bumpy ride.

The plane flew low enough now, below the clouds, that Katie could look down and see the grey water flowing away to the horizon, dotted with brown and green islands. The plane took a heavy jolt every minute or two, and each time, some passenger would groan or sigh. At one point, a woman in the back made a high-pitched squeak, like a mouse. There wasn't much confidence in this cabin. There wasn't much reason to be confident.

The airline had a strange name. Coastal-Piedmont Carrier Air Express – it was enough to make Katie laugh. It sounded like they kept tacking on words so nobody would know who to blame when the plane went down. She had never liked flying, but commercial air travel was an especially iffy thing these days. The company could be gone next week – these airlines winked in and out of existence like lightning bugs.

Flight 5599 from Charleston to Key West was a small turboprop that sat all of thirteen people. It was like a flying mini-bus, complete with the seat across the back where three people could cram themselves together. The engines worked hard and loud, and never quietened – she could feel their vibrations in the walls and in the floor. Katie guessed the ceiling wasn't quite six feet high. There was no bathroom. Riding in that plane gave her the sense of being in a mine right before the collapse. The plane was buffeted by high winds, listing to the side, lurching up and then dropping down. Rain sprayed against the windows.

The captain had come on the intercom soon after take-off. 'We'll be seeing some turbulence on this flight. Looks like we'll be riding the tiger most of the way.'

He wasn't kidding.

She looked around the compartment. Eight people were on this flight, headed into Key West when most everyone else was leaving. She thought of going around and doing a little survey of the other passengers. *Why are you on this flight? Do you realise there's danger up ahead?*

She wondered if any of them thought of it that way. Once they landed, probably none of them were in any real danger except her. She took a deep breath and closed her eyes. This was a trip all the way out to the end of the line. She couldn't know what was going to happen when she arrived there. Finding Jonah and Gordon should be easy enough – she could call the Bloodhound company and ask them where her own car was parked. But her heart sank when she thought of seeing Tyler. The image of Tyler's photograph came back to her, but she pushed it away again. For Katie, on the aeroplane, it was almost too much to think about. She was headed straight for him.

The steward's voice came on the intercom. 'Attention passengers. We will now make our final approach into Key West International Airport. Please note that the fasten-seat-belt signs are on. It's already raining in Key West – lots of cloud cover and about seventy degrees. As you know, we're in for some heavy weather during the next twenty-four to forty-eight hours, so we ask you to keep safe, keep dry, and enjoy yourselves. We'll see you on the flight back.'

The plane turned and banked. They were going down. God help her, Katie was going down.

Gant lay on top of the bed, ignoring the TV news across the room.

His head felt stuffed with cotton and his tongue felt glued to the roof of his mouth. From where he lay, he could look past his nondescript room and out the large window. The rain was starting to pick up. He saw dark skies and various pieces of garbage rolling along the wharf, blown by the wind.

The wind was picking up, too – some of the gusts were real howlers. Nobody was out.

Things were shaky right now. He needed to firm them up. He'd made some mistakes, and he had to stop doing that. He'd called Katie several times and yelled at her voicemail – he didn't really remember what he'd said. Then, as exhausted as he was, he'd stayed up half the night, drinking and watching TV. He'd slept a long time, and when he woke, it was already two o'clock in the afternoon. The bottle of Chivas Regal was empty. That was an hour ago.

He had given Howe the go-ahead last night to send his men. They were coming today. He should expect them at the boat by 6 p.m. tonight – roughly three hours from now. They hoped to be back on their plane – Jesus, with Gant riding along – by 8 p.m. Land at the island by around 10, then hit the water towers sometime after midnight. By late tomorrow morning, half the people on the island should already be dying. And all of that was fine and dandy. Terrific – it was what we were here for. But if Gant had it to do over again, now, while sober, he probably would have told Howe to wait another day.

Gant was tired, and not looking forward to the long night ahead. To make matters worse, he hadn't spoken with anyone on his team yet today. Five minutes after waking up, while still lying there in bed, Gant had called Vernon. There was no answer on Vernon's phone, so Gant called Big Mama. Also no answer. What did that mean? Was the cell service out? He double-checked his own phone. No, it was working fine. He tried them both again. Again no luck.

Vernon wasn't answering. That was strange. Gant had known Vernon three years, and in all that time, Vernon hadn't been late once, and hadn't failed to return a call. Not even once. Mama might flake out and disappear from time to time, but laid-back Vernon was as punctual and reliable as the tides.

One possible scenario began to develop in Gant's mind. Vernon had gone to find Katie and put her out of commission. Sure, that made perfect sense, and was exactly what Gant had asked him to do. That's why he wasn't answering his phone. Meanwhile, Mama was slacking off in bed with the girl-friend. That's why she wasn't answering. OK, so if all that was true, the boat was right where he left it yesterday, and in all likelihood, when Gant went to meet Max one hour from now, Vernon would turn up there as well. Then the three of them would head out to the boat together and be ready to make the transfer to Howe's men.

Gant liked that storyline – he liked its optimism. But were there other, darker, possibilities? Here was one: Katie had called the cops about her suspicions, Vernon had been busted by the police, and he had rolled over on the location of the boat. Gant didn't like that one at all, and he didn't believe it. If it were true, the cops would have come storming in here by now – both Vernon and Mama knew where Gant stayed in town.

Still, it would reassure him just to talk with Vernon and find out everything was going fine. He picked up his cell phone and dialled Vernon's number.

'Vernon, you son of a bitch. Pick up the phone.'

'It looks pretty easy to me,' Gordo said.

He walked with his hands stuffed in the pockets of his shorts. He practically had to shout over the wind. He was getting drenched from the rain, and so was Jonah. The shoulders of Jonah's sweatshirt, and his hood, were soaked through.

They had arrived in Key West less than an hour ago, and were walking from the Schooner Wharf bar back to their motel – it was that close. It needed to be close in case they had to take Gant somewhere private to soften him up a bit. They had gone to the bar early just to take a look at it, get a sense of what they were dealing with.

It was a wide open place, all but deserted today, with huge windows along three walls and an outdoor patio section on the side of the building that was completely deserted. Gant would probably sit by a seafront window and look out at the water. When they spotted him, they'd come from two different directions – Jonah through the front door and Gordo from the patio. Jonah puts the gun to his head, Gordo wrestles the cuffs on him.

Flash the badge at the bartender on the way out and it's all over – then on to the next thing.

Now, the rain started to pour and they picked up their pace as they walked towards the motel. The streets were narrow with leafy canopies overhead. White clapboard houses behind picket fences vied for space with large homes with gables, pediments, and columns set back from the street. Many houses were trimmed with intricately carved moulding. Windows were protected by wooden louvred blinds. At one house the sloping front roofline all but covered the top-storey windows, like eyebrows over tired eyes. A lot of places were boarded up for the storm.

At a blinking red stoplight, a gaunt old man, shirtless and with skin like tanned cowhide, bicycled past with a small black dog in his handlebar basket. Rainwater ran off both man and dog. The big heavy stoplight swung crazily in the wind. No one else was around.

'Easy,' Jonah said. 'Just like this whole job has been. We go from one easy thing to the next, thankful that we didn't get killed by the last easy thing.'

'Well, we're still here.'

'Do you think Foerster's still here?'

That gave Gordo pause. He hadn't thought about it at all. He figured that if Gant showed up to meet Max, then it went without saying that Foerster was still in town. But Gant could have moved him elsewhere ahead of the storm.

And stayed behind? Why do that? Why not just tell Max to meet him somewhere else? It occurred to Gordo that Max might have slipped a code word to Gant during that phone conversation, warning him to take off. But if he had, Gordo hadn't caught it. Anyway, it was better not to think about these things. The best thing to do was to move forward with confidence, as if everything was going according to plan.

'Yeah, he's still here. I feel sure of that.'

The motel was up ahead, a place called the Anchor Inn. The big parking lot was nearly empty. Just the egg and a few other cars sat out in the wind and rain. Across from the lot was another wharf where a couple of orphaned dinghies were still tied. Waves kicked up and broke right on to the wharf, slamming the dinghies against the wooden dock. If the owners of the dinghies didn't come and get them soon, there'd be nothing left of them by later tonight.

Leaning on the egg, half-concealed by shadow and by the driving rain, was a hooded person holding a dark umbrella.

'Watch it here,' Gordo said to Jonah. 'We got a visitor. Gant might know we're here. That would be just like him, sending someone to take us out on our doorstep.'

Jonah's hand slipped into his sweatshirt pocket. They came closer. The shape was all wrong for a hitman. The person wore a stylish red rain slicker, pulled tight to what began to look like an hourglass body. Had Gant sent a woman to kill them?

As they drew near, the woman looked out from under her umbrella. 'Hi,' Katie Gant said. 'I've been wondering when you would get home.'

'Son of a bitch,' Davis Foerster said to nobody, and smiled.

He knelt in the bottom of an inflatable rubber dinghy tied up to the wharf. The waves repeatedly drove the dinghy into the dock. The motion was violent, but somehow, this close to land, it didn't bother Foerster. In fact, at this moment the pouring rain, the crazy wind, the storm itself was hardly on his mind. Maybe fifty yards away, the two dickheads from New York had just met a woman in front of the door to their motel room. Foerster, wearing a rubber rain poncho but soaked to the bone anyway, had just watched the whole transaction with Vernon's binoculars. They were good glasses – they put the action right in the palm of Foerster's hand.

He'd watched them the whole time. Vernon's laptop had helped Foerster find the car. He'd confirmed it by the vanity plate on the back – *GANT2*. Was he surprised when it turned out to be these two jackasses driving it and not Gant's wife? Sure, sure. But hey, anything was possible. Gant had clearly been deceived. If these two were here, that probably meant they knew about the boat. What else could it mean?

Foerster had followed them down the street, lurking in the shadows, and had watched them as they scoped out the bar. When they'd run into the woman leaning on the hyper-modern bubble car, he'd crept here to the dock and into one of the dinghies. It was a brand new feeling, and a good one, to be the pursuer rather than the pursued. Foerster was invisible out here in the darkness, laying low with the water rats. He could see them but they couldn't see him. He knew where they were, but they had no idea where he was. For once, the element of surprise was in his favour.

While he watched through the glasses, the woman took her hood down and let loose her blond hair. Then she hugged both men in turn. The three of them went upstairs and into a room, Room 207 to be exact. Of course, he remembered where he'd seen the woman's face before. The lovely Mrs Gant, whom Foerster had met briefly before Gant had knocked him out with the butt-end of a gun, was making time with the boys from New York. What did that mean?

It meant opportunity. Today was a day of opportunities for Foerster. Everything was lining up just right. In fact, even though Foerster was currently drenched and miserable, five blocks away from here comfort awaited. There was a one-storey bungalow – set back from the street behind thick bushes, boarded up, darkened. The city was almost deserted, and this house was no different. In the front of the house, beneath one of the wooden boards, a window was missing. Foerster had knocked it out himself. You could pull that board back, slip underneath, and climb through the empty window. If you did, you'd have to allow a moment for your eyes to get used to the almost total darkness in there. Then you would move through the house to the back bedroom.

The girl was there on the bed. Her arms reached above her in a Y. Each of her wrists was tied to one of the bedposts. In fact, her ankles were tied to the bedposts at the bottom of the bed. She was spread-eagled. Her body was something to see, even in the darkness. This wouldn't be immediately obvious to the casual observer because Foerster had covered her in blankets to her chin just before he left. 'I'm cold,' she'd said to him in her little-girl voice just before he put the gag in her mouth, and he'd taken pity on her. Wouldn't want her to catch her death while he was gone, would he?

But when he first tied her to the bed, she'd been exposed to him in all her glory. Her eyes had watched him as he paced around the bed.

'You know I can kill you any time I like.'

The girl nodded.

'And you do want your freedom, right?'

It went without saying.

'Well, I'll give you your freedom in a little while. But first you have to do anything I say, anytime I say it. How does that sound?'

It sounded just fine.

Yes, it had been one hell of a red-letter day, and if events went where they appeared to be headed, it could turn out to be an even better night. Foerster would just have to wait here a little while longer and see.

Jonah shut the door against the storm. He and Gordo had just had a long conversation about Katie out in the wind and the rain. Gordo was not pleased that Katie had shown up. In fact, he was pissed. After they had talked, he had stalked off to eat some dinner before they did the job.

After locking the door, Jonah turned around, and as soon as he did, she was there. Their eyes locked and she came to him. She had changed into a terrycloth robe while Jonah was outside on the street. He slid his hands inside the robe and found she had nothing on underneath.

They made love standing up, without preamble.

Her hands gripped the back of his neck as he lifted her against the wall. She was ready, and in a moment he was, too. She groaned as he entered her. Dimly, he heard the things she said. She had abandoned all pretence of being a lady. Later, she bit him. Her nails clawed into his back. She wailed, a sound like a cat in an alley on a still, sweltering summer night.

Later, a tenderness came upon them, and they did it again, more slowly the second time. Then they sprawled in the bed together, naked under the covers. They ran their hands along each other's bodies, taking their time, no goal in mind, no hurry. Clocks ticked away outside the hotel-room door, but in the room a kind of eternity had set in. Jonah felt the onrushing world, its desire to smash that door and seize this moment away from them, but he pushed it away for just a little while longer. They lay in each other's arms.

'Katie, don't get me wrong,' he said. He touched her hair. 'If things were different, I'd love you being here with us. But things might get rough from here on out. No, scratch that. I know they're going to get rough. I think you should go home till it's all over.'

She stood and went over to her bag. 'I have something to show you. It's the reason I came here. I think you should give up this chase and just leave Tyler alone. Both of you.'

She dug in the bag and came out with a photo, an old Polaroid. He hadn't seen a Polaroid in years. He noticed that she didn't look at it. She passed it to him. He stared at it for a moment. It was a black woman, eyes open, with some kind of bloody wound to the head, maybe a gunshot wound. She was lying on a pavement somewhere. The picture didn't show anything below her shoulders, which were bare.

There was a long minute of silence.

'Gant did this?' Jonah said.

Katie nodded. 'He gave me the photo before he left. As a threat. I have no idea who the woman is, but I think he killed her. Where else would he get it?'

'It might have been evidence,' Jonah said. 'From when he was a cop.'

Katie shook her head. 'I tried to think that. But I found it in a book with a lot of other photos and newspaper clippings, all of them about murders. Some of them took place before he was a cop. Some while he was a cop. Some after. I think it was a book of trophies. I think Tyler has killed a lot of people. I think he was responsible for the anthrax attack two years ago.'

Her big eyes looked at Jonah.

'Katie, come on.'

'Jonah, it's true.'

'And where is the book now?'

She shook her head. 'I don't know. When he left, it was gone. He must have it.'

Jonah found that he didn't want to go to the place where all this was leading. He'd been hoping that the cholera thing was a ruse – a sick joke – that Max had concocted so they would let him go. Gordo seemed to be leaning that way. Jonah also wanted to be careful not to reveal anything they knew to Katie. The last thing he needed was to have her spiral into a panic. 'So let me get this straight. Your husband is a mass murderer. He's even a terrorist. And if I get too close to him, he's so dangerous that he's going to kill me, too.'

'Yes. You and Gordon.'

Jonah put the photo face down on the bedside table. He took Katie into his arms. 'Baby, Gordo and I are not that easy to kill.'

Gordo sat alone.

He'd eaten a sandwich and had finished his second beer. A cup of coffee had just landed in front of him. The food and the drinks were making him feel better. For a while, he had wandered along Duvall Street, but the emptiness of the place had only given him a queasy feeling. It seemed like only a few lost souls were still in town. Thick plywood had appeared on most of the windows. *LOOTERS WILL BE SHOT* was scrawled in spray paint on a few of the wooden panels. At one point, a military transport had passed him, the soldiers on board looking wet and miserable and more than a little hostile.

Gordo didn't want Gant's wife here. He'd told her as much back at the motel room. It was too dangerous. There were too many emotions involved. She was going to get in the way. Gordo and Jonah had left the room and gone out to the street. They talked about it, hammered by the wind and the rain.

'It's just a lot of shit getting in the way,' Gordo said.

'I know. I'm sorry it happened. You know, this is about her husband, and she lent us the car, and there's this whole other thing maybe going on . . . Listen, give me some time to talk to her.'

Gordo nodded. 'Good enough. We have about exactly an hour. Now I'm going to get some food. And you go do whatever you have to do to convince her.'

'Convince her of what?'

'That she's gotta go,' Gordo said. 'I don't care how you do it. She damn sure can't be in our room. We might need it. Unless she doesn't mind sitting around and watching me bust her husband's teeth out to get him to talk.'

'Where is she supposed to go? She's not going to be safe anywhere but in our room.'

'And if we happen to need the room? If we need to take Gant somewhere?'

Jonah shrugged. 'I guess we'll have to take him somewhere else.'

Gordo had said nothing to that. Now, he looked around this little sandwich shop. It was just about the only place open. Two other people were hunkered down at another table. Outside the window, the rain drummed hollowly on the front awning. Gordo watched the raindrops plunk into deep puddles on the street. He sat and stared and sipped his coffee. He shook his head.

Gant's wife. Good grief.

Nevertheless, Gordo began to get that feeling – that confident buzz he often got right before a job. Maybe it was having some food in his stomach. Maybe it was just a growing sense of excitement, and of danger. But the feeling told him that this was going to be the time. They were finally going to nab Foerster, once and for all. They were going to get the money. They might even break open an international terror ring. How was that for a night's work?

He looked at his watch. Twenty-five minutes to five. OK. It was time to break up the little huddle back at the motel room.

It was time to rock and roll.

Jonah lingered in the doorway before he left her. Leaving that room was like being torn in half. Gordo was waiting downstairs on the street.

'Do you really have to go now?' she said. 'In a hurricane? You're going to get killed out there. It's not even safe to be in here, never mind out there.'

Jonah didn't want to say too much about their intentions – about the fact that in the next ten minutes, they planned to grab her husband at gunpoint. 'We have to go. Anything could happen if we wait till morning. It has to be now.'

The look in her eyes told him everything he needed to know.

'It's going to be OK,' he told her. 'You just lay low tonight and nothing will happen. Keep the door locked and don't open it for anybody but us. We'll go out to that boat, get this guy, and be back in a few hours. Then I'll come by here, and tomorrow we'll get out of town. Leave your husband behind, leave it all behind.'

'And go where?' she said.

'I don't know. Do you want to come back to New York? I've got a great apartment. It looks right out on the water.'

'We'll talk about it,' she said. 'Just come back safe.'

'I will.'

They kissed again, a long one, their bodies and spirits entwined. At least, Jonah thought, for now.

Foerster watched the two men walk away, beaten by the rain and the wind. He stood about a block away, up the street from the motel. He watched them from beneath and behind a thick tree, its branches waving crazily in the wind above him. He imagined that if they looked this way, which they didn't, they would never notice him. He wore a dark blue hooded rain slicker, and he watched them with Vernon's same binoculars.

Mighty handy, binoculars. He wondered why it had never occurred to him before to own a pair. He could see everything clearly with those glasses. He could see clearly that the black guy and the fat guy had walked off together, leaving Gant's wife alone in her room. He could see them leave the room, then close the door tightly behind them.

Foerster watched closely. He watched as the black guy looked around as they walked, just checking it all out. The fucking guy nauseated Foerster. He and his fat friend. It was hard to believe they had followed him all this way, but follow him they had. They would never stop, he realised. Not till he taught them a lesson. Well, it was about time to do exactly that.

Gant's wife was the lesson.

'You like her, don't you?' Foerster said. 'Yeah, I can tell.'

He was no master of disguise, Foerster knew that about himself, but in the past few days he had grown the beginnings of a beard and moustache. He looked better. If someone were using an old mugshot of him, they'd have to do a double take to make sure they had the right guy.

Beneath the rain slicker, he was dressed in a maintenance man's uniform and an old, oil-stained Caterpillar baseball cap he had found in the deserted bungalow where he and the girl were staying. The uniform had the name *Steve* sewn across the left breast. He looked right for a maintenance guy. The beard and moustache helped the look – just some good old boy working a night job fixing leaky pipes.

He'd packed a gym bag with a few items that he might need. He had the flashlight he'd taken from the boat – the better to play the handyman role. He had a box cutter with a retractable blade. He had a one-litre container of alkaline water teeming with active Cholera B. And he had a small metal hatchet with a rubber grip which he'd found in a dilapidated tool shed in Steve the maintenance man's backyard. He slipped the box cutter into the pocket of his overalls.

Gant's tasty wife, alone in a room. Boy oh boy. Foerster's part in the project was over, and that was too bad, but he would still find out if the cholera worked. It would satisfy a certain curiosity that he had, and it would kill two birds with one stone, as it were. He had kind of toyed with testing it on the girl, but she was too much fun to kill so soon. So it was down to Gant's wife. She would make the perfect test.

He'd have to move quickly and right away. There was no telling how soon those guys would be back. He had no idea what they were doing. They might ride out to the *Sea Dog*, they might not. If they didn't, they could return at any time. *Act now!* a voice shouted in his head. *Before time runs out!* He walked down the block and across the deserted roadway in the rain. The upstairs room was near the end, away from the main office. That was good, although the office itself was dark, which was even better. It looked like management had gone home to wait out the storm.

He climbed the stairs, went right to her door and knocked.

'Hello?' came the voice.

'Maintenance, ma'am.'

He felt her peering through the eye hole at him.

The door opened a few inches. The metal restraining chain was still on.

'Ma'am, the office sent me down to look at the pipes in the bathroom. We've had some flooding in recent weeks, and the way it's coming down tonight, we're afraid we might see some more. We might even have to ask you to change your room assignment.'

'Southwinds?' she said. 'Isn't this the Anchor Inn?'

He glanced down at his uniform. 'Well, yeah. I work for Southwinds, but this place always hires me to do little odd jobs for them on the side.' He put his forefinger to his lips. 'Don't tell nobody.'

She shut the door again. He heard the deadbolt latch. 'Do you mind if I call the office to make sure?' she said from the other side.

Foerster smiled and dug his hatchet out of the bag. 'Of course not,' he said. 'Go right ahead.'

He reared back with the hatchet and struck the door right next to the lock. The sharp blade sank into the wood. From the inside, he heard her scream. He yanked the axe out and did it again. And again. And again. And again. The wood splintered and the lock collapsed from its seating. He pushed the door open.

She stared at him, her blue fuzzy robe pulled tightly around her body. Foerster's eyes wandered to the hint of cleavage at the top. He stepped inside the room and closed the door behind him.

11

'Hurry the fuck up, kids. We ain't got all night.'

Marco Dolby stood on the floating dock in the darkness, smoked a joint and watched the team load up the go-fast boat with MP5 submachine guns – silencers already attached – and boxes of 9mm ammunition. Dolby was squat and muscular. He swayed with the rolling movement of the dock and cupped the joint with his hand to keep it out of the rain. He liked to get high for action like tonight's. It put a weird glow around everything.

The boat, bobbing and weaving in the heavy swells, was thirty-two feet long with huge engines and enough cabin space under the long foredeck to hold all the shit they were taking from Gant tonight. The team was himself, Smith and O'Neil – two crazed shooters much like himself – and Martins, a former Navy Seabee who would pilot the boat through the storm. Under their clothes every man on the team wore a Kevlar soft ballistic vest. Smith and O'Neil stacked padded crates in the cockpit – the guns were safe and dry inside the crates. Martins stood at the helm, buckets of water running down his rain poncho. He yawned.

'You bored, Martins? Why don't you take a nap?'

Martins flashed a gap-toothed smile and raised his middle finger.

The load-up took all of five minutes. When they were ready, Dolby pulled out his phone and called the number Howe had given him before they left the island. Three rings and the man himself answered.

'Gant.'

'Mr Gant, this is a friend of a friend. I've been sent by a man to make a pick-up. In fifteen minutes, we can be at the coordinates you gave us. Are you there?'

'You're early,' said the voice on the other end. It sounded like an accusation. Dolby remembered the voice, and the attitude. He'd been standing in the runway shack when they'd strip-searched Gant just days before.

'Yes, we are, but we're on a tight schedule, so . . .'

'Well, I'm not there. I'm in Key West, picking up one of my guys. If you want to head out to the spot, my people will—'

'My friend told me to deal only with you.'

Dolby winced, hoping the lie came out smooth. Howe hadn't exactly said to deal only with Gant. What he had said was to make sure Gant was on the boat before going there. What he'd also said was to shoot every person they found on the boat, leaving no one alive – especially Gant. In fact, Howe had instructed the team to refrain from head shots so they could be sure to make a positive identification of Gant. He had to be confirmed dead before Dolby transferred a single container from the lab to the speedboat.

This was your standard double-cross. The man who had masterminded the cholera attack – and likely his entire crew – would be dead before the attack ever took place. When islanders started dying horrible deaths tomorrow morning, there'd be no trail back to where the disease had come from. No loose ends.

Dolby shook his head. Smith and O'Neil were a couple of trigger-happy nutjobs who couldn't be counted on to refrain from anything. And Howe was an idiot. Gant would be fish food before the night was out – Dolby could guarantee that much. But he couldn't guarantee it would be pretty.

'Well gee, that's wonderful,' Gant squawked over the cell phone. 'It's nice to be wanted. Give me half an hour, maybe forty-five minutes, and I'll meet you out there.'

Dolby signed off and slipped the cell phone into his pocket. 'Motherfucker.'

'Is it go?' Martins said.

'It most definitely is not go. We gotta sit here in the rain at least another half-hour till this shitbird goes home.'

'That sucks.'

'It really does. You know what? I'm gonna kill Gant one time because that's the job. Then I'm gonna kill him a second time for making me wait.'

Martins flashed that goofy grin again. Not for the first time, Dolby wondered if Martins wasn't a little soft in the head.

Gant hung up the phone and gazed through the window at the roiling sea.

He was starting to feel a little better. He sat alone at a corner table in the Schooner Wharf, watching the storm outside. At times, the rain blew sideways past the glass. There was almost nobody in this whole place – so few people that the bartender, a bearded, heavyset fellow with a bright red nose, was doing double-duty as the waiter. Gant's third whiskey had just arrived in front of him, and he was climbing neatly up and over the hangover that had plagued him earlier in the day. In fact, he felt pretty mellow yellow. His next drink would be an Irish Coffee, and the jolt of caffeine would help him get ready for the evening's festivities.

Now, if only Max would get here. Or if Vernon would call and confirm that everything was a go. Either one would be nice. In another five minutes, if Max didn't show, Gant would head out to the lab by himself. Max could call in and find out what was up.

Fucking Howe . . . the man was relentlessly neurotic and impatient. He'd pushed Gant to make the transfer today – OK. But now his men were here early and waiting around, probably because Howe had sent them from the island too early. Logjams like this were exactly how jobs went wrong.

Didn't matter. The hand-over would go smoothly. Gant would make it work. If Howe's men had to stand around on the boat for half an hour because things weren't quite in order, that was Howe's fault for speeding the job up. But Gant doubted even that much would go wrong.

Then a man put a gun to his head.

'Don't move. Don't even twitch.'

Gant saw the gun there on the left side of his peripheral vision. He didn't turn his head or make any move at all. A brown hand held the gun. Now a large white man, heavyset, appeared on his right. The man grabbed Gant's wrists and pulled them around behind his back. Gant felt the bite of steel manacles as the man cuffed his wrists together. Fuck. Maybe he was getting old. He hadn't even seen these guys coming.

'Police?'

'Try again.'

Gant turned his head as they yanked him up from the table. Tall, good-looking black guy, light brown skin. Gant remembered the motel card with the name scribbled on it. Jonah. And here was his buddy, the no-named husky one. The big man could use a shave.

'I thought you guys were dead.'

'Surprise.'

'I guess this means Max isn't coming tonight?'

'Good guess,' the big man said. 'Now don't give me any hassles getting out this door. Don't say a fucking word to anybody, or I will make your life very hard. Understood?'

'You're the boss.'

Gant's mind was racing too fast to give anyone a hassle. They had broken Max, and made him roll over. That in itself was out of sight. Max was a tough guy. But they'd also got Max to call and pretend everything was OK. That was almost too much to believe. Still, there had to be a way out of this mess. These guys weren't professionals, not in the sense of the term that Gant normally understood. They'd been lucky so far, but they were bound to make a mistake – probably a big, glaring one.

They walked Gant through the nearly empty bar. A few people at tables turned to look as they went past. The big man flashed a badge at the bartender. 'Police business. This man is under arrest.'

The bartender shrugged. Gant said nothing. Then they were outside on the street, battered by the rain and the wind.

'OK,' Gant said. He practically had to shout. 'What now?'

'Now you take us out to your boat,' the big man said. 'You give us Foerster, and we go away. You can keep your little drug lab, whatever it is your friend Max said you were doing. All we want – all we ever wanted – is Foerster.'

Gant nodded, and had to suppress a smile. Here came the mistake, right on schedule. Let's make a quick trip out to the ol' drug lab, where these two cockroaches would get caught between the rock of Vernon and Big Mama, and the hard place of Howe's men. It was anybody's guess who would do the actual killing, but if Gant managed to get these manacles off before it happened, he hoped to take that pleasure himself.

'I'll give you Foerster,' he said. 'I don't mind doing that, as long as everything else stays intact. To tell you the truth, he's kind of a pain in the ass.'

'Let's go, in that case.'

'Fine. The boat's about fifteen minutes out.' Gant gestured with his head. 'My dinghy is tied up over that way.'

The thin man in the maintenance uniform took a long drag from his cigarette. 'You know who I am, right? I mean, here you are in this mess, you should at least know who I am. That's what I'm thinking.'

He sat across the room from Katie, stationed in a chair by the window, peering out down the street. He played with the box cutter in his hand. He pushed the lever forward over and over, the blade of the razor snaking out. Then he pressed the lever down, pushing the blade back in. It clicked each time he did so. The clicking sounded loud to Katie's ears. She knew exactly who he was. He looked a little different from a few days ago, with the trace of a beard and a baseball cap on, but it was him, all right – the man Tyler had beaten with the gun. Foerster, the man Jonah and Gordon were searching for – the rapist and murderer.

'It's a hell of a mess you're in, am I right?' He took another long drag.

He was right. It was a hell of a mess.

Katie couldn't move. She was bound hand and foot, her wrists secured to the headboard of the bed, her ankles secured tightly together. Her mouth was gagged, an ankle sock stuffed in there, then secured with a sports bra, which was wrapped around the back of her head. The ropes bit into her wrists and ankles, and the sock distended her mouth, making her jaw ache. She wore only the underwear she'd had on beneath her robe when she answered the door. The robe was now on the floor, stuffed in the crack beneath the bottom of the room door, keeping it shut.

Her whole body trembled.

It had happened so fast. The knock on the door. She wrapped herself in her robe. An innocuous little man outside, wanting to check the pipes. Suddenly he crashed through the door with an axe. Then he had the knife in his hand and the sharp point was against her throat.

'Say even one word and I will slice you open.'

It had been a small matter for him to bind her hands, then lash her to the bed. The knife had never left her throat.

Foerster took his attention off the window and gazed at the length of her body. She longed to cover herself, but it was too late for that. He stood and came towards her, carrying a small bottle of some liquid. He took the cap off as he approached.

'Are you listening?' he said now.

She nodded.

'Those friends of yours have been chasing me up and down the coast. I'm just trying to get them to stop. To leave me the fuck alone.' He laughed. 'I think this is gonna do it, boy. When they get back here and find you . . . I wish I could stick around to see their reaction. When they find you . . . I wish your husband could be here, too. Of course, I'm not going to wait around for that. By the time anybody finds you, I'll be long gone.'

He crouched down, getting eye level with her. His cigarette dangled just inches from her face. His skin was sweaty. He smelled foul.

He ran a hand along her stomach.

'Mmmm-hmmm, you are something. I'll say that much. I wish we had the time to really play together. When it comes to that, I'm as good as any man.' He winked. 'Maybe one day you'll find out.'

He was all mouth now, all teeth. Like a shark. Like a monster.

He indicated the bottle in his hand. 'I see you looking at my water. It's good stuff. You want a drink? Sure, I'll give you a drink, if you promise not to scream when I take that gag off.'

His hands were on her then. He undid the gag and pulled the sock from her mouth.

'You know the drill. No noise, now.'

She worked her jaw to get some of the feeling back into it.

He raised the open bottle near her mouth. 'Here ya go. Down the hatch.'

Gordo already disliked Gant. Never mind that he hired Foerster to make a disease, or hired Max to murder them. Personality-wise, the guy was just a prick.

'Sorry,' Gant said with a smirk as they stood on the dock. 'I have no life jackets. I don't wear them.'

'That's OK,' Gordo said. He showed Gant the big gym bag he was carrying. 'We brought a couple of our own.' Gordo shrugged into one, then handed one to Jonah. The life jackets were bright yellow, and each came equipped with a light that would turn on automatically if the wearer fell into the water.

They'd also managed to pick up an Epirb – it had cost more than Gordo had hoped, but they got one. That little beauty was in Gordo's pocket at this moment. Its distress signal would come on if he fell in the water, or he could turn it on manually. His plan was to turn it on and leave it at the houseboat after they grabbed Foerster and called the Coast Guard. The Feds could deal with this whole cholera mess. The Government was on a losing streak these days, and were probably feeling pretty mean. With any luck, they wouldn't just put this piece of shit Gant in jail – they'd put him *under* the jail.

On that score, Gordo felt pleased, almost absurdly so. The grab had gone just as smoothly as he had said it would. Gant put up no resistance and bought the 'we only want Foerster' story without any fuss. It couldn't have gone any better if Gordo had written the script himself.

In the darkness, they muscled the handcuffed Gant across the gap from the dock to the inflatable zodiac-style dinghy. The rolling of the heavy swells threw Jonah off-balance and he fell into the puddle at the bottom of the boat, dragging Gant with him. Gordo slid across afterwards, nearly crashing down on top of them.

Gordo fished the key from Gant's pocket, unlocked the motor, and dropped it into the water. A couple of tugs and the boat roared into life. Gordo took off slowly, getting the hang of the choppy water before opening the throttle.

Further up in the boat, Jonah wedged a knee against the rubber gunwale, and wedged a foot in the deep puddle along the bottom. He held on to Gant by the chain between his handcuffs. Gordo felt the wind and the sea spray tear into his face as they accelerated into the blackness. The lights of Key West dwindled into the distance behind them. A moment later, the harbour mouth dropped away and they were in open sea.

Gordo felt sharp and alert. His mind was perfectly blank, following Gant's shouted instructions – 'Right!' 'Straight ahead!' – and responding to what the sea brought in each new moment. The surface of the water was white with foam. Spindrifts detached from the waves and blew through the air. They ran up the slopes of monster twenty-foot swells and down the other side. He saw lights bobbing violently here and there, but it was impossible to make out any details. The water sprayed by on either side of the boat. Everything had become indistinct, fuzzy. They had entered another world. For three long seconds, Gordo closed his eyes and felt the exhilaration of dark speed.

In another ten minutes, he powered down the engine again. Up ahead, maybe thirty yards away, was a large houseboat. It was long and rectangular, and had a deck protruding from the end. Lights were on inside. The houseboat was getting creamed by the waves – huge sprays of water washed over the sides of it. That was about all he could make out behind the sheets of rain.

'That's it,' Gant said. '*The Sea Dog.*'

'OK,' Gordo shouted. He huddled up close to the other two men. The dinghy rocked and rolled. Jonah looked sick from all the motion. 'Jonah, look alive, man. It's show time. We'll pull up real quiet. We go in, put Foerster

down, slap on the cuffs, and we're out of here. Gant, if you have people on
that boat, and you don't want them to die, I'd better hear you shouting "Don't
shoot!" when we go in there.'

Gordo gave the throttle a half-turn, and the dinghy sidled up to the *Sea
Dog*. The boats slammed together, fell away, then slammed together again.
So much for real quiet. Jonah scrambled over the gunwale of the dinghy and
jumped across to the *Sea Dog*'s deck. Gordo threw him the rope, and Jonah
inexpertly made a few loops with it and tied the dinghy tight to the back of
the houseboat. Gordo manhandled Gant, practically lifting him across to Jonah,
then followed him, one step behind.

They stood on the back deck. Then a small, reddish-brown dog bounced
up and down in the doorway, barking its tiny, high-pitched bark. Then it
started to growl. A festive red bow was tied around the dog's head.

'That's the dog,' Gant said. 'Versace.'

'Versace?' Jonah said. 'Come on.'

'That's what they call it.'

The dog knew they were here, but he was the only one. For only a second
or two, Gordo reflected on how odd that seemed.

He peered through the doorway and into the main cabin. An overhead
light was on, which was very dim, but brighter than the night outside. The
three men stepped inside, Gant first, and there was a living-room area, with
a long couch, a couple of chairs and a bulkhead. The low ceiling gave it the
feel of a cave. On a table mounted in the corner was a large radio, with a
hand-held microphone – the VHF. The radio had been smashed apart.

Two bodies lay together on the floor. One was a tall, muscular man with
no clothes on and the back of his skull crushed in. He was covered in tattoos.
The other body was a large woman, lying on her back in a flannel nightgown,
a pair of scissors protruding from her chest. Gordo's heart did a funny dance
as he moved to the bodies and knelt by them. He looked up at Gant.

'Do you know them?'

Gant's eyes seemed large in the dim light. He nodded. 'They both work
for me.'

Gordo shook his head. 'They used to. Any idea what happened to them?'

Gant shrugged. 'Foerster, if I had to guess. There was an extra dinghy tied up here before. It's gone now.'

The boat leaned way up to one side – for a second, it seemed like it might roll over. It creaked and groaned as it went. BANG! A wave slammed hard against the outer wall. A whistle sounded outside somewhere, maybe far away across the water. It was impossible to tell.

'I thought we were gonna flip that time,' Jonah said.

'Nervous?'

He nodded. 'Yeah.'

Gordo barely moved his head. 'I think we need to take a look around. Doesn't seem like anybody's home, but you never know.'

Arms braced against the walls, they moved through the cabin and into the narrow back hallway. The boat rocked and lurched, knocking them from side to side. Gordo didn't like it. It looked like nobody was here. It felt like nobody was here. But he didn't trust it.

Jonah, gun in hand, opened a door and peered inside a small bedroom. He lodged himself in the doorway to keep his footing. He glanced back down the hall at the rain coming in through the back doorway. Gordo recognised the look on Jonah's face – the man was starting to turn green. He was getting seasick.

'Listen, maybe we should get the fuck out of here,' Jonah said.

Gordo could sympathise. He was getting a little lightheaded and sick himself. He had to be careful. It was the kind of thing that could come on very fast. He took a deep breath and raised a hand. 'OK. One more room and then we'll blow.'

The door to the back room was open and swinging with the movement of the boat. Gordo stuck his head inside. This was clearly the lab. There was a worktable in here and various kinds of equipment – all of it bolted down. On the floor squatted several big plastic containers. Each one had orange and black biohazard stickers plastered on it. Each one had a lot of what looked like water sloshing around inside.

Gordo gave the room the once-over. Anybody in here? Sure didn't look like it. Any apparent places to hide? No. Well, maybe not. Too much motion made it hard to tell. He had trouble concentrating on any one thing. He backed out of the room and turned around. The passageway seemed narrower than before. He and Jonah headed along it to the main room. The boat swayed and Jonah lurched to the couch. He sat heavily and slumped down.

Gant had wedged himself in the rear doorway with his legs and his back. Suddenly, something outside caught his eye and he went out into the rain.

'Where's this jackass going?' Gordo said. 'He's liable to fall in.'

Gordo staggered through the hatch, following Gant outside. On the deck, the storm was more real, more immediate. It seemed even worse than before. The rain came in stinging needles, and the wind howled and shrieked like the souls of the damned. Gordo grabbed Gant by the handcuffs, then stumbled to the right and leaned hard against the side railing, gripping it, bracing himself against it, the water raging below him.

He was so dizzy he could barely stand. When had that happened? He peered out at the night. All around him, the sky was dark. The ocean was white and alive. The waves were monster breakers, foam flying everywhere. There was no pattern to it – just clashing, crashing, gigantic water. The boat was puny in comparison. There was something beautiful about it, but it also horrified him. He had never feared death before, not till this moment. But here was the thing that could kill him.

He noticed another boat nearby, coming right towards them. It was a long speedboat, the kind drug runners used. It came sliding down the face of a wave. Listening hard, Gordo could just make out the engine's whine as it faded into the wind. They had bright lights over there, like flashlights, pointed in this direction.

Gant shouted something. To Gordo, it sounded like: 'Hey! Hey, over here!'

Then Gant was shot. He started to jitter and jive as bullets pierced his upper body. Precious seconds passed while Gordo looked on, not understanding. He felt a sharp pain, like a bee sting, and looked down at his hand.

A hole had appeared in the centre of it. As he watched, blood flowed – the stigmata.

A huge wave hit the boat and Gordo lost his feet. He fell, banging his head against what seemed like a green metal park bench bolted there to the deck. He had no chance to break his fall – he hit that damn thing hard. Water surged across the deck, then retreated into the sea, nearly taking Gordo with it.

He clambered to his feet again. Bullets whistled all around him, tearing up chunks of the boat. Another beesting in his upper arm. Another in his leg. He glanced around. Gant was gone, just totally gone, probably in the water.

'What the fuck?' Gordo croaked. 'What the fuck?'

He put a hand to his head, to the spot that had hit the bench. His hand came back bright red before the rain washed it clean. The blood flowed down his face and mixed with the rain, getting in his eyes. He slumped hard against the railing, but his grip was weak. The dark world spun around him.

The boat lurched. He could not feel his legs.

Jesus, don't fall in the water!

'Jonah,' he said, trying to shout. 'Jonah.'

His fingers slipped along the railing. Then the railing was gone.

Where was the door?

He spun around. Dimly, Gordo had the sensation of falling, falling through the sky. A long time passed. He crashed into the water and for a moment the darkness was all around him. There were no sounds except the muffled sounds of the deep. He thought about floating in the womb, bathed now in warm light. It occurred to him that the emergency light on the life vest had activated. Then the vest brought him to the surface, back to the roar and the spray. He gasped for air and paddled madly. He had to warn Jonah. For a moment he could not see the boat. Then he spotted it.

It was already drifting away. But then so was he. Spots of the blackest darkness danced before his eyes, growing larger all the time. He knew he was done. Thank God, he thought. Thank God for the vest.

A breaking swell washed over him and he thought no more.

* * *

Jonah sat on the couch, the whole room spinning around him.

His vision blurred. He had no idea which direction he was facing. He was ready to puke, and starting not to care what happened, one way or the other. He didn't care any more if he drowned. He had wriggled out of his tight life vest because he felt it constricting his air passages. He had unzipped his jacket as well.

He stared across the room at a small round window – a porthole, somebody would probably call it. Through the porthole, he thought he saw the lights of some boats anchored nearby. He watched all those lights bobbing and rolling madly. Somewhere very close, maybe under this very couch, Versace the dog growled and barked.

Jonah daydreamed, something about a bright sunny day, and a child running down a hillside of tall grass and yellow flowers. The child fell and tumbled down the hill, carving a path with his rolling body through the endless blades of green and yellow. The child was laughing with the excitement and innocence of youth. It was nice, but it made no sense. As a child, Jonah had rarely seen a hillside, never mind run down one.

Gant appeared in the doorway.

Jonah had wandered so far, at first he thought it was Gordo. A moment passed. His eyes focused on the bright blue windbreaker Gant wore, and sent the message to his brain. This was foe, not friend. Then where was Gordo? Had they missed each other out there?

Gant came stumbling into the room. His hair was matted from the storm. Jonah sat facing him, like a critic watching a song-and-dance routine. He felt the weight of his gun in the pocket of the jacket he was wearing. Then Gant collapsed at his feet.

Jonah looked back at the doorway. Chunks of it were tearing away. Holes appeared in the wall, as if by magic. Next to the doorway, a plastic window pane crashed apart. The overhead light shattered and went out. The room went dark.

Jonah slid to the floor. He kneeled and propped Gant up against the opposite wall. Gant's eyes rolled. His breathing came in angry shrieks.

His windbreaker was all torn to shit. Without really looking, Jonah could see that the man was covered in blood.

Only then did it click – somebody was shooting at the boat. Gordo? Why would he do that? It didn't make sense.

Gant's eyes found Jonah. 'Don't let them have it.'

'Who? Have what?'

'Howe's men.'

'What? What the fuck are you talking about?'

Gant's jaw tightened. Veins stuck out in his face and neck. 'It's a double-cross,' he said through clenched teeth. 'They want the cholera. Bastards. Don't give it to them.'

Big holes punched through the wall to their right. Shards of fibreglass sprayed Jonah, biting into his skin. He pulled the gun from his jacket and fired twice through a hole in the wall. The sound was terribly loud. His ears started ringing. The muzzle-flash blinded him for several seconds. Pointless, random shots, and now he could barely see or hear.

He looked at Gant again. Gant gestured with his head. He was having trouble speaking. Great. Jonah was just now having trouble hearing. He put his ear close to Gant's mouth.

'Grenades,' Gant rasped. 'In the bulkhead there. In a box. Just pull the pin. Blow it up. Don't let. Them. Have it.'

Jonah glanced up at the bulkhead over the couch. It seemed impossibly high and far away. He'd have to stand up to open it. It was bad planning to stash grenades up there. The entire room was falling apart – bullets flying everywhere. He turned back to Gant.

'Where's Gordo? Where's my partner?'

'Dead.'

'Shit.' Jonah didn't have much time to think about it. Gordo dead? How could that possibly be? Gordo was too big to die.

Gant stared at him, eyes wide, jaw gone slack. For a second, Jonah thought he must be dead. Then he spoke. 'What are you waiting for?' he said, calmly, almost conversationally, with none of the straining from before.

An instant later, a bullet passed though his head, spraying blood and bone and bits of grey matter all over the wall, and on the front of Jonah's T-shirt and jacket. Gant's body slid sideways.

'Jesus.'

There was nothing left to do. In another moment, Jonah would be dead like Gordo and Gant. He didn't even think. He just sprang up and lunged for the bulkhead. He fumbled with the latch, flipped up the door, and pawed through the contents. All kinds of shit in there. Coiled rope. Tools. Junk. Here was a flat wooden box. It was heavy. Jonah seized it and dropped to the ground again.

Jonah lay flat on his belly, his head pressed against the floor, the box in front of him. It opened easily. Three grenades lay inside, nestled in little egg-crate-style wombs. Jonah hefted one. OK, how did it work? Here was the pin mechanism. Just pull it out of there? And then what? His inner child, raised by television, hiding deep inside the man, answered for him: Throw it, of course. But how long before it blew?

Jonah looked up at the ragged main doorway of the boat. A man crouched there, silhouetted against the night sky. He held a weapon of some kind, a rifle maybe, or a machine-gun, with a flashlight attached along the top. He swept the room with the light, then moved inside. Behind him, another man appeared.

The last seconds of Jonah's life ticked by. No more time to wonder. Jonah pulled the pin and tossed the grenade.

Gant's wife turned her face away. 'I really have to pee first,' she said.

Foerster held the bottle of tainted water above her. He could force her to drink it – that much was true. But he could also wait, couldn't he? Seeing her body there on the bed had stirred him.

He glanced at the window. What if they didn't come back right away? What if they didn't come back all night? That meant he would have hours to stay here and play with Mrs Gant. Or maybe he could somehow get her back to the bungalow. That would be even better. The girl could help him tie her up and then watch what he did to her. Oh my God, wouldn't that be something? After it was all over, Gant's wife could still drink the water. Certainly, Foerster didn't want to give her a deadly disease before he got his fun in.

He looked at the window again. Should he risk it? It had been a red-letter day. Every risk he'd taken had worked out in his favour so far. You didn't get too far in life without taking a chance now and then, right? So fuck it. Let it ride. He put the cap back on the water container.

'I'll tell you what,' he said. 'I'm going to let you pee. Then we're going to put your nice red coat back on and we'll take a little walk, OK? It's just a few blocks. How's that sound?'

Foerster undid her wrist binds from the bedposts, then re-tied them in front of her. He untied her ankle binds.

'OK. Let's go.'

He stood in the doorway to the bathroom, the bottle in one hand, the box cutter in the other, and watched her sit on the toilet. There was something about watching her crouched in there . . .

'Do you have to watch me?' she said.

'I have no choice. Can't exactly trust you alone in there, can I? I mean, I untied you, didn't I? That's about as far as I can go.'

'Well, can you at least close the door halfway?'

He smiled. 'Nope.'

She closed her eyes and began to tinkle. Her face turned red in what Foerster guessed was embarrassment. But it might be something else, too. Foerster was starting to think this woman liked being here with him. He thought of the way she spoke, the way she moved . . . well, she was flirting with him. They really needed to get out of here. It could be some night ahead of them.

'I'm thinking I want to get some beer, if any place is open. You look like a lady who drinks a beer now and then.'

He had smoked his cigarette down to the filter. He wanted another one — his nerves were bothering him just a little. Now where was that lighter? He must have left it back on the table. He looked over there. Sure, the lighter was on the table. He would get it in a minute. He glanced at the window again. You know what? This was taking too long. It was time to go.

He turned back to the girl – just in time to see the top of her head ram into his jaw. The force of it drove him backwards. He tripped and they fell together. His head slammed to the floor.

BETRAYAL. The word blinked bright in his mind. The bitch had betrayed him. She'd attacked him as soon as he wasn't looking.

He had dropped the box cutter. His hands searched the carpet, but he couldn't find it. She was on top of him. She was all over him, scratching at his face, her wrists still bound together. Her breasts pressed against his chest. She squirmed across him like a snake. Stinging pain came as her nails tore down his cheek.

He reached for her hair and got a big chunk of it in his fist. He pulled, yanking her sideways and down. She grimaced. He banged her head against the floor.

She exhaled fiercely.

Oh, she was gonna get it. She was really gonna fucking get it.

The explosion was LOUD.

Jonah shut his eyes against the blinding flash of light. Just before it blew, he rolled himself into a tiny ball. He tried to make himself disappear. He covered his hands with his ears.

No matter. He went deaf anyway. All he could hear afterwards was his ears ringing. Stinging shards of whatever – plastic, wood, metal, bone – sprayed his back. Seconds later, he realised he was still alive, and he got moving.

Jonah crawled fast and encountered bodies on the floor – the man and woman who were dead when he first arrived. He squirmed over them like an eel. He dragged the wooden box along with him as he crawled along the passageway towards the lab. He tried to control his breathing, which he could not hear but which must be loud, loud, LOUD.

He glanced back towards the doorway, the main hatch where he had thrown the grenade. It was gone. The entire back of the boat was ripped wide open. Water rushed in through the gaping hole. Licks of flame danced here and there in the darkness.

Two flashlights swept the inside of the boat. A muzzle flash went off, then another. They were still alive, at least two of them. Muzzle flash after muzzle flash, white paint splashed on black velvet, on and off, on and off. All around the room they fired. Deep into the boat. Jonah blinked and saw huge white infernos floating.

The boat rocked violently. Jonah squeezed himself against the floor. A gunshot ripped a chunk from the wall a foot above his head. He didn't move. He knew where they were. They didn't know where he was. But the advantage degraded as each moment passed. Soon their flashlights would find him, trapped in this narrow corridor. Then he would be dead.

The floor was wet now, too much liquid to be blood. Water, maybe three inches deep, sloshed around. The boat was taking on water through that massive hole in the back. No surprise there. Jonah himself was soaking wet – from water or blood, or a combination of both.

He froze and held his breath. The men were much closer now. As Jonah had crawled along the floor, they had crept into the room. The first one was RIGHT THERE, at the opening of the hallway, not ten feet away.

It was a shallow breath Jonah had held. Already his body begged for more air. The moment stretched out like all the hours that had crawled past since the beginning of time. The pressure built in Jonah's lungs.

Very carefully, he inched backwards toward the lab. He reached behind him. OK, here was the door. He slid back some more.

Suddenly, the hallway was filled with the light from the man's gun. Jonah slithered through the threshold as gunshots ripped open the walls, the floor, the entire hall. He slammed the door and crawled to the side of it, staying low against the wall. As he watched, the door fell apart. For a moment, it turned to Swiss cheese, and then it simply collapsed. Bullets sparked off surfaces throughout the room. A large container of water burst open. The cholera – it had to be the cholera. If he swallowed it, he would die.

But that was a long-term worry. The men would come blasting in here any second.

Jonah yanked another grenade from the box. He pulled the pin and tossed the grenade out the door. Again he rolled into a ball. Again he covered his ears. Again he closed his eyes.

He saw the bright flash through his eyelids. He felt the shockwave throughout the room. All around him, the walls and equipment blew apart.

For a moment, Jonah just lay there, blessedly still. Long minutes must have passed. He swayed with the motion of the boat. There was something comforting about that movement. It seemed like he could stay this way for ever. Then he remembered the water. He was lying in it and it was deeper than before. It half covered his body. It must be infested with deadly bacteria. Either way, the boat was going down, and soon.

OK. He opened his eyes.

The boat was hollowed out. The explosion had destroyed the walls of the passageway, slicing open the whole length of the boat. The small bedroom was gone. Jonah lifted his head just a bit and found he could see right out to the back deck. The boat was on fire. Water really poured in. No living thing moved anywhere on board. Outside, he caught a glimpse of a power boat, its running lights bounding away across the big water. It was gone a second later.

Jonah pulled himself slowly to his feet. He stepped through the wreckage and into the main cabin. Pieces of the attackers – an arm, a leg – were strewn here and there. Jonah tried not to look at them. A few feet away, Gant's corpse lay against a wall. Jonah approached him, came very close. Yes, he was dead, but right now Jonah felt nothing for him, or for anyone. He went past Gant and groped around on the floor for the life vest. Another wave hit, the boat turned nearly on to its side, and white foam surged into the room.

On his hands and knees Jonah crawled from place to place. Time passed, maybe a long time. Finally he found the damn thing, the vest. He stood up and worked his way towards the back. He braced his hands against the wall and his legs against the floor. The boat rocked and rolled, and he stumbled along till he found a metal pole, which was one of the boat's main supports.

He looked down and the dog was at his feet, jumping and barking. It was soaked and shivering. Jonah realised he could just hear its bark, a high-pitched yap. It sounded far away. Jonah clung to the pole. White light danced before his eyes like a spirit leaving this world for a better place.

Later, Jonah spent an eternity in the water.

He paddled but the bulk of the life vest made it hard to move his arms. He kicked with his feet but giant waves washed over him and he panicked. The violence seized him and he urged himself forward. Sometimes a wave would slap his face and for a moment he would be gone. The rain beat down. He swallowed seawater, vomited, then swallowed some more. He passed out and woke vomiting. The panic raced through him again and he paddled in a frenzy. He screamed but heard no sound except for rushing water. Then he realised struggle was no use and he began to grow calm.

He couldn't see over the swells. Now and again he floated to the top of one and could see for a few seconds – endless water. He turned back the way he thought he had come. The *Sea Dog* was gone.

The rain never lessened. The waves never lessened. Up and down, Jonah was ploughed under into the darkness, the only light the yellow beam from his vest. He held his breath as long as he could, until his lungs ached, until he thought his head might explode. Then he was shot out like a cork into the air. He gasped for more breath. The air was filled with water.

He lost himself.

Was he being swept out to sea? Swept in towards land? Where would he be if he was alive in the morning? Alone with the sharks? It didn't seem to matter.

Time stopped.

He thought about nothing. It didn't seem worthwhile to start any train of thought. He would be dead soon. A dark mass loomed ahead, a deeper darkness in the absence of light. It came fast. In his terror he thought it was a monster. Huge gaping jaws. At the last second he put his hands up. Impact. It rammed into him and over him. His hand scraped along it as it passed. It was made of wood. A chunk of something, some wreck. Then it was gone.

A moment or an hour later, he was flat on his back. Then he was aware of nothing. He was not in touch with his body. No pain. No feeling.

Emptiness.

He welcomed the emptiness and just let himself drift. That seemed best. At last he felt at peace.

Then something grabbed him. He was pulled out of the water. The noise was incredible. Then he dangled in mid-air, flying through high winds and rain. Hands and arms. Shouts. He fought them, or so it seemed. NO! Let me sleep.

A bright light shone in his face.

'Is he alive?'

He opened his eyes, then covered them with a hand scraped raw and bloody.

'Hey, man, can you kill that light?' he said.

Somebody laughed. 'He's OK.'

He turned and vomited more seawater on to the floor.

'That's it, buddy, get it out.'

Jonah raised his head and looked around. Gordo was slumped across from him on the floor, wrapped in blankets. Two men in jump suits and harnesses stood nearby. Heavy rain blew through the open doorway.

'Where am I?'

One of the guys grinned. He was a young guy, maybe early twenties, with a crew cut and all-American good cheer. 'You're on a United States Coast Guard helicopter,' he shouted. 'We got your distress signal. Found your buddy and he said to keep looking, you were out here somewhere. I'm Lieutenant Ryan. I was your rescue swimmer tonight.'

'Thank you.'

The kid's smile broadened – the look of a man who loves what he does. Jonah couldn't remember the last time he'd seen a smile like that one. 'No problem,' the kid said. 'All in a day's work.'

Jonah looked at Gordo – again. Gordo's face was battered and bruised. He had a nasty gash across the forehead. He smiled too, despite everything. 'Rough night,' he said.

Jonah nodded. Then he put his head to the floor and passed out again.

Key West was under water.

Jonah and Gordo stumbled along, picking their way through the flooded streets. They wore clean T-shirts and slacks, and their various wounds were patched up and bandaged, courtesy of the United States Coast Guard. The sky was dark, but the worst of the storm seemed to have passed, at least for now. The wind had let up, but the rain still came down, sometimes in a light drizzle, sometimes in sheets. Tree branches and other jetsam flowed by.

They turned up the block towards the motel. Jonah was thinking of sleep – sleeping for hours in Katie's arms and putting this whole experience out of his mind. He would also have to find a way to tell her about her husband. That would make it hard to sleep. Face it – the bad stuff wasn't nearly over.

He sighed. It was going to be a long night.

'What's going on here?' Gordo said.

Jonah looked and saw two Key West police cruisers parked in front of the motel. Blue and red lights flashed. A small crowd of onlookers had gathered. An ambulance sat there, too. But its lights were off. It was in no hurry to get anywhere.

Right away Jonah knew. Foerster was slippery, like a snake. Foerster was a rapist. Foerster was a murderer.

They had gone out to the boat and left Katie behind as a sacrifice.

How could they have been so dumb? How could they have left her alone? 'Oh my God,' he said, and started running. His feet splashed through the flood.

A sombre-looking cop stepped in front of him, raising his cop hand. 'Hold on, sorry, sir. We're going to have to ask you to step back away from here.'

Jonah burst past the cop.

'Oh my God,' he said again.

Then he saw her.

She stood among a couple of cops, dwarfed by their size. She was barefoot, wrapped in the same robe she had worn earlier. A big cop held a black umbrella over her. She laughed at something one of the cops said. She shook her head, then turned and saw Jonah approaching. She gave him the brightest of bright smiles.

'Hey, Jonah, you'll never guess what happened,' she said.

He stopped running. He walked towards her. She stepped out from under the umbrella and came to him.

'What is it?' Jonah said. 'What happened?'

They embraced and Jonah looked around. Foerster was in the back of the open ambulance, strapped to a gurney. His face looked all scratched to hell. He strained against the leather straps, trying to get loose. The veins in his neck and face stood out in sharp relief. He ranted at the cops and the ambulance medic – a torrent of words. His eyes were wide with panic.

'Look, man, you gotta get me to the hospital right now. I only have hours to live. You gotta call the Centers for Disease Control and fly some experts down here. I have an extreme form of cholera. If I don't get help I'm gonna die.'

Jonah turned back to Katie. They gazed into each other's eyes.

'It was a terrible fight,' she said. 'But I took him. He's not half as tough as Tyler. And the police have been so nice. Can you believe it?'

'Listen to me! Would you listen to me? The bitch gave me cholera. I'm gonna fucking die.'

The medic slammed the back door of the ambulance, enclosing Foerster in there and muffling his ravings. 'Fucking guy is out of his mind,' the medic said.

Gordo had appeared. He went to the cop standing nearest to Foerster and whipped his detective badge out of his jacket. 'Detective Robert Darker, NYPD. The man in that ambulance is my prisoner. He's wanted for multiple felonies in New York.'

The cop seemed unimpressed. 'Get in line, pal. We got him on multiple felonies right here.'

Gordo stepped away from the cop and took a deep breath. Jonah and Katie went and stood next to Gordo in the rain. Katie punched him on his meaty shoulder. 'Not bad for my first fugitive, eh?'

'Not bad,' he agreed. 'But you haven't really caught him unless you're the one who's bringing him in. Nobody's gonna pay a reward for a guy already in the custody of the Key West police.'

Katie's smiled died. 'Oh.'

'By the way, did you really give him cholera?'

Katie shook her head. 'I don't know what he's talking about. He tried to make me drink some goop he had in a bottle. By the time I finally beat him, I was so mad I forced him to drink some of it instead. I'm not proud of it, but I poured it right down his throat. Then he freaked out. I think he must be crazy.'

Gordo gave Jonah a long look.

'Sure. He's crazy. That must be it.'

9 November: Miami Beach

Jonah awoke from a nightmare.

As soon as he opened his eyes, he remembered none of it. For a moment, he lay in the cool darkness and stared up at the ceiling fan spinning slowly around. Next to him, beneath the thin silk sheets, Katie made a noise like a sigh and inched her warm body closer to him. She was having nightmares, too.

He reminded himself she had lost a husband in all this. The scars were still fresh. Jonah didn't know when, if ever, she'd be able to return to her big house in Charleston and wrap up her affairs.

They had to get out of this room, he decided. Days had passed since either of them had felt the sunshine. To Jonah's left, there was an east-facing, floor-to-ceiling, wall-to-wall picture window. The light streaming through the gap in the big heavy curtains told him it was already full daylight outside.

He squirmed away from Katie's grasp and padded nude to the window. He peered through the slats. Ten stories below, the dark green of the mighty Atlantic beckoned. A small white sailboat moved out on the water.

The room phone rang. He jumped to pick it up.

On the bed, Katie grunted and covered her head with a pillow.

Jonah spoke low into the receiver. 'H'lo?'

A woman's voice, brisk, businesslike: 'Yes, Mrs Katie Gant, please.'

'Sorry, you must have a wrong number.'

'Sir, what is your name?'

Jonah smiled. 'I don't have a name.'

'Sir, this is Maggie Reed of the *National Report*. Please tell Katie that we're ready to offer her a substantial sum for exclusive, world-wide serial rights to her story. This is a story that needs to be told, and I think she'll agree we're the best ones to tell it. If I could speak to Katie, just for a moment, I'm sure—'

Jonah hung up the phone. Katie's cell phone was full of messages. The landline at her house was full of messages. Now, somehow, the jackals had found her here at the hotel. They all wanted to talk to the beautiful wife of the man behind the Illinois anthrax attack and the recent thwarted cholera attack. Her high school yearbook photo had been running in the tabloid press for days.

Foerster had died, of course. It had taken less than a day for him to become a wizened, dehydrated caricature of a human being. His cholera was so virulent that the entire hospital – patients, staff and visitors – had to be quarantined. The media swarmed all over the story. They were camped outside the hospital twenty-four hours a day till the quarantine was lifted.

It had all been on the TV. Before he lost the ability to speak, Foerster was debriefed by operatives from Homeland Security. Afterwards, one of Foerster's co-conspirators – a young woman – was taken into custody. She was found tied to a bed in a Key West bungalow. Later, a force of US Marines invaded a small Caribbean island and rescued an American named Roscoe Fielding – the heir to a real estate fortune dating back two hundred years, and the apparent target of the terror plot. Fielding was well despite his ordeal, and recuperating at his sumptuous penthouse apartment on Central Park West in New York City.

Homeland Security had given the media Tyler Gant's name during a press conference. Twenty minutes later, the whole world was looking for Katie.

The phone rang again. Jonah grabbed it on the first ring.

'Listen. Stop fucking calling here. OK?'

From the other end came Gordo's voice, robust and jolly. 'Hey, man, this is the first time I called you all day. I'm trying not to annoy you too much. How's it going over there?'

He was staying in the same hotel, two floors down. Katie's money – *Gant's money* – was paying for it all. They'd met Gordo in the ground-floor restaurant for dinner two nights ago. Some kind of water main had burst just outside the building, and the sodden carpet in the lobby had squished under their feet.

Jonah smiled at the memory. 'It's going pretty good.'

'Did I wake you?'

'No, I was up.'

'Good. Listen, did you see anything on television about the triple murder that happened in Overtown a few days ago? The one where the guy is suspected of killing his ex-girlfriend and two other guys she was with?'

Jonah scratched his head and yawned. 'I might have seen that, yeah. I remember something about it. The guy is some kind of psycho. After he shot the two guys, he stabbed the chick like forty times with a carving knife.'

'That's him. OK, you did see it. Well, it turns out there's a lot more to the story. The deal is this: the girl was rich, a wandering daughter story. Her parents have money. Two days ago they put out a $25,000 reward on the guy.'

Jonah's mind couldn't seem to wrap itself around the problem. He glanced back at the window, thinking about heading down to the beach and taking a swim. He hadn't shaken the last of his fitful sleep.

'So?' he said.

Gordo's smile came through the phone lines. 'So get dressed, man. We have a job to do. I happen to know where the guy is hiding out.'

Katie was fully awake now. She watched Jonah, her eyes showing a devilish glint. She whipped the sheets away, revealing her body. She waved him over. Jonah smiled and moved towards the bed, phone in hand. The phone was attached to the wall with a cord. The cord wasn't long enough to reach the bed.

Gordo was still talking. 'I got a call from a guy this morning. He's an agent in Hollywood. He thinks there might be a TV show in this work we do. You know, stylish black guy, tough white guy, tracking down criminals. He wants to call it *Freelancers*. The only thing is, if there's going to be a show, we actually have to do the work, you know what I mean?'

'I need to call you back,' Jonah said into the handset. 'Give me an hour.' He hesitated, halfway across the floor. Katie waited for him. It was time to put the phone down.

'I got a call from *People* magazine, too,' Gordo said. 'They're talking about maybe doing a photo of us with a little blurb. My idea is that we bring the photographer out in a boat and do the shot where the coast guard first pinpointed our distress signal. You know – right here is where the laboratory of death was anchored. That kind of thing.'

'I'll tell you what,' Jonah said. 'Make that two hours.'

Acknowledgements

Deepest thanks as always to literary agent Noah Lukeman, without whom none of this would have happened.

Thanks again to Joy Scott for her patience and for ten (mostly) great years.

Thanks very much to Lliam Harrison, Director of Research Compliance, and Tom Wood, Director of Operations for Research Administration, both at the University of Southern Maine (USM). Lliam and Tom gave generously of their time, walked me through the microbiology labs at USM, and taught me a little bit about growing bacteria. These guys are super-knowledgeable. Any mistakes in the book are, of course, mine.

Thanks to Brian Dunleavy for once more reading early versions of the manuscript and giving me invaluable advice on improving it.

Thanks to Sara Goldenthal for an awesome new author photo.

Very special thanks to editor extraordinaire Marion Donaldson for her insightful work on the story, and the entire excellent team at Headline Publishing Group, including of course Editorial Assistant Sarah Douglas, Ross Hulbert in Publicity, Jo Liddiard in Marketing, and Laura Esslemont in Production. Craig Fraser nailed the cover design once again. Thanks to him for that. And thanks to copy editor Marian Reid for finding and gently pointing out various gaffes and miscues, improving the book a great deal in the process.

Numerous people have been writing books and blogging on the internet for years about an approaching financial, and possibly societal, collapse. Their work puts the lie to the idea – currently popular in government, investment banking and mainstream media circles – that no one could have predicted the recent (and as of this writing, ongoing) economic meltdown. A few of these writers are James Howard Kunstler, John Robb, Matt Savinar and Dmitry Orlov. Hats off to them and their kind.